Wildflower Promise

life imperfect book three

Wildflower Promise

life imperfect book three

a novel by

katherine turner

This is a work of fiction. Names, characters, places, and incidents either are the product of the author's imagination or are used fictitiously. Any resemblance to actual persons, living or dead, events, or locales is entirely coincidental.

First edition: April 2023

Editing by Kayli Baker and Olivia Castetter
Cover design by Murphy Rae
Print formatting by Shanna Hammerbacher
E-book formatting by Jo Harrison
Cover photography by Zhao Chen

Library of Congress Control Number: 2022910961
Library of Congress Cataloging-in-Publication Data available upon request.

ISBN 978-1-955735-08-7 (ebook)
ISBN 978-1-955735-09-4 (paperback)

Josha Publishing, LLC
Independent Publisher
www.joshapublishing.com
Haymarket, VA

Printed in the United States of America

for my soulmate

it wasn't easy, but that didn't stop us

prologue

rob

"**Why do we** have to move again, Charlie?" I asked my older brother, out of breath from trying to keep up with him.

"They said we're too much trouble, bro," Charlie responded.

"That's what they all say. Maybe if we tried to behave, if we just—"

"Fuck that," he interrupted, looking back over his shoulder to glare at me. "We don't need to change for anyone. If anyone gave two shits about us, we wouldn't have to. But they don't because we're not good enough for their uppity families. Get used to it, bro, 'cause it ain't never changing. All we got is each other. We'll never be good enough for anyone else."

"But if we—"

"I'm telling you, man, it won't matter!" he shouted, finally coming to a stop after what felt like hours of moving quickly through the dark, sticking to shadows. He turned to face me as I gasped for breath, the large brick wall comprising the back side of our local strip mall a few feet to my left. "Trust me. Not even Mom and Dad gave a shit about us. Remember? I don't get why you cared that they died, dude. They were never around. And they died because they were out getting high with their dealer and wrapped their car around a tree. They didn't care about us. No one cares about us. I'm the only one who's got your back and the only one who ever will. Now enough bitching, you pussy. Let's go."

I glanced over my shoulder, my stomach twisting. "I don't know, Charlie. I don't..." I swallowed before finishing, my voice small. "I don't want to."

"Of course you do, you little shit. How else are you going to toughen up and learn to fight? Besides, those fuckers have it coming, walking around with sticks up their asses just because their mommies and daddies have some money. Here—drink this. Liquid courage, bro."

Charlie produced a bottle of amber liquid from somewhere deep inside his black trench coat. There were also knives in there somewhere, I knew, but I tried not to think about those—or what he might be planning to do with them—as he held the bottle toward me. I hesitated; I really didn't want to go start a fight with a bunch of people. I'd seen Charlie come home bleeding and with broken bones enough times to know how it would end. And they were all bigger than me; I was just a short, skinny, barely-ten-year-old kid.

"Come on. Drink up," he said impatiently, shaking the bottle in my direction. "You keep whining about wanting to hang out with me—this is what you gotta do. Drink it. Now."

He shoved the bottle into my chest, and I grabbed it from him instinctively as I stumbled backward a few steps.

"Come on, asshole, I don't have all fucking night. Unless you're too scared?" he sneered, his eyes filling with venom.

I *was* scared, but there was no way I'd admit that to him; there wasn't much Charlie hated more than people showing fear, and there wasn't anything scarier than when my brother was angry. With a deep breath, I wrapped my lips around the opening and tipped the bottle up as I squeezed my eyes shut. On the first swallow, I doubled over, sputtering and coughing violently as liquor spewed from my mouth to coat my shoes and the ground.

Charlie laughed. "Don't worry, it gets easier. Take a few more."

I did as he instructed even though my mouth, nose, and throat all felt like I was breathing fire. Because I knew what to expect, this time I was prepared enough to fight the urge to spit it out, and I suppressed my vicious cough into something more subdued.

"That's it, much better, bro," Charlie said with a nod of approval as he snatched the bottle back from my hands and clapped me on the back so hard I had to step forward to keep my balance. With a harsh laugh, he flipped the bottle upside down and guzzled the remaining contents in one go as if it was a bottle of water; I couldn't even drink a can of soda that fast.

"Whoo!" he shouted after the last drop was gone, followed by a low growl as he flung the bottle into the brick edifice, where it shattered and sprayed glass in all directions. "Yeah! Let's go fuck some shit up!"

The liquid courage was already working its magic and my body was warm, a strange but pleasant numbness settling into my limbs, my worries about moving for the sixth time since our parents had died three and a half years ago already fading. High on the praise from Charlie, the rare look of pride and approval in his eyes, I raised my fist into the air.

"Yeah!" I shouted in reply. "Let's do it!"

Walk away
from whatever
weights you down,
from whatever keeps
your heart from opening
and your soul from singing.

Walk away from anything
that doesn't fit,
feel right,
or bores you to death.

Life is too short
to waste your time
with anything
that doesn't feel
like love.

-Mark Anthony

chapter one

———

annie

My heart skipped in anticipation as Rob pulled into the parking lot at his friend's tattoo parlor. My hands shook and my knees threatened to buckle with each step as we approached the front door, and I had my doubts about whether I was brave enough to go through with it. In fact, Rob's palpable excitement was the only thing keeping me from declaring I'd changed my mind.

I'd thought the weeks since I'd told Rob I wanted the tattoo would be enough to get used to the idea, but the time had passed faster than I ever could have imagined. It felt like only the day before that I'd left the hospital after my aneurysm and moved in with him in Stockwood, instead of six weeks earlier. But those six weeks, interrupted by having the coiling procedure to prevent any more aneurysms from bursting, had somehow flown by, though I'd spent most of my time sleeping or reading in my library or lounging in the hammock at the Hideaway. It seemed no amount of rest was enough to make up for months of working around the clock and a serious medical scare. I'd never been more content to do absolutely nothing—not even when I was living at my mom's house the year before.

"I wish you would tell me what you're getting," Rob said for about the hundredth time as he reached for the handle of the front door to the parlor. "The anticipation is killing me."

A nervous giggle escaped as I quirked an eyebrow. "I already told you, it's a surprise," I responded, repeating the same words he'd said to me less than a year before on the way to surprise me with the house he'd bought for us. I'd threatened to have the words tattooed on my ass if he said it again, which—of course—he had.

No one knew what I was getting except for me—I hadn't even told my best friend, Haley. Actually, I hadn't even told Jax yet, aside from the fact that I wanted something on the back of my left shoulder. Jax was the owner of the tattoo parlor, the artist who'd done all of Rob's post-high-school tattoos, and who was going to be doing mine. He had assured Rob that I'd be fine without an initial consultation since what I was going to have done was small.

"Hey, asshole, what's up?" Jax called out as we stepped inside. "I'm all ready for y'all."

Rob removed his arm from my shoulders long enough to shake Jax's hand and exchange a quick half-hug. Jax was several inches taller than Rob, and I guessed at least fifty pounds heavier, all of which appeared to be muscle. He wore snug-fitting, faded black jeans and an equally faded, skin-tight black t-shirt with tall, lace-up black boots. Tattoos covered his arms and the backs of his hands and climbed all the way to his chin from under his shirt in the front and up the back of his neck to cover most of his bald head. He also had a beard, but it was much longer and wilder than Rob's. Punctuating his bad boy look were two enormous spikes in his ears that looked like they could easily be used to impale someone. But he spoke with a rolling southern drawl, had an easy-going smile, and his hazel eyes were warm and kind as they twinkled with good humor.

"Hey, man, how's it going?" Rob said. "Thanks for doing this on your day off."

Jax had agreed to do my tattoo on the one day a week the parlor was normally closed, a request Rob had made. I wasn't sure if the reason was—as he'd told me—because I'd be more comfortable if there weren't any other people around, or if it was really to assuage his jealousy whenever there were other men within eyesight; a jealousy that seemed to only be intensifying with each passing day, something I assumed was at least partially because of my friendship with Lucas. I'd repeatedly assured Rob that Lucas and I were only friends, but it hadn't made any difference. Neither had the fact that I'd moved in with Rob and we were as together as any couple could possibly be… even if I hadn't been able to bring myself to have sex again since Eddie's assault in the hospital room—my hesitation compounded by my ever-present exhaustion.

"Anything to meet the famous Annie," Jax responded, shifting his gaze to me. He seemed to be searching for something and assessing me at the same time as he spoke, his eyebrows drawn together and eyes narrowed ever so slightly compared to when he was looking at Rob. "Nice to finally make your acquaintance, Annie."

My face heated under his scrutiny, and I had to look away, but not before shaking the hand he was holding out to me. "Nice to meet you, too, Jax," I said with a timid smile, my mind racing as it tried to determine why he was studying my face the way he was.

"So, y'all ready to get started?"

My eyes darted to Rob's face for a split second before they turned back to Jax. "Actually, I don't want Rob to see anything until it's done."

"Making him wait until the last second?"

I offered another smile and a short nod. It wasn't that I didn't want to speak, but I was too nervous—I knew if I tried to, it would probably be indecipherable. Hopefully he wouldn't find me to be rude or unfriendly as a result.

"Alrighty then, we can do that. You got the design?"

Again, a nod was my only response, though I was contemplating turning and walking back out the front door.

"Relax, darlin', ain't nothin' to it," Jax said, interrupting my thoughts before they'd had a chance to spiral further out of control. He turned, placed a hand on my shoulder, and started walking me toward the back of the building. "Don't worry, Rob, she's in *real* good hands," he said with a deep laugh as we walked down a long, narrow corridor with walls plastered with tattoo designs and photographs. There was so much to see at once, and for some reason, that made me even more anxious, as if I was expected to have noticed everything on the walls by the time we reached the end of the hall.

"That's my fucking wife, Jax!" Rob called down the hallway. His voice had changed from when he'd greeted Jax, the friendliness mostly gone, and my stomach flipped.

"You're just worried she's gonna want a real man instead of your puny ass."

"You may be bigger than me, but I can kick your ass any day, man."

Jax maneuvered us into a small room with something that resembled a black dentist's chair, surrounded by walls decorated in the same fashion as the hallway. I knew Rob never would have brought me to see Jax if he didn't trust him, and it seemed as if Jax was only joking, but it was apparent that Rob's anger was on the rise, and I felt the need to warn Jax.

"Rob's definitely the jealous, possessive type and can have a short temper," I spoke quickly, my voice irritatingly quiet and uncertain.

Jax chuckled as he closed the door behind us, a grin stretched wide across his face, his eyes twinkling as he gave me a wink. "I know. I'm just having a little fun with him. You can go ahead and pull out whatever you brought to show me for the design and take your sweater off so I can see where it's going."

While I removed my cardigan and slid the strap of my tank top to the side to expose my shoulder, Jax's eyes filled with mischief that reminded me so much of Haley when she was up to something it was almost uncanny. He looked toward the door and raised his voice to a boom as he replied to Rob.

"Is that so? Well, at least let me give Annie what she wants first, right darlin'?" He barely got the last word out before he burst into guffawing laughter.

"Fuck this!" Rob shouted.

He burst through the door a second later. Jax was doubled over with laughter, but Rob was breathing heavily and had his fists clenched. I was frozen in place, unsure what would happen because Rob certainly looked like he was going to start swinging.

"Man, you should see your ugly face right now," Jax said between laughs, slapping his thighs. "I don't know what you're all worked up about, man," he continued with affected innocence.

"Fuck you, Jax," Rob responded with his jaw clenched.

Jax laughed even harder, completely unaffected by Rob's murderous expression. Once his laughter had subsided into quiet chuckles, he addressed Rob again. "Calm down, asshole. I'm just screwin' with you. Payback for all that pain-in-the-ass script you wanted. Now get out, she didn't want you in here."

Rob stared hard at him another minute before tearing himself away to look at me. His anger was fading to be replaced by uncertainty and indecision, his face tight. "I want to stay in here with you," he said gruffly.

Honestly, a large part of me wanted him to stay, too—I was so nervous about what I was about to do—but I also wanted it to be a surprise. After everything he'd done for me, it was the only thing I could offer in return. And my desire to do something meaningful for him was sufficient to conquer my fear.

"I don't want you to see until it's finished. Please."

His lips parted, his brow drawing further down in obvious disapproval, but instead of arguing as I'd expected, he bent to cup my face in his hands and kissed me long and hard.

"Okay, love," he said.

"You call that a kiss?" Jax teased as Rob stood.

Rob glared at him as he walked toward the door, flipping his middle finger. After he pulled the door closed behind him, he shouted, "Don't touch that fucking lock or I'll break the goddamn door down!"

Jax laughed again as he shook his head in amusement. Turning to face me after his laughter tapered off, his expression turned more serious, as did his voice.

"Now, show me what you got in mind for your design."

Jax offered some ideas to develop the designs a little more after studying them as well as the areas the tattoos were going. Before I knew it, they'd been traced on my skin and it was time to get started. We were beginning with my shoulder, so I was sitting up but leaning with my chest against the back of the chair, my face turned to the side. I'd intentionally turned to face away from Jax in case the roiling in my stomach ended with me vomiting. The grip my hands had on a bar across the back of the chair tightened when the tattoo gun touched my skin.

"How you doing, darlin'?" Jax asked a moment later, his voice kind.

Embarrassed and trying to hide the fact I was battling tears, I replied, "I'm fine."

"Alright, tough girl. Well, tell me if you need to stop for a bit, though it'll get sort of numb soon."

I nodded, not trusting my voice if I spoke again.

"You know," he started a few minutes later, "Rob spent a lot of time in this same chair, talking about you. Telling me the stories behind everything he wanted inked. He told me about how you guys met, and you turned his life upside down, and he knew right then that he never wanted it flipped back the other way. He told me about your parents, too, and about what those men did when you were a little girl. About how brave you were, moving on and finding something positive from it all."

He stopped and cleared his throat as I tried to mask my sharp inhale of relief at the unexpected reprieve from the needle. While I'd heard his words, the pain in my shoulder was all I'd been able to focus on.

"When Rob first came in here, I was mad. About everything. Nothing was good enough and I felt like the world was against me. I didn't make enough money. I didn't have a nice enough car. You name it, and I was mad as all hell about it. But when he told me about you, I realized how lucky I really was. I'm not rich, but I love what I do and wouldn't choose to do anything else. Nobody's ever really hurt me. I got both my parents. And there I was, just mad for no good reason when I had so much."

He bent and pressed the tattoo gun to my skin again as he continued. "Anyway, hearing about you changed my life. I stopped thinking about everything I *didn't* have and started thinking instead about everything I *did* have. And I've been so much happier ever since. And for that, I thank you."

I couldn't believe Rob had told him about my childhood. There was no real reason to be upset, I knew, though that knowledge did nothing to stop a sense of betrayal from washing over me. But there was nothing to be done about it at that point. At least it had helped someone; in a way, it was like that meant that what I'd gone through hadn't been for nothing. And as uncomfortable as I was with anyone knowing my past, if it helped them to be happier... maybe that was worth the discomfort.

Once Jax completed the main tattoo, he brought over a hand mirror so I could see how it turned out. It looked amazing, though the thought that it was permanent made me queasy.

The tattoo was of a dark storm cloud with Rob's name scripted in to look like silvery mist in the bottom lining, and three words included in the top lining. The final element was a willow tree beneath the cloud. It had turned out better than I'd expected and gave me the final burst of courage I needed to follow through with the next one.

"He's going to love these, darlin'," Jax assured me.

"I hope so," I breathed out. I knew I was getting them for me, but I wasn't sure what I'd do if Rob didn't also like them.

As Jax started on the second tattoo, he asked, "You got any idea how much that man out there loves you? I've never seen anything like it. I haven't seen him since I did that last poem on his forearm, and I almost didn't even recognize him. I've known him a long time, and I've never seen him happy like he is now. Closest was when he was sitting right here, tellin' me stories about you. It's good to see him like this. I don't think you would, but do me a favor and don't break his heart again."

My saliva was thick as I swallowed. "I'll try not to."

As he finished the second tattoo, he turned to me, giving me another warm smile like the one when he first met me.

"It was good to meet you, Annie, and a pleasure to work on you today." His smile broadened further. "I'm glad you're back in Rob's life."

My face leapt into flames, and I didn't know what to say, so I just nodded and looked down at the ground in silence.

"I'll cover these for you after you show Rob," he said, standing.

I took that as my cue to stand as well, and we headed down the hallway toward the front of the shop. As we neared the lobby, Jax gave me a wink and that Haley-like mischievous grin, and my stomach dropped.

"Well, darlin'," he said loudly. "That was certainly the nicest ass I've ever worked on."

I cringed, then glared at Jax as I heard a growl accompany a scraping sound, unsure why he was so determined to stir up Rob's jealousy, but he was looking into the lobby and paying no attention to me. Rob was there a split second later, standing in front of me and breathing fire.

"He didn't go anywhere near my ass," I said immediately, hoping to placate him. "He's just messing with you again."

"You're a dick," Rob said to Jax, though his words held no ire. Then he turned to me, a glimmer of excitement in his eyes. "Can I see now?"

I rolled my eyes in mock annoyance and then gave a small smile. Spinning slowly, I gave him time to examine my shoulder. There was no doubt he was inspecting it closely because his breath fanned across my aching skin, his fingers feathering around the tattoo, leaving enough space to avoid causing me any more pain. Though he could see it, I explained the bulk of what he was looking at.

"What about the top of the cloud?" he asked.

Trying to suppress a laugh, I said, "I told you I was getting a surprise."

I knew he'd noticed the top lining was made up of the words "it's a surprise" when he snorted. Turning, I tried to give him a serious expression, but failed miserably, unable to keep myself from grinning in response to his deep, baritone laughter as it filled the small lobby area of the parlor.

"I know I said I'd get it tattooed on my ass, but my shoulder will have to suffice," I added as I suppressed a giggle.

Rob was still chuckling softly when he bent and kissed me hard on the lips. "I love it," he murmured.

"There's one more thing," I said, surprised he hadn't yet noticed the angry skin where my second tattoo was.

I held up my left hand and Rob looked down as he grabbed my fingertips. On my ring finger was a miniature version of the same Celtic heart that was on Rob's back, the band formed by intertwined willow branches that wrapped all the way around my finger, all done in a tan ink that was slightly darker than my skin. Jax had done an incredible job with it considering the intricate detail it had required.

Several moments passed and Rob had yet to move or in any way react. As each second ticked by, I became more certain he didn't like it and convinced that I'd made a mistake. My face heated with shame, and I tried to pull my hand back, but Rob wouldn't release my fingertips.

He sniffed harshly and I saw there was moisture gathering in the corners of his eyes; he was trying to hold back tears. His thumb smoothed back and forth across the backs of my fingertips as he stared at the permanent wedding band. Without warning, he yanked me into his arms, engulfing me in a tight embrace, though managing to avoid my sore shoulder.

After a long moment, he moved to grasp my head in his hands, his eyes staring into mine as he whispered through his harsh breathing.

"I fucking love you."

"I love you, too," I replied.

"Well, you better, considering that you've permanently marked yourself as mine," he said, laughing.

Then, as if he couldn't help himself, he wrapped his arms around my waist, lifted me and twirled me around in circles, his laughter giddy, the biggest smile I'd ever seen stretched across his face. It dawned on me as the man I'd loved for over half my life gazed at me, continuing to spin us in circles, that Jax had been right; Rob *was* happy.

And in that moment, so was I.

chapter two

rob

It **was a** pleasantly cool evening, unusual for mid-August, as Annie and I meandered together along the path toward the Hideaway holding hands. Ever since the tattoos Annie had gotten the month before had healed, I couldn't keep myself from looking at them and touching them whenever there was an opportunity—doing so gave me a thrill—so my fingers rubbed over the tattoo on her finger as we walked.

"I'm so glad you closed on your house today, that you're finally completely free of it," I said, grateful for her house in the city to officially be sold.

"Yeah, I agree," she replied softly with a quick glance up at me.

Using my free hand to scratch my chin through my beard, I stopped walking and pulled Annie to a stop along the path. I needed to make sure she was telling me the truth and I needed to be able to look into her eyes to do that.

"Do you, really?" I asked, searching her face for any sign to contradict what she'd said.

"What do you mean?" she asked, her brow furrowing.

"I mean, are you glad to be free of it?"

She shuddered. "Of course. Now I'll have money to contribute around here until I'm working again. Why?"

"I told you, you don't need to worry about that," I sighed. "I meant, are you glad to be free of it, aside from what happened there with Eddie?"

She smiled, looking deep into my eyes for a moment before she replied. "Yes."

I stared back at her, hoping she was telling the truth; for some reason, my ability to discern whether or not she was eluded me. My heart was beating an erratic rhythm and felt as if it had migrated into the base of my throat as my eyes searched.

She laughed a little, but the sound was hollow, and her eyes began darting around. "What's going on?"

"Nothing, love. You ready for your surprise?" I asked, changing the subject.

"For once—yes—I'm actually excited about it."

Her eyes twinkled in the dim glow from the string lights along the path while her hair blew gently in the breeze. We were surrounded by a chorus of crickets and frogs, everything framed by a sky that would soon be overflowing with stars. The beauty of the moment, of the woman standing in front of me, was suddenly overwhelming and my breath caught.

Right then, I wanted to turn around and walk back to the house with her, keep her to myself instead of sharing her with the group waiting at the Hideaway to surprise her. I'd missed so much time with her—so many years of our lives—and I wanted to make up for it by never sharing her with anyone else for any reason. But I knew she'd like the surprise I'd planned as an early birthday gift, not to mention that I had something important to do, something I'd planned and practiced so I could do it during the celebration. So, instead of turning back to the house, I pressed a kiss to her lips and began walking toward the Hideaway again.

As we approached the clearing, we could make out shapes of people ahead, and I knew at any second Annie would figure out the surprise.

"Rob," she said, dragging my name out as excitement creeped into her voice. "Is that—"

"Yes."

"I didn't even finish my sentence!" she laughed.

"The answer is yes no matter what name you append to that sentence," I explained. "All your friends are here. For you. For your birthday."

She squealed. "I can't believe you did this!"

"Why?" I asked, winding my arms around her and pulling her into my chest. "I know how much you love your friends. And I regret I was never able to take you to senior prom. This seemed like the best way to have everything; a night dancing under the stars, but with only your friends."

"Rob," she exclaimed breathily, sounding like a giddy teenager. "This is perfect!" She threw her arms around my neck and pressed a hard kiss to my lips before breaking off suddenly. "Wait, my birthday isn't until next month."

"I know, but this was the closest date that everyone could be here at the same time."

"Thank you," she whispered before giving me a peck on the lips and then tearing herself out of my arms to crash into Haley's.

I reached into my pocket and pressed a button on the small remote and music filled the air around us. I smiled, walking slowly along the rest of the path and taking in the scene before me. Annie was talking animatedly with Haley, Carol, and Lori, her hips swaying to the beat of the music. Linc, Jax, and Lucas stood around them, each holding a beer. Linc and Jax seemed to be carrying on their own side conversation, Linc stealing an occasional glance toward the group. Lucas, however, was openly watching Annie, seemingly oblivious to anything else around him. And every few seconds, Annie would glance in his direction, and they'd exchange smiles.

My fist clenched by my side as I watched him watching her, the urge to hit him sweeping over me. Instead of indulging in that desire, however, I took several slow, deep breaths and they did seem to just take the edge off. I hadn't wanted him there to begin with—hell, I didn't want him talking to Annie again, ever—but I hadn't really had a choice about inviting him if I wanted to avoid another fight with her, and I definitely needed to tonight— especially after we'd been arguing about him just hours before when she spent over an hour texting him.

After he'd shown up unannounced at our house the week after she got out of the hospital from her burst aneurysm in June, I'd demanded she explain to me exactly what the deal was between them. She'd turned bright red and promised me they were just friends, that they'd become friends again while she and I were apart, but that it was nothing more. I didn't believe her though—I was sure I'd walked in on them about to kiss in the hospital. But when I told her she couldn't be friends with him anymore, we argued for days until I caved to keep her from walking away from me. If I hadn't invited him, she'd have been pissed at me again. Besides, he needed to be there to see what was going to happen tonight so that he'd know she was never going to be his again.

I forced my eyes away from Lucas and back to Annie as I thought about what I would soon be doing. She seemed happy, which helped to calm my nerves, though only slightly. I needed to wait for the right time, but damn if I wasn't already a nervous wreck. I came to a stop at the end of the path and leaned my shoulder against a tree, watching everyone catch up and enjoy themselves. Despite Lucas' presence nearby, I felt my face soften as I watched Annie. Something about seeing her animated and happy always made me happy, too. Until she left the group of women to greet Lucas, Jax, and Linc. She hugged them all, lingering with Lucas, then the two of them were having a private conversation.

At least ten or fifteen minutes passed before Haley left the chatty group and sidled up next to me. "Hey there, hot stuff," she greeted.

"Hi, Haley," I said, rolling my eyes.

She laughed before her face turned serious. Reaching out, she squeezed my hand briefly. "How're you doing?"

I snorted. "I'm fucking terrified."

"You know there's no reason to be, right?" she replied.

"Ha."

"Trust me. This is going to be amazing, even if it's so sweet it makes me want to projectile vomit." She squeezed my hand again. "I promise. You're nervous for no reason."

I gestured toward the group on the platform with my chin. "Bullshit," I said, my voice low. "I know there's something between them."

"No, there's not," Haley replied sternly. "I've told you—they're friends. That's it."

"Yeah, so you say."

"I do. You know what else I say? That guy right there?" She pointed to Jax. "He is positively delicious."

I laughed. "You guys have been out here for a while, haven't you talked to him?"

"Fucking duh, of course I did. Told him how gorgeous he is and everything," she replied. Huffing out a frustrated sigh, she leaned her shoulder against the same tree supporting me.

"Okay, so what's the problem?"

"He fucking laughed at me! Can you believe it? He laughed! Then he said, and I quote, 'That the best you got, darlin'?"

I was powerless to stop the laugh that rocked through me as I pictured the interaction Haley had just described.

"It's not funny, asshole," Haley gritted out. "No one has ever said something like that to me before. In fact, the only other rejection I have *ever* gotten was from you. And that guy is beyond fucking hot, way hotter than *you*, no offense—"

"None taken."

"—and he completely blew me off! What the fuck? And every time I look at him, I get all hot and bothered, but he won't do anything except laugh every time I catch his eye."

She huffed and I continued to chuckle. Haley had met her match, it seemed. Jax reminded me of a countrified and tattooed male version of her. I wondered if it was just her bruised ego or if it was Jax that had her so upset about what was happening, but I completely lost my train of thought when Annie started toward me.

In the time since she'd gotten out of the hospital, Annie had gained some weight, something I attributed to her eating regularly again, and I fucking loved it. I had always been captivated by her curviness since the day I had first seen her in literature class. She'd never been like everyone else who was stick thin and straight as a damn pole. She was self-conscious about it then, sometimes even teased for being heavier than other girls, but she seemed to be more accepting of it now, which meant she was healthy and beyond gorgeous.

As she neared, I could see the quick stab of doubt and self-consciousness in her eyes before she had a chance to hide it. She should never feel that way, and I needed to do something about it.

"Excuse me," I murmured to Haley without taking my eyes off Annie. Pushing off the tree, I moved toward Annie as she continued to sway her way over to me, meeting her a few steps from where I'd been. As soon as we reached each other, I wrapped my arms around her and gave her a long, hard kiss, eliciting catcalls from some of our friends.

I paused then, nervous. This wasn't how I'd planned it, but it seemed to be the perfect timing. Logically, there was no reason to be anxious, but that didn't stop my heart from hammering in my chest, my lungs from forgetting how to function, my stomach from flipping over. I wanted this to be perfect for her—Annie deserved nothing less. I grasped her head between my hands, giving her a chaste kiss on her lips, then stepped back, lowering my back leg to the ground so that I was on one knee as my hands slid down her arms until I intertwined our fingers.

"Rob, what're you—"

"Ever since the day I met you," I interrupted, "I have been captivated under your spell, living for you, breathing for you. I was an angry, cocky, know-it-all delinquent when I met you, but you saw through it all... you saw *me* and changed my life for the better." I swallowed, willing away the tears that had appeared in my eyes. I wanted to make sure I got out everything I wanted to say; there was a speech I'd memorized, but not one word of it was coming to me.

"I knew only darkness and pain until you loved me. You taught me there was also light and happiness. You taught me how to love because that's what you did. You taught me how to appreciate what I had instead of focus on what I didn't, because that's how you lived. You showed me the person I was inside, the person I didn't even know existed before you. You taught me how to find a silver lining in every situation because that's the kind of person you were. From your untamed curls to the freckles on your face, your expressive eyes to your infectious laughter, your quirky sense of humor to your intense compassion for others in need, your passion for life to your selfless devotion to those you love—there is beauty in every facet of your personality, in every movement you make, in every inch of your skin, in every word you say." I cleared my throat and then laughed nervously. I sounded like a blubbering idiot, but I couldn't stop now.

"Anyway, what I'm trying to say is that you are and always will be the only woman for me. All my love is yours. I am forever under your spell, and I want to spend every second of every day of the rest of our lives together, doing everything I can to make sure you know it. I know we already signed papers at the courthouse, but what I want to know is…" I cleared my throat again. "Will you marry me, Annie? Walk down an aisle for all to see, pledge before everyone we know to let me worship you until my dying breath? Because—fuck—that's all I want in this world."

She looked down at me, tugging on my hands, but I couldn't move until she spoke. Even though we'd eloped at the beginning of the year, that had been a spur-of-the-moment decision and I needed to know it was what she actually wanted.

"You're killing me, here, love," I croaked out.

She giggled. "Only *you* would propose *after* we got married."

"All the same," I said tightly, not finding her lack of a response at all funny. "Will you marry me? Again, I guess?"

"Of course, always, as many times as you want." She laughed.

Rising to my feet, I cupped her face. "You know, I had a plan, I knew exactly what I was going to say, and a specific time for it and then, as usual, you flipped everything on its head. My planned speech was much more eloquent… I'm sorry I couldn't wait a moment longer."

"Sorry? This was incredibly romantic."

"I don't know. There was a song, and then—fuck!" I shouted, cutting myself off.

"What's wrong?"

"Nothing's *wrong*," I bit out, angry with myself for having fucked up the most important part of the evening. "I just completely forgot the ring. I'm so sorry, love, you deserved a better proposal than that train wreck you just put up with."

She snorted. "That wasn't a train wreck. And I don't need a ring."

"You don't understand—I have one, I just forgot to pull the damn thing out of my pocket."

Her smile stretched across her face. "Even so, I don't need one; I've got one already that can never be removed."

"Well, you can wear *this* one for everyone else to see, then, so they all know that you're taken... that you're *mine*."

"Oh, I get it," she said, laughing, as I fumbled to pull the ring out and slide it onto her finger. "You're marking your territory, like a dog peeing on a hydrant."

I barked out a laugh at her completely, utterly, perfectly unromantic description of what wearing my ring meant. "I fucking love you."

"I effing love you, too," she replied.

chapter three

annie

Despite the late night of dancing and the seemingly endless exhaustion that still plagued me, I woke early. My bladder had insisted. Jax and Lucas had driven home the night before since they both lived close by, but everyone else was staying for the weekend, and they were all still sleeping. I smiled, thinking back to the night before as I padded down the hallway in my pajamas toward the kitchen to start a pot of coffee. Looking down when I reached the kitchen island, I studied the ring on my finger, getting my first good look at it in the light.

It was exquisite. The band was carved from white gold like the twisting, wispy, stubbled branches of a willow, with a diamond forming a bud in the center. I slipped the ring off, noticing the similarity between the band on it and the band of the tattooed ring on my finger... he must have had the ring custom made to match. Just as I was slipping the ring back on, something caught my eye. Closer inspection revealed the inside of the band had been engraved with the words *You and Me, Always.*

Rob's leathery scent reached my nostrils as I read the words, but before I had a chance to process what that meant, his arms were already wrapped around my waist from behind. He nuzzled my ear as he pulled my back into his bare chest. "Do you like it?" he asked, his voice deep and scratchy like it always was first thing in the morning.

"Eh, it's okay," I replied with a shrug, trying to keep my voice even, but failing to suppress a giggle.

"Well, maybe I should just return it, then," Rob replied, snapping the ring from my fingertips.

"No!" I shrieked, laughing and trying to reach for it, but Rob's other arm was still wrapped around my waist, holding me in place.

"Shhhh, don't wake everyone up," he laughed, holding the ring high over his head.

Futilely, I reached up as far as I could, but I was too hopelessly short to reach his hand. Jumping was also useless with his arm around my waist preventing me from moving more than an inch or so off the ground. After a few minutes of laughing struggle, I gave up and rested my head back against his shoulder, looking up into his face.

"Okay, I give up," I whispered, smiling. Rob's face changed as we gazed at each other, the laughter in his eyes shifting to desire. Butterflies took flight in my stomach as my blood became hot and pounded in my veins. I barely noticed when he lowered his hand and slipped the ring back onto my finger. The fingers of his free hand tipped my chin away from him and he bent his head to kiss my neck.

My body shuddered, all playfulness gone, as his facial hair scratched my skin in that way I loved. Equal parts desire, anticipation, and anxiety filled my bloodstream. Ever since Eddie had attacked me in the hospital and in my house in the city, I'd been assaulted by relentless, violent flashbacks. Both Eddie and Charlie invaded my mind anytime Rob and I came close to having sex, even though Eddie was over an hour away and Charlie wasn't going to be released from prison until December. Even Rob's efforts to keep me tethered to the present—efforts that at one point had been successful—had been failing.

Rob, of course, had been understanding and patient, but I hated that I'd regressed from where I'd been earlier in the summer before Eddie and my aneurysm. I wanted so desperately to feel that connection with him again. To experience intimacy without the intrusion of violent memories.

My thoughts slipped away again when Rob turned me in his arms, his lips finding mine. As he kissed me, that same all-consuming and mesmerizing kiss he'd always had, I lifted my left hand from bracing me against the counter and rested it on his cheek. Rob broke our kiss to nuzzle my hand with his cheek, his eyes closed.

"I feel your ring catching the hair in my beard," he whispered, his voice gravelly and harsh. "I fucking love it." With a sharp inhale, he lifted me onto the edge of the island countertop behind me.

"Rob," I whispered, the skin on my face heating, "there are people—"

He cut me off with a kiss, his hands grasping my thighs. "Exactly why we need to stay quiet—so we don't wake them up," he rumbled in my ear before his teeth nibbled the lobe.

My body shivered involuntarily, forcing my breath out in a burst. "Please," I breathed out, leaning back and turning away. "Someone could walk in."

Rob let out a sigh and stepped back, his shoulders falling. "Okay," he said, stepping over and starting to make coffee. After it was started, he remained where he was, facing the coffee pot with his back to me.

I slipped off the counter, my chest heavy with guilt. "I'm sorry," I said quietly as the coffee finished brewing, feeling the need to apologize for having said no to what was happening between us. I knew he missed having sex; I could see it in his face every time I stopped us. "I—"

"Do I smell coffee?" Linc interrupted as he wandered into the kitchen yawning.

"Sure do," I replied, staring at the floor. "Help yourself."

Turning, I slipped out of the kitchen to get dressed. Not only was I uncomfortable around Linc in my pajamas, but I knew it would stir up Rob's jealousy and wanted to avoid yet another argument with him about who I was friends with.

chapter four

annie

Carol, **Haley, and** I were lounging in the library, catching up while Lori was still sleeping. Rob and Linc were supposed to be heading to the basement to spar, but instead they walked into the room. While Rob walked toward me, Linc stopped just inside the doorway, staring at Carol, who was looking the other direction, completely unaware of his attention.

"Hey, I thought you and Linc were going downstairs?" I asked, smiling up at Rob as he reached me.

"We are, love, I just wanted another kiss first."

He cupped my face as he bent over to kiss me. After a few hard, chaste kisses, he pulled back. Without another word, he turned and left, Linc on his heels. I watched them go, shaking my head, smiling, though I still felt unsettled about what had happened between us in the kitchen that morning.

Once the door had closed behind them, Haley began talking about her lingering frustration with being blown off by Jax the previous night. I'd never seen her so agitated about a guy before and listened in amusement. Surely, there was something more to it than frustration about being rebuffed.

"I think I might be pregnant, guys," Carol interjected when Haley paused for breath.

My jaw dropped, and a glance revealed Haley's countenance mirroring mine. The thought of Carol having sex outside of a committed relationship was shocking—she was practically the opposite of Haley in that regard—and we weren't aware of her having a boyfriend.

"Who's the guy?" Haley asked.

Carol looked down at her hands, her cheeks pink. "I don't know for sure that I'm even pregnant," she said quietly. "I haven't taken a test yet. But I'm almost always regular and I'm late."

"How late?" I asked.

"Two weeks."

"Who's the guy?" Haley asked again, her voice more forceful this time.

Carol's face shifted from pink to red, but she didn't say anything. I remembered Linc watching her the night before, Carol steadfastly avoiding eye contact with him and blushing when she couldn't. And then Linc had been gazing at her just minutes ago, not even having noticed Haley or me.

"It's Linc, isn't it?" I asked gently.

She nodded in response.

"I knew it!" Haley shouted triumphantly, her arm shooting into the air. "I *knew* there was something going on between you guys!"

I shot Haley a look, then asked Carol, "Why are you embarrassed? Are you guys seeing each other?"

"We only slept together once," Carol responded. "He wants more, but... I can't."

"Why the fuck not?" Haley asked.

"Because!" Carol shouted in reply.

"Because why?" Haley persisted, shrugging. "I don't see the problem."

Carol turned to glare at her. "Of course you wouldn't. I'd be dating the guy who screwed one of my best friends and was in love with the other. Besides the fact that it feels like I'm betraying you guys. He must just be desperate or something, anyway, you know—like, I'll do since options one and two didn't work out." Carol's voice broke on the last word.

"Not true," I said, getting up and walking over to sit down next to Carol, pulling her into a hug. "You're better than both of us; you're beautiful, smart, loyal, caring, kind, fun, sweet, determined, successful, level-headed, rational—should I keep going? I can do this all day."

She offered a small half-smile. "No, I get the point—you think I'm great. But it's true that I'm third choice."

"That's not a fair assessment, Carol," Haley chimed in. "You didn't even meet Linc until after I'd met him, and the thing with Annie was completely contrived because I wanted her to get laid. And if you remember, Linc was a douchey male whore until then. He never would have had a chance with you because you were just way too good for him." She hmphed. "Still are, really."

Carol snorted in response, but there was a softening of her features and a hint of a smile on her lips. "Thanks for the pep talk, guys, but I still don't want to be pregnant with his baby. Or at all, actually. I'm not ready for that."

"Well, I can go get a pregnancy test so we can find out for sure," I offered. "There's a pharmacy not too far down the road."

"I already got some," Carol replied. "Actually, I've had a multi-pack of every brand in the grocery store in my purse for the last four days. I've just been too scared to take them."

"We'll take them with you!" Haley shouted, jumping to her feet. "Come on, it'll be fun."

I shook my head. "If peeing on sticks is your idea of fun..."

Haley winked at me, pulling Carol to her feet. "Come on, let's do it. How many do you have?"

"Eighteen tests," Carol said sheepishly.

"*Eighteen?*" Haley balked.

"Eight brands. Six are two-packs, and two are three-packs."

"I think you're set for life," Haley muttered. "Come on, let's go pee on some sticks."

While waiting for the results to show on the tests, we went to the kitchen to start a fresh pot of coffee, Haley keeping Carol distracted with complaints about Jax's response to her despite her best efforts to proposition him. Once the coffee was happily brewing away, we meandered back to the bathroom to take a look.

We all froze as we stepped in and looked at the counter. Two negatives and one positive. I glanced up sideways at Haley and Carol, who were looking from the countertop to me.

"I think I'm losing it," I laughed, though my heart was racing. "Which test is mine? I thought it was in the middle but it can't be."

"Mine was left," Haley said.

"And mine was right," Carol chimed in.

I looked back down again at the test, at the very dark second line that indicated a positive pregnancy result, and my breath whooshed out of my lungs. "That can't be," I whispered. "Someone switched the tests."

"There's no one *to* switch the tests, babe," Haley said.

"But *that—*" I pointed to the middle test on the counter, "isn't possible. I had a period a few weeks ago, and I haven't had sex since before my aneurysm." Though my period *was* much lighter than normal. But stress could do that, and my period had never been predictable anyway; it wasn't the first light period I'd ever had.

"Okay," Carol jumped in, her hands held up. "This is easy to solve. Just take another test."

"We'll *all* do it again," Haley agreed.

I nodded, and we proceeded to select three more tests and pee on them. This time, however, we didn't leave the bathroom and we stood right in front of our own tests. But it didn't matter. I didn't have to wait the full two minutes to know the result of mine; the second line appeared right away as the moisture moved across the results window.

My eyes glued to the test on the counter, I stumbled backward into the wall, then slid down to the floor. *Pregnant. I'm pregnant. I'm going to have a baby. The gynecologist told me I'd have trouble getting pregnant, but here I am.* I tore my eyes from the test and looked up at Haley and Carol, who were both beaming at me.

"Congratulations, babe!" Haley squealed.

"That's so exciting!" Carol added.

I stared back at them, still processing the news. Having a family with Rob one day wasn't an idea I was averse to, exactly, but it was something we hadn't even discussed yet, something that had been safely far in the future. Except that it wasn't in the future anymore—it was right now. What would Rob think?

"I can't be pregnant, guys. I'll take another one tomorrow," I said, swallowing. "It must be a false positive. I told you—I had a period a few weeks ago."

"That could have been implantation bleeding," Carol said. "Trust me, I did a lot of research—"

"You've gotta be wrong," I interrupted. "The test has to be wrong."

"Babe, I know it's not convenient, but... is it really such a bad thing?" Haley asked as she squatted down in front of me, placing her hands on my knees. "You guys love each other, you're happy together, you're financially secure, you have space, you have support. And don't you guys want kids one day anyway?"

"I don't know," I whispered. "I don't know if Rob wants kids. I don't know how he'll react to this."

Haley snorted. "I'm sure he does, and he'll be over the moon. Anything with you makes him happy."

"But I'm taking blood pressure medication, what if it causes birth defects? I should stop taking it—"

"Don't you fucking dare," Haley cut me off. "I was there when the doctor told you that stopping suddenly can give you a heart attack and fucking kill you. Don't even consider it. I'll tell Rob to shove those pills down your damn throat if he has to."

"You can't tell Rob! Not yet. Not until I'm sure."

"You can't hide it for—"

"And what if I lose it?" I cut Haley off.

"You mean miscarriage?" Carol asked. "Most miscarriages happen before you even know you're pregnant."

"But what if it happens? What then? Rob—if he wanted a baby—he would be devastated."

They continued speaking, but I couldn't hear their voices. My mind was playing through different scenarios for how Rob might react to the news. Would he be happy? Or angry? Or disappointed? I could predict how he'd react to most things and act accordingly, but this was unfamiliar territory. Would he lose his temper? What would he do if he did? My stomach lurched at that thought and the room started to spin.

"Hey guys. What's going on?" Rob's voice floated into the bathroom from the hall.

I curled tightly into my knees and willed my breathing to normalize so the room would stop spinning. Haley and Carol filed out of the bathroom without a word, leaving me alone with Rob. At least they'd thrown away the pregnancy tests before he appeared.

"Love? Are you okay?" he asked.

I looked up into his face, covered in a sheen of sweat, a big drop about to fall from his forehead. Reaching up to where he was stooped over me, I swiped it before it had a chance to drip on my face.

"I'm fine," I said quietly, studying his eyes for any hint of how he might take the news that we were going to be parents.

"Why are you on the floor?"

My heart skipped as my mind raced to come up with an excuse. "I'm just a bit dizzy," I said when I could come up with nothing else. At least it was true.

"Okay, love," he murmured, reaching his hands out for mine. "Let's get you up, and then we're going to the doctor."

"No, I'm fine, I promise. I'm just a little hot."

Rob's forehead knit together as he looked at me. "It's not that warm in here, Annie."

"I swear I'm fine," I insisted. "I don't need to see the doctor."

He studied me, the slight shift in his expression giving away that he suspected I was hiding something. I wished he would just let it go and leave me to go do whatever he was going to do when he saw us all in the bathroom. Having him so near to me was making the dizziness worse, and now I was feeling sick.

"When did you last take your blood pressure?" he asked.

"Yesterday. And it was low. Really low, actually—the lowest it's ever been in my life, so I'm fine. I promise."

"I don't know, Annie—"

"I said I'm fine! Just leave me alone!" The shout escaped unexpectedly, and guilt rolled over me. He didn't deserve to be yelled at. A glance revealed hardened features and hurt in his eyes. "I'm sorry." I looked away, feeling faint. "I didn't mean to yell at you. It's just that I'm fine. I'll lay down for a while, okay?"

His narrowed eyes probed me for a long moment. "Okay, go lay down," he said, his voice low and dubious.

The next morning, I woke dazed and exhausted. My dreams had been filled with memories of my biological mother, and I woke several times soaked in sweat. When I'd lived with her, I'd existed in a constant state of fear, never knowing when she would have a bad day and lose her temper on me over something small or even non-existent. As a child, I had no idea what I might say or do that would result in her screaming at me or bruising me somehow.

Rob hovered more than usual, his drawn and tight features betraying his worry and suspicion, but I kept to myself and continued insisting I was fine. I couldn't even sort out my thoughts about my childhood, let alone about the fact that I might be bringing my own child into the world.

First, I needed to take more tests so I'd know for sure that I was pregnant. And to do that, I needed Rob out of the house. I contrived a reason for him to run out to the store after Carol and Linc had left, and while he was gone, I took all the remaining pregnancy tests. They all told the same story: I was pregnant.

"Talk to me, babe," Haley said, leaning into the kitchen counter, facing me.

I shook my head as I gazed at her. "I don't even know," I muttered. "I have so many different feelings and thoughts whirling around like a tornado and it's like I can't find solid ground."

"Any of them happy feelings?"

I nodded. "Yeah. Some of them."

"Focus on those, then."

"But what if he doesn't want kids?"

"If it's with you, I'm sure he does."

"And Haley... how can I be a mother? I don't know anything about being a parent."

She laughed. "No one does before they have kids."

"That's not what I mean. My mom—my biological mom—she was... well... I mean, I loved her, but..." My voice cracked and tears started sliding down my cheeks. Using my palms, I cleared them and continued. "My mom was a horrible parent. What if I'm just like her?"

Haley pulled me into her arms and rubbed my back. "You're not your mom," she said gently. "You're nothing like her. And you won't parent like her."

"You don't know that."

She pulled back and looked me straight in the eye. "You won't. Because I'll tell you if you ever do. I promise you."

I nodded, sobbing into her shoulder for a few minutes before her words really sank in. She was right—I wasn't anything like my mom had been. My mom had yelled at me for no reason and never apologized; she'd drank to excess regularly, while I rarely drank at all. We *were* different. That didn't mean I wouldn't be a terrible parent, of course, but at least I had a better starting point. Pulling back, I snagged a tissue from another counter and blew my nose. With a final swipe across my cheeks to dry them with my hands, I turned to Haley and smiled. After confessing that fear to Haley and crying, I felt better than I had since I 'd seen the first positive test.

"You're right," I said. "I'm not her. I'm me, and I can do better."

"Damn straight," Haley agreed with a grin. "You already are. All you need to do is tell Rob the news."

My smile faltered, but I forced it to return. "Okay."

"He's going to be so happy about it, babe. You're going to call me laughing and feeling stupid because you were so afraid of nothing."

"You're probably right."

"Of course I am," she replied shamelessly.

I laughed, a wisp of excitement coursing through me. Maybe she was right. Maybe I was afraid of nothing. Maybe it was just my fear patterns of old taking over again.

"Okay." I smiled. "Once I figure out how best to do it, I'll tell him."

Lori walked into the kitchen at that moment, yawning. "Tell who what?"

Haley smirked. "That you're gonna be an aunt."

Lori stopped short. "Wait, really? That's awesome!"

A grin broke across my face as it heated. "Really. I just found out. So please don't say anything to Rob when he gets back. I'll tell him after you guys leave."

"I won't," Lori said quickly. "Promise."

Then, with a squeal, Lori rushed forward and hugged me. It was possibly the first time she'd ever spontaneously hugged me before and it felt... good. Strange, but good. And for some reason, I felt a little more excited about my unexpected pregnancy.

Lori left right after lunch and Haley a few hours later. Once they were gone, I was looking forward to some time to myself to try to sort out all my thoughts and feelings about being pregnant and to figure out how and when to tell Rob. However, I didn't get the time I was hoping for. Within moments of Haley's departure, Rob was back in the house from his workshop. Something was bothering him—he was watching me constantly, scowling, and I could feel his tension and anger. I wanted to do something to help but was too distracted by how much I had on my own mind to even try to figure out what was wrong.

By dinnertime, the tension was so heavy I had trouble eating. As I pushed my food around my plate, seeing the positive pregnancy tests in my mind, I made an effort to start a conversation.

"Thank you again for the party," I said, looking up and offering a genuine smile—I really had enjoyed the surprise he'd planned for me. "It was great to see everyone."

Rob stared at me expressionless for several long seconds without moving. "Everyone? Or Lucas?"

"What?" I asked with a small headshake.

His jaw ticked. "It was obvious how happy you were to see *him*. You barely even noticed anyone else."

My heart skipped, making my chest contract painfully for a moment, before beginning to race. "What are you talking about? I spent time with everyone."

There was a loud clatter as Rob dropped his fork onto his plate. His arms crossed in front of him, and I could see how tense every muscle in his body was. "I'm not fucking blind, Annie. I saw the way you guys looked at each other all night. I saw you guys touching each other every fucking time you talked."

My face leapt into flames. Lucas hadn't been looking at me any differently than he always did, and I hadn't looked at him any differently either. And he hadn't touched me in a way he shouldn't have. "We're friends," I said slowly, already knowing what was coming next.

"Bullshit, Annie! He's your goddamn ex—you shouldn't even be talking to him!"

My stomach clenched and I swallowed the bile rising in my throat as my vision began to tunnel. "Rob," I started in as soothing a voice as I could muster, my hands now shaking wildly, "you and I are *married*. That—"

"And that's why you shouldn't be fucking talking to him," he cut me off.

"Who I'm friends with is *my* decision, and I am not ending my friendship with Lucas," I asserted, just as I had countless times over the summer. As afraid as I was of how angry Rob was, I refused to let him cut Lucas out of my life this time. Not losing Lucas again was sometimes the *only* thing in my life I was sure about; having done so the first time was a mistake I wasn't going to repeat.

"Goddamnit, Annie!" he roared. "Be friends with whoever the fuck else you want, but end it with *him!*"

My jaw trembled and my eyes filled with tears, but I refused to back down. "No."

He shoved away from the table. "I'm going for a walk," he muttered, then strode out of the room.

As he went, a breath I'd been holding whooshed out of me. I hated fighting with him, and I especially hated that it was about Lucas. Maybe the pregnancy and the idea of starting a family together would help calm his jealousy. I certainly hoped so... I couldn't imagine having him blow up like that in front of our kids.

Still shaky, I cleaned up the table and the kitchen, but Rob wasn't back yet. I knew he was out in the woods somewhere, likely hitting a tree, though I hoped not. Just in case, I set out supplies for him to clean up his hands on the counter in the bathroom. I wasn't sure I'd ever felt more exhausted in my life.

Even so, I couldn't fall asleep after I laid down. While I was lying there, I got a message from Lucas that my sister had just left after an hours-long date at the brewery. He said the guy seemed alright, but they'd left separately after exchanging numbers. I responded, thanking him for looking out for her, and then thanking him again for coming to the party. I knew he didn't like being around Rob and appreciated that he'd come anyway.

We chatted over text for several minutes, and while I didn't feel right sharing the news with him before telling Rob, I did tell him I had some news that I was worried about, and that I'd tell him what it was soon, but asked him to wish me luck. I knew when he didn't respond right away that he must be busy with customers and set my phone back down with a yawn.

Just texting with him had helped me to feel calmer and more optimistic and I was finally sleepy. I'd get a good night's rest, and the next day, when Rob had had time to calm down, I'd tell him the news. He'd realize how ridiculous he was acting, and then we'd start a new chapter in our lives.

chapter five

rob

Annie was hiding something from me, without a doubt—she had been since I'd found her sitting on the bathroom floor two days earlier. It had crossed my mind every few minutes that it could be that she'd changed her mind about us and decided she wanted fucking Lucas.

And hell, I'd seen her and Lucas interacting the night of her mini surprise party. Seen the way his eyes devoured her, the way she smiled in return. The blush that crept onto her cheeks whenever they made eye contact. The way she was so comfortable with him touching her, which he did every fucking time he spoke to her. I wasn't an idiot—they obviously had feelings for each other, no matter what Annie and Haley had said about them only being friends.

Why else would she be so stubborn about staying friends with him? She wouldn't listen to reason when it came to him. And the morning after the party, she'd pushed me away and it had nothing to do with a flashback. Was it because she was thinking about him instead? What the fuck did she see in him, anyway? When *he'd* thrown her a surprise party, he'd fucked it up in every way. She'd loved what *I* did for her. Didn't she see that I knew her better than he ever would?

I was tempted again to check her phone. I'd sat staring at it while she was sleeping the night before, at the preview for a message from Lucas that said "It'll be okay. I'm here no matter what—I'm not going anywhere."

What would be okay? And he wasn't going anywhere? What the hell did that mean?

I'd managed to lay down without invading her privacy, but after a restless night, I was as tempted as ever to read through her messages and see for myself if there was something going on between her and Lucas. But if there wasn't, Annie would never forgive me for snooping on her, so I refrained.

I finished taking my frustration out on my heavy bag and trudged up the stairs from the basement. After showering, I found Annie in the library, but she wasn't reading, or even sleeping, which she seemed to do a lot nowadays. She was just staring off into space with a small smile on her face that faltered as I entered. I sat down across from her, trying to figure out how exactly to talk to her about Lucas in a way that she would understand she couldn't stay friends with him—*without* yelling at her again. But before I had a chance, she spoke.

"I want to talk to you about something," she said, her smile back in place, though I could see the hesitation in her eyes.

"It's about damn time," I bit out, my eyes boring into hers. My whole body was already tensing in anticipation of what she was about say.

Her smile disappeared and her brows drew in. "U-um," she stuttered, then fell silent, her eyes falling to her lap.

I studied her as I waited for her to speak. Was I really about to lose her to Lucas? No—there had to be a way to fix it. I'd make sure of it. My saliva was thick and stuck in my throat when I swallowed. I was upset and angry, vacillating between the two rapidly as I waited.

"Annie, just tell me what the fuck you're hiding from me and get it over with."

Her eyes darted up to mine, now filled with so much fear my heart stuttered, then looked away again quickly. I reached across the space between us to clasp her hand and she flinched away, her body stiffening. In that moment, I knew I was right that it had to do with Lucas—there was no other explanation for my touch being so unwelcome that she'd recoil. My anger reached boiling just under the surface—I wanted to beat the living hell out of him. But I had to keep myself in check a little longer... I wouldn't be able to fix anything if I hauled off and started hitting shit first. Instead, my hands balled into fists.

"Rob," she whispered, her voice wavering, "I'm pregnant."

My thoughts stalled for a moment, and I stared at her, trying to process her words... she was pregnant.

"Are you sure?" I asked, my words drawn out as reality sank in.

Her head moved up and down, her glassy eyes wide and now trained on me. My blood pounded in my ears.

"Maybe you're wrong," I rushed out, desperate for her to be mistaken. "Did you take a test?"

She inhaled slowly, her lips trembling as she did, then huffed out that breath before whispering in a watery voice. "Fourteen of them."

Annie was pregnant. Everything made sense now. And I was so goddamned stupid. So in love with her that I deluded myself into thinking she felt the same way because I so desperately wanted it to be true.

"No." I pushed up from the chair to my feet, my head shaking back and forth as if denial could make it any less true. "No, no, no! This can't be happening." My body began to tremble and the pain morphed into burning rage. "I fucking loved you, Annie! I would have done anything for you! And you just... you..."

The sounds of Annie's sobs filled the silence in the room when words failed me, but she said nothing.

"Don't you have anything to say?" I shouted. "Anything? Fucking say something, goddamn it!"

"I-I didn't mean for it to happen. I'm... so... sorry," she whispered between sobs, hugging her knees to her chest.

"You didn't mean for it to happen? You're *sorry*? Fuck sorry, Annie!" I stared at her hunched form for a moment, trying to breathe through the crushing weight of betrayal. I could have found a way to deal with anything she revealed... except this. "Get out," I ground out through my clenched jaw, my hand jabbing toward the front of the house. "Now. And don't ever fucking come back."

Turning, I strode through the house, outside, and into the woods. I needed to get away for a while—away from our home... away from the woman who'd just destroyed every reason I had to live.

chapter six

annie

It was several minutes after Rob left before I could make myself move. I had played out in my mind dozens of possibilities for how he might react to the news that I was pregnant, but not a single one was as bad as reality. He'd been enraged, disgusted. He'd spoken as if the pregnancy destroyed his love for me. I never would have thought him capable of reacting like that, but he had. Not only that, but he'd told me to leave... and never come back.

I told him I'm pregnant, and he's kicking me out.

A panic attack was imminent—it was rising like a wave of terror in my chest that made it nearly impossible to breathe or think or see. And I was completely and utterly alone. Except for the life growing inside me. A life that depended on me for survival—I had to provide it with oxygen, which wouldn't be possible if I didn't somehow calm down enough to breathe. Action would provide a distraction that would allow me to function—at least for a while. And what I needed to do was find somewhere to go.

Mom was out of the question. She'd only make things worse with her constant questions and need to say she told me so about Rob. One day I'd be able to handle her, but not yet. Haley and Carol were hours away and I couldn't wait that long for them to arrive. Rob could return any time and he wasn't in control of himself—that much had been obvious, from the ticking vein in his temple to his fists and harsh breathing. I was afraid of how he might act, of what he might do to me, if I was still there. It was the first time I'd ever seen the violence in his eyes directed at *me*, and now, for the first time, I found myself truly, deeply afraid of him.

Clearing the tears off my face, I stood unsteadily against the sudden spinning of the room and searched the house until I found my cell phone still plugged up in our bedroom. Snatching it off the nightstand, I fired off a text to Lucas, telling him I'd explain later but that I needed him to come get me as soon as possible—there was no way I could drive right then. Next, I texted Haley to tell her what had just happened.

Almost immediately, my phone started ringing. Answering and talking to Haley would lead to another breakdown, something that couldn't happen again just yet. First, I had to get safely away from my house. After sending the call to my voicemail, I texted her to explain that we'd have to talk later. Then, with as deep a breath as my lungs could manage considering it felt like a tank was sitting on my chest, I pulled out a suitcase and started packing.

I hadn't been on the front porch with my suitcase for more than a minute or two before Lucas' car flew up the driveway, spraying gravel in its wake. After coming to a stop only a few feet from the porch steps, Lucas jumped out and started jogging toward me. I stood and reached behind to grab my suitcase, but the sudden motion combined with the dizziness that hadn't subsided in the last few days knocked me off balance and I stumbled sideways.

"Whoa!" Lucas shouted as he leapt up the remaining porch steps to steady me. "Are you okay?"

"Yeah," I responded, my voice small. My body felt weighed down with grief and exhaustion and speaking required more effort than usual. "A little dizzy, that's all."

"Leave the suitcase, I'll grab it once we get you into the car."

"I'm fine."

"No, I don't think you are," he responded, his eyes scanning my face. "You almost fell over."

He wrapped one arm around my back and held the other out for me to grab onto, and despite what I'd just said, I was grateful for his help; the world was still spinning around me. Once he'd settled me into his passenger seat, he returned to the porch to retrieve my suitcase and then hopped into the driver's seat. Worry was etched into his features as he looked at me before putting the car in gear.

"Where are we going? The doctor?" he asked.

"No—I'm alright. I've always had dizzy spells when I'm emotional. And my blood sugar is probably low because I haven't eaten much—I'll be fine once I do."

"I don't know… I've never seen you just stumble like that for no reason."

I reached over and squeezed his hand, forcing a small smile so he'd believe me. "I promise." Looking away, I added, "Can I go to your house for a while?"

"Of course," he replied. "But what's going on?"

I shook my head and allowed my gaze to roam the woods by the side of the house as Lucas shifted the car into gear and started to drive. The air in my lungs rushed out when I spotted Rob there, standing amongst the trees where they met the yard. His hands were fisted and bloody, but the worst part was the chilling expression in his eyes as he stared at me: pure, unadulterated hatred.

"Shit," Lucas breathed out. "What's going on, Annie?"

"We had a fight," I whispered, my eyes filling with tears.

"*That*—" Lucas replied, lifting a hand and pointing toward Rob, "—looks like more than just a fight."

My jaw started trembling as I tried to make the words come, but they refused. I couldn't tear my eyes away from Rob and the look on his face that would haunt me for the rest of my life.

"What did he to do you?" Lucas asked forcefully a few seconds later, his voice hardening.

When I glanced over, his eyes were frantically scanning my body. "Nothing. I mean, he…"

"Annie, you promised me this summer you'd tell me if he ever hurt you. You can trust me. What did he do?"

Once I could no longer see Rob, I shifted to face Lucas, studying his face as he drove for a moment. When he glanced over, I turned away, already shrinking down to take whatever his reaction might be. After Rob's explosion, I had no idea what to expect from anyone anymore.

"I'm pregnant," I said as my voice broke.

Lucas swallowed but was otherwise silent as we pulled from the driveway onto the paved back road that would lead us into town.

"I found out Saturday," I continued. "I told Rob this morning and he lost his shit. He told me to get out and never come back."

As soon as the last words left my lips, the sobs I'd suppressed while I packed and waited for Lucas to arrive returned, and I rested my face in my hands as my body heaved and struggled to draw in air.

Lucas slowed and pulled over onto the shoulder. As soon as the car stopped, he was pulling me into his arms. Turning, I removed my seatbelt and fell forward into his chest, crying so hard my ribs hurt. He held me in a tight embrace, patiently letting me cry until my tears dried up, a hand gently stroking my back, his head resting against mine. He never spoke, but it wouldn't have made any difference if he had—there were no words that could make what had just happened hurt any less.

chapter seven

lucas

Annie **was crying** in my arms on the side of the road and I still wasn't convinced Rob hadn't done something more to her than what she'd told me. Not that throwing her out wasn't bad enough. Anger flared in my chest at what he was putting her through. How callous would someone have to be to throw out their pregnant wife?

I wanted her to tell me everything that had happened since I'd left the party Friday night, but it wasn't the time, even if my mind was running through different possibilities. What she needed in that moment was to let everything she was feeling out the way she was, and there was nothing I could say that would help—I knew that from when my mom died—so I didn't even try.

The only thing I could do was hold her for as long as she needed and then be there for her, whatever came next, whatever it meant. I'd make sure she was taken care of, that she'd have the support she needed if she was keeping this baby. I was sure she would, though—I couldn't imagine her *not* keeping it, even if Rob didn't want to, which seemed obvious from what happened.

God, what an asshole he is.

There was another flash of anger as I imagined what might have transpired when he threw her out, seeing his face as I had moments earlier as we were leaving. Annie deserved so much better than to be exposed to that kind of violence. Anyone did, but the thought of it being turned on *her* made my chest constrict.

I continued smoothing my hand slowly up and down Annie's back as her sobs tapered off and I felt her body get heavy against my chest. Soon she'd stopped crying, but I didn't move away; I'd hold her until she was ready.

"Do you have any tissues?" she asked, her voice flat and quiet as she pulled back out of my arms, sniffling.

"Napkins okay? That's all I've got. In the glove box."

"That's fine." She pulled some out and blew her nose. Then with a loud inhale and deep sigh, she replaced her seatbelt. "I'm okay now. We can go."

"Are you sure?" I asked, pulling my own seatbelt slowly across my body.

"Yeah. Thank you. I'm sorry I fell apart."

"Don't be sorry, Annie," I replied gently.

After several miles passed, I decided to ask. "Will you tell me everything that happened?"

She nodded, and then told me in detail everything that had happened that morning leading up to her texting me. My hands tightened on the steering wheel as she told me about him yelling at her.

"You said he was already angry this morning. Do you know why?"

"I... yes, I do. I think."

She swallowed loudly, looking out the window.

"Are you comfortable telling me?" I asked.

Her breathing became louder and choppier. "We had a fight last night, too. About something else. Something we've been fighting about all summer. I think he was still mad about that."

They'd been fighting all summer? Annie and I at least texted daily, and she'd never once mentioned any discord between her and Rob since she'd gotten out of the hospital in June. Why hadn't she told me? Was there more to it than arguing... had he done something to her, and she'd been too afraid to tell me?

"What was the fighting about?"

She inhaled sharply. "You."

My eyes darted to hers, but I had to look back to the road before I could make out her expression. "You guys fight about me?"

"Yes," she said, her voice watery as she started crying again. "All the time."

"Oh, god, Annie. I'm so sorry."

"It's not your fault, Lucas. It's Rob—he doesn't like that we're friends. He's wanted me to walk away from you since he and I got back together, but I won't agree to it."

"And you've been fighting about that all summer?"

She nodded, breaking into another sob. We were almost to my house, so instead of pulling over, I reached over and gently grabbed her hand, giving it a squeeze. I hadn't expected what she told me. When I thought about it, it wasn't all that surprising that he'd tried to cut me out of her life again, but the thought hadn't crossed my mind because Annie hadn't mentioned anything, and she and I had only grown closer in the months since I'd helped her set up for her mom's birthday party. Even after I'd nearly told her I still loved her and come close to kissing her in the hospital, she hadn't put any kind of distance between us. But if the whole time Rob had been trying to make her do so, I could only imagine what she'd been going through to keep her friendship with me.

I swallowed over the sudden lump in my throat as I pulled down the street I lived on. Knowing what she'd done for me—for us—made my heart swell painfully at the same time I was furious that she'd ever had to. But she wouldn't have to anymore. He may have kicked her out, but she would always have a home with me, and I'd never treat her the way he did.

chapter eight

rob

Once the pain in my hands had blunted my anger into a dull roar, I'd tried to figure out how it was possible Annie had betrayed me the way she did. Had I really been that wrong about her? I'd needed to understand what happened, to know if she'd never loved me as much as I'd thought or if I'd done something to drive her into his arms. But when I'd decided to go back to the house and talk to her, I looked up and saw Lucas, Annie in his arms as they walked to his car before he grabbed her suitcase from the front porch. I'd told her to get out, but if she'd loved me, she'd have tried harder to stay. There's no way she would have left that easily unless that's what she already wanted to do. Maybe even what she'd already been planning to do—the thing she had actually wanted to tell me.

After standing rooted in place until well after they'd driven away, I'd barreled inside to hear my cell phone ringing somewhere; when I didn't answer it, the house phone started ringing, too. But the one person I'd have wanted to talk to had just proven she didn't love me. I'd ended up wandering from room to room, seeing Annie everywhere, but instead of seeing her with me, I'd seen Lucas. Lucas holding her. Lucas laughing with her. Lucas kissing her. Lucas undressing her. Lucas making love to her.

After ripping the phone and the entire outlet from the wall, leaving a gaping hole, I pulled out the liquor the previous owners had forgotten and left there. I was going to drink until it no longer hurt.

"Arg!" I shouted, suddenly wide awake and drenched in ice-cold water. My eyelids began to lift, but that was a huge mistake; instead, I closed them again, but not before seeing that Haley was standing in front of me.

"Get the fuck out of my house," I bit out.

"No," she replied in a voice made of steel. "We need to talk."

"There isn't shit for us to talk about."

"Oh yes there is, asshole. And we're going to do it right now."

"Nothing you have to say in her defense is going to fucking work."

"Rob, I'm not just here because of her. I'm also here because we're friends and you're not answering your phone."

"Friends? Really? Fuck you. If you were really my *friend*, you would have told me what she did a long time ago."

"What she *did*? Seriously? She can't get herself pregnant, you jackass."

I laughed mirthlessly. "Nope, and I can't do it for her either."

Haley snorted derisively. "Accidents happen when you have sex, dickhead, even when you take precautions. Do I need to explain to you how babies are made?"

Anger drove me to my feet, the pain from my hangover fading into the background. With my face inches from Haley's, I shouted, "Oh, I know *exactly* how babies are made—when my *wife* fucks someone else, just like the slut Charlie said—"

My words were cut off when Haley's fist connected with my nose; I hadn't even noticed her about to hit me, but she had. And it couldn't have been the first time she'd punched someone in the face—she'd hit me perfectly and broken my nose. It had happened to me enough times in my life for me to know. I laughed, welcoming the physical pain as blood flowed freely from my face.

Haley glared at me before speaking, her voice calm and quiet and threatening. "Don't you *ever* talk about Annie like that again. I don't know why you think she would cheat on you, but she never has and never would. She is pregnant with *your* fucking baby. I thought you were better than this." She glanced away quickly before returning her glower to me. "Get your shit together, Rob, and take care of your damn family before you lose them."

She turned on her heel and started walking away. Obviously, she believed every word she'd spoken, but she was wrong. And I wanted her to *know* she was wrong, that she'd misjudged Annie, too.

"I *couldn't* have gotten her pregnant, Haley!" I shouted after her. "I had a vasectomy twelve years ago!"

"If that's true," she shouted, "you might want to consider filing a malpractice suit on your way to beg for Annie's forgiveness!"

As she slammed the door behind her, I picked up the empty liquor bottle and threw it at the wall, the shattering glass reminding me of my own broken heart.

chapter nine

"I told you that you didn't have to come out here," I said after finding Haley at Lucas' front door. I'd been aiming for playful but was too tired to succeed. Between what I knew now were pregnancy hormones, the days of anxiety and fear, all the crying I'd been doing since I told Rob about the pregnancy the day before, and the nightmares I'd had all night, my energy was in short supply.

"You know I always do what I wanna do anyway," Haley replied with a wink. Then she stepped over the threshold and wrapped me in a hug. "How're you doing, babe?"

I snorted. "Well, the good news is that I think I'm physically incapable of producing any more tears."

My attempt at a smile ended up as more of a grimace. With a shrug, I shut Lucas' front door behind her. But then I turned around too quickly and stumbled over my feet, catching myself against the wall.

"Damn it!" I bit out. That was at least the fifth time since Lucas had picked me up the day before.

"You're dizzy?"

"Yeah," I sighed. "It comes and goes."

"You need to go to the doctor."

"No, I'm fine. It's normal to get dizzy with low blood sugar in pregnancy, or so I read. I just need to eat more frequently, that's all, and it'll get better. I just haven't been able to stomach much food the last few days." I shrugged.

"Annie... I..." Haley huffed out a breath. "I went to your house before I came here." She scrutinized my face for a moment as I froze. "I saw Rob."

My breath hitched. "Then you know I wasn't exaggerating. He hates me and... this baby." My hand moved of its own volition over my belly, as if it could protect the life growing there from the reality that its father wanted nothing to do with it.

Haley opened her mouth like she was going to say something, then closed it, looking away from me as she put her hands on her hips.

"What is it?" I asked.

"Come on, let's go sit," she replied, ushering us further inside. "Is Lucas here somewhere?"

"Just tell me, Haley."

"I will—after we sit. Is Lucas here or at the brewery?"

"He's at the brewery, thank god. He's been hovering over me since he picked me up yesterday, especially after I threw up this morning."

"Okay, good," she murmured absently, nodding. "Let's go sit."

With another sigh as we sat, she looked me directly in the eyes, her expression earnest and intense. Whatever she was about to say was going to be bad... I knew because she was scraping her index finger against the side of her thumb. When we lived together in college, I figured out that was her tell that her anxiety was ramping up. Back then it meant she was going to drink until she was shit-faced. Sometimes that was still what she ended up doing.

"I'm guessing you don't know this," she said slowly. "Rob... he just told me... he got a vasectomy twelve years ago."

"Okay," I started, shaking my head slightly and my mind spinning as it tried to figure out why that mattered. "I wish he'd told me, of course, but I don't under—" My voice disappeared as the pieces of the puzzle snapped together in my mind. "Oh my god, Haley. Oh no. I've only been with Rob since he moved into my mom's house last December. I swear, Haley, it must be ineffective, something, I don't know, but—"

"Shh," she interrupted, waving her hand between us. "Babe, I know. I don't for a second think you slept with someone else."

"But Rob does." The realization was crushing. He thought I'd had an affair, that I'd cheated on him. I couldn't decide what hurt more—that he assumed I would do that without even talking to me or knowing how much pain he was in and not being there to help him through it.

"Haley… I have to do something."

Her hand rested gently over mine where they were clasped in my lap. "You can't. Not until he admits the possibility that his vasectomy wasn't effective. I'm sorry, babe."

"Do you know why he got a vasectomy?"

"I don't. I also don't see how it could possibly make a difference."

I swallowed and turned to stare at the wall. "I never asked him to tell me about those years after I left, when he was back to drinking and drugging with Charlie. That means something during that time is what prompted him to sterilize himself. What if—"

"Stop speculating, babe. You can ask him when he comes to apologize and then you'll know."

"How are you so sure he'll come?" I asked, my voice frail.

"He will. Just give him a little time to process."

My eyes darted to hers briefly, then I nodded.

"Oh, and don't get mad," she added offhandedly with a stretch as she looked up toward the ceiling, "but he was being a dick, so I broke his nose."

"You *what*?" I asked.

She shrugged. "I didn't mean to hit him quite that hard, but he hit a nerve and he deserved it."

"A broken nose? I don't know about that."

"He fucking did. Trust me. He said something he shouldn't have."

"What did he say?" I asked.

Haley glanced down at her hands, up at the wall, then back down at her hands. "You don't wanna know. Seriously. I shouldn't have even said anything, I just didn't want you to be surprised that he's got a broken nose when his dumb ass eventually shows up."

"Whatever he said can't possibly be any worse than the way he looked at me after I told him. Or the way he was looking at me when I left with Lucas." I didn't add that every time I thought of the way he'd been looking at me, my chest seized in fear. It was the same way Charlie had looked at me the night he attacked me on my mom's porch the year before. "Just tell me," I added.

After a loud inhale and exhale, she spoke quietly. "He said Charlie was right about you, basically. But he didn't mean it, babe, he was lashing out because he was hurt. And I broke his nose for saying it, so..."

Haley's voice disappeared as the pounding of blood through my ears got louder, black beginning to encroach around the edges of my vision. Now that I was thinking about it again, I couldn't get Rob's face out of my mind, except that it wasn't just *his* face, it was also Charlie's. It was both of them, looking at me with hatred—the kind of hatred that meant my life was in danger.

"Babe, you okay?" Haley's voice finally came through, laced with concern as her now cloudy blue eyes bored into mine. "You're really pale."

"I feel like I might pass out," I admitted, focusing on the area between her eyes and willing the room to stop spinning.

Haley swallowed loudly. "Lean on me, babe, so you don't fall. We're going to the hospital."

"No, I—"

"This isn't normal, Annie."

"I'm fine, really. It's just—"

"I don't give a shit what you think it is!" she shouted. "It's not fucking normal. And I can't go through the you-almost-dying shit again—I can't. We're going to see a doctor right now."

My mind flashed back to all the times I'd been in the hospital over the last year, to my former boss's attack during the most recent stay after the aneurysm. Back to all the strangers examining me and touching me to do so, and my stomach lurched with nausea. I couldn't do that again—not yet. "I'm not going to the hospital," I stated, looking directly at her. "That's a big fuss for nothing. And I'm so sick of hospitals right now. I'll make an appointment with my primary care doctor. I promise."

Haley's face drew in. "Do it now."

"Seriously?"

"Yeah, seriously." She handed my phone to me, and I took it, rolling my eyes.

By the time I had made an appointment for the upcoming Thursday, my irritation had subsided. "I'm sorry for being bitchy," I said.

She waved her hand dismissively. "I know that, babe. I understand. What I *don't* understand is why you're here. Why not go to your mom's house? Or my place? Or Carol's? Why, of all people, did you choose Lucas?"

"I'm not ready to tell my mom. She already hates Rob—you know that. She'll give me that look that tells me how disappointed she is in me and say she told me so. I can't handle that right now—not her disappointment or her insistence on talking about how she always knew Rob would do this to me. It's too raw."

She nodded in understanding. "But what about me or Carol?" she persisted. "You're not working right now, so it's not like you have to be in Stockwood for any reason."

"You guys have enough on your plates without dealing with my problems. I've been enough of a burden."

"Oh, for Christ's sake, Annie! I love you, babe, but I swear to god I'm going to duct tape your fucking mouth closed if I ever hear you talk about being a burden to your friends again. This is what friends are for. We're all here for each other, through thick and thin, right?" She groaned, then said, "I know you're emotional and hormonal right now, but you seriously have to stop. So, now that we've established you have no reason to feel like a burden, why don't you just come home with me? You can stay for as long as you want."

"I have my appointment on Thursday. Can you drive me down? I'm not comfortable getting behind the wheel with all this dizziness."

Haley checked the calendar on her phone. "Fuck, I can't. I'm actually going to be up in New York for the day for another meeting with some investors—I can't bail on this one. We can see if Carol or Linc can take off work to drive you down."

"Why don't I just stay here until after my appointment? And if Rob still won't talk to me... then I'll move in with you or my mom."

"It's a little early to be talking about moving in with anyone. Rob will realize he's a stubborn fucking idiot sooner or later, don't worry." She was thoughtful for a moment. "Actually, I have an idea. Does Lucas have a printer?"

About an hour later, Lucas reappeared from the brewery, bearing dinner in the form of a variety of pasta dishes from the local Italian restaurant. Despite everything going on, my mouth watered as soon as I inhaled the aroma. After days of barely eating, it seemed I was now ravenously hungry. It surely helped that I was no longer in a constant state of fear—there were other emotions threatening to drown me, but fear of Rob's reaction was no longer one of them.

"It smells incredible, Lucas," I said, standing close by and watching as he pulled all the food containers out of the bag in the kitchen. He didn't really need help—I just wanted to be close to him. Being near him made everything seem less bleak. "You really didn't have to do all this, especially when you were at the brewery."

"I wanted to. And the brewery is fine right now—it wasn't that busy when I left."

"Well, thank you. Really."

He flashed me a warm smile, though I could see the beginnings of circles under his eyes giving away that he was tired—I wasn't the only one my nightmares had prevented from sleeping the night before. Pausing in his endeavors with dinner, he reached out a hand and smoothed it across my lower back.

"You're welcome, sw—" he said, cutting himself off by clearing his throat.

My heart skipped when he nearly used his endearment for me. He didn't use it anymore after I'd spent the summer reminding him to stop because it felt too intimate for friendship. But right then, I didn't want him to stop. After the last several days, hearing him call me "sweetheart" was all I wanted.

"Lucas," Haley called from the area where the kitchen turned into the dining room. Something was bothering her—the skin above her eyebrows was wrinkled more than it had been before Lucas arrived. "Let me get your thoughts on something."

"Sure, what's up?" he asked, sliding his hand from my back and finishing with getting the food from the restaurant containers into serving dishes.

"So, I talked to Rob today." She paused, watching Lucas as he ferried food and dishes and silverware from the kitchen to the dining table. "This whole fiasco is because he had a vasectomy over a decade ago and I guess thinks they're fail-proof, which they're not, so he's determined that his wife had an affair, which she would never do, obviously. So, I did some research and printed it all out. It proves that vasectomies aren't one hundred percent effective and includes a copy of the legally required waiver he would have had to sign that states that explicitly. I was thinking I'd swing by and drop it off for him, tell him to read it when he's done being a dick and ready to come apologize to Annie—his wife, who we all watched him propose to just last weekend. What do you think?"

I'd barely followed what Haley was saying, too distracted by her referring to me as Rob's wife as if I wasn't even there and she was talking to a stranger. What was going on with her?

Lucas shrugged, his posture stiffening as he moved around. "I think he won't read it if he doesn't want to. And while that explains his reaction, I suppose, he's still being an asshole."

"Pot, kettle?" Haley said with a raised eyebrow as she stared hard at him.

He went rigid for a split second. Then his shoulders fell as he set the last pasta bowl on the table. "I never said I haven't been an asshole before," he replied soberly. He turned to me, his mouth turning down at the corners as he grabbed both of my hands in his and looked into my eyes with urgency. "Again, Annie," he said, slow and quiet. "I'm so sorry about everything I did and everything I said to you when I was hurt."

"I know, Lucas," I said softly, giving his hands a squeeze and looking him in the eye. "You've been apologizing to me for months. I've already told you I forgive you, and that I'm not upset about it anymore. I meant it."

"Yeah, I know..." he replied, his voice tapering off as he got a sad, faraway look in his eyes. "I just... I would go back and do things differently if I could." His focus returned to me, and he smiled, though this was also tinged with sadness. "Okay, you guys ready to dig in?"

I listened to Haley and Lucas talk about the brewery as I ate, sensing an undercurrent of tension between them. But I was too tired and hungry to try to dissect what was happening. Then, before we were finished eating, Lucas got a call; he needed to head back to the brewery.

"I'm sorry I have to run, ladies, but enjoy," he said after practically inhaling what was left on his plate. "If you just pop the leftovers into the fridge, you can leave the rest—I'll clean everything up when I get home tonight."

"No," I said, shaking my head. "You're already letting me inconvenience you. Haley and I can clean up."

"No, please, leave it," he called from the kitchen, where he was setting his dishes in the sink. A second later, he reappeared and rested a hand on my shoulder, his eyes shining bright as he looked down at me. "You're not an inconvenience, Annie. It's really nice to have your company. And I want to do these things for you, so please don't worry about it, okay? You can get some rest and leave the mess for me."

I nodded in response, swallowing, though my saliva stuck in my throat. For some reason I couldn't fathom, my face was heating and my heart speeding up under his gaze.

"Okay, I have to run," he murmured a moment later, finally breaking eye contact to glance at the clock on the wall. "I'll see you guys in the morning—I'll try not to wake you up when I get in later." His hand moved to smooth across my back a few times. "Tomorrow's a new sunrise—a new day." With a smile and gentle squeeze of my shoulder, he turned and left.

Haley and I finished eating in silence; she appeared to be as lost in her thoughts as I was. Though it was doubtful hers were a swirling, confusing mess of contradictory emotions: pain and comfort, a desire to both cry and smile, feelings of worthlessness and love and fear and safety.

"Why don't you go ahead to bed, babe?" Haley asked, raising her chin toward me when I finished eating. "You're falling asleep—I'll take care of all this."

I yawned, my eyelids so heavy I couldn't open them all the way. "Okay. I'm exhausted."

"Yeah, I'm sure you are. Are you dizzy at all? Do you want some help walking?"

"Yeah, I am," I sighed as the room began to spin the second I got to my feet. "I would appreciate that."

She stepped to my side and wrapped an arm around my waist. "Lead the way."

We walked down the hall on the other side of the living room. When we reached the doorway at the end, Haley stopped.

"Is this Lucas' room?" she asked.

"Yeah," I replied on the tail end of another yawn. "He doesn't have a bed in the guestroom yet."

"I hate to ask you this, babe, but where is *he* sleeping?"

I pointed a thumb over my shoulder back in the direction from which we'd come. "He was on the couch last night. I'm not sure about tonight, though, because he said he was going to pick up an air mattress for the guestroom on his way in to work, if he could find one, but I don't know if he did or not."

"Oh. I didn't see any bedding or pillows out there."

Another yawn escaped. "He knows that clutter bothers me, so he put it all in the linen closet when he got up."

I walked into the bathroom, brushing my teeth and washing my face, comforted by the smell of Lucas that surrounded me; it was a scent I associated with calm and safety. With my eyes closed, it was easy to conjure him next to me, with his steady heartbeat and gentle aura. Between his imagined presence and the very real one of my best friend, my body felt heavier as it relaxed more than I could remember it ever having done.

Haley was still standing in the same spot in the doorway when I walked back out, watching me thoughtfully. When she was still there after I'd changed into my pajamas, I finally asked, "What are you doing?"

She sighed. "Just thinking."

I climbed into bed, too tired to try to figure out what was bothering her or even care right then. "I almost forgot—that means you're sleeping in here with me."

She snorted. "No shit—I certainly wasn't sleeping on the couch with your ex."

My eyes were already closed, my body becoming heavy with sleep. "Good night, Haley," I murmured.

"Night, babe."

chapter ten

rob

After Haley left, I made my way to the bathroom to find some pain killers to take the edge off from my broken nose and hangover. But once in the bathroom, Annie's scent enveloped me. How I could smell her with my nose fucked up the way it was, I didn't know, but I could. My hands caught and supported my weight on the sink when my knees buckled. Each breath felt like someone was tearing into my chest with a machete.

Looking in the mirror, I saw that my hair and beard were still dripping with the water Haley had dumped on me not ten minutes ago, mixing with the bright red blood still flowing from my nostrils. The rest of my face was pale, and I had the beginnings of two black eyes from Haley breaking my nose. My hands were covered in dried blood from punching trees the day before.

What would Annie think if she could see me now?

I knew what she would *do*—she'd clean and bandage my hands one at a time, moving slowly to avoid hurting me. She'd drive me to the doctor to have my nose set, and then she'd carefully clean my face and wash my hair for me in the sink. Closing my eyes, I could feel her fingers in my hair, smell her bending over me, hear her voice telling me she loved me.

But in reality, I'd never experience any of those fucking things again. She was gone—she'd chosen Lucas over me. My body gave out, and I collapsed onto the floor. Charlie had been right every time he'd told me no one would ever give a fuck about me.

After jerking awake during a dream about Annie and Lucas together for the fourth time, I decided more alcohol was needed to drown it out. It was Sunday morning, though, which meant the liquor store was closed all day and no bars would be open yet. *Fuck.* But I had to leave anyway. I couldn't be in the house where I'd had this nearly perfect life with Annie for a few months.

It didn't take long to shower off all the blood and sweat caking my body, chuck a handful of clothes into a duffel bag, and leave my house behind. Stockwood was small, with a motel near the middle of town, so that's where I was headed. Every bar we had—as well as the liquor store—would be within walking distance from there. I'd never have to leave.

After checking in at the motel, dumping my bag, and downing the last of the liquor from the house, I set out on foot toward the closest bar, but it was still closed. I knew they all opened at two o'clock and moved to check my cell phone to see how much time I'd have to wait, only to find I'd forgotten it somewhere. My fingers flexed into a fist with irritation, sending a wave of pain through my hand as the damaged skin was stretched taut. With a sharp inhale, I unclenched my fingers and decided to walk to the central town square—the clocktower there in the courtyard outside the old courthouse would tell me how much longer before there'd be another drink in my hand. A car slowed as it passed me and when I glanced back, it was parking on the street. Then Haley stepped out and started toward me.

"Fuck off," I growled.

"Yeah, yeah, I know—you don't want to talk to me. But I don't give a shit."

"I don't feel like having another heart-to-heart with you, so unless you're planning to shut the hell up and get plastered with me, you can turn the fuck around and walk away."

"Someone woke up on the wrong side of the bed this morning, huh?" she retorted, her voice cold. "I just wanted to give you this," she added, waving around a stack of paper held together with a binder clip as she continued to approach me.

"I don't fucking want it."

"Grow the fuck up, Rob—take the damn papers and read them before it's too late." Now right in front of me, she slammed the stack of papers into my chest with a glare.

Snatching the stack, I stepped around her, heading down the street toward the town square. I'd drop it all in the first trash can I came across.

"You know, vasectomies aren't a guarantee. You should have signed a waiver that said as much. Shit happens sometimes!" she shouted after me. "Read the fucking papers!"

I ignored her and kept walking.

"You're gonna lose her, you stubborn asshole!"

Fuck Haley. And fuck Annie. And fuck Lucas. Fuck everyone, actually. The further I walked down the street, the quieter the string of expletives Haley was flinging in my direction got. But the less angry I became… the more I could feel the pain in my chest, the one over my heart that felt like it would kill me if I didn't find a way to keep it at bay.

The clocktower read one o'clock. *Shit.* I still had an hour before I'd be able to get a drink anywhere. Spinning in a slow circle as my mind raced to figure out what the fuck I was going to do with myself for that hour, I spied the sign for Stockwood Brewery. I knew exactly what I was going to do—I was going to go to Lucas' house and beat the hell out of him.

As I rushed up the street Lucas lived on, Haley's voice came back to me on repeat. Her telling me to file a malpractice suit if I'd had a vasectomy. Her telling me that vasectomies could fail. Her telling me I was losing Annie, as if she wasn't already gone. And through all of it, her voice so full of conviction. My steps slowed and I lifted the stack of papers I was still holding on to, my eyes scanning the contents. Near the bottom of the stack of research was a copy of a medical waiver; signing it would mean acknowledging that the vasectomy could be ineffective, that you agreed to come back to have your semen checked after twelve weeks.

My hand fell to my side as I searched my memory for the day I'd had the vasectomy done, but it was hazy. I'd been fucked up out of my mind that day, like I was every day back then. I had no idea if I'd signed something. Probably not—the doctor was only doing it because his brother owed Charlie a favor. And fuck if I knew if I'd ever gone back. Everything for a few years was just a haze with flashes here and there.

Maybe it really was possible that I wasn't sterile. And that would mean it was possible that baby *was* actually mine. My breath rushed out of me at that thought, but an instant later, I remembered seeing Annie leave our house in Lucas' arms. If it was really mine, why had she left so quickly with fucking Lucas?

I scrubbed my hand down my face, looking up as I neared Lucas's house, the sight of it igniting rage. Even if there was a good reason she'd called him, even if the baby really *was* mine, I'd seen the way they acted together, the way he looked at her. He needed to stay the fuck away from her, and I was going to make sure he did. Annie would be pissed, but I'd figure that out later—better to have her pissed at me than have that fucker around her.

My hand slammed the doorknocker down repeatedly after I arrived, then jabbed the doorbell. After a breath with no answer, I pounded on the door with the side of my fist. The more seconds that passed, the angrier I became. I'd beat the damn door down if I had to.

"Open the fucking door!" I shouted.

After a few more bangs, the door began to swing open slowly and I stopped short as I was about to shove it open and start swinging. It was Annie. I'd watched her leave our house with Lucas, but—for some reason—I hadn't expected to see her there at his house. I realized right then I'd expected he had taken her to her mom's house, not that she would still be with him. And yet, there she was, gazing at me with fear in her eyes as her face paled. Seeing her was like a punch to the gut, leaving me winded.

The flicker of hope I'd irrationally had was doused. How was I so fucking stupid again? She was there because she was having an affair with Lucas. And that was his baby she was carrying—not mine. All those years of fucking anyone and everyone, I'd have a shitload of kids at this point if the vasectomy had failed. But not one woman came and told me she was pregnant. No, I was sterile. And my wife cheated on me. The pain tearing through my body was at least as strong as it had been two days earlier when she told me she was pregnant. She was talking, a pained and haunted expression on her face. But I could hear nothing over my thoughts. We were really over.

With that thought, I shoved the door the rest of the way open, stepped inside, and wrapped my hands around her biceps, moving so forcefully she thumped against the wall behind her. In that instant, I wanted to kiss her one more time. But the intense fear in her eyes gave me pause.

I'd seen that fear in her eyes the other day after she told me she was pregnant. It was the same fear I saw when she had flashbacks about Charlie. But why the fuck would she be afraid of *me*? A long, tense moment passed, her held against the wall, me at war with myself about what to do next as I searched her eyes.

"I love you," she whispered, her jaw trembling, eyes wide and full of tears.

It was a new sensation for those words to hurt... They'd only ever felt healing to me before, but this time, they ripped my heart apart. I growled, then crushed my mouth to hers, pouring my rage and heartache into it. And then I remembered where we were. In Lucas' home. Up against *his* wall. I was kissing the same lips he'd probably been kissing before I got there. My head reared back, though my hands still held her in place. The fear in her eyes grew stronger, eclipsing anything else that may have been there, and she started crying.

"Rob, please," she pled. "I don't—"

"I know you don't want me!" I roared. "You never fucking wanted me!"

"Annie!" I heard Lucas shout from somewhere inside, followed by rapid footsteps. Fucking perfect. Lucas rounded the corner a second later, hair wet, slowing when he saw me.

"Rob," he said slowly, with an expression that clearly meant he wasn't happy to see me.

I glared back at him, the desire to beat him into a pulp flooding my veins. I knew right then that if I started, I wouldn't stop until his body was lifeless. Annie made a strange sound and we both looked toward her.

"What the hell is wrong with you?" he shouted, leaping forward. "Let go of her!"

My eyes fell and I saw my fingers were white with tension against Annie's reddening skin and my hands ached where they'd fisted so tight around her arms that she'd made the kind of sound I'd once sworn I'd never be the source of—one of pain. My hands dropped to my sides, and I jumped backward, staring at them as if they belonged to someone else.

"Rob," Annie breathed, her voice cracking.

Looking up, I saw a bead of blood on her lip and my thoughts scattered, leaving me with only the intense desire to hold her in my arms and pretend none of this had happened. To shower her face with kisses and apologize as many times as it took to undo having put that fear in her eyes, undo having physically hurt her. "Annie," I scratched out.

She lifted an arm toward me as she stepped away from the wall and I thought for a second I'd get what I wanted. But then she was stumbling and Lucas was reaching out for her, and before I could close the distance between us, she was in *his* arms... not mine.

Concern over what had happened flickered in the recesses of my mind, but my attention was focused on where Lucas' hands were in contact with Annie's body. I tore my eyes away from his hands and glared at Annie. "Charlie was right about you—you're a slut."

"You're an idiot and an asshole," Lucas ground out through clenched teeth, his eyes filled with loathing. "Get the hell out of here."

I watched in detachment as he turned back to Annie, positioning himself between us as he murmured something into her ear. Worry continued nagging at me deep down, but it was slowly replaced with my old, familiar friend—anger—as the seconds passed. Only the top of Annie's head was visible, but it was enough to see that she was nodding at whatever Lucas was saying to her.

Fuck them. Spinning on my heal, I bolted.

- 63 -

chapter eleven

annie

Once the sound of Rob's footsteps had faded away along with his alcohol-saturated breath, my knees gave out. I sank to the floor with my back against the wall and Lucas followed, sitting with one arm around my shoulders and the other wrapped around my front.

"I'm so sorry," Lucas rushed out, his thumb smoothing back and forth along my arm as he pulled me sideways into him. "If I'd gotten here sooner, I could have stopped him from talking to you like that. I could have stopped him from hurting you."

"It's okay, Lucas," I sniffled, noticing that my bottom lip was sore.

"No, it's not—I saw your face and heard that noise you made when he was pinning you to the wall—he left marks on you, for god's sake."

Lifting my head from Lucas' chest provided a clear view of my arms, and sure enough, there were red handprints on my biceps. My eyes were stuck, unable to look away. *Rob did that to me. Rob left marks on me. Rob hurt me.* At the same time the thoughts crossed my mind, I rejected them. It wasn't possible. Rob would never hurt me. And yet... he had.

"Oh, god, Annie," Lucas said, his eyes turning glassy as his hand raised to hover near my mouth.

"What is it?" I asked, defeated.

"Your lip is bleeding," he replied quietly. "And it's swelling."

I touched my fingertips to my sore lip and when I pulled them away, there was blood on them. I shook my head harshly to clear it; I couldn't reconcile what had just happened, let alone the handprints on my arms and a bloody lip, with the man I'd loved since I was a teenager. The first—and for most of my life, the only—man I'd ever trusted not to hurt me. Without a word, I allowed my head to fall back into Lucas's chest and the tears to flow freely until the strong, steady beat of his heart soothed them away.

"He's wrong, you know," he said after a while.

"What?"

"What he said about Charlie."

My breath caught in my throat. "I know. And I know he doesn't mean it—not really."

"Mean it or not, he never should have said something like that," Lucas retorted, his voice hard.

Lucas was right, of course. But I couldn't bring myself to say that aloud. Instead, I focused on Rob's appearance.

"He looked awful. He needs to go to a doctor so they can set his nose, and his hands were destroyed, too. If he doesn't clean them out and cover some of those cuts, they could—"

"Don't worry about him," Lucas interrupted, his voice firm. "Let's just focus on you. Would you like something to eat before I leave? I can make you some lunch, or go grab something and bring it back. What would you like?"

I shook my head at the thought of food. "I'm not hungry. I just want to lay down."

Lucas nodded. "Okay," he said, standing and grabbing my hands and pulling me to my feet.

"I think I'm fine to walk," I muttered, embarrassed that I wasn't more self-sufficient.

With a flash of his irresistible boyish grin and a wink, he replied, "Humor me. I'd feel responsible if you fell because I didn't help."

After watching as I climbed into bed, Lucas grasped the back of his neck as he stared at something, his face drawn and jaw set tight. I followed his gaze to the darkening marks on my arms, and my stomach turned, my heart racing as I remembered the violence in Rob's face when he barreled through the door, grabbing me and pinning me against the wall, squeezing until it felt my bones would break, kissing me so hard it hurt and made me bleed while I'd stood frozen in fear. My tongue darted out over my swollen lip and my eyes flooded with fresh tears as they flitted up to catch Lucas' gaze. My body began to tremble. In that moment, I desperately didn't want to be left alone with my fear and my memories.

"Can you stay a while?" I asked, my voice watery, feeling weak for having done so.

His eyes looked to the alarm clock.

"You don't have to," I rushed out before he had a chance to speak, wishing I hadn't asked. "I know you have to go. I'll be fine." I forced the corners of my mouth to turn up slightly. "I promise." But then I started crying again.

Without a word, he climbed onto the bed with me, sliding under the blankets and pulling me into his chest. As I cried, he used one hand to slide his cell phone from his pocket and, using his thumb, typed out and sent a text message before setting it on the nightstand.

An hour later, when I was all cried out and my body was heavy and sleepy and secure in Lucas's arms, he slid from the bed and stood. His gaze rested on me for a long minute, his eyes clouded. Eventually, he reached down and cupped my cheek, his thumb whispering across the skin. "I'll put a plate of food together for you and leave it in the fridge. But if you need anything at all while I'm gone, just call my cell or the brewery, and I'll be back right away."

I nodded. "I will."

His hand withdrew and he headed toward the door.

"Lucas?"

He turned, his eyebrows raised in question.

"Thank you."

He smiled softly, though his eyes looked sad. "Get some rest."

I was running for my life, for my baby's life. Turning to look behind me, I saw nothing, but I knew someone was there just out of sight. My legs continued to pump, carrying me as fast they could through a long, dark tunnel, though I didn't know if there was a way out of the other end. I wanted to stop, but there was nowhere to hide. I ran harder and faster as I sensed whoever was behind me closing in, my hand over my swollen belly in a feeble attempt to protect my baby. But no matter how fast I ran, the footsteps grew closer and closer. Again, I turned to look behind me; again, I saw no one. When I turned back around, Rob was now in front of me, laughing, but his laugh sounded like Charlie's. In my confusion, my feet got tangled with one another and I pitched forward, landing hard on my belly.

My eyes flew open in terror from the nightmare as the first morning light was beginning to brighten the windows. I was drenched in sweat, my skin clammy, and my next ragged inhale brought with it an intense wave of nausea. I tried to sit up so I could get out of bed to go to the bathroom, but I was too dizzy. Even with my difficulty breathing, I shouldn't have been as dizzy as I was.

I called out for Lucas, knowing he'd be there in seconds. As soon as I was able, I'd call my doctor and tell them it was urgent.

———

The visit to my primary care physician later that afternoon confirmed my pregnancy, and we discovered that my dizziness and possibly some of my frequent nausea was because my blood pressure was too low. After everything that had happened only a few months earlier because of my chronic high blood pressure, I never would have guessed low blood pressure could be the culprit. What we learned, though, was that pregnancy causes a drop in blood pressure as a result of an increase in blood volume. With my blood pressure already on the low side after several months of medication and a change in lifestyle, the result was blood pressure that was *too* low.

The issue could be corrected by discontinuing my blood pressure treatment, though I had to be weaned off the medicine slowly or risk a heart attack. So, while the end of all the dizziness was in sight—and hopefully some of the nausea—it would take some time and the decrease in symptoms would be gradual. Relief at having answers and knowing I'd be okay overshadowed anything else, however, and I didn't mind that it could take a few weeks before the symptoms would fully subside. The only other thing Dr. Miller had to say was that I needed to see an OB/GYN as soon as possible, considering how far along I was.

Just when I thought she'd say we were good to leave, though, Dr. Miller had asked Lucas to go to the waiting room because she needed to talk to me alone for a few minutes. He'd complied, his brow creased as he went.

"Annie," the doctor said as she closed the door behind him, "we noticed you've got some fresh bruising on your arms and your lip is swollen. Can you tell me what happened?"

I glanced away, my voice catching in my throat as my arms crossed and my hands instinctively covered my biceps where I knew the bruises were under my cardigan. I'd been keenly aware of how noticeable they were when I'd removed my sweater to have my blood pressure recorded, but had never expected anyone would say something. How could I answer her question? I hadn't spoken about it to anyone since it had happened, except Lucas, because he'd been there at the time and had seen what transpired. How could I explain that my husband, the father of the baby I was carrying, was responsible?

"It's okay," she continued after a moment or two. "It's just us in here. You can tell me. I just want to make sure you're safe. If you need help, we can help you."

It dawned on me as she finished speaking that she'd sent Lucas out of the room because she thought *he* was the one who'd hurt me. I felt panicky as I processed that realization; I couldn't imagine Lucas *ever* putting his hands on someone in anger the way Rob did to me and didn't want anyone to think otherwise.

"The man who came with me didn't do this to me," I said firmly. "He would *never* do something like this. It... it..." That was all I could manage before I dissolved into tears. "It was someone else," I explained between gasps. "The—the father." Each syllable was a struggle because I was still in shock that Rob had done something to me that made my doctor concerned for my safety.

"Are you in a situation where he could do this to you again?" she asked, handing me a box of tissues.

I shook my head. "No," I whispered. "He's gone."

Once I was able to stem the flow of tears, I made my way to the waiting room where a very worried-looking Lucas stood as soon as I walked in. He strode over quickly and wrapped an arm around my shoulders to balance me as I walked. My arms crossed tightly over my chest and I gave him a weak smile, knowing my eyes would give away that I'd been crying. His face fell further, and once we'd exited into the hallway, he spoke.

"What happened? Is everything okay?"

I nodded, glancing up at him before looking away again. "She wanted to know about the bruises and my lip."

His body tensed. "What did you tell her?"

"The truth," I replied quietly, my voice cracking again.

Lucas stopped us just before we stepped outside the building and turned to me, his hands gently grasping my shoulders. I was staring at the floor but could feel his gaze on me. A wave of pain and fear welled up as what transpired with Rob that day replayed again in my mind and I leaned forward into Lucas, my cheeks already damp again. But I could feel the pain softening and the fear dissipating as soon as he wrapped his arms tight around me, holding me close enough I could hear his heart beating.

"Would you like to stop somewhere for dinner?" Lucas asked with a sideways glance when we were en route to his house from Dr. Miller's office.

"No, that's okay. I can eat something at the house. I'm sure you need to get back to work." I already felt guilty that Lucas had been away from the brewery almost all day because of me. And from what I'd learned about the brewery from him, the busiest time of day was about to begin. Looking down toward my lap, I watched the fingers on one hand scrape the nails on the other. I didn't want to do what I was about to suggest but felt like it was the right thing to do. "In fact, it's time for me to go stay with my mom. I can't keep asking you to help me."

Lucas lifted a hand from the wheel, reached across, and rested it over mine with a gentle squeeze. "I *want* to help, Annie. It makes me happy to be here for you, even though I'm sorry for the circumstances. I mean it." He paused, shifting his hand until we were palm to palm. "If you want to go stay with your mom, or Haley, or whoever, that's fine. But if you *want* to stay with me? Well... I want you to stay. Just think about it, okay? And if you still want to leave and stay somewhere else, I'll take you."

My head nodded lazily up and down, my eyes shifting to stare out the window as we cruised down the highway. What was the right thing to do? I didn't want to tell my mom anything yet, though I'd have to if I went to stay with her. I also didn't want to be back in the city like I would if I stayed with Haley or Carol because of the risk of running into Eddie, especially since I knew he'd wriggled out of any legal repercussions due to his family's connections, even though he'd assaulted me multiple times just a few months ago. But all that aside... I simply *wanted* to stay with Lucas.

I liked being around him so much. He was calm and caring, which meant I felt cared for and calm and sometimes even happy when the comfort of being with him made me forget for a few moments why I was there in the first place. I liked smelling him in the house, knowing there was never a reason to worry about his mood or how he might react to something that was said. I liked the way he watched me and was always gentle when he touched me and made me laugh even when I was upset. The way I never looked at him and felt gut-wrenching fear about what he might be about to do next or pressured to do what he wanted me to. The way I felt so safe in those moments I somehow ended up in his arms.

But how could I want those things from him when they were all so different—the opposite even—of Rob? And what did it say about me that, when I closed my eyes, all I wanted was to be in

Lucas' home… not even my own? What did it mean that, instead of missing Rob right then, I was thinking about life with Lucas? I loved Rob, deeply, but after several days away from the constant anxiety around him, the constant uncertainty about his mood and what he was going to do, I mostly felt relief.

"So," Lucas said a few minutes later. "Dinner. What would you like?"

"It doesn't matter," I responded quietly, still distracted by the direction my thoughts had been going before he spoke. "I don't want to go anywhere, though."

"Breakfast for dinner? I think I have what I need to make pancakes, eggs, and sausage, and we still have some fruit salad. How does that sound?"

Though I had always loved eggs, just the thought of smelling them made my stomach twist. "Except for the eggs, that sounds good," I replied, turning my gaze toward him.

His eyes darted to mine, and he grinned before turning back to the road. "Breakfast it is, then—minus eggs, of course."

The rest of the drive passed in a comfortable silence aside from the music playing quietly through the car speakers. Lucas was exuding contentment, and it was infectious. With my head turned to look out the window and my gaze softened so the scenery passing was a gentle blur, my thoughts drifted away to leave me in a relaxed meditative state that was strangely refreshing. By the time we exited the highway, I felt a lethargic sense of peace.

A few miles from his house, Lucas' eyes darted over to me, and he ran his hand through his hair—something was making him nervous. Before I had a chance to try to figure out what, however, he turned up the radio so it was now loud enough to hear clearly; the song was "Treat You Better" by Shawn Mendes. As I listened to the lyrics, Lucas continued to glance over nervously, and a deep blush leapt to life on my face and neck. It was as if whoever was on the other end of that radio station had been listening to my thoughts and chosen this song on purpose.

The song ended a moment before we pulled into Lucas' driveway, and neither of us spoke about it. Instead, when we went inside, Lucas drew a bath for me, insisting I lounge and relax while he prepared dinner. And because it *did* sound wonderful to sit in a tub full of warm water that could draw some of the tension out of my body, I was more than happy to agree.

The door was left ajar so he could hear if I needed help, but that also meant I could hear *him* as he moved around in the kitchen and when he answered his phone. He was speaking in hushed tones, though he didn't need to. Listening to his voice was soothing—it reminded me of the year before when he and I were developing our relationship and I'd sit on my mom's porch, my head resting on his shoulder as he told me about growing up in the Midwest.

I determined that he was talking to Haley, then he relayed everything we'd learned a little while ago from my visit to Dr. Miller. Haley must have asked about my living situation next because Lucas responded that he'd take me wherever I decided I wanted to go. Though he also informed her that he'd made arrangements to be around for the next week or two until the dizziness was gone so I wouldn't be alone. *When did he do that?* My heart skipped as I grasped that meant he was counting on me staying with him—he'd meant what he'd said in the car.

My thoughts scattered as Lucas' voice shifted—he was irritated.

"I can take her to her mom's if she wants, but it's up to her."

There was a brief second of silence, then Lucas spoke again, his words clipped and loud. "Yeah—I *do* want her to stay here. So what?"

They were arguing... about me. My body slipped down into the water until my ears were submerged and I was surrounded by silence. Why did they have to argue? I was closer to the two of them than anyone else, and I wasn't sure I could handle them being at odds with one another. My desire to know more about their disagreement took over and I pushed myself up far enough out of the water that I could hear again.

"—not since he was here," Lucas was saying. "I heard that he's been at bars in town all day the last two days, and that he left with random women more than once."

They had to be talking about Rob. My head tipped back so my ears were again submerged, and my eyes stared at the ceiling. That same numbness I experienced when Rob and I were fighting before I moved back to the city in the spring took over, and I didn't feel sad or angry or hurt, just... nothing. Though I knew that wouldn't last; sooner or later, all the pain would hit. Sighing, I slid my engagement ring off my finger and held it a few inches from my eyes. It really was an exceptional piece of jewelry; so much thought and skill had gone into designing and making it. *I should find out who made it and return it so they can find someone who'd be able to wear it; it's a ring that deserves to be worn.*

Sitting up and setting the ring carefully on the side of the tub, I gazed at the ring tattooed on my finger—the ring I *couldn't* remove. It would be a permanent reminder of what had once been and never would be again. I pulled the plug, though I made no move to get out while the water was draining. Instead, I stared into nothingness, unseeing, thinking about my tumultuous history with Rob. All the love and laughter, all the pain and tears. The best moments in my life, as well as some of the worst, involved Rob; he was part of me and always would be. Losing him was akin to losing a limb; I would forever miss him.

And, if it survived, I would have this baby to remind me of him every day. A baby I would be raising alone, except... I couldn't do this alone. I couldn't be a single mother. I wasn't equipped for that. I couldn't keep *myself* happy—how the hell could I keep a baby happy? Give it a good life? Teach it to live well? But I would have to; Rob was clearly not going to have a change of heart if he was out doing what he'd wrongfully accused me of—sleeping around.

With the water now drained, my body shook with cold, my teeth knocking painfully against one another, but my body was frozen in place. The pain that had been noticeably absent only moments before was now drowning me, punctuated by images of him having sex with other women, doing things I thought he'd never do again with someone other than me. A sound that was part moan, part wail escaped my lungs, and then I was sobbing so hard I couldn't catch my breath.

Lucas burst into the bathroom a few seconds later, but I had nothing left for anyone. I couldn't speak, I couldn't look up—nothing save cry. A towel wrapped around me from behind, and then Lucas was using another to dry my hair.

"You're going to stay cold unless we get your body dried off," he said gently. "Let's stand up so we can dry the rest of you." He wrapped his arms around me from behind and pulled me up as my body shook and spasmed from the force of my cries, supporting me with one arm around my back while he used the same towel he had used on my hair to quickly dry my legs.

"Come on, let's go get some clothes."

After a moment of unsuccessful attempts to walk myself, Lucas bent over to slide an arm under my knees and carried me into his bedroom. I sat on the edge of his bed, bawling with a damp towel hanging around my shoulders while he rummaged through my suitcase, then his dresser drawers. When he walked back over, he had a pair of my underwear, one of my t-shirts, and a pair of sweatpants and a sweatshirt of his.

"I'll turn around while you get dressed," he said as he placed them on the bed next to me. "I don't mind helping you, I just..." He cleared his throat and turned his back to me.

I wanted to thank him for being so considerate while I was such a mess, but the thoughts refused to translate into words; it took too much effort right then. I couldn't even make myself speak once I'd managed to pull on the clothes.

After several minutes had passed, he turned around slowly, his eyes scanning my face. "What do you need? What can I do?"

I shook my head back and forth and pulled my knees up to my chest, hugging them in tight as if that would somehow diminish the pain there. Lucas's hand started smoothing slowly up and down my back.

"Do you want me to go?" he asked.

Again, I shook my head. I wanted to be alone, but I also desperately didn't.

"Okay," he breathed out in response.

Sitting, he wrapped his arms around me, pulling me into his warmth, and we rocked like that for a while until he eased us down onto the floor. He leaned back against the bed with me curled in his lap as I cried for what felt like an eternity. Through it all, he smoothed a hand slowly along my back and cradled my head, murmuring occasional reassurances to me that he was there, that he would always be there, for me to let it all out.

"Are you ready to eat?" he whispered into my ear, breaking the silence that surrounded us after I'd stopped crying but hadn't moved.

A refusal was on my tongue—I wasn't hungry and wanted to just stay in the bubble created by his arms around me—but then I remembered: I was pregnant and hadn't eaten in hours. Like it or not, I needed to eat something. It wasn't just about me anymore.

I sat at the table a while later, forcing myself to nibble at the fruit salad while Lucas moved around the kitchen reheating the sausage and making us fresh pancakes.

"I would eat the cold ones that you made. You didn't have to make fresh just because I lost my shit for a while," I said. My voice sounded hollow even to me.

"I don't mind. Besides, reheated pancakes are rubbery and nasty. What kind of host would I be if I served stuff like that to you?"

Lucas was being playful, but I couldn't even force myself to look at him right then. Nodding, I continued to stare at the wall from my seat at the table. My entire being felt drained and empty.

"Thank you," I said weakly, giving my best effort to smile when Lucas set my plate of fresh, hot food down in front of me.

"You're very welcome," he replied with a bright smile, but I could see how he really felt in his eyes—uncertain and worried.

"I heard you," I whispered. "When you were talking to Haley."

His fork froze mid-air, and he stiffened. "I'm so sorry, Annie," he breathed out a tense moment later. "I didn't know you could…" His voice trailed off, then he mumbled, "Shit."

"He's not coming back," I said, shaking my head as I stared at my plate. "And I'm not sure I could even look at him, let alone take him back, if he did. But what do I do now? I can't do this alone, Lucas. I'm not cut out to be a single mother. I'm not even sure I'm cut out to be a mother at all."

"Why do you think that?" he asked.

I inhaled slowly, still staring at my plate. "I don't know anything about how to be a mother, let alone a good one."

Lucas's fingertips tipped my chin up until I raised my eyes to look at him. Holding my gaze, he lowered his arm and grabbed my hand. His eyes were luminous with intensity and emotion. "Listen to me, Annie. First, no one knows how to be a mother before they become one, but you'll be an incredible mother no matter what. I know it. This baby will learn how to care about people, be compassionate and kind and caring, and it has your genes, so will obviously be brilliant." He winked and grinned. "Second, you will never have to raise this baby alone. There are a lot of people in your life who love you and will support you in any way you need. It takes a village, that's the saying, right? And you have a dedicated village."

"But I'll still be an emotionally unstable single mother at the end of the day," I bit out, my jaw trembling.

Pain swept across his features. "Don't say things like that. It's not true. You aren't emotionally unstable—you're scared and hurting, and that's different. And Annie…" He swallowed, looking down to where he shifted his hand to slide his fingers between mine and clasp my hand tightly. With a deep breath, he raised his gaze back to mine and spoke softly. "Sweetheart—you will only be a single mother if you want to be."

chapter twelve

annie

It **didn't take** long for Lucas and me to settle into what felt like a natural routine together. First thing upon waking, my morning sickness had me bent over the toilet and he always joined me to hold my hair out of my face and gently stroke my back. When there was nothing left in my stomach, he'd help me stand to brush my teeth and then to get into the shower, always returning to be close by as I dried off, just in case I fell. And as easy as it would have been, he never took advantage and looked at me while I was naked, instead keeping his back turned or his eyes averted.

Next was breakfast. Though he would never admit it, he must have been sick of making the same thing every day. But ever since he'd made breakfast for dinner the day I saw Dr. Miller, the only thing I could stomach in the mornings was pancakes, fresh fruit, and yogurt. At first—like with everything Lucas did for me—I'd apologized profusely for not being able to do those things myself, but after several days of Lucas brushing off my apologies, I'd done what he asked and stopped making them, with a promise to start helping and contributing as soon as I could.

After breakfast was the best part of the day. Depending on the weather, we alternated walks around the neighborhood with watching movies, playing his twenty questions game, and taking naps, always doing everything together and always with a snack handy. And we spent at least a couple of hours a day together reading several pregnancy books. At some point, I needed to think about getting a job—I couldn't live off the money from the sale of my house forever—but for the time being, work wasn't an option, and I was enjoying my time with Lucas.

As wonderful and carefree as it was to spend each day with Lucas by my side—who was seemingly as content with the arrangement as I was—the nights were dreadful. After a dinner of take-out or something Lucas picked to make out of the *Easy Recipes for Kitchen Newbies* cookbook he'd bought expressly so he could cook for me sometimes, I was exhausted and ready for bed. It didn't sit well with me that Lucas was still sleeping on an air mattress in the guestroom of his own house, but he'd laughed at me like I was crazy when I suggested we switch so he could take his bedroom back.

Not that it mattered anyway—regardless of what room we were in, Lucas would be visiting me several times a night. My nightmares were more frequent than they had been in a long time and my shouts and screams roused him from his sleep. He'd wake me, cradling my body against his chest as I shook and sweated and cried, murmuring into my ear long, beautiful descriptions of the property he'd grown up on, speaking as if he would take me there one day. My favorite was when he talked about the meadow full of tall grasses and dotted with flowers where he used to watch the sunrise with his mom. I could picture it so clearly the way he described it, and gradually the terror would fade from my body, and Lucas' soft voice and steady heartbeat would lull me back to sleep. He always went back to the guestroom, though I never remembered him leaving since he waited until I was sound asleep. If it was a good night, this would only happen once; on bad nights, it could be three or four times.

But the night before had been a good night with only one nightmare, leaving us both a bit more rested than usual. While Lucas cleaned up from breakfast, I kept him company, leaning against the counter behind him. As he placed the last dish in the dishwasher, he looked back over his shoulder.

"Twenty questions?"

I grinned. "Sure. You can go first."

He rinsed and dried his hands on a towel, then leaned back against the sink, mirroring my stance, and made eye contact with a soft smile. "What's your earliest memory?"

My heart skipped and my eyes fell to the floor—that was a memory I wished I didn't have. After a moment, I shook my head, still staring at the linoleum under my feet. "New question," I said after a pause.

"Why?"

"It's not something you want to know, trust me. I wish *I* didn't know, that I could forget it."

"Look at me," he said gently. When I did, he continued. "I *do* want to know, whatever it is. That's why I asked."

My eyes became unfocused, and instead of Lucas, I was looking into my own past. "I think I was about three," I started in a voice scarcely above a whisper. "I'd fallen on the concrete stairs to the front door and scraped my knee. I went inside the house, crying, to find my mom. But she was having a bad day."

The rest of the story got stuck in my throat and I sniffled harshly, trying to will away the moisture pooling in my eyes. After staring wide-eyed at the ceiling a moment, I turned back to Lucas with a half-smile and a shrug.

"What happened?" he asked, his brow creased and voice gentle.

I laughed, the sound cold, as my arms crossed tightly in front of me. "The same thing that happened anytime she had a bad day and I was anywhere near her." My eyes darted away again as my jaw trembled. "She screamed at me for crying so loudly and getting blood on the carpet, then pulled down my pants and spanked me with a wooden paddle until I was bruised." I stole a glance at Lucas, who had tears in his eyes. "See? I told you that you didn't want to know."

Lucas crossed the few feet that separated us and engulfed me in his arms, his chest shaking slightly against me. "I'm so sorry," he whispered.

"That's all I knew," I whispered back. Then, for some reason, I had an urge to keep talking, to tell him about my deepest fears.

"And it's the biggest reason I'm so afraid of raising a child, not to mention alone. What if... what if I'm just like her?" My voice cracked on the last word, a few tears slipping out.

"You're not," Lucas said forcefully, holding my shoulders as he pulled back and studied my face. "And you won't be."

"How do you know that? It's in my genes to be like her—to be abusive and addicted and mentally ill. And what right do I have bringing a baby into the world with genes like that? Not just from my side, but from Rob's, too. What chance do I—do *we* have?"

"Annie. You're nothing like her—you already aren't. It doesn't matter what she passed on to you—you're a different person and you can always choose your path in life. That goes for you, for your baby, for anyone. Your family history doesn't determine who you are or who you become. My mom used to say 'tomorrow is a new sunrise—a new day' because it was always a chance to start fresh and it was never too late to make the right decisions. You aren't like your mom, sweetheart. You don't have to be, and you won't be."

I nodded, looking at my crossed arms. No one really knew if I would be or not. But I didn't want to dwell on that right then. I wanted to go back to the pleasant morning we'd been spending together... get back to forgetting my earliest memories.

"Your turn," I said. "What's your earliest memory?"

Lucas got a faraway look and his face softened. "I don't know how old I was, but I was young enough that I was still wearing those one-piece footie pajamas—you know the ones?"

I nodded.

"It was cold, though what season, I have no idea. Mom woke me up wearing a jacket and tiptoed down the stairs with me half-asleep in her arms. I remember her feeling so warm and that she smelled like vanilla where my head rested on her. She grabbed a thermos off the kitchen table and situated a blanket over me. It was still dark outside, but Mom knew the farm as well as she knew the house and didn't need any lights to find her way. It was the first time she took me out to watch the sunrise with her. I remember huddling together under the heavy, scratchy wool blanket and sipping hot chocolate as the sun came up over the horizon."

My voice was watery when I spoke. "That's beautiful, Lucas."

He nodded, smiling. "That was Mom."

"She sounds like such a wonderful mom."

Again, he nodded. "She was," he said. His voice sounded so sure, as if there was no doubt, no other possibility. And then he added, in the same voice, "And you will be, too."

"I hope you're right," I murmured.

"Of course I am," he said playfully, then stepped back. "I'm always right." He winked and flashed me his trademark grin with an eyebrow raised.

I couldn't help but roll my eyes. "Naturally."

He laughed and wrapped an arm around my shoulders, tugging me away from the counter and walking us to the living room. I sat, but kept shifting around, trying to find a position in which my favorite jeans weren't digging uncomfortably into my waist to no avail. With an annoyed sigh, I looked up at Lucas and asked him if he'd mind taking me clothes shopping. While there were few things I'd have preferred to avoid more, it was impossible to continue denying that my midsection was rapidly growing as I neared the end of the first trimester, and I didn't have many dresses. Besides, I hadn't brought any of them with me when Rob kicked me out—I'd only emptied my drawers and forgotten about anything hanging in the closet.

"Sure," he replied. "But I thought you hated shopping."

"I do, but I need clothes." My face leapt into flames. I was pregnant—there was no reason to be embarrassed about getting bigger, but it seemed so early for it. "Mine are getting too small already."

"Oh!" Lucas' eyes widened. "I hadn't thought about that. Where do you want to go?"

I shook my head. "I don't know. I've never paid attention to where I've seen maternity stores. I'll have to look something up, I guess."

"I can ask Nick if you want—I remember him telling me he took his sister when she was pregnant with Jayden. Then we can leave whenever you're ready."

I agreed, and while Lucas called Nick and started getting us ready to leave, I texted Haley to tell her I was going shopping. She texted back a moment later that she was shifting around her afternoon so she could come with us. Her enthusiasm about my growing baby bump ignited a flicker of excitement in my chest and I smiled. Until she asked if I'd heard anything from Rob and the dark cloud of sadness that was never far away returned. I responded, telling her I hadn't, and that Lucas was keeping tabs on him, though he didn't know I overheard him doing that almost every day.

Haley responded that Rob would come to his senses sooner or later and I stared at the words on the screen, my eyes flooding with tears. Would he? From what I'd overheard, Rob was drinking and maybe even doing drugs and screwing other women. And even if he *did* come to his senses and I could get past what he was doing, could I ever feel safe with him again? Did I even want to try?

"Hey, what's wrong?" Lucas asked as he walked back into the room and sat in the chair next to me, a small backpack slung over his shoulder. His fingertips skated gently along the skin on my arm as he studied me.

I shook my head, clearing my cheeks of moisture with a rough swipe of my hands. "I'm fine. I'm just a little hormonal thanks to this little one," I said, my hand automatically resting over my belly. "Did you find a store?"

"No, I didn't, unfortunately," he responded. My eyes moved up to find his dancing and the corners of his mouth twitching. "I actually found four."

A short laugh escaped my lungs. "Lucas!" I admonished, rolling my eyes. "I can't believe I fell for that."

It was the exact same joke he'd played on me the year before when he took a few days off after Thanksgiving to spend with me. I giggled, shaking my head when he winked at me and his familiar cheesy, boyish grin stretched across his face. That damn irresistible grin… apparently it was enough to disarm me even when I was upset because there I was smiling back at him, my conflicted feelings and sadness already fading.

"Do you mind a bit of a drive? They're all at the outlet mall in Caperton. Maternity jackpot, it seems. And they're also the only stores within an hour of Haley."

"No, that's fine. I just need to pee, of course, and grab my purse."

"I'll grab your purse. I've got water and snacks already." He winked and patted the strap of his backpack, then gave me that disarming grin again. I could suddenly see him as a father, always prepared and happy—it seemed like something that would be so natural for him. "But I haven't figured out how to pee for you yet."

I snorted, the sound mixing with his infectious laughter as he stood and pulled me to my feet. We stood there, studying each other's faces as our laughter tapered off. The playfulness in Lucas' eyes was fading, and as it went, my heartbeat got louder in my ears, for a moment drowning out the signals from my bladder. He swallowed and my eyes were drawn to watch the slow movement of his Adam's apple. For some reason, that made my heart flutter, and my eyes came back to his face.

"I love making you laugh, sweetheart," he said, the words soft and slow.

As he spoke, one hand reached up to tuck my hair behind my ear, his fingertips searing my skin where they brushed around my ear and along my jaw. My breath caught as a pleasant shudder moved through my body. But as it passed my midsection, pain signals broke through, making my legs weak, and I nearly peed my pants.

"Oh my god," I breathed out, wincing and grabbing the back of the chair next to me for support. "I have to pee right now, or I might explode."

Lucas burst out laughing as he stepped back to give me space to walk around him, and I couldn't help laughing, too, even as I mused how natural it all felt living in his house, laughing together over the most normal experiences along the road to parenthood.

chapter thirteen

annie

It **turned out** I didn't mind the drive at all; within a few minutes of leaving, the soft music Lucas played, his spicy-sweet scent that surrounded me, and the warm sunshine on my skin through the windows relaxed me and I dozed off. I woke as Lucas pulled into the enormous parking lot, yawning and stretching, feeling both sleepy and rested. My mouth pulled up at the corners while I studied Lucas's profile as he searched for an open spot and then navigated his car into it. He seemed so relaxed and content, his features focused on the task at hand, but not tense. My hand itched to reach out and touch his face the way he sometimes touched mine. I wanted to bury my face in the crook of his neck just below the open collar of his short-sleeve button-up and know again what it was like to be there, to feel his arms around me, holding me close to him when I *wasn't* crying. As soon as he shifted into park, his eyes darted over to catch me looking at him. A blush spread across my cheeks, and I turned to look out my window.

The zipping sound of Lucas's seatbelt filled the air—along with my pounding heart—then his hand was covering mine as he raised the volume of the music and the lyrics to "Wait for You" by Tom Walker surrounded us. I shifted back toward him at the contact. His face was intense, his eyes bright, and my gaze was trapped in his. Once the song ended, he lowered the volume and swallowed slowly, and my eyes were drawn to the movement in his neck again. Then my phone chimed loudly, and I jumped, pulling my hand out from under his and looking toward my purse. Lucas cleared his throat, placing his hand on the steering wheel and looking out his window as I read the message from Haley.

"Haley's here," I murmured. "She's waiting at Little Peas for us."

He nodded with another throat clear, then climbed out of the car. Offering me his arm once I'd reached my feet as well, we headed through the oppressive heat toward Haley. As we approached, she grinned at me, her eyes flicking over us.

"Hey, babe!" she called.

I smiled at her in return, looking through the front windows of the shop, surprised to see how cute the clothes were. I'd always assumed maternity clothes would be frumpy. Comfortable, but frumpy and unattractive. Anticipation stirred deep in my belly and my smile broadened into a grin. I was actually a little excited about the day.

We spent a few minutes talking logistics, telling Lucas where and when to meet us since Haley was insistent that shopping for clothes was a girls-only thing. Lucas took in everything we said, his eyes resting on me, nodding as he listened. And then, with a last look, he started down the walkway toward the other end of the mall.

Once inside, I was expecting to be daunted by the volume of clothes to choose from, but the friendly, helpful staff and Haley were happy to do the choosing for me. I tried on outfit after outfit that they'd selected and was rapidly tiring as I neared the last in the pile.

"What do you think about this one?" I asked Haley, stepping out of the dressing room. It felt like the thousandth time I'd asked her that. The linen shorts I was wearing right then with a slightly fitted white cotton blouse might have been my favorite.

She examined me in silence for a moment, smiling. "Best one so far, aside from one or two of the dresses."

"Yeah?" I asked, turning and looking in the mirror again. "I think it makes me look more pregnant than I am, though."

"It does, but it works. You look fucking hot."

The skin on my neck heated and I wondered what Lucas would think of it. Then the heat shot up onto my face at the direction of my thoughts. What was wrong with me? Lucas and I were friends. That's it. What did it matter what he thought of what I was wearing?

Even so, I changed into the new outfit after checking out and balking at the total for the mountain of clothes I was purchasing. Maternity clothes were more expensive than I'd expected. I reasoned it was worth it, though, to be comfortable throughout my pregnancy. And as long as I got a job sometime in the next few months, I could afford it.

We exited the store, Haley carrying half of my bags, and turned right to head toward the next maternity store—this one specializing in maternity underwear and bras. We had a bit less success there, but I still managed to find a few things that would make me more comfortable and changed into one of the new bras. When I walked out of the bathroom after changing, Haley shook her head.

"Damn, babe," she said, her eyes dancing.

"Would you stop saying shit like that?" I laughed, my cheeks hot.

She shrugged, then laughed, linking our free arms together. "I'm just saying, this baby's got a smokin' hot mama."

I rolled my eyes, but my chest felt buoyant. I was actually enjoying myself—it was the first time I'd ever enjoyed shopping for clothes. As we walked through the store, I caught a glance of my profile in a mirror and sucked in a breath. Haley was exaggerating, of course, but I actually liked my reflection. Had I *ever* liked my reflection before? I paused, staring, and set my bags down, moving my hand over my belly... over my *baby*.

"Holy shit, Haley," I breathed out, my eyes still fixed on my reflection. "I'm having a baby."

"I know," she said, her voice uncharacteristically gentle.

I turned my head and we grinned at each other as she set down the bags she was holding and moved her hand over mine on my belly. I giggled and my eyes glassed over—happy tears this time.

In that instant, my heart ached and expanded, and I was suddenly madly in love with the tiny being growing inside me. My breath whooshed out of me as this new kind of love washed over me and I half-laughed, half-cried, watching Haley's eyes fill as her smile split her face.

It felt like we soared through the next hour as we browsed at the other two stores, and then it was time to head back to the first store to meet Lucas so Haley could get back to work.

"How much longer are you living with Lucas?" Haley asked as we meandered slowly through the heat.

I shrugged, keeping my eyes fixed straight ahead. I didn't want to think about the inevitable day I'd have to leave. I wanted to just pretend I'd be there forever. "I don't know."

"I still don't understand why you never came up with me after your appointment, babe."

Again, I shrugged, and she sighed. My spirit started floating back down to earth as the reality of my situation sank in again, though I fought desperately to hold on to the wonderful, optimistic feeling I'd had.

"I think," Haley started slowly, "it would be better if you weren't living with your ex when Rob gets his shit together, Annie."

Anger coursed through me. If I hadn't been dizzy, I'd have yanked my arm from hers.

"What about *me*, Haley? Huh? What about me? You talk about Rob getting his shit together and coming back around as if I'm just expected to take him back. What if I don't want to? I can't even *think* about him without thinking about what he's doing right now."

"He's fucking up, yes, but you're telling me you wouldn't forgive him? With your history together?"

My history with him flashed through my mind. All the happiness, and all the pain. I couldn't *not* love him. And my first thought was that I'd forgive him for anything. But my second was revulsion and anger and fear. "He's sleeping around, Haley," I seethed. "He's not just avoiding me or something—he's having sex with other women. Sex! Why is it expected that I'd just forgive him? Especially when he kicked me out?"

The other things he'd done—leaving bruises on me and making my lip bleed—rose into my mind, but I couldn't bring myself to tell her, too ashamed of what had happened as if it was my fault. I knew it wasn't, but I still felt like it was.

"I know," she said quickly. "Of course you don't have to."

We continued in silence, my thoughts swirling with trying to figure out what I'd do if Rob came back apologizing. Turning the last corner, I could make out Lucas already waiting for us, though he was staring ahead of him at something and couldn't see us. With Rob on my mind, I couldn't help but start mentally comparing the two. If Rob were standing there instead of Lucas, I'd be nervous at the way he was standing with his arms crossed and looking into space. With Rob, it usually meant he was brooding about something that pissed him off, which meant he'd be easy to set off. His jealousy would be ramped up. He'd probably yell and might lose his temper and hit something. But watching Lucas as we neared, I knew none of those things would come to pass with him. Whatever his thoughts were, he wasn't about to start yelling or hitting something, even if he was frustrated. Instead of being nervous about reaching him... I was eager.

"Hey, Lucas," I called when we were about twenty feet away.

I saw his grin break across his face as he turned toward us. "Hey, Ann—" his lips halted, and his voice stopped, his grin fading as his eyes scanned me from head to toe before returning to my gaze.

"What's wrong?" I asked, my previous thoughts scattering, my skin warming.

Lucas cleared his throat and glanced away briefly. "It's just..." His eyes flitted back to mine. "You look..." He shook his head, his mouth curving up slightly, then ran his hand through his hair as his face got red.

A blush spread like wildfire up my neck and stained my cheeks. His eyes were shining and filled with emotion, communicating something unspoken to me as we stood there. It was overwhelming and confusing, but I couldn't look away. Whatever was happening, I liked the way it made me feel and wasn't ready for that feeling to end. However, the spell was broken a moment later when Haley spoke.

"Well," she said loudly, tugging slightly on my arm before holding the bags she was carrying out toward Lucas. "I have to get back to work."

I placed my bags on the ground and turned to wrap my arms around her, our conversation about Rob forgotten for the moment. "Thank you for doing this with me."

She quirked an eyebrow. "Like I would have let you do it without me. You'd have been so determined that comfort meant ugly that you'd be walking around in a muumuu right now."

I snorted, shaking my head. "No, I most definitely wouldn't."

She smirked. "Yeah, you would." After a last squeeze, she stepped back. "I really do have to go. Love you, babe."

"Love you, too, Haley."

She and Lucas inclined their heads toward each other, and then she was heading to the parking lot.

"Ready for lunch?" Lucas asked, his eyes scanning me again.

My head spun, though I wasn't sure if it was from the heat or from Lucas's gaze. "Not yet," I replied. "But I'd love something cold. Like ice cream."

He tilted his head toward the other end of the mall. "Not far that way was a frozen yogurt shop."

"Yes! That's perfect," I said, grinning.

Lucas grabbed up all the bags before I had a chance and wrapped an arm around my shoulders. Before we had taken a single step, however, a familiar voice reached me.

"Annie, honey, is that you?" my mom called out from across the walkway, Mrs. Renner by her side. "And Lucas? What are you guys doing here?"

I froze, not prepared to deal with what was bound to unfold. Lucas knew I hadn't told my mom yet—and why—and shot me a reassuring smile as he squeezed my shoulder and whispered into my ear.

"It'll be fine. I promise."

I nodded, but how was I going to explain to her what happened with Rob? I could already hear her voice telling me she told me so about him. It was exactly the reason I'd avoided talking to her since everything happened, and I still wasn't ready to hear it.

"Annie!" Mom exclaimed, her eyes darting to my midsection. "Why didn't you tell me? Congratulations, honey. How far along are you? You must have just found out if this is the first I'm hearing of it, but look at that belly already! Where's Rob? How are you feeling? Are you having morning sickness?"

"Wow, Mom," I laughed, trying to suppress the panic brewing in my chest as we exchanged hugs. "Slow down. We were heading to the frozen yogurt place down a ways, would you guys like to join us? Then we can talk once we're out of this heat."

They agreed to join us, and we moved as a group toward the shop as Mom explained that she and Mrs. Renner were there to get some gifts for the pregnant granddaughter of one of their knitting group members.

For a moment, Lucas and Mrs. Renner were busy talking about the brewery just behind us, and Mom turned to me as we walked. "Honey, why didn't you tell me?" she asked, her eyebrows drawn, her voice tinged with hurt.

I sucked in breath, unsure how to answer that question, but was saved when my increasing dizziness caused me to stumble off-balance. In an instant, Lucas had steadied me and kept his arm around me until we reached the yogurt shop. He held the door, and Mom and Mrs. Renner passed inside first, heading over to the self-serve area. As I stepped over the threshold, Lucas suggested I go ahead and find a seat, and that he'd grab our frozen yogurt. "Half vanilla, half cookies-n-crème?" he asked.

I smiled that he'd remembered my favorite flavors from one of the days we'd played his twenty questions game. His was chocolate, I'd learned that day. "And maybe some fresh strawberries if they have any?"

"Sure thing."

After sitting, my eyes roamed around the small, busy shop as I drank in the cool air. There were a few couples, but mostly families with young children. The sounds of kids playing and talking and laughing was sweet and brought back my own memories of getting ice cream cones on hot days with my mom when I was growing up.

"What are you thinking about, honey?" Mom asked as she sat down across from me, interrupting my reverie. "You've got a faraway look and are rubbing your belly."

I smiled, glancing down. Rubbing my belly had somehow already become a habit and I rarely noticed when I was doing so. "I was thinking about when Lori and I were little, and you would take us out for ice cream cones on really hot summer days as a special treat. Remember? That little mobile soft serve business that set up in the drugstore parking lot?"

"Oh my, yes, I do." She smiled. "You girls took so long to make up your minds about what kind of ice cream you wanted, even though you almost always got the same thing."

Lucas sat down in the chair to my right, placing a cup and spoon in front of me. I smiled in thanks before responding to my mom.

"Well, it was hard to decide—I loved two different kinds and couldn't get them in one cone!" I laughed.

"What did you go with today?"

I held my cup out toward her after taking my first bite so she could see inside. "Mm, so good. A little of each. What did you guys get?"

"Vanilla, of course," Mom replied.

"I decided to try the mango," Mrs. Renner said.

"Chocolate," Lucas chimed in. "Though I almost got the same thing you did so I could see what all the fuss is about."

"The fuss is because it's amazing. Try some." After carefully scooping up a bite of only cookies-n-crème, I held the spoon out for Lucas, and he leaned forward to eat the frozen yogurt from it.

"Mm, that might be better than my chocolate," he said.

"Now try the vanilla," I said, holding another spoonful out.

This time, he made a face. "Why would anyone voluntarily pick that flavor?"

"Hey now!" I said, feigning offense. "Mom and I have great taste, thank you!"

We laughed and debated the merits of different frozen yogurt flavors, agreeing unanimously after we'd tasted it that Mrs. Renner's mango was okay at best. I had completely forgotten the events of the last couple of weeks, simply enjoying the company of three people I cared about, when the inevitable happened.

"So, Annie, tell me about this pregnancy!" Mom said. "How does Rob feel about having a baby?"

My heart lurched and my mouth hung open, silent. I couldn't see because my eyes suddenly filled with tears. My breath was coming in short, ragged bursts, and it felt like thousands of eyes were watching and waiting for me to respond. But then Lucas' palm was on my back, his thumb moving rhythmically back and forth, providing just the encouragement and support I needed in order to speak.

"Well," I began with jaw trembling. "He... uh... he doesn't believe it's his, so... he's... we're not..." I couldn't make myself finish that sentence. It was ridiculous, but I felt like saying it out loud to them would be admitting that I'd failed in some way. I was embarrassed by everything Rob had done, as if it was somehow my fault.

"Is it?" my mom asked.

"Are you serious, Mom?" I shouted, shocked by her question. "Of course it is! I can't believe you would even ask me that."

She shrugged, glancing pointedly at Lucas. "If he's so sure it isn't his, I just figured there's a reason."

"There is, but he's wrong." I inhaled and exhaled sharply. My emotions were getting out of control, and I didn't want to cry somewhere so public and busy. "Excuse me."

Forgetting that standing suddenly was my enemy, I shoved up from the table and nearly fell over. Lucas jumped up, reaching out to steady me, but I shoved him away from me. "I'm fine—I don't need anyone's help!"

It took about ten minutes of splashing icy cold water on my face while locked in the bathroom, but eventually my tears dried up and I thought I could keep a handle on my emotions long enough to finish the conversation that was waiting for me. My movements were slow and deliberate in order to avoid losing my balance again as I approached the silent table and sat down. But before turning to face my mom and her questions, I turned to Lucas, grabbing his hands; he deserved an apology, though I couldn't keep eye contact while I was speaking and stared at where our hands were clasped instead.

"I'm so sorry, Lucas. I shouldn't have yelled at you. And I didn't even mean it."

He dipped his head until he made eye contact with me. "It's okay, Annie. Don't worry about it."

I nodded, though I *was* worried about it... about pushing him away after everything he was doing for me. With a deep, slow breath in and out, I turned to the other members of our group as Lucas gathered up and disposed of everyone's garbage. Mom was staring at me, and Mrs. Renner was staring at Lucas, but the only thing that mattered right then was getting through this conversation so it would finally be over.

"I didn't find out until after I discovered I was pregnant, but Rob apparently had a vasectomy years ago and that's why he thinks the baby can't be his. But it is. They aren't always effective, but Rob has blinders on because he's convinced himself that I had an affair."

As I spoke, my mom shook her head in her signature disapproving way—the headshake that precedes a lecture—so it was obvious what was coming next, and my heart sank.

"Annie, honey," she started, "I hate to say it, but—"

"Then don't," Lucas interjected, his voice quiet but forceful. I gaped at him, stunned that he'd said what I'd been thinking.

"Lucas!" Mrs. Renner chastised.

"Look," he said, his jaw ticking as he reached around my back to grasp my shoulder. "I don't mean to be rude, but what's the point in saying something like that? Annie's going through enough right now. How about just being supportive?"

My chest was filled with gratitude for the way Lucas had just stood up to my mom on my behalf, and it took considerable effort to ignore the urge to fling my arms around his neck right then and there.

"Well, what happened, then?" Mom asked after an uncomfortable pause.

"He, um..." My words were trying to stick in my throat, but I needed to get them out. "I told him I was pregnant and then he kicked me out. I found out about the vasectomy later."

"That bastard," Mom muttered. Mrs. Renner winced, and her mouth pressed into a thin line as Mom asked, "When did that happen?"

"About two weeks ago."

"You've been gone for two weeks!" Mom exclaimed, her eyes wide with incredulity. "Where have you been this whole time?"

I watched my finger slide along the edge of the table, not wanting to answer her question. Not wanting the judgment I knew would come—the suspicions that Rob was right. Knowing how to explain why I'd gone to Lucas at first, but not why I'd stayed. Or why it was the only place I wanted to be.

Lucas gave a light squeeze to my shoulder and pulled me a little closer to his side. "She's been staying with me," he said.

"Wait a second—" Mom started.

"I didn't know who else to call when it happened," I rushed out before she had a chance to continue. "I couldn't go to you and hear you tell me that you told me so about Rob like you just did when it was so fresh. Haley and Carol were at work for god's sake, and Lori... who knows, she isn't always dependable anyway. So, I called Lucas."

"But you've been living with another man for *two weeks,* Annie?"

My face leapt into flames and my mouth hung open, wordless. *Yes, I have been, Mom. I've been living with another man. And I might just keep living with him, because I like living with him.*

"I've been taking care of her," Lucas chimed in, filling the tense silence.

"Taking care of her?" Mom pursed her lips and drew her head back. "She's barely pregnant. Annie, surely I've done a better job of raising you to be independent. You don't need to have a man to take care of you!"

"Maybe not," Lucas replied before I had a chance in that same quiet, forceful voice, "but she does need *someone* to take care of her right now. Haven't you noticed her losing her balance? Her blood pressure is out of whack and will take a few weeks to normalize. Not only that, but she has severe morning sickness."

Mom shifted her gaze to me without responding to Lucas. "You could have come to me. You *should* have come to me."

"No, I couldn't," I replied. "Like I said, I couldn't hear what you thought about Rob, about the situation. It's hard enough... hurts enough..." my voice cracked, and my jaw trembled as I fought to keep my tears from falling.

"I'm sorry, honey. But now I know, and we've talked about it. I'll try not to say anything else about it, so you can come live with me now. I can take care of you as long as you need, and Lucas can get back to his life."

"I know," I said, guilt stabbing through me. "I've been an incredible burden on him. I should—"

"Annie," Lucas cut me off, shifting to face me. "Look at me," he said, his voice filled with urgency. My eyes lifted from staring through the tabletop to meet his gaze. "I've told you already—you are *not* a burden. I like taking care of you. And nothing's changed. You don't have to go anywhere. If you want to stay... well, I'd like that." He swallowed, then added in a soft voice, "I'd *really* like that."

"I can't do that to you," I replied quietly. Everything around us faded away as I focused on him. "You haven't gotten a good night's rest since I arrived because of my nightmares, you're away from the brewery all the time, you have to drive me everywhere I go, and you're sleeping on a damn air mattress. I can't ask you to keep doing that for me."

"You're not asking me to do it. I'm asking you to *let* me do it."

His expression was bright and intense; he was looking at me in that way that made my skin prickle and get hot, the way he'd looked at me since that night at the brewery when he spent the night and our friendship morphed into something more over a year earlier. That realization hit me hard, stealing my breath. I shouldn't even consider staying with him—the right thing to do was move in with Mom, or Haley, or even Lori. Anyone but Lucas. Yet, the words wouldn't come. Being with him made me feel normal and accepted. He had this uncanny ability to anticipate my needs and know what I needed, even though I didn't tell him. No one had ever understood me better than Rob, and yet it seemed Lucas did... at least he did *now*. He hadn't always. How had that changed? Or was *I* the one who was changing? Maybe my needs weren't the same as they used to be?

"Annie!" Mom said sharply. "You can't seriously be considering staying there any longer. You should be with your family. Who else is going to be there to help you raise a child? No offense, Lucas, but not a young, successful, unattached guy who isn't the father."

My gaze shifted to my lap. Mom was right, even if I didn't think living with her was the right long-term solution—staying with Lucas definitely wasn't. "I don't know what I'm going to do right now, Mom. I need to think about it. Things could also change with Rob, I guess..." My voice trailed off with the last sentence. Could they really? Even if he came crawling back, would it make any difference?

"He left you because he thinks you're carrying another man's baby. He's not coming back. And he doesn't deserve you after doing that, anyway."

There was nothing I could say in response, and a tense silence began to stretch between us all until Lucas changed the subject to focus on the pregnancy itself, insisting I show them all the clothes I had bought. His efforts to change the atmosphere around us were successful—by the time we were standing to leave, I'd regained some of the happiness and excitement I'd found in the maternity stores.

"Lucas, can you hang back and talk for a minute? Miriam can walk with Annie, and they can have a moment alone as well."

That was the first time Mrs. Renner had spoken since we'd talked about her mango-flavored frozen yogurt. During the rest of the exchange, she had simply listened, looking back and forth between Lucas and me.

"Of course, Grams. I've got the bags, Annie. Do you want to give me your purse, too?"

After passing over my purse and thanking Lucas, my mom and I linked arms and started slowly down the sidewalk toward the parking lot. After passing several stores, Mom broke the silence.

"You okay, honey? You feel like you're wobbling a bit."

"I'm fine," I replied. "It's much better than it was."

As chance would have it, however, I stumbled hard just as the last word left my lips, dragging my mom down with me. Luckily, there was a man walking past who saw what was happening and reached out to help. Unluckily, he could only keep one of us from falling, though he chose the right person: my mom. At her age, a fall could have resulted in a broken hip or arm. I landed hard on my palms and knees, my skin scraping along the concrete.

"Annie!" Lucas shouted from behind. A second later, he was there, his arms around me as he helped me stand. "Are you alright?" he rushed out, his eyes searching me rapidly.

"Yeah, I'm fine—just scraped my hands and knees a bit, but I'm not hurt."

He sighed, gazing at me with brows creased. "You're dizzier today than you have been the last few days. Maybe we should go see Dr. Miller again."

"No, it's just this god-awful heat. It makes it worse. I'll be fine once I cool off."

"Here," he said, steering us in the direction of the nearest door. "Let's go inside for a minute." We'd entered a restaurant and Lucas guided me toward some benches near an air conditioning vent. "Sit here. I'll be back with the car in a few minutes to get you, okay? Just wait here for me, alright?"

My nod was feeble as I sat and basked in the cool air blowing over my head. It was a relief to sit since the adrenaline from the fall had left my limbs shaky and unsteady. Leaning against the back of the bench, I sighed. "Okay, I will. I'll be here."

Mom sat as Lucas returned to the blazing heat outside, speaking even as she was getting comfortable. "I can't pretend to agree with everything you do, because I don't. But thinking about it, I can understand why you felt you couldn't come to me. And I'm sorry that I'm like that, honey. I care and I wish you felt comfortable coming to me about things. And I would really like for you to come live with me until this mess gets sorted out with Rob— we can hire someone to be around to help you since we just saw how helpful *I* am when you get dizzy—I'll fall right with you, apparently."

She laughed, shaking her head, then continued. "Anyway, I think you should come live with me, so think about it. Lucas is a nice young man, Annie, but he's not going to want to give up his life to raise someone else's child. He may think that now, before the baby is born, but that will change, honey. And then you'll go through heartbreak all over again. And even if it doesn't, is it really fair to ask that of him?"

"Mom, for once in my life, I'm not thinking that far ahead. Right now, I'm just trying to be as calm and happy as I can for this baby."

"When are you due?" Mom asked a moment later.

My gaze shifted to study my fingernails. "I don't know. I haven't been to the doctor yet."

"How far along are you?" she asked, looking concerned.

"About three months," I replied.

"That's what I thought you'd said earlier. You should have already been, honey. Make an appointment as soon as possible."

"I did make one—it's for Tuesday."

"Okay. Are you going to come stay with me in the meantime, honey?"

"I don't know, Mom." I let out a long breath; thinking beyond the next day seemed impossible at the moment. "I just don't know."

She wrapped an arm around my shoulder and pulled me into her side like she used to do when I was young. With my eyes closed and my head resting on her shoulder, I could almost pretend life was as simple as I'd always wished it was.

chapter fourteen

lucas

After settling Annie in the air-conditioned restaurant, Grams and I made our way toward the parking lot. I wished I'd been walking with her so I could have kept her from falling. She assured me she was fine, but I'd seen her go down and she'd landed pretty hard; she must have been in more pain than she let on. I glanced back over my shoulder for probably the tenth time to make sure she hadn't decided to walk after she'd agreed to stay put; Annie could be obstinate about doing things herself.

"Lucas!" Grams' voice cut into my thoughts.

"Sorry, Grams, I was thinking about something," I muttered, turning my attention back to her.

"Grandson, I can see exactly what you were thinking about," she retorted, her voice admonishing me. "You're in love with her again."

There was no point in denying it—not to Grams. She'd see right through it. "No—not again, Grams. I never stopped."

"How do you see this playing out?" she asked.

I pondered her question before responding, closing my eyes for a brief moment. In my mind was Annie, her dark curls shining in the sunlight, her skin glowing. We were walking next to each other, holding hands, her other hand resting on a very large baby bump, her eyes luminous and crinkled at the corners as she laughed at something I said.

"I... I don't know, Grams."

"Rob will figure things out and come back eventually, you know."

"I think you're wrong," I said, my jaw taut as I remembered Annie falling apart when she found out what he was doing. "You know he's sleeping around?"

"And how would you know that?"

"Nick—he's friends with the bartender at Midtown Tavern, where Rob spends most of his time now."

Grams swore under her breath, shaking her head. "He'll get it together at some point," she said. "He always does. And when he does, he'll be back for her. What then?"

My chest tightened at the thought. "I don't know. I guess it depends."

"Depends on what? That's *his* baby she's carrying—not yours."

"You think I don't know that?" I asked loudly, frustrated. I didn't need a reminder about Annie's relationship with Rob. It was under the surface at all times already.

"You aren't acting like you do," she said with a sharp look.

"Look, if he comes back around—and that's a big 'if'—*and* if Annie wants to go back to him—another big 'if'—it's not like I can do anything about it. But I don't think he will, and I don't think she'd take him back if he did." *At least, I hope she wouldn't.* "There are things you don't know, Grams."

"Then tell me."

I shook my head. "Not right now. I need to get back to Annie."

She stopped walking, holding out a hand so I'd stop as well. "Lucas, listen to me. I'm worried about what you're doing right now. I'm sure Rob will be back, and when that happens, he and Annie will be okay. They'll figure it out—they always do. And the longer you're involved with her before that day comes, the harder it's going to be for you to let her go."

I exhaled loudly, absently scanning the horizon.

"You know it's not just her anymore?" Grams prodded.

"Obviously. And even the possibility of raising a child with Annie? I can't describe it, Grams, but I want that more than I've ever wanted anything else—even the brewery. I love her, and I'll love that baby, too, if I get the chance."

———

After stopping on the way back from shopping to pick up a few replacement taps, we needed to swing by the brewery to drop them off before heading back to my house. Once I was parked, I told Annie I'd run in quickly, but she needed to use the bathroom, so we headed inside together. I waited for her outside the staff bathroom, wanting to be close by if she was dizzy. When she came out, I slipped my arm back around her shoulders and we headed toward the bar.

"Thanks for taking me shopping," she said, turning to smile up at me.

I smiled back at her, wanting to see her face the way it was right then—soft and content when looking at me—every day. I wanted her to be happy, and I wanted that to be with me. "You're welcome, sweetheart," I replied. "Besides," I added, broadening my smile into the grin she liked so much, "if Haley's to be believed, I didn't really have a choice—we couldn't have you walking around in a muumuu."

She snorted and her eyes crinkled at the corners as she burst into laughter, and my heart thumped against my ribs as I watched. On impulse, before I really even knew what I was doing, I pulled her into my side and leaned down to kiss her temple. It had felt so natural that I'd done it without thinking but was immediately worried I shouldn't have. Annie, however, only continued to smile, though a beautiful blush tinged her cheeks.

As we rounded the corner into the dining area, however, Annie's body stiffened and her face fell. I lifted my eyes from where they'd been studying her as we walked and froze.

chapter fifteen

rob

After being drunk for days on end, thinking about Lucas and Annie, I'd been itching to punch the fucker in the face. He'd fucked my wife. I should have known better than to let him near her—anyone could see he was still in love with her. But *her*? That had been unexpected. She'd fooled me—I'd really believed she loved me.

Nick told me they weren't at the brewery, but I refused to leave, even though he said he wouldn't serve me any beer. Didn't matter, though—I'd found two out-of-towners eyeing me, batting their fake eyelashes every time I looked at them, and they were happy to give me their drinks. At least one of them would be willing to fuck me after, too—I was sure of it. If I could do it this time. I'd been trying, wanting to fuck Annie out of my mind, do to her what she'd done to me, but I hadn't been able to yet. Maybe that would finally change.

The third beer the two chicks had gotten for me from the other bartender when Nick wasn't paying attention was about half gone when I knew Annie was there. Even drunk, I could sense her presence somehow. My blood started pounding in my ears, heightening the feeling of intoxication and drowning out whatever shit the blond chick was droning on about.

When my eyes found her, she took my breath away. She was radiant. Her face was positively glowing, framed in the soft curls I knew so well, her cheeks pink as she smiled up at Lucas. My eyes fell, taking in the shirt that accentuated her curviness, her hand resting over a noticeable belly. Again, I couldn't breathe—what if that baby really was mine? My eyes darted up to Annie's, trying to figure out what was real and true. Tears were now tracking down her cheeks as she looked at me and she took a small step in my direction. My gaze was drawn back to her belly. *Wow! There's really a baby in there!* I had known that already, but in that moment, I really *knew* it—it wasn't just something Annie had said to me.

I glanced back to Annie's face; she was pale and her eyes were filled with fear and uncertainty and pain. Why was she looking at me like that? My conviction about her infidelity was wavering, doubt chipping away at what I had been sure was fact. I shook my head violently, trying to clear the alcohol fog so I could think clearly. When I looked back, though, nothing had changed. Not the expression in Annie's eyes or Lucas standing with his arm around her as he glared at me.

"Rob?" Annie spoke unsteadily.

My steps faltered when I heard my name coming from her, my gaze landing on her belly again. "No!" I roared, willing the anger to the surface to replace the pain in my chest. "I loved you so goddamn much and you fucked somebody else. Would you have ever even had the decency to tell me if you hadn't gotten yourself pregnant?"

She swallowed, her tears coming so fast it was like a river down each cheek. "Rob, I swear I didn't—I would never—"

"The fuck you didn't!" I spat. "It doesn't matter what you say, I know I'm not the father—I *can't* be."

"Rob, please—"

"No, goddamn it!" I shouted, breathing heavily, my chest heaving. "I already signed and returned the divorce papers you so conveniently sent to me before. I should have just signed them the day I got them and saved myself from discovering I'd married a whore. But don't worry, *love,*" I added, spitting out the last word. "I've learned my lesson this time. We're over for good—I won't make this fucking mistake again."

My glare shifted to Lucas. As much as I wanted to beat him unconscious, the pain in my chest was beginning to eclipse my anger; I needed to get away from Annie. But not before I gave her a taste of the pain she'd caused me.

"Hey, wife-fucker, I'll catch up with you later—I'd like to show you how much I appreciate you taking care of my wife. But right now, I'm going to go enjoy my newfound freedom with those two gorgeous ladies over there." I jerked a thumb behind me. "Who—by the way, Annie—would *never* turn me down for sex."

Turning slowly so I wouldn't stumble, I winked and smirked at the women I'd been drinking with as they dissolved into flirty giggling. When I reached the table, I slung an arm around each of them, suggesting we head back to my hotel room, and the three of us made our way out.

Despite the fact that she'd betrayed me, guilt slammed heavily into my chest—so heavily it was nearly impossible to breathe—for intentionally hurting the one person in the world I'd ever truly loved. For everything I'd already said and done... and all the vile and reprehensible shit I knew I was going to do. Not that it mattered—Annie didn't care, not really. I could have saved myself a lot of heartache and trouble if I'd just listened to Charlie when we were kids—he'd been right.

No one really gave a shit about me, and no one ever would.

chapter sixteen

lucas

After Rob's comment about the women not turning him down for sex, the blood drained from Annie and her posture crumbled. Her eyes were lifeless and unfocused. At her request, I'd driven her to Haley's after packing her a bag while she waited in the car. The entire trip, she stared out the window with her hands on her belly, silent, even when I spoke to her. After we arrived, she thanked me softly without raising her eyes to mine, then disappeared with Haley without looking back once.

Not even half the drive back home had passed, and already I felt empty—an emptiness I'd only felt when I'd lost my mom and during the few months after I'd screwed up with Annie in the fall. Annie had said she was going to stay with Haley only for the weekend, that she needed to be away from Stockwood for a few days to clear her head, and while I wished she hadn't felt the need to be somewhere else, I also understood it. I'd just have to distract myself from the void she left by getting myself caught up at the brewery after my extended absence.

She was hurting over the confrontation with Rob, I knew, but I felt angry that she'd run to Haley's. Why couldn't she see that I was right there in front of her? What else could I possibly do?

My dad's voice materialized in my mind in response to that question—the same question I'd asked him in the winter not long after Annie had left Stockwood and before I showed up to help her set up for her mom's birthday party.

"Hi, Dad," I said, trying to smile at the screen of my cell phone when his face appeared. It had been a long time since we'd had a video call, but I needed to see his face for this conversation. It surprised me every time I did how quickly he seemed to be aging. The guilt I harbored for having left him to run the farm alone so I could pursue my dream of running a brewery reared its head, but I ignored it. If my dad had asked me to, I would have stayed. But instead, he'd insisted the farm was his dream and that it was time for me to follow mine. Though he'd never expected to live that dream of his alone—Mom was supposed to be there by his side. "I want to talk about Mom."

My voice had cracked saying her name—the pain of losing my mom when I was a young teen was still so raw and fresh. I missed her as much right then as I had when she'd died all those years ago. And I knew Dad did, too—he was already crying before he responded. Talking about her was like losing her all over again for us, so we'd rarely done so after she was gone.

There were things I needed to know and understand, though. I'd always known—even when I was really young—that my parents were different. They loved each other in a different way than other parents I met. It had always seemed almost like they were an extension of one another, and you could feel their happiness together, even when things were hard or they disagreed. Before Mom got sick, I'd vowed to never settle for something less than what they had. And then after... I'd seen what losing her did to my dad. He'd never been the same again— some of the light and life I'd always known in him was lost and he never got it back. That's when I decided it was better to never have it than to lose it.

Until I'd met Annie and suddenly couldn't seem to remember why I'd made that decision. And as challenging as our relationship was at times, I'd loved her deeply and had no intent to ever let her go. But then the way I'd never dealt with losing Mom got in the way, and I'd lost her anyway after I walked away from her. I'd tried to get her back, but it was too late. Still, I couldn't seem to accept that it was truly over.

Dad nodded, wiping at his eyes, though it didn't help—more tears replaced the ones he dried.

"How did you know Mom was the one?" I asked.

Over the next half an hour, Dad told me stories I'd heard when I was little, but he gave me the full unabridged versions this time. He told me about the first time he met my mom when they were seniors in high school. She'd just moved to the area from the city when a tornado had ripped through the county, destroying several properties. For months, almost everyone in the county, as well as several neighboring counties, pitched in to help rebuild the demolished homes and barns. She'd walked onto the farm where he was working on the third morning, scared and tearing up every time she looked at the destruction around them, but determined to help.

"As soon as our eyes met, it happened. I was a goner. I didn't realize that's what was happening until later, but that was the moment I fell in love with her. I could see so much in her eyes— everything I ever needed to know about her was there. I insisted she follow me around so I could keep her from getting herself hurt—she had no idea what she was doing. It could easily have been someone else there, though. I was just drawn to her and didn't want to be away from her."

My heart skipped listening to his words—he was describing exactly how I'd felt when I met Annie. That there was just something about her, and I didn't realize it until later, but that was when I fell in love with her.

"But, how did you know she was it?" I asked. "That it wasn't something that would pass?"

"I didn't know it when I met her—your mother didn't even tell me for months, not until the day I told her I loved her, actually— but she was engaged already."

"What?" I exclaimed. That was a part of the story I'd never heard. My mom was engaged before she married my dad?

Dad let out a half-sigh-half-chuckle. "Yeah. She was. To some rich asshole—pardon me—from where she'd grown up. She'd known him since they were toddlers, and their families were close and pushed them together."

"It was an arranged marriage?" I asked, trying to imagine my grandparents as I knew them forcing a marriage on my mom.

"Not exactly. They weren't told explicitly they had to marry, but it was expected of them. One of those inevitable things, you know, when a boy and a girl grow up together. So they'd gotten engaged officially right before she moved to our town."

"Dad... what did you do?"

This time there was no laughter in his sigh, and he got a faraway look in his eyes. "Well, for starters, I was pretty pissed off that she'd never told me. And then I was even more pissed off when she refused to end the damn thing. It had never occurred to me that she didn't realize what was so damn clear to me—that she and I belonged together—but she didn't. She was confused and torn between her feelings for me and her sense of responsibility to her parents."

He told me how he'd cut ties with her after a few weeks—told her she'd have to choose him or her fiancé and that she'd chosen her fiancé.

"And until your mother died, son, those weeks after I walked away from her were some of the worst days of my life. But the thing was, they weren't just bad... each one was worse than the last. I lost interest in everything—stopped planning for my farm one day, stopped doing my schoolwork, stopped doing my chores at home. I just didn't care about anything anymore. And then it hit me that I couldn't live without her. That even if she married someone else, she was the only one for me and I needed her any way I could get her. So, I walked over to her house one day and apologized and asked her if we could still be friends."

"I'm guessing she agreed?"

Dad laughed softly. "Sort of. She told me I couldn't go around professing my love for her anymore, that it wasn't appropriate when she was engaged to another man. I agreed to do my best, but was clear that I was making no promises. She gave me a stern look—you know the one—then told me she accepted my terms.”

My mouth curved into a smile—that sounded just like Mom to be all feisty like that. “Did she end up marrying that guy?”

“Hell no,” Dad snorted. “Though she came close. Their wedding was planned for about a year and a half after we met. During that time, we spent just about every waking minute together. Her folks lived in the same house they did when you were little—that big house in town—and had maids and gardeners and all that, so she had a lot of free time. But I didn’t because I had to help Mom and Dad, and I was working toward getting this farm. So she started helping me with everything I did. That’s how she fell in love with the farm, too, you know. Your mom loved being out here and working with her hands, though her parents didn’t really approve of it.”

I laughed to myself, remembering my grandparents on Mom’s side. I hadn’t known them long before they both passed away, but I couldn’t imagine them doing manual labor a day in their lives.

“Anyway,” Dad continued, “about a week before the wedding, her parents and her fiancé sat her down and told her that she needed to end her friendship with me by the time she walked down the aisle because it wouldn’t be right for someone of her social stature to spend time with someone who worked on a farm, and that it wouldn’t be appropriate for a married woman to be such good friends with a man who wasn’t her husband.”

“Oh, god, Dad, I’m so sorry,” I breathed out.

“It’s alright, son. I’ve never been ashamed of the life I’ve lived—not then and not now. They thought they were better than me because they didn’t get dirty to work, but I didn’t buy into that. I knew neither of us was better than the other—we’re all just people at the end of the day.”

“Yeah,” I agreed. “So, what did Mom do?”

“She ran to my house and told me everything they’d just said. She was a mess, sobbing and shouting, and I couldn’t make heads nor tails of anything she was saying at first, so I walked her out

here to this property, telling her again what I wanted to do with it one day, and she eventually calmed down enough that I could understand what had happened. I was scared I was losing her, but I'd done all I could, really. We'd been walking for hours, and the sun was starting to set, so I took her out to the back side of the barn, and we sat down side-by-side, watching the sun go down together as we had a habit of doing almost every day. She said she couldn't believe she was watching the last sunset ever from right there. And I told her, no matter what she did or where she went, that sun was gonna keep right on setting in that same place on the horizon every day. That it wasn't going anywhere just because she was leaving and would be right there for her to watch if she ever came back."

Dad paused, smiling, though he had tears running down his cheeks. I was crying, too, and smiled back at him. "That's the same thing you said to me before I moved out here with Grams," I said.

"Yeah," he said, his grin widening. "Well, your mom, she told me the next day that when I said that to her was when she realized she could live without her fiancé and her money and her nice house and her parents' approval, but that she couldn't live without me and our sunsets together. She'd gone home once the sun was down and broken off her engagement. Then she came back at sunrise the next day, told me what she'd done and why, and then I asked her to marry me at the exact same time she asked me to marry her."

We both laughed through our tears—I remembered that part of the story, that they'd gotten engaged after both of them said "will you marry me?" simultaneously. After a moment, I asked, "But, Dad, when she was engaged to someone else, how did you... how did you get her to love you back? How did you deal with knowing she was with someone else?"

"I never stopped loving her," he said, sniffling.

"I know that, Dad, but what did you do?"

"Lucas, listen to me," he said, staring intently at me from the screen. "The only thing I did was never stop loving her, the best I

knew how. That's it. I couldn't tell her how I felt as often as I wanted or in the way I wanted, I couldn't kiss her or hold her hand whenever I wanted, but that didn't change that I loved her. And I never stopped showing her that. All the other ways I showed her I loved her after she left that jerk were the same ways I'd been showing her before."

I nodded, mulling over his words for a few moments. "And how did you handle knowing she was going to marry someone else anyway?"

"The same way, son. It wasn't my decision, as much as I might have wanted it to be. I recognized every time I got angry it was because I wanted to control her decisions, but they weren't mine to control. It wasn't easy, but once I figured out how to stop trying to control what would happen, I could just enjoy loving her in any way I could—the only thing I had any real control over anyway. And as much as it hurt sometimes, some of the best memories of my life are from loving her over that year and a half when she wasn't even mine."

chapter seventeen

annie

Hormones were surely to blame for it, but my mood had been swinging between devastation from the confrontation with Rob that solidified for me that there would never again be an "us" and a growing excitement to see the baby for the first time on Tuesday. Fear of losing the baby was fading, often leaving me in a state of wonder about what was going on inside my body.

The weekend had been spent in a whirlwind of activities with Haley, Carol, and Linc—what Haley and Carol had not-too-secretly dubbed Operation Keep Annie Too Busy to Be Sad. From walking through baby stores to an improv comedy show, and everything in between, by the time Haley had gone into work Monday morning, I was completely and utterly exhausted and ready for a break.

When I texted Lucas to tell him I was going to stay with Haley for a few more days, I half-expected, and mostly wanted, him to insist I return, but he didn't. Instead, he only asked if there was anything I wanted him to bring up for me and reminded me about my appointment on Tuesday morning. His responses were unusually brief for him, leaving me with a sense of unease. I tried calling him, but he never answered when I did—not even in the middle of the night. I knew it was because he was working, that he would be busy after missing a week for me, something he'd never done before. But I also had the sense that he was working more than usual, and it reminded me of when I had my job in the city, when I was working so much because I *wanted* to keep myself busy so I wouldn't have time to think about other things.

Was *that* what Lucas was doing? Was he burying himself in work on purpose? He'd told me twice that he wanted me to stay with him if that's what I wanted, and I could see the hurt in his eyes after the confrontation with Rob at the brewery, and when he dropped me off at Haley's. Had I driven him to working around the clock?

I shouldn't even consider living with him again. Mom was the most responsible choice—at least until I found a place of my own, though I wasn't sure I'd be ready to do that before the baby was born. As much as Haley kept offering, I could never live with her—her life was too fast-paced. Even if everything else was confusing, there was no doubt I never wanted to go back to living the way I had for so long. Not only that, but anytime I was outside of her downtown condo, my anxiety skyrocketed, and I was constantly looking over my shoulder, afraid of seeing Eddie.

He was out there somewhere, I knew. But surely after everything that happened, he wouldn't come after me out in Stockwood, especially since my restraining order remained intact. But right then I wasn't in Stockwood—I was in *his* territory.

No, Haley and Carol still weren't options, just as Lori was never really an option. Which meant I was back to square one: Mom or Lucas. And no closer to figuring out what I should do. Though my mom was right—Lucas *was* young. What guy still in their twenties wanted to be tied down with a woman and child, let alone a child that wasn't his? He was different from other men, more of what Mrs. Renner would call an old soul, but still... what if he grew to resent us?

Yawning, I padded to Haley's bedroom to nap, but twenty minutes later I was still just lying there, thinking about Lucas and his short responses to my messages. It felt too risky to call him—though a large part of me wanted to—so I texted him instead.

I miss you, I typed out. As soon as my finger hit send, I wished I could take it back. Even if things were over with Rob for good, even if we were divorcing, it wasn't final yet. I was still technically married and had no business even thinking about Lucas as much as I was, let alone saying things like I missed him. One hand picked at lint on Haley's blanket while the other held my phone, waiting for Lucas's response, afraid he wouldn't return the sentiment—equally afraid he would. When there was no response after several minutes, I fell into a fitful sleep, filled with confusing dreams where people like Rob and Lucas turned into people like Eddie and Charlie.

When I woke some hours later, drenched in sweat, the only message I had was from Haley checking in on me. After responding to her, I opened my chat with Lucas and typed another message.

> I'm sorry—I shouldn't have said that. Good news, by the way, my dizziness is improving and I'd guess will be gone in a few days, so I'll finally be able to drive again and won't be so dependent on you when I come home.

Now I was officially babbling in text form. And it dawned on me when it was too late because I'd already hit send that I'd said "come home" about going back to his house. I could feel my emotions cycling through, aggravated by pregnancy hormones, and I was suddenly both angry and upset about everyone and everything: Rob for being so cruel and for hurting me, Lucas for suddenly being so distant, Mom for disapproving of my choices, Lori for being a flake, Haley for thinking Rob deserved another chance, and myself for being pregnant in the situation I was in, for having turned my back on Lucas the year before, for having ever gone back to Stockwood, and more. I threw my phone across the room and then buried my face in my palms, shocked there were any more tears to come out.

"Annie! Wake up! Wake up!" Haley was shouting at me.

My eyes flew open, my chest heaving, my whole body soaked in sweat.

"You okay? It was just a nightmare."

My head shook from side to side as I fought to swallow down the taste of fear and despair that lingered in my mouth.

"It's alright, babe, it wasn't real," Haley said again, rubbing my back soothingly. "Try to calm down. I can feel your heart racing. You need to breathe for the baby, okay?"

Her words were muffled by the memory of the dream that was fighting its way back into my consciousness. My palms pressed into my eyes sockets as my body shook and heaved with my sobs.

"Do you want to talk about it?" Haley asked gently.

I shook my head quickly—I wasn't sure I even could. In the dream, I'd gone home for my birthday. My toddler daughter was with me, but when we walked into the house where everyone I had ever cared about was waiting, no one even knew who I was. I tried to remind them, but they just stared at me, then called me a stranger and pushed me back out the front door as I protested. My daughter had run inside ahead of me just after we'd arrived, and when I called for her, she no longer knew me, either. Chilling laughter was coming from behind me, and when I turned around, Charlie and Eddie were standing next to each other, grinning.

Eddie spoke, saying, "You took everything from us, and now we've taken everything from you. Well, *almost* everything." He'd laughed and they'd lunged. Haley woke me just as they'd grabbed my arms.

I reached up and wrapped my arms around Haley, clinging to her, afraid if I let go, she would no longer know who I was. "I love you, Haley," I sobbed out.

"Shh," she soothed, one arm hugging me back and the other cradling the back of my head. "I'm right here, babe. I love you, too. Everything will be fine. It was a horrible, shitty dream, but it was just a dream."

I nodded, though I didn't loosen my hold on her, just in case. After a few moments, Haley began to hum. The song was one she'd made up when we lived together in college. The words, which I'd long-since forgotten, had been nonsensical and intended only to make me laugh, but the tune was calming when she hummed it.

And sure enough, my sobs eased and then ceased altogether. Before long, I was sound asleep.

chapter eighteen

---

lucas

On Saturday, I caught up on all things Stockwood Brewery with the employees for the first hour or so after arriving before the rush started. What became clear after talking to everyone was that business was booming—more than I'd ever expected considering the size of the town—and some changes were in order.

First, I needed to hire some more people for just about every position in the business, and it needed to happen right away. Second, it was time to think about opening a secondary location, and I knew exactly where it should be: Clarksburg. If the property was still available, anyway. There was an old abandoned church there in the historic district that would be perfect. In fact, that had almost been the location for the brewery to begin with, but it was a bigger financial investment, and ultimately I'd decided to go with Grams' suggestion to get the business started in Stockwood where real estate was more affordable. But expanding would have personal consequences, too, that I needed to consider... It would take me away from Stockwood for at least a few years, if not permanently. Something I wasn't willing to do if I had a chance with Annie—I wanted a life with her more than I wanted to expand my brewery.

A knock at the office door as it swung open distracted me from my thoughts. Nick, my general manager and right-hand guy at the brewery, walked in.

"What are you doing here still? I told you that you could go home and take the weekend off after stepping up to cover for me all week."

"I know, but I think I'm addicted to this place. I don't really want to take a few days off. Besides, we'll be swamped later and could use at least one extra set of hands out front, so I can fill in."

I studied Nick for a moment. He was a good employee. A *great* employee, actually. "I was thinking it was time to do some more hiring, too. Sit, tell me what *you* think we should be doing right now."

An hour later, it was clear that Nick had a very shrewd mind and had both a serious love and intuitive understanding of the business.

"I'm sorry to say it, but I've underestimated you, Nick. I can't believe you decided to come here and work at the bar. You could have gotten a management position anywhere."

He shrugged. "Yeah, but I love this town—I don't want to go anywhere else. And besides, you told me there was growth opportunity here. I didn't mind starting at the bottom and working my way up. Better experience that way, anyway."

"Well, I'm glad you decided to do that—the brewery's lucky to have you. I need to sleep on some of this stuff and then in a few days we can nail down a plan together."

He nodded, though his eyes had widened slightly. "Sure, of course, man."

We talked a few minutes longer about the expectation for business for the weekend before Nick got up to leave. He paused at the doorway, turning his head. "It's not really my business, but is everything okay with Annie? I hadn't expected you to be in until sometime next week. Did something else happen with Rob after he left here?"

Without looking up, I replied, "She's okay. And everything will work out as it should one way or another."

He nodded. "Alright, man. Let me know if you need me to cover for you again or if you just want to grab a beer and talk about it. I happen to know a great place to grab one," he added with a chuckle.

I snorted. "Thanks, Nick. Appreciate it."

———

For our usual Saturday dinner, Grams had made pot roast—the same meal that had been my favorite my whole life. And because she'd taught both of my parents how to cook, it tasted like my childhood. Someday soon, I needed to find the time to go back home for a nice long visit with my dad. I missed him and my childhood home.

We talked at length during dinner about the brewery and then about some odds and ends around the house Grams needed some help with, but she carefully avoided mention of Rob or Annie.

"I know what's on your mind," I said, sitting back in my chair after clearing my plate of a second helping.

She waved a hand at me dismissively. "We don't need to talk about that stuff right now, honey. Who knows what's going to happen? No point in rubbing salt in fresh wounds."

I sighed. They were fresh alright. Grams placed her silverware on her plate and made a move to stand.

"Uh-uh, Grams," I said, jumping to my feet. "Sit. I'll clear the table and clean up."

"No, you sit, Lucas, and let me take care of you."

I laughed, reaching out and grabbing her plate. "When have you *not* taken care of me? And everyone else for that matter? Even when I was living with Dad, you called and wrote letters and sent care packages after Mom died. And I never would have gotten the brewery off the ground without you. I might not have even had the guts to try if you hadn't believed in me." My head shook side to side. "Let me do it, Grams."

She didn't reply, but she didn't try to stop me, either. Instead, she watched, her eyes following me as I cleared the table and then cleaned up the kitchen. Once the last dish was dried and put away in the cabinet, I turned, leaning into my hands that rested on the edge of the countertop.

"Can I make you a cup of tea before I head out?" I asked her.

"You're a good man, Lucas," she said, instead of replying to my question.

I smiled. "I'm glad you think so, but you're my grandmother—you're supposed to."

"And since when do I do something just because I'm supposed to?" she asked, raising her eyebrows.

"That's true," I laughed. "More like the opposite. But you always end up right in the end, as annoying as that is for everyone else."

"Not always," she replied, her voice suddenly soft and sobering. "Sometimes I'm wrong. Not often, I know," she added with a small smirk. "But really, it does happen." Sighing heavily, she continued. "And I think I was wrong about this."

"About what, Grams?"

"About you. And about Rob."

I froze. "What do you mean?"

"You're a good man, like I said—you always have been. You're young, though. And inexperienced. But what I was mistaking for the stupidity and stubbornness of youth—sorry, Grandson—I think was something else. I think you're more insightful than I gave you credit for. And I think you know what you want in life with a clarity that's unusual for people your age." She cleared her throat before continuing more softly. "You're just like your father in that way. You remind me so much of him when he was young."

Her assessment surprised me in a good way—I was proud to be likened to my father—but what I really wanted to know about was the part she hadn't said yet. "And Rob?"

"I thought he had healed some from his past, but he just became more adept at hiding from it. And hiding that from me. His behavior right now... his determination that Annie would just decide she didn't value their relationship? That's from his past. But if he's doing it now, he'll do it again and again until he deals with the parts of his past that are responsible. Annie and that baby need better than that—better than what he's capable of giving them right now."

"No shit," I muttered bitterly.

Grams looked up at me sharply. "Why do you say that?"

I glanced at the clock on wall. "Like I said the other day, there are things you don't know."

"Enlighten me, then, Grandson."

I sighed, feeling pain and anger course through me as I thought about what Rob had done to Annie in my house. "He came to my house two days after he kicked her out. He was drunk. He called her a slut. And he hurt her."

Grams winced. "I can only imagine how much that hurt her."

"No," I said, my voice hard. "He *hurt* her, Grams. He pushed her against the wall and kissed her so hard her lip was bleeding, and held her arms so tight she had bruises on them for weeks."

She gasped and tears filled her eyes, then began spilling over.

"What's wrong, Grams?" I asked. The last time I'd seen her cry was when my mom died.

She shook her head and held her hand up as she got a distant look in her eyes, more tears spilling over. My heartrate sped up as I started to get worried. I'd never seen her like that.

"Grams? Are you okay?" I asked as I sat down next to her and rested a hand over her forearm.

She turned to me, her eyes focusing on me, and swallowed, pulling a handkerchief from her pocket and blowing her nose, her hands shaking as she wiped the tears from her face. "Do you remember your grandfather at all?"

"A little. He died when I was eight, I think? I just remember him walking around the farm with me, holding my hand and asking me questions about all our animals."

She nodded, smiling sadly. "Yes, he loved listening to you talk about them." She paused to blow her nose again. "Bernie was my second husband. He wasn't your father's daddy—not biologically, I mean."

I stared at her for a minute. How was that something I'd never known? "Does Dad know?"

She nodded again. "He does. He was old enough to remember his biological father when that ended."

"What happened to him?"

She shook her head. "What happened to him doesn't matter. But he was not a kind man. He had a hard life, and it gave him a mean streak... which he took out on me."

My heart stopped for a second at the thought of someone hurting my grandmother. "He... he..."

She cleared her throat and sat up straight. "He beat me, Lucas. Almost every day for years."

"Oh my god, Grams. I had no idea. I'm so sorry."

She held her hand up to stop me from continuing. "I'm fine. It was a long time ago. And Bernie, the grandfather you knew, was a wonderful man, nothing like my first husband. We had a good life together. It's just, what you told me made me think about things I haven't in a long time." She sighed, her features pulled down so she looked sad in a way I'd never seen before. "My heart hurts for all of you, Grandson. Maybe especially Rob. He's just a broken little boy at heart, thanks to circumstances beyond his control, and he's throwing away his chance of becoming whole because of it without even realizing it. He's doing things that he can never undo."

I nodded. For just a moment, I thought about the things Rob had been through independently of the current situation and I felt the same ache I knew Grams had. I didn't know a lot of detail about his childhood, but what I knew was harrowing all the same. No child should ever go through the kinds of things he had. But it didn't change what he'd done to Annie... or the fact that I was in love with her.

"What should I do, Grams?"

"Do just what you're doing, Lucas. Be there for her. Make sure she knows she doesn't have to go back to someone who hurts her. And be patient with her as she works through everything. That's all you can do."

Basically the same thing Dad said—just love her, the best I can.

My phone vibrated as I mulled over what Grams had said, and I slid it out of my pocket, looking at the screen. A text had just come in from Nick that the brewery was getting swamped.

"Grams, I have to go," I said as I slid the phone back into my pocket. "Thanks for dinner... and the pep talk. Where's the box you need me to drop by the library for you?"

She rose and gestured for me to follow her to the living room, where a large box sat, filled with books. "You can just leave it at the reception desk—they're expecting it. Whenever you get a chance in the next few days is fine."

"Alright. I'll drop it off tomorrow."

"Thank you."

"Of course, Grams," I said, giving her a hug, then picking up the box. "Love you."

"Love you, too, Grandson."

I popped my trunk and groaned as I set the heavy box of books on the ground so I could make space. Why was cleaning out my trunk always put off? It was littered with beer growlers, keg taps, random office supplies, flyers and other marketing materials, and swag for the brewery. As I shifted things around, I saw a branded box like we used for customers tucked in the back behind everything else, though I wasn't sure why that one would be in my trunk. Flipping it open revealed the box was filled with small, folded pieces of notepaper.

The one on top read *I am thankful for Miss Turner for giving me and my family food so we wouldn't be hungry* scrawled across it in messy handwriting. I pulled out another that read *I am thankful to have Annie in my life, the best friend a girl could ever ask for.* A third said *I'm thankful Ms. Turner made this dinner so my family can eat and be happy this year.*

They were the notes from the Jar of Thanks at the Community Thanksgiving Annie and I hosted together at the brewery the year before; I couldn't believe they'd been sitting in my trunk, unnoticed, for the last nine months. That meant Annie had never seen them, and she should—she deserved to know what she meant to people. I pulled the box out and put it in the front passenger footwell so I'd remember to take it inside once I was home later.

chapter nineteen

Haley and I arrived at the doctor's office so early that we still had twenty-five minutes to spare after I'd completed the required paperwork. My stomach was twisted into knots, a concoction of anxiety and excitement, but even more prominent was a deep sense of sadness. It felt as if a part of me was missing, like there was a hole in my chest that couldn't be filled. This wasn't how it should have been happening: sitting in the waiting room to see my baby for the first time without its father.

"Everything's going to be fine, babe," Haley murmured, pulling her hand out of my iron grasp to respond to some work emails on her phone.

"I'm not ready, Haley," I whispered furiously, feeling panicky. "I don't want to do this. I... I'm going to get some fresh air."

"Hang on, I'll come with you," Haley said when I stood and started toward the exit.

"No, don't. Please. I need to be alone. I'll be back in a few minutes. Come get me if they call me back early."

I pulled the door open, stepped through, and rushed down the long hallway. It felt like I might suffocate before I made it outside, and when I reached the end, I shoved the doors open and burst onto the sidewalk. Several quick steps down the sidewalk so I'd be out of the way of anyone coming or going, my body bent over, supported by my hands on my knees. My breath was coming in shallow bursts and my vision was narrowing—a panic attack. Tears stung the backs of my eyes. I just felt so crushingly alone, like I must have done something to wrong the universe except I couldn't figure out what it was. Leaning back against the wall of the building, I crumbled to the ground, wrapping my arms around my bent legs and crying into my knees.

Only seconds later, there were rapid footsteps nearby and I hoped whoever it was wouldn't stop to ask me if I was okay.

"Annie, wasn't it?"

That soft voice was as unmistakable as the question. My head lifted a few inches as a blurry Lucas sat down beside me.

"Lucas? What're you doing here?" I asked tearily.

His eyes clouded and he seemed uncertain for a moment. "We were planning to come together, weren't we?"

"Yes, but Haley's here, so I'm not alone. I didn't think you'd still come. You didn't have to."

"You think I'm here because I feel obligated?" He looked away, swallowing loudly before turning back to me. "I'm here because I *want* to be. Because there's nowhere else I'd rather be right now than here with you."

My shoulders shook as I started sobbing again, his words making the pain even more raw. "Everything just... hurts."

Without speaking, he wrapped his arms around me and pulled me into his chest, running a hand slowly up and down the length of my back. Eventually, my sobs had tapered off to be replaced with drowsiness. Within Lucas' arms, it felt—at least for that moment—as if I was protected from the sadness and pain I'd been carrying, leaving me weary.

"Come on, let's go in," he murmured after a while. "We don't want to miss your appointment."

After untangling himself, Lucas stood and pulled me to my feet, wrapping his arm around my shoulder as we began to walk. I was no longer unstable on my feet and didn't need him to steady me, but it was comforting nonetheless, so I didn't say anything.

As we were walking down the long hallway, Lucas said, "I missed you, too, by the way." A moment later, he added, "You look beautiful, Annie."

I snorted, shaking my head. "My eyes are red and puffy from crying, I've got circles under my eyes because I haven't been sleeping well, and my skin is blotchy and pale from being upset. Not to mention that I'm getting flabby already. I don't know what you're looking at," I muttered.

"I'm looking at you. And you're as beautiful as I've ever seen you."

Feeling myself blush, I opened my mouth to argue, but mumbled a "thank you" instead.

Haley looked up from her phone as we walked through the door, her eyes darting back and forth between Lucas and me. "Hey, babe, feeling a little better?" she asked before greeting Lucas.

"A bit better, yes," I replied as Lucas nodded his head at Haley to acknowledge her greeting. "I'm ready to go back now. Or at least as ready as I'm ever going to be."

"Good." She smiled. "I hope they call you back soon, I can't wait to see this—" She was interrupted by her phone ringing. Shaking her head and sighing in exasperation, she muttered, "Fuck, man. I told them I was going to be out today, I don't understand why they can't handle things for a single day without me holding their hands. I'm sorry, babe, I have to take this. I'll be right back."

As soon as Haley disappeared into the hallway, a nurse appeared and called my name. My heart hammered into my chest and my stomach flipped over a few times. I stood, swallowing and trying to steady the shaking in my hands. Lucas was on his feet a second later.

"May I—"

"Yes," I interrupted, grabbing his hand and squeezing. I was terrified and didn't want to do this alone. "Please."

With an answering squeeze to my hand and a warm smile, he walked with me toward the nurse.

Instead of leading us back to an exam room, the nurse led us into an office and shut the door.

"Welcome to All Female, Mrs. Weller. I'm Nurse Gina. Are you Mr. Weller?"

Lucas tensed beside me.

"No," I replied quietly. "Mr. Weller isn't in the picture."

"I'm sorry about that! It's an assumption I shouldn't have made, goodness me! I really do apologize." Gina flashed us a bright smile before continuing. "Now, we typically do this earlier in the pregnancy, but since this is your first visit, we'll go through all the information on the practice, what to expect from us and pregnancy in general, basic health tips, payment expectations, that sort of thing. We've got a bag of products for you to take home and try, and we'll also chat briefly about each of those items. Finally, we'll go through a questionnaire to determine which genetic abnormalities you are at a higher risk for and discuss what each of those mean so you can make an informed decision about which genetic screening tests you would like to perform, if any. Questions so far?"

"Um," I swallowed, having trouble breathing. "May I use the restroom first?" I asked. I could always go these days, but I'd asked just so I could have a moment alone to collect my thoughts and calm down. I could feel tears trying to fill my eyes and my vision tunneling already.

Nurse Gina let out a friendly laugh. "Of course, Mom, it's actually the next door down. We need a urine sample from you today, anyway, so grab one of the cups from the basket inside, write your name on it with one of the markers there, and then put it into the little passthrough in the wall when you're done."

My head nodded mechanically up and down. "Okay. Thanks."

After peeing into the cup as instructed and washing my hands, I paused. Gazing at my reflection in the mirror, ignoring the circles under my red-rimmed eyelids and blotchy cheeks, I looked into my eyes and said, "You've got this, Annie. Listening to and remembering large volumes of information is easy for you. You've been doing it for years for your career. You can do this."

The words portrayed more confidence than I felt. And at least Lucas was there with me; he could help me remember everything.

There was a simultaneous stab of pain that Rob was *not* there and rush of warm gratitude that Lucas *was*. Sighing, I shuffled back to the office and sat down, steeling myself for the quantity of information to come my way.

After covering all the office policies and some basics on what to expect at different pregnancy stages, we moved on to family histories, during which I had to explain somewhat awkwardly and tearfully that Lucas was not the father, that he was a friend, and that the father was not involved, though I provided what information I could. Through all of it, Lucas held fast to my hand, though I wouldn't have blamed him for wanting to leave instead. Most surprising of all, Gina seemed to be sympathetic; I couldn't detect any of the judgment I'd expected to encounter.

The slight confidence that inspired in me, however, was crushed a few minutes later when we were presented with what I decided to dub the Horror List: a list of nearly every possible genetic defect, regardless of how low the likelihood. My panic resurfaced as my mind raced through all the different things that could be wrong with my baby.

"Gina, is it possible we could have a few minutes alone?" Lucas asked.

"Of course!" She smiled. "I know it's a lot to take in. I'll be back in a few minutes."

As soon as the door was closed behind her, Lucas separated our hands and folded me into a tight embrace.

"This baby is going to be perfect, Annie. The chances of any of those things happening is almost zero. I know it's a long list, but even if you combine all the statistics, the chance of your baby having even one of them is *still* almost nil."

My head bobbed up and down. "I should test for them, though, right? I mean, to make sure."

"That's up to you. But I wouldn't. Like I said, this baby is going to be perfect, however he or she is."

I pulled back enough that I could see Lucas' face. "You really believe that?"

"I do," he said forcefully, holding my gaze. "And *if* this baby has something on that list? Won't make him or her any less perfect."

"But what if…" I started but wasn't even sure how to sort out my racing thoughts enough to finish the question.

"Can you tell me that you would love this baby any less if it had a birth defect?" Lucas asked. "I would find that hard to believe."

"Of course not!" I exclaimed.

"Then what purpose would the testing serve?"

"Well, I would know."

"Do you really need to? I mean, will that change or help anything?"

I paused, thinking about it. "I mean, I'd know. I don't like the unknown. But otherwise? No."

"Then why put yourself through the heartache of doing the tests and then waiting for the results?"

"You really think everything will be okay?"

Lucas's gaze was unwavering as it held mine. "I do. And even if something were to happen, I'll be here for you through all of it."

Promise? I thought as I fell deeper into the intensity in his eyes. And then, as if he could hear my thoughts, he nodded slowly, his lips moving into a soft smile.

Gina walked in just then, and we pulled apart.

"Okay, are you ready to continue?" she asked brightly. "Do you know if you want to perform the tests or not?"

I looked back to Lucas who still wore that soft, encouraging smile, his eyes steady. Warmth washed over me, dousing some of my fear. "I don't want to," I replied to Gina with my gaze still on Lucas.

"Okay," she continued. "Since this is your first visit, we'll do a quick transvaginal ultrasound today. It will allow us to confirm the pregnancy and record the heartbeat, but you'll need to pick an imaging specialist for a more detailed ultrasound—here's a list of providers you can choose from. Typically, you would have one at twelve weeks and another one at twenty weeks' gestation and that would be it, but with the history of vaginal trauma that you indicated earlier, it is likely you'll need more frequent scans. Dr. Nadiri will take a look around today and let you know the best course of action." She paused, smiling at us again. "Any more questions before we head back to an exam room?"

"Not yet," I squeaked. "But I have a friend in the waiting room who will come back when she's done with her call if that's okay?"

"Sure! Okay, you can follow me."

When we reached the exam room, I stood on a scale so they could record my weight, then sat down while Gina took my blood pressure.

"Every visit, we'll get a urine sample and record your weight and blood pressure," she explained. "Do you recall your starting weight before you got pregnant?"

My face leapt into flames as I told her; I'd already gained eighteen pounds and still had two trimesters to go.

Gina smiled kindly. "Don't worry, mom. Everyone puts on weight during pregnancy. We monitor in case we see unexpected changes that could indicate a problem, but there's nothing to worry about right now." She handed me a sheet covered with dark pink, pale blue, and bright yellow ducks. "You'll need to take off everything from the waist down so Dr. Nadiri can take a look around and do your ultrasound. She should be in shortly. Can I get you a snack or some water while you wait?"

"No," I replied softly with a small shake of my head. "I've got some things in my purse. Thank you."

"Okay. The doctor will be in soon."

Lucas set my purse down on the extra chair in the room after Gina had closed the door behind her. Turning to me, he asked, "Do you want me to send Haley in when I go to the waiting room?"

My heart skipped and my eyes watered. "You're leaving?"

His eyes bored into mine for a moment before he spoke. When he did, it was soft and slow, as if he was choosing his words carefully. "I would love to stay and be part of this, but I figured you'd be more comfortable if I wasn't here for what comes next."

I nodded, my eyes falling to my clasped hands. He was right. "Thank you."

"Okay. I'm gonna go, then. I'll send Haley back if she's off the phone."

Instead of leaving, though, he continued to stand where he was for a minute or two. What he was doing was a mystery, but I couldn't make myself look up. Finally, he sighed and walked out. His absence brought an immediate chill to the room and my eyes flooded with tears. I felt alone in a way I didn't want to be— especially for seeing this baby for the first time.

"Lucas!" I shouted, his name rolling off my tongue before I even knew what I was doing.

The door swung open, and Lucas' frame filled the doorway. "What's wrong?" he asked, worried.

My tears spilled over. "I don't want to be alone," I confessed.

"You want me to stay?"

"Yes," I breathed out.

"Okay," he responded, closing the door behind him. "I'll give you some privacy, though."

Lucas turned his back to me, leaving me alone with my conflicted emotions for a moment. I wanted him to stay. His presence comforted me and made me feel calm and strong in a way no one else's did; that was one of the reasons it had been so easy to love him after spending time with him last year, and one of the reasons it was so hard not having him in my life for a long time.

"Thank you."

I wiped my eyes with the backs of my hands, then grabbed a tissue from the counter to blow my nose. Just having Lucas nearby was making it easier to breathe, easier to believe I could do this. With a deep inhale and exhale, I removed my pants and underwear, folding them neatly and placing them on top of my purse in the corner of the room before sitting back on the exam table and unfolding the sheet over my lap.

"Okay," I said, picking at the lint on the sheet. "I'm covered."

Lucas turned, offering me a reassuring smile as he pulled the extra chair up to one side of the exam table. Sitting down, he reached up and rested his arms on the table next to my waist. Without thinking about it first, I rested a hand over his. After a beat, he shifted his arm and laced our fingers together, his thumb stroking rhythmically across the back of my hand. I closed my eyes and focused on the soothing pressure of Lucas's touch assuring me that I wasn't alone.

chapter twenty

lucas

Dr. Nadiri explained in a gentle, lyrical voice what she would be doing and why, but I missed most of it because I was so focused on the screen. So far, it looked like television static, but she'd assured us we'd be able to see something in a moment.

"Oh, here we go. See this here," Dr. Nadiri said, pointing to a fuzzy blob on the screen, "that's your baby's head, and this is a little arm, another arm here, and—oh, baby's a wiggler, that's for sure. Okay, right here, these are the legs. And can you see that light pulsing right there? That's the heartbeat. Now, I'm just going to take some cursory measurements to confirm your expected due date and record the heartbeat, but on first glance, everything looks fine."

It was the most incredible, most magical thing I'd ever seen—a teeny, tiny, little baby flipping around inside Annie's belly. "Wow..."

"I know," Dr. Nadiri said. "It really is a miracle. Congratulations."

I glanced over at Annie to see a look of wonder in her eyes, her temples damp. There was a beeping sound as Dr. Nadiri hit a button twice and two little photos of the baby spit out of a printer. She removed the ultrasound wand from between Annie's legs and the image on the screen faded back into meaningless static.

Turning toward Annie, a broad grin stretched across my face. "It's an actual baby!" I laughed, giddy all of a sudden.

"I know..." Annie replied dreamily.

Her face was soft, her eyes glowing as she gazed at me, and my heart skipped. Somehow, I'd just fallen even more deeply in love with her than I already was. I reached up to cup her cheek, her skin so soft under my fingertips as she tilted her head into my hand. For a second, I forgot about everything else except us and leaned forward, pressing our foreheads together.

"Here you go," Dr. Nadiri said, holding out the printouts.

Sitting back, I accepted the two slips of photo paper. My finger whispered over the image of the baby—I was transfixed. My heart was painfully swollen with joy and excitement and love in a way I'd never experienced before. I wondered briefly if that's how it had felt for my dad when my mom was pregnant with me.

My breath caught with that last thought—how was I getting so attached? I needed to remember that it wasn't my baby. Rob could still come back, and at the end of the day, Annie could still decide to take him back. And if that happened, I would have no place in her life or that of her baby. Grams had been right; I was already going to be devastated if Rob suddenly came back in the picture. I'd thought I could just keep loving her like my dad had done with my mom, but it seemed he was stronger than me; I wasn't sure I could keep going without knowing I'd have Annie at the end. But looking back down at the image of the baby and Annie's hand that was still clasped tightly in mine, I wasn't sure I could distance myself, either.

Haley burst through the door, out of breath. "Did I miss it?" she asked as she closed the door behind her.

"Excuse me, but who are you and why are you in my exam room?" Dr. Nadiri questioned.

"It's okay, she's my friend and she's welcome," Annie responded before turning to Haley. "Yeah, you did. But we have pictures!"

Haley stared pointedly at mine and Annie's clasped hands a moment before accepting the printouts I was offering. Her eyes fell to the printout on top and widened as she grinned. "Holy shit!"

Annie giggled, her face blissful and dreamy. "I know."

"You're good to go, Ms. Weller. You can get cleaned up and make your next appointment here for four weeks from now. Go ahead and schedule your first ultrasound as soon as possible. If you call the center in the building next door, they might be able to fit you in today. You do have quite a bit of scar tissue, so I'd like you to get monthly ultrasounds as well, okay?"

Annie nodded, her features falling a bit.

"Don't worry," Dr. Nadiri said with a warm smile. "As long as you keep your regular appointments, you'll be fine. It's just a precaution anyway. Try not to stress."

"Okay," she breathed.

"Alright, see you in a month," Dr. Nadiri said, then slipped out the door.

"It's a fucking baby!" Haley shouted, her eyes glued to the ultrasound picture.

Annie sighed contentedly and the sound made my heart skip. "I know." She looked back and forth between Haley and me, grinning so widely a small dimple appeared in one cheek.

As Dr. Nadiri suggested, Annie called the ultrasound center as soon as she'd checked out and was able to get an appointment right away. We meandered next door together as Annie and Haley chatted excitedly about the baby. Everything seemed more beautiful when we walked outside—the sky was bluer, the sun brighter, the birds louder. My chest was filled with optimism. I grinned and slid my arm around Annie's shoulders, pulling her into my side. She glanced up at me and smiled before turning back to her conversation with Haley. We continued the rest of the way to the ultrasound office this way, my fingers skimming up and down her bare arm.

"I should go check in," she said, still smiling when we arrived. "I'll be right back."

As soon as Annie walked away, Haley stepped closer. "You should leave her alone," she said in a hushed tone. "It's just going to end up in heartbreak all around when Rob comes back."

"He won't."

"Yes, he will—he'll get his shit together at some point."

"You don't know him as well as you think you do. It's not going to happen. And Annie won't take him back even if he does." *At least that's what I keep telling myself.*

"So what's your plan, then, huh?" she hissed. "Just capitalize on being her rebound—"

"Screw you," I cut her off, my voice rising. "I haven't done a damn thing except be there for her. How can you possibly hate me for that when you're supposed to care about her?"

"Shh!" Haley hushed me before letting out a sigh. "I don't hate you, you know. I just think you're confusing her and going to make things harder for her. I'm glad you were there when she needed you, I really am, and I know you're good to her, I just think you're being selfish—it's fucking obvious you want some sort of a relationship with her and that's not fair to her right now."

"I've done nothing but be her friend," I retorted, purposely not responding to her accusation that I wanted more than that.

Haley narrowed her eyes. "Whatever. Just remember I warned you to leave her alone before you made things worse for her."

"I'm not trying to make anything worse for her," I replied, my chest tightening at the thought. *I just want another chance to love her... and to see if she can find a way to love me again, too.*

chapter twenty-one

annie

The clarity with the abdominal ultrasound was unexpected after the fuzzy images I'd received from the transvaginal ultrasound—there was so much more detail. I stared at the screen in fascination, barely registering what the technician was saying as she snapped digital images of different measurements. On the opposite side of me were Haley, with a hand on my leg, and Lucas, one hand clasping mine and the other resting near my hairline. When I glanced over, their expressions mirrored the wonderment I felt as they watched the shifting images. A wave of warmth washed over me, a sense of being whole and loved and not alone, and excitement for the future filled my chest and buoyed my spirits.

"Here are some pictures for you to keep," the technician said, handing a stack of printouts to Lucas and patting my hand. "The doctor will be in shortly."

"Can I see them?" I asked.

"Of course."

I inspected the images Lucas handed me, each one presenting a slightly different angle or focusing on a different part of the baby. "Wow... look at that—it's a little tiny nose! Can you believe it?"

"It's incredible, babe," Haley said, sounding dazed. "It really is."

The smile stretched across my face made my cheeks ache as I looked through the images again and again until the doctor came in. The doctor was a soft-spoken older woman and put me at ease about as much as was possible considering my midsection was bare. She looked through all the images and measurements that were logged in the machine from the ultrasound technician, then used the wand to look around and take a few additional measurements. But the longer she looked at the baby without saying anything, the more anxious I became until it was more than I could bear.

"Is everything okay?" I squeaked.

"I'm just checking a few more things, but so far, so good, Ms. Weller."

So far, so good? That meant something could still be wrong. Even counting my breaths with my eyes closed, my heartrate continued to accelerate.

Lucas' forehead pressed gently into my temple. "Everything is going to be fine," he whispered into my ear. "This baby is perfect, no matter what, okay? Well, unless you were hoping for extra arms or legs, in which case it looks like you should prepare for disappointment."

His words were so unexpected that I snorted, then began laughing. Lucas sat up with his signature cheesy grin—the same one I'd been a sucker for since the day I met him—as he winked and chuckled. For the moment at least, he had successfully dispelled my worry and panic.

"What's so funny?" Haley asked.

I shook my head as my laughter began to taper off. "Lucas is just ridiculous."

"Okay, Ms. Weller," the doctor said, then launched into an explanation of everything she was looking at and what she was expecting to see. But the only thing I cared about was that everything looked normal, with no apparent indicators of birth defects or abnormalities. She echoed what my other doctor had said about the frequency of my ultrasounds because of my medical history, but based on what she saw, she didn't anticipate any complications.

Joy at having confirmation that the tiny being growing inside me was healthy eclipsed everything that had been weighing so heavily on me: Rob, my living situation, my future as a single mom, what I was going to do for work, all of it.

Haley received a work call and headed outside while I checked out and scheduled my next appointment. With the appointment reminder card in hand, Lucas' arm slid around my shoulders, and we headed into the long hallway that led from the office to the building exit.

"I can't believe it," I squealed, wrapping an arm around his waist and squeezing. "I was so sure something would be wrong, but..." I laughed in relief, my eyes filled with tears as I looked up at him. "He or she is perfect."

Lucas' face mirrored mine, down to the watery eyes. I'd known he wanted things to go well for me, but this seemed to be different—he seemed to be happy like I was happy, in that deep, gut-wrenching way.

We had stopped walking while I was lost in my thoughts and were now just standing near the middle of the empty hallway. Lucas faced me with one arm still wrapped around me, though it was now around my waist, the fingers of his other hand slowly tangling into my hair. Where tears had been a moment ago was a deep, unreadable expression that made my blood rush through my ears and my heart skip the longer we gazed at each other. Something was happening between us, and not for the first time. But every time we found ourselves like this felt more intense than before. As he drew closer, I felt myself also leaning forward. My arms lifted seemingly of their own accord until my hands rested against his chest. His lips were so close to mine now, maybe only an inch away, and I knew it was going to happen this time. *I'm going to kiss Lucas.*

That last thought yanked me from the bubble I'd been in. I couldn't kiss someone who wasn't Rob—I couldn't do that to him while we were still married, no matter what he was doing to me. "I can't," I said, stepping back quickly out of Lucas' embrace, out of whatever had been passing between us just as our lips began to touch.

Lucas' face fell and he shoved his hands into his pockets. Averting his eyes, he said quietly, "I'm sorry, Annie. I... I shouldn't have done that. It was a mistake. Come on."

As I followed him down the remaining stretch of hall and out into the scorching late-summer heat, my feelings were a jumbled mess. It had felt like someone stabbed me in the chest when he'd called our near-kiss a mistake.

"Work is killing me!" Haley laughed as we approached, having just ended her call. "Who am I kidding? I love it even when it makes me fucking nuts. Anyway, let's grab some lunch to celebrate having a healthy baby and healthy mama in our midst."

Lucas cleared his throat, still avoiding eye contact with me. "I'll have to pass, unfortunately. I need to get back to the brewery. Congratulations, Annie, really. It's incredible."

I was rooted to the spot as he turned and started walking toward the other end of the parking lot.

"Fuck, it's hot! Come on, babe, let's get in the air conditioning. And then you can tell me what the hell I just missed between you guys."

With a nod, I trudged after her.

"Annie, wait!" Lucas called out after we'd made it a few steps, striding quickly over to us. "I almost forgot." He held out the stack of ultrasound pictures he had been holding for me. "Here."

When I accepted the images, I noticed the one on top, one of the close-up profile images of the baby's face, was the same one that Lucas had been drawn back to repeatedly when we were inside, stroking his finger down the side of what would be the baby's cheek. As he started to turn, my hand reached out and grabbed his.

"Take this one," I said when he faced me, releasing his hand and holding out the picture.

But when he only stared at it without making a move to accept it, I gathered he didn't want it. *Of course he doesn't want it—why would he? It isn't his kid; why would he want a picture of it?* I groaned inwardly, embarrassed and aggravated that I was tearing up again. Stupid hormones.

"Sorry, I didn't mean... I just thought... never mind," I babbled, not even able to put together a coherent sentence as I lowered my arm.

"I want it," he said, his voice thick as he reached out and slid the picture from my fingers. "Thank you."

I chanced looking up at him and his eyes stopped me from moving, filled with a mixture of emotions that seemed to be torturing him as he stared back at me. My heart sputtered and then sped up, much like it had in the hallway only moments earlier. Neither of us moved, but it was happening again—that something that was passing between us. It was as if every time it happened, there were threads passing back and forth, tethering us more strongly together. It was a new kind of feeling for me—nothing like how I'd always felt with Rob—and it was as unnerving as it was exhilarating.

Haley cleared her throat, and Lucas and I dropped our gazes. I wanted to say something, but didn't know what that would be, so I just stood there awkwardly until Lucas thanked me again for the picture. I nodded but couldn't make eye contact again. After a moment, he turned and walked away.

"Annie..." Haley said, drawing out my name. "What the fuck did I just miss?"

I swallowed, a blush creeping up my neck to my cheeks, and started toward Haley's car. "Nothing."

"Babe, you're still married."

My veins flooded with sudden anger, and I spun on my heel to face her. "Yeah, Haley, I fucking remember," I seethed. "I'm married to a man who's screwing anyone who'll spread their legs. A man who called me a slut and told me that the man who *raped me* was right about me. A man who kicked me out when I told him I was pregnant with his child. A man who won't let me have even five minutes to talk to him. The same man who's divorcing me, for god's sake! But thanks for that reminder."

"Look, babe—"

"No!" I shouted. "I'm so damn sick of everyone else thinking they know what's best for me. Maybe I don't always make the best decisions, but they're *my* decisions to make. Not yours, not Mom's, not Lucas', not Rob's—no one else's! Just... stop." I had lost steam at this point, the anger fading in the face of the crushing pain in my chest, and my voice was flat when I continued, tears streaming down my cheeks. "I know everyone means well, but I can't take it anymore. I know you love me, and I know you want me to be happy, and that you think that's with Rob... but he's not coming back, Haley. He's not. As much as that hurts to say, it's true. It doesn't matter how much I or you or anyone else wants things to be different, they aren't. And even if he *did* change his mind, there's no way I could take him back after what he's done." I swallowed, my heart racing. No one except Lucas and Dr. Miller knew what I was about to say. "Haley... he hurt me."

"I know, babe—"

"No, Haley," I interrupted. "Not upset me—*hurt* me."

She stared blankly at me for a moment. "What? When?"

My gaze landed on the ground between us. "The day he came to Lucas' house."

"What did he do to you?"

"He..." I swallowed again. It was harder to talk about than I expected. "He pushed me into the wall and held me pinned there while he kissed me angrily. He left bruises on my arms and my lip was swollen and bleeding afterwards."

Haley's eyes filled with tears and her jaw opened and closed a few times. "I'm so sorry," she finally said quietly. "I had no idea he... I never thought... fuck, babe. I can't believe that bastard hurt you. I've been pushing you to forgive him, and the whole time he'd hurt you. I never would have done that if I'd known. *Never.* I swear."

"I know."

"Why didn't you tell me?" she asked.

I shrugged and looked away as my eyes watered. "I'm embarrassed, I guess. And I feel like it's partially my fault, like I should have known something like that would happen and shouldn't have been in a relationship with him, so it's my fault it happened. And I also don't want you to hate him. He wasn't himself, he was drunk—"

"That doesn't fucking make it okay," Haley bit out.

"I'm not saying it does. I'm just saying he *was*, and that he's never touched me in violence otherwise. As fucked up as everything is that he's doing, as much as I don't think I could ever forgive him, I don't think he's a bad person, Haley. I know why he is the way he is, and what's happening tears me apart because I know how much he's hurting. And I don't want you to hate him because he's in pain right now."

"Listen to me, babe," Haley started, her voice hardened. "It doesn't matter how much he's hurting or how much pain he's in or how much he had to drink—he had no right to do what he did to you. And you shouldn't try to protect him from the fallout from what he did."

I nodded, my cheeks now soaked. I understood what Haley was saying, but my emotions weren't that clear cut.

"And you shouldn't even consider taking him back," she added.

I nodded again. "I know. I'm not. It doesn't matter what he does now—it's too late. He and I are over for good."

She leaned forward and wrapped her arms around me, and it felt like I might melt into the pavement.

"I appreciate the moment," I sniffled, pushing her away, "but I'm so hot I think I might pass out—please don't touch me right now."

Haley laughed as she cleared the moisture off her face with a rough swipe of her hands. "Come on, let's go somewhere to cool off."

chapter twenty-two

lucas

A **few days** had passed since Annie's appointment, and she was still at Haley's. It was for the best, considering I'd unintentionally crossed a line with her and recognized I should probably be putting distance between us, but that didn't mean it was sitting well with me any more than the lack of communication between us in that time. I was going crazy with wanting her around... I missed her. And the more time that passed, the harder it was to remember why I thought it was a good thing for us to be apart.

At Annie's request, I went up to Rob's house to collect her mail and the rest of her belongings. The only thing that would be left was her car. When I'd arrived, the yard was in complete disarray—Rob had obviously not yet returned to the house since he'd left. Or if he had, he certainly had done nothing while he was there.

There were two envelopes in the tower of mail I separated that were obviously not bills—one for Rob and one for Annie. It seemed odd they both had yellow mail-forwarding labels from the post office on them; Rob's had been addressed to his last house and Annie's to her mom's house. They were both addressed in the same handwriting, and neither included a return address. I thought about texting Annie before opening hers, but figured she'd be fine with it since she'd asked me to open whatever was addressed to her and keep anything that looked important.

The envelope addressed to Annie contained a piece of lined notebook paper like I'd kept in three-ring binders in high school. One side was covered in large, messy handwriting.

Annie—

Been a while, have you thought of me often? I've thought of you every day. And I've had plenty of time inside these walls to think about the perfect reunion. Trust me—you're gonna die over it. Are you as excited as I am?

-C

A second read-through of the short letter revealed I wasn't missing anything to indicate who'd sent it. But why would someone send such a vague letter with no indication of who they were?

And then it all clicked. It must have been from Charlie. Seconds later, my eyes were scanning the lines of the letter addressed to Rob.

Little Bro—

I can't believe you left me here to rot, motherfucker. After all the shit we've been through, you threw it all away over a slut from the past. Well, I always said if you can't fix the problem, get rid of it, right? And this is definitely one problem that can't be fixed. Just remember, this is all your fault for choosing pussy over your blood.

-Big Bro

I stood frozen for several long seconds, my stomach bottoming out. Annie had told me Charlie was getting out of prison in a few months, and now he was planning to do something—I had no idea what—to Annie. There was only one person who might be able to figure out what he'd have planned and maybe even know how to stop him. Clutching both letters, I rushed from the house and tore down the driveway.

Before I made it to town, though, I realized my plan to enlist Rob's help wasn't well thought-out. Rob didn't care anymore, and even if he did, he couldn't be trusted. Instead, I began formulating a new plan. One of my roommates from college owned a private investigation and security firm—I'd reach out to him. He'd be able to advise on what to do next.

In the parking lot at the brewery after leaving a message for Joel, I texted Annie to find out when she was coming back. My resolve to put some distance between us didn't matter right then—even though Charlie would be locked up for another few months, I was worried she might already be in danger. I wished she'd decide to come back soon.

I knew I should probably tell her about the letters I'd found, but couldn't bring myself to do it over text—I needed to be able to sit down with her to tell her about it. And I wanted to talk to Joel first. There was no doubt how much stress the letters would cause for her, which I remembered learning could be dangerous for the baby. If I could have a plan for how to ensure her safety first, I could keep her from becoming too anxious and scared. I'd tell her—in person—as soon as I talked to Joel and had some idea for how we could react.

When she replied, however, she said she'd finally decided she was going to live with her mom, that Haley would bring her down to get her things from my house in a day or two. And while the thought of not having her in my house anymore made me feel restless, I said nothing to try to convince her to stay with me. I wasn't confident I was capable of being just friends with her anymore, and it would be even harder with her under my roof.

chapter twenty-three

annie

Less than a week after my first appointments for the baby, I had moved in with Mom and begun volunteering at the library again for something to do. Sitting around all day with nothing to do but read books about pregnancy or watch television was starting to get to me. I'd briefly considered taking a part-time job at the brewery to help in the office since it would give me some income as well as something to do, but ultimately decided against it. Everything about my relationship—my *friendship*—with Lucas was so confusing, it seemed better to keep some distance between us until I could figure it all out.

Lucas must have decided the same thing because he'd definitely been distant since we'd almost kissed after my ultrasound—all our communication was via sporadic text messages. Though, to be fair, he was looking into opening a second brewery location in Clarksburg.

Aside from the lawyers who assured me he was adamant about moving forward with the divorce, no one had heard anything from Rob. And while just thinking about him deeply hurt, I was glad he hadn't changed his mind and decided to fight the divorce. It was now only a matter of time; once a year had passed from the day Rob kicked me out, our divorce would be finalized. Haley, Carol, and Linc had gone up to the house for one last pass to make sure I had nothing left there and picked up my car when I'd moved to my mom's from Haley's. I hadn't been able to bear the thought of going up there myself with all the memories within those walls. Unless he one day realized he'd made a mistake and wanted to be a part of his child's life, I knew it wasn't likely I'd ever see him again.

———————

The day after I'd moved back in with Mom, I'd found myself in the living room after she went to bed, unable to sleep. Much like the first time I'd found it a year and a half earlier, I pulled down the album with my name on it even though I knew it would be better to leave it alone—possibly never open it again. It wasn't the photos that drew me to it this time, though; it was the folder inside. I compulsively read through every paper it contained: every court document, every social worker note, every report on my biological parents. At times, I felt I would suffocate because I couldn't breathe. At other times, I felt nothing and even laughed as I read some of the notes—my sister and I had been placed in foster care because of the things they noted, and yet what they saw was only a fraction of what happened in those years before they removed us.

They knew about a few times that my mom's friend, Dwayne, had touched me, but they didn't know how many times that had happened. They didn't know about how he'd hurt me if I tried to stop him. They didn't know that Dwayne wasn't the only one who'd done so or that my dad made me promise not to tell anyone that my cousin had, too. They knew my mom was an alcoholic, but they didn't know how mean or violent she could be or how often she screamed at me. They knew my parents struggled to take care of us, but they didn't know how often we went without food for days on end or what it felt like to be that hungry. They knew they were pulling us out of a bad situation, but they didn't know what it was like to be removed and told we'd never see our parents again without warning or an opportunity to even say good-bye. They didn't know I'd end up harming myself for years just to cope with being alive.

My mind had fixated on the documents and my thoughts, and the sun rose with me in the same place, everything scattered around me. When I'd heard Mom leaving her bedroom and realized I'd been there all night, I'd known I needed help; I couldn't risk obsessing that way once I had a baby to take care of. It was time for me to return to therapy.

I'd made an appointment with a new therapist in town—close enough to walk to from my mom's house. Selena was at least a decade older than me and everything about her put me at ease immediately. She dressed casually, was relaxed in demeanor, had an earthy quality to her voice, and intelligent, warm, caring hazel eyes that seemed to understand what I was trying to say even when I couldn't articulate it.

In our first appointment, I brought the folder and picked lint from my jeans while she scanned the documents, contemplating every few seconds if I should just get up and leave. But remembering I was pregnant and had a baby to think about kept me in my seat. We'd talked a bit about what was in the folder and things that had happened since, and she'd asked me why I was seeking therapy. I told her about the night I'd stayed up unintentionally, I told her about my history of self-harming, about my anxiety, and my intense fear of becoming a parent because of my own childhood.

We'd agreed to meet three times a week for a few weeks before backing down the frequency, and Selena had given me homework. She'd explained that many people with the kinds of trauma in their pasts that I had found it helpful to connect in some way to others with shared experiences and had given me a few websites to look at. I was to read articles by others like me and explore other online sources of information if I found it helpful. And I *did* find it helpful to know I wasn't as alone as I'd always thought, so I spent some time every day online, finding and reading stories and articles by other women who'd experienced the kinds of things I had and struggled with life the way I did.

"I'm so sick of feeling sad, and hurting, and feeling out of control of my life. I'm just... sick of it." It was our fourth appointment, and I was crying, having one of those days when I was feeling sorry for myself, with no confidence in my ability to be a single mother or ever find lasting happiness.

Selena gazed at me with a sympathetic expression for a moment, then said, "Okay, then don't."

"Very funny, Selena," I said through my tears. "It's not that simple."

She cocked her head to the side. "Why not?"

"I can't just say I'm not going to feel a certain way and have it happen."

"Sure you can," she replied with a nod of her head.

"No, you can't," I said, starting to get angry.

"Why not?"

"Stop asking me that!" I burst out. "I have wanted to feel differently for almost my entire life, but that hasn't made a damn bit of difference. Because it doesn't work that way."

She sighed softly, studying my face. "Okay, let's say you have two cars in front of you."

"What kind of cars?"

"Doesn't matter for this," she replied, shifting her weight in her chair to get more comfortable. "But you've got two cars in front of you, and we can assume they're both identical from the outside. With me so far?"

I nodded, though I had no idea why she was talking about cars.

"Okay, so there is no question that the way the steering wheel is connected to the axles or whatever else in the car, I don't know much about how cars are built, but it's going to be complicated, right? If you mess up one small thing, it can cause the steering to fail, there are a lot of parts, they all have to be connected properly and in a specific order, and so on. Would you agree?"

Where is she going with this? "Okay, sure."

"But steering the car is simple, right?" she continued, raising her arms as if she was holding onto an invisible steering wheel in front of her. "I mean, you turn the wheel to the left and the car goes to the left, you turn the wheel to the right, the car goes to the right. Yeah?"

"Yes."

She let her hands fall back to her lap. "Okay. Now let's just say for the sake of argument that one of those cars has power steering, while the other one does not. What does that change about the steering?"

"Well, one car will be much easier to steer," I replied, thinking about the only vehicle I'd ever driven that didn't have power steering—it was Rob's first truck, an old used pickup truck he bought for a few hundred dollars when we were dating in high school. It had felt nearly impossible to steer and made me so nervous I'd refused to drive it ever again.

"Right, exactly. But the mechanism for steering, turning the wheel to the left to go left or right to go right, will that change at all?"

My head shook slightly side to side. "Mm-mm."

"So, would you say it's a fair assessment that the *simplicity* of the steering was completely unaffected, even though it will be much more difficult to accomplish with one than with the other?"

The proverbial light bulb had gone off as soon as she said the word "simplicity." "Yes, I get it. You're telling me that, while it might not be easy, it doesn't have to be complicated."

"Exactly."

There was a quiet moment as I digested her words, letting the concept roll around in my mind. "But I've already wanted this for decades without success... What can I do that will make any difference?"

"Great question," she said, smiling. "There are lots of things people can do—not everything will work for everyone. But I think affirmations are a good place for *you* to start. We've already talked about your negative inner dialogue, which will need to be dismantled, and affirmations are a great way to do that. You create personalized affirmations, which we can do together before you leave today, then you repeat them to yourself as needed—at least several times a day. Every day. Frequency and consistency are key. Over time, it becomes second nature, automatic, and will drown out that negative voice in the back of your mind. Easier said than done, yes, but also not complicated—simple."

We spent the remainder of the appointment coming up with my affirmations together and I'd started on them right away, eager to see some amount of progress. I kept the affirmations we wrote together in my pocket at all times until I had them all memorized, and I made sure I looked at myself in the mirror and said them out loud at least five times per day at Selena's suggestion. Sometimes I said them more—especially when I became aware of my negative inner voice beating me down.

Between therapy sessions with Selena, reading other women's stories, my affirmations, and volunteering again, I began to notice a sense of balance internally—a kind of balance I'd never really felt before. The closest had been when Lucas and I were dating the previous year. But this time was different because it wasn't born of hiding from the past—this time I was facing it. And it was coming from me alone; I wasn't dependent on someone else for that sense of balance, which sprouted the beginnings of a kind of self-confidence and optimism I'd never had before. I realized that a lot of shitty things had happened to me in my lifetime—and many more shitty things might still happen—but despite a plethora of setbacks, I would make it through to the other side as long as I kept trying.

Of course there were good days and bad days, thinking about everything I'd lost and missed out on in my life—from my birth parents to missed opportunities for friendships in my youth to everything that had happened with Rob, and even Lucas. But thanks to Selena, I now had my affirmations to bolster me when I began to spiral into the self-doubt and feelings of worthlessness those thoughts triggered.

I appreciated that I now had tools to turn to that I'd never had before. Tools to help me through in ways I couldn't have imagined even a few short months earlier. And having those tools changed everything because it meant I had a chance of making sure I didn't make the same mistakes my own mother did with me.

chapter twenty-four

annie

"I'm coming!" I called, making my way toward the front door in my mom's house to see who was knocking. "Ooof!" I mumbled as my feet tripped over the edge of a rug that I hadn't seen was turned up thanks to my growing belly. Honestly, I wasn't sure how I was going to make it to the end of the pregnancy without having exploded with the rate my belly was already growing when I was only sixteen weeks along. Even though no one saw my clumsiness, my face flushed with embarrassment as I laughed at myself and swung the front door open, one hand still protectively covering my growing belly.

Standing on the other side of the screen door was Lucas, wearing khakis and a black button-up shirt with a Stockwood Brewery logo on the chest, the top couple of buttons undone and the sleeves rolled up to the elbows, looking nervous as a hand ran through his hair and the other held a beautiful bouquet of wildflowers. My heart skipped a beat, causing my breath and movements to stall for a moment. I hadn't seen him in a month, and he hadn't told me he was going to be back in town.

"Lucas!" I exclaimed a second later, beaming, fluttering in my chest as I pushed open the screen door.

His broad, boyish grin stretched across his face, and I walked into his waiting arms as he set the flowers onto the bench on the porch.

"God, I missed you," he breathed out, still holding me tight.

"I missed you, too," I replied, leaning back so I could see his face. "What are you doing here? I thought you were still out in Clarksburg indefinitely."

He stared at me for a moment before he spoke. "You look more beautiful every time I see you," he said.

His gaze roved over me as he stepped back. His hands moved down between us and hovered in front of me for a moment, his eyes darting up, his eyebrows raised. I nodded, and he rested his palms over my bump. His eyes came up to mine, rounded in awe, before he looked back down.

"Wow..."

I laughed. "I know. Every day it gets bigger. I swear to you I'll be the size of a hot air balloon by the time this baby comes out."

He looked back up at me, his hands still resting on the sides of my belly, though he wasn't saying anything—he just stared at me intently.

"What is it, Lucas?" I asked softly, my forehead creasing as worry set in.

After a deep breath, he leaned forward to rest his forehead against mine. "Nothing, sweetheart. I'm just really happy to see you."

My breath caught hearing him call me "sweetheart" and my body warmed. "I'm happy to see you, too—I thought you were out of town."

"I was," he replied, dropping his hands from me and putting a few steps between us. "But you have your appointments today, right? I didn't get the date wrong, did I?"

"No—they're today. But I figured you wouldn't be able to make it."

"No way I was missing this."

I blushed. "Thank you. But the appointments aren't until this afternoon, you know."

He smiled softly. "I know. I was thinking—well, hoping—we could have lunch together. We can go out or eat at my house— whatever you want to do—I'd just like to spend some time with you."

My eyes cast down to the bricks under our feet, trying to sort out my thoughts and feelings. Spending time with him sounded wonderful, but I was confused by his distance since the last appointment, confused by the pull to him that had reappeared as suddenly as he had, confused about what it all might mean.

"I'd love to have lunch with you," I finally said, smiling at the hopeful expression on his face. "And I can go for anything, honestly, I'm just hungry in general," I laughed, rubbing my belly. "But tell me where we're going so I know what to wear."

"You can wear whatever you want wherever we end up going. You're always beautiful."

Blushing and giggling to cover my discomfort, I said, "Okay, enough of the compliments, Lucas. You're making me self-conscious."

"It's not a compliment, Annie, it's the truth. You have no idea, but you are."

The way he was looking at me certainly made me feel beautiful, but that wasn't a word I'd ever associated with myself. When I was growing up, my body had always been on the plump side, with disproportionately wide hips and thighs, my hair unruly, my breasts too large, and I was short—barely five feet tall. Rob and Lucas were surely the only people who'd ever thought I was attractive.

"Um, okay, I'll just grab my purse and some water. And go pee, of course." Lifting the flowers from the bench, I inhaled their sweet fragrance. "These are lovely, Lucas."

His eyes glowed. "I wanted to bring you more of the wildflowers I found earlier in the year, but there aren't any blooming anymore. This was the closest the flower shop had."

My face heated more than it already was as I held his gaze. "Thank you. I love them. Just looking at them makes me feel happy."

His grin broke across his face. "Do you know what wildflowers represent?"

I shook my head. "No, actually."

"I just learned this myself—the florist told me. They represent joy."

I stared at him intently for a moment as my chest lurched. "Thank you for bringing me joy," I said quietly, meaning more than the flowers.

We decided to go back to Lucas' house for lunch since it was too early to go out anywhere anyway—only a quarter to ten when we left my mom's house.

"I'm sorry I missed your birthday dinner," Lucas said as we sat on opposite sides of the sofa. "I feel horrible about that."

"Please don't. It's fine. My god, Lucas, there's only so much time in the day. Really. I would have liked to have seen you, but I certainly wasn't upset with you."

"Everyone else was there?"

"Yeah—even Lori made it." My thoughts traveled back to that evening. Lori hadn't only shown up for dinner when I didn't really expect her to, but she'd surprised me a second time when she'd impulsively hugged me in the middle of our conversation. And then she'd whispered to me that I seemed different—in a good way—than I had with Rob and that she was glad I wasn't with him anymore.

Lucas' lips tipped up on one side. "You seem like you're doing well, Annie. Like, really well. You seem... happy."

"I am," I agreed, my eyes drawn again to his kitchen where the ultrasound picture I'd given him was held to his refrigerator door with a flower magnet he said he'd picked up because it reminded him of me. "I mean, I have bad days, but there are fewer of them than I ever would have expected. I started seeing a therapist again, a new one, Selena, and she's amazing. The last time I felt this settled and balanced was last year when you and I were dating."

Lucas' face fell and he looked away. "And a few months ago. With Rob."

My face flushed and my eyes shifted to my hands on my lap. "Actually, no," I replied, running a finger over the texture of the couch. "I mean, I was happy with Rob, I guess, kind of, but that's not the same thing—I wasn't balanced or settled. When I was dating *you*, though, you did that for me. But now, I've figured out how to do it for myself." A flicker of self-pride warmed my chest—it wasn't easy, but I was giving this healing thing all I had. Looking up, I found Lucas studying me and offered him a soft smile. "So, yeah, I'm sad about things, but I'm also happy. Or at least getting there—like I said, I have good days and bad days. Today's a good day. Well, no, it's not—it *was* a good day, but then you showed up on my porch, so now it's a *great* day."

His cheesy, boyish grin stretched across his face as he gave me a playful wink. I laughed until he reached down and pulled my feet onto his lap, beginning to massage one of them; then my eyes fell closed, and I groaned with pleasure. It was the relief to my aching feet, but it was also just his touch, the way every spot his fingers contacted buzzed and sent shockwaves up my legs, straight to my heart.

"Oh my god, Lucas, that feels incredible. I'd tell you that you don't need to do it, but I don't want you to ever stop."

He laughed lightly and easily and continued to work on my feet as a comfortable silence settled between us. After several minutes, he said, "So, I've been looking at properties for a possible second location for the brewery in Clarksburg recently."

My eyes opened and I looked up at him. "That's what you said. Congratulations—I'm happy for you. It's wonderful that business is so good. I hope you don't spread yourself too thin, though, trying to run both on your own."

"Well, it won't be on my own, that would be asking to fail. I decided I needed a partner, so I brought Nick in two weeks ago. He's got the business background, the experience and know-how, he's invested in the success of the brewery—it's a perfect fit. The only thing we're missing is funding. I can't fully finance a second location yet. But I've been talking to some investors and banks and I'm not too worried about it. The brewery's success speaks for itself."

"That's great! I guess Nick is willing to relocate, then?"

Lucas' hands stilled and rested on my ankles. He was studying me attentively, silently, and an odd feeling took root in the pit of my stomach. Something wasn't right.

"What is it, Lucas?" I murmured.

He spoke slowly, his eyes boring into me. "Nick wouldn't relocate—he'd stay here."

I was confused now. "Then who would run the Clarksburg location?"

Swallowing dryly, he replied with his eyes locked on mine, "I would. I'd move to Clarksburg."

My body was suddenly cold, numb. Despite the circumstances and his recent distance, I was closer to him than to anyone else in my life, except Haley. Even though we hadn't talked much over the last month. Even though our history was messy. Even though I was pregnant with someone else's baby. Even without a romantic relationship, I had thought he would always be in my life. But he was leaving—leaving Stockwood, leaving me. Just like everyone always did. Because I was never worth it enough to stay.

Damn it! My negative inner voice was taking over, I noticed, as my chest constricted and the desire to flee washed over me. I swung my feet off Lucas' lap and stood abruptly. "Excuse me, I just need a minute," I said, rushing to the front door.

"Annie, please..." his gentle, pleading voice followed after me as I slipped on my shoes and dashed outside.

The sky was dark gray like a storm was moving in, the air whipping around me, but I didn't care. The fresh air was exactly what I needed. As I made my way down the street, I whispered my affirmations to myself. On my fourth time through, Lucas appeared next to me.

"Please don't go," he said.

"I'm not going anywhere. I just needed a few minutes. I'm coming back, I promise. But you can join me if you want."

He continued by my side, silent. After about fifteen minutes, I turned to start walking back, having quieted the unwanted voice in my head. Neither of us had said anything yet, and the silence hanging between us was tense and uncomfortable—nothing like the ease we'd experienced when he was rubbing my feet.

A loud clap of thunder startled me from my thoughts and when I looked ahead, there was a wall of rain moving toward us.

"Oh, shit," Lucas muttered. "We're going to get soaked. I'll run back home and grab the car."

"Lucas! No!" I shouted after him as he began sprinting away. When he slowed and turned, I added, "Walk with me. I love the rain."

"But—"

"Rain is refreshing. Come on."

After a moment's hesitation, Lucas returned to my side. Before long, the rain pelted us as we walked, and I basked in the sensation of my soul being cleansed. I had forgotten how revitalizing it was; I hadn't walked in the rain since I was in high school. As the thunder rumbled almost constantly around us, preventing any attempt at conversation, the rain washed away my self-doubt, my negative thoughts, my fear. We were soaked, hair plastered to our heads and faces, clothes clinging to our bodies, but I didn't mind. I wasn't even cold; my skin was hot and buzzed with Lucas' proximity.

When we reached his house, I came to a stop on the porch. "The downside of walking in the rain," I shouted to be heard over the downpour, gesturing at the water running off me in rivulets. "I don't want to get water all over your floors."

"There's only one thing I really care about, Annie," he shouted back, "and it sure as hell isn't my floors."

He searched my face, growing closer as he did until we were only inches apart, our eyes locked together. It was there again, that tether between us, drawing us together with an inevitability. I swallowed against the fear that bubbled up, focusing instead on how his nearness made my blood rush through my veins and a blush warm my face. How my breath caught when he reached out to rest one hand along my side and cup my cheek with his other. How I could feel his accelerated heartbeat under my hands when they rose to rest against his chest. How I knew as we stood there, his thumb caressing my cheek, that we were going to kiss even before he bent his head to touch his lips to mine.

He kissed me slowly, teasing me with chaste kisses first until his tongue softly touched my lips, coaxing me to open. My blood was steadily heating in response to his gentle, spellbinding touch, my breath ragged between kisses.

"I've *missed* you," he whispered against my mouth.

I knew he didn't mean just over the last the month of barely talking, but over the last year since we had broken up. And damned if I didn't miss him, too, in that same way. "I've missed you, too," I whispered back. And then I kissed him, pouring my thoughts into my actions.

His hand slid from my cheek to the back of my head, the other from my side to my lower back, pulling me against him as our mouths became more insistent. Each breath now carried with it a yearning I refused to fight against as much as I refused to name. Feeling desired by him was energizing and made my head spin in the best way.

Lifting his hand from cradling my head, Lucas opened his front door, his hands returning to my body as he walked me backward through the doorway without breaking our kiss. Kicking the door closed behind us, he continued to guide us, unhurried, through his house.

When we reached his bedroom, he broke our kiss. His voice and body shook as he spoke with our foreheads pressed together. "Annie, I want you. I never stopped wanting you. Tell me you want this, too."

"Yes," I breathed out, knowing he meant more than the physicality of what was transpiring in that moment. For such a small word, it carried a lot of weight, and uttering it to him was intimidating enough to have kept the word in even a few weeks earlier—but not anymore. I was getting stronger and was determined not to continue as a slave to fear.

The pressure from Lucas' lips returned to mine, sending a shock of electricity through my body. The sensation called forth a well-known voice in my mind that insisted I was dirty for and undeserving of what was happening, but the difference this time was that I was ready for it. I ran through my affirmations silently as Lucas and I kissed until the voice faded away into nothingness.

And then all my thoughts deserted me when his hands slipped under the knee-length hem of my dress and slowly skimmed up my thighs, dragging the wet, clingy material with them. He paused to grasp my hips and pull me against him, and my heart hammered against my ribcage. And then his hands were traveling further up my body, leaving fire in their wake, until I raised my arms and he peeled my dress the rest of the way off, tossing it on the floor.

Lucas' arm circled my lower back and held me compressed against him for a moment as we kissed feverishly, and then he lifted me onto his bed. He unbuttoned his shirt, his lips never leaving mine until he peeled the material away from his body. My arms, which I was leaning back on, wobbled as I took in his exposed torso. His breath drew in sharply as he watched me watching him remove his pants, then he climbed onto the bed, straddling my hips as his hands slid under my back to unhook my bra, his lips pressed against my sternum. Once my bra had released my pregnancy-swollen and sensitized breasts, he lowered his body over me, shuddering as he dropped his head to press our foreheads together.

"I can't describe for you the way your skin feels against mine," he said, his voice husky and raspy. "It's incredible."

His voice, his words, the way his body felt on top of mine all fanned my blood further. My hands skated up and down his back as the sounds of our labored breathing filled the air around us. Something tugged at the recesses of my mind, trying to pull me away from the moment, but I steadfastly ignored it. I wanted nothing to ruin what was transpiring.

Lucas tilted his head, and our mouths began a sensual dance, our bodies shifting against one another. He kissed along my jaw to my ear, breathing heavily before whispering, "I didn't do things well the last time, in my eagerness and ignorance of what you were going through. That won't happen ever again, sweetheart—I promise."

I nodded my assent, doubting I could find my voice, and trying not to think about anything except how it felt to be with him right then. His lips traveled down the side of my neck, over my collarbone, down until he reached my belly, nuzzling me. His short facial hair was scratchy against my skin and sent a jolt from my head to the tips of each finger and toe. His fingers hooked into my underwear, and he dragged them haltingly down my legs, the sopping material not willingly cooperating.

After fighting to remove his boxer briefs, he asked, "Are you sure?" His eyes moving rapidly back and forth between mine, searching.

With a swallow, I nodded, lifting my hands to his sides.

"Stop me if you change your mind," he said, his voice soft.

I nodded again. "I will," I whispered.

Lucas lowered his body on top of mine and began kissing just under my ear, sending a shiver throughout my body and spreading goosebumps across my skin. He moved a hand to caress my cheek as his lips explored my face.

My neck.

My chest.

Slipping his hand from my face, he shifted his weight again so he was straddling my legs. Ten fingertips dragged at an excruciatingly slow pace along my skin for the length and breadth of my body, starting at my jaw and moving down my neck, across my shoulders, down my arms and my sides, over my hips, and continuing along the outsides of my legs all the way to my feet. I had never experienced something like the way he was touching me, and my breath was stuttering painfully in my chest, my mind both spinning and blank at the same time.

"Oh my god, Lucas," I breathed out, my hands clutching the blankets under my hands.

The sensations he created in my body built on one another, intensifying with each caress. He lifted my ankles, placing my feet flat on the bed so my knees were bent, then began working his fingers in tiny massaging circles up my calves. Then my hamstrings. My eyes watered when I realized Lucas' hands were trembling where they touched me. Reaching down, I grasped his hands and pulled him up. Articulating what he was making me feel wasn't a possibility right then, but maybe I could show him. He held his weight off me, his hands on the bed on either side of my head. I clasped my hands around his neck and pulled him down, kissing him deeply.

Our tongues tangled, the kiss somehow becoming more passionate by the second while remaining slow and sensual, and Lucas' weight slowly lowered onto me. As his erection pressed between my legs, my mind suddenly recalled the last time I'd had sex: with Rob the weekend everyone thought he'd kidnapped me four months earlier. The weekend I got pregnant.

"Stop, I can't do this," I said frantically, scooting myself away from Lucas to curl up on my side. The shame was overwhelming as I hugged my knees into my chest, wishing I could disappear into nothingness. How could I share this kind of intimacy with Lucas when I was still technically married, let alone so soon after the end of my relationship? Everything Rob had done to me recently didn't change how much I'd loved him most of my life, and what was happening with Lucas felt like a betrayal to what I'd once shared with him.

"Annie, what's wrong? What happened?" Lucas' breathing was labored, his voice filled with concern. "What did I do?"

The hand he rested carefully on my arm would have been comforting if it weren't a reminder that I was naked in bed with someone other than Rob. I flinched away, out from under his touch.

"Talk to me, sweetheart," he pleaded breathily, a twinge of panic entering his voice as his words became rushed. "I don't know what I did—please, tell me."

Now sobbing harder than I had in a couple of weeks, the guilt from what had just transpired crushing me, I choked out, "He was right. I'm a cheater."

Every movement slow and gentle, Lucas tried to hold me, but his touch made everything hurt so much worse because of how desperate I felt for it. "Don't touch me. Please. Just leave me alone," I wailed.

"Annie—" he started, his voice cracking.

"Please, Lucas... just go."

After a while, he finally stood and walked out of the room, picking up our discarded clothing as he went and pulling the door closed behind him. He returned about an hour later with my clothes, still warm from the dryer. My tears had stopped, but my chest ached, and nausea consumed me.

"I dried your clothes," he murmured. "I'll leave them here for you. I'm making some lunch, too. It'll be ready in about twenty minutes."

He left a minute later after I'd been unable to respond, closing the door behind him again. I wanted nothing more than to open my eyes to find this had all been a dream, but that wasn't going to happen. Instead, I needed to get dressed, eat something for my baby's sake, and then give Lucas the explanation he deserved. What had happened wasn't his fault and he should know that. At the same time, I felt incapable of performing any of those tasks; instead, I walked into the bathroom and showered, hoping that would help.

In fact, though, showering had been a terrible idea—now I couldn't escape Lucas' scent because it was on my body and in my hair. The way smelling him made me feel—aching to have him hold me—heaped on more guilt and shame. Not only had I nearly had sex with him, but even now I still wanted to be in his arms.

Aside from the sounds of Lucas plating food, it was silent in the kitchen when I sat down. He stole glances at me, his expression guarded, but he didn't speak until after our plates were filled with fruit, waffles, and sausage, and he'd sat down across from me.

"Annie, I'm sorry," he began. "I—"

"No, Lucas, *I'm* sorry," I interrupted, staring at my hands clasped in my lap. "I don't want you to think you did something wrong. You didn't... everything was perfect—*you* were perfect." My voice broke and I took a deep breath in an effort to control my overwhelming conflicting emotions. "It's me. I... I'm still married. Nothing Rob's done or doing changes that. And I can't betray him that way. Not any more than I already have, anyway." A humorless laugh escaped. "Turns out he was right about me after all—I just didn't know it yet."

"That's bullshit, Annie," Lucas said, his voice hard, much like it had been when he stood up to my mom in the frozen yogurt shop. "You haven't done anything wrong."

My eyes lifted to his face. "How can you say that? I'm still *married*! And you and I... we almost—"

"No," Lucas interjected, his jaw set and eyes blazing as his words came rushing out of his mouth. "I'm sorry, I know you don't want to hear this, Annie, but you can't keep doing this to yourself. Rob *left* you. You guys are getting a divorce. You don't owe him *anything* anymore—nothing."

"He's still my husband," I replied, my voice rising.

"No, he's not!" Lucas said vehemently, his eyes boring into me with a startling intensity. "No husband treats his wife the way he's treating you. And he *hurt* you—don't you remember? He grabbed you so hard you had handprints on you for weeks. Bruises, Annie! And he made you bleed!"

"He didn't mean to," I retorted, though my response was weak—I was aware I was defending Rob's violence and was disgusted with myself. I wasn't even sure why I was doing it.

"Whether he meant to or not, he did it, Annie. He physically hurt you. You think you owe him *anything* after that?"

I stared back at Lucas in silence, tears slipping down my cheeks as I tried to breathe. It was obvious in the way his jaw trembled slightly, the way his eyes were glassy, the way his chest heaved, even his wavering voice, how much everything was hurting him, too.

Lucas continued a few seconds later, his voice having lost the anger, leaving only sadness behind. "You think he deserves your loyalty until your divorce is final? He doesn't deserve *anything* from you."

My head fell into my hands, my lungs seizing under the heavy truth of Lucas's words, my body crumpling under the weight of shame and guilt and confusion. I needed space to sort through everything, to figure things out. I couldn't do it right then—Lucas's presence just made my feelings even more confusing.

"I need to go home now," I whispered.

"Please stay," he rushed out, the panic returning. "Don't push me away. Eat with me, let me take you to your appointments as we planned. Please. We don't have to talk about any of this stuff anymore today, and I promise I won't touch you if that would make you more comfortable. Just please don't go."

I wanted to stay, wanted him to hold me and comfort me, as screwed up as it was to want Lucas to soothe my pain from Rob. But I also felt worthless, like trash for wanting that when I was still married... when the person I was still married to was *Rob*.

"I have to, Lucas," I replied, my voice watery and thin. "I need some space to sort through my feelings. Please, just take me home now."

chapter twenty-five

lucas

When Annie learned the news about me moving to Clarksburg for the brewery expansion project, I'd scrutinized her reaction. Expansion was without doubt the best decision from a business perspective, but I wouldn't move forward if there was a future for Annie and me and she didn't want to relocate to Clarksburg with me. Before we'd gotten that far in the discussion, though, we'd ended up tangled in each other's arms.

But none of it mattered anymore—she was determined that what was happening between us was somehow wronging Rob. My mind raced as the car slowly navigated the short distance to her mom's house through the pelting rain. Her hand was already reaching for the door handle as we slowed to a stop in her mom's driveway, and I still hadn't figured out what to say to her, how to tell her I was willing to give her space, but I didn't want her to leave—I could be patient as she worked through her conflicted feelings.

"Annie, wait," my words rushed out desperately as I reached over and grabbed the back of her hand. "Look at me, please."

She looked up, her features tortured as she waited. I shifted to release the back of her hand and slid our fingers together. When mine bent, so did hers, our hands now tightly clasped together.

"If you want space, I'll respect that and give you space," I said. "But I want you to know first how I feel so there is no doubt as you sort out your own feelings." I paused, taking a deep breath. "I love you with everything I am. I never stopped loving you, and my love has only grown over the last year in a way I never thought possible.

You are a part of who I am now. The only life I really want to build has you in it. I'm sorry that I got carried away and let things go too far too quickly today. Haley warned me that I would hurt and confuse you if I didn't back off, and she was right. I'm so sorry."

I sniffed and turned my head away, blinking to dry my eyes. When I turned back, I cupped her face, smoothing my thumbs across her cheeks. "May I kiss you?" I asked.

Her mouth turned down at the edges and I knew she was trying not to cry, but she nodded her head up and down. Our lips pressed together for a long moment. When the kiss was over, our foreheads and noses touched. "I love you so much," I whispered.

She nodded again, her shoulders shaking as she began to cry. Abruptly, she turned away and climbed out of the car without saying a word. As I watched her rush through the rain toward the porch, feeling helpless, something caught the corner of my eye— the birthday present in the back seat that I hadn't given to her yet.

"Wait, Annie!" I called as I jumped from the car with the gift. "I forgot your birthday gift," I added, holding it out to her once I'd reached the porch.

"It's okay, Lucas, you don't need to give me anything."

"Please take it, sweetheart. It's yours."

I handed her the large, shallow, white box tied with a burnt orange ribbon, now dotted with raindrops. She accepted it reluctantly.

"Open it. I think you'll love it," I smiled.

She nodded, her gaze cast down near her feet as she turned away from me once more.

"Wait!" I called out again. Her steps halted, but she remained facing her mom's front door. "Can... can I call you? Text you?"

Slowly her head moved from side to side. Stunned, I watched—helpless—as she opened the front door and walked across the threshold, disappearing inside as the door closed behind her.

chapter twenty-six

annie

The day after almost sleeping with Lucas, I walked into Selena's office and everything I'd been trying to hold inside for the last day came rushing out in a tidal wave of emotion.

"Take a few deep breaths, Annie," she soothed, a hand on my back as she guided me to the sofa I always sat on. "That's it... calm down... breathe... there you go..." She disappeared for a moment and returned with a glass of water. "Have some water, then you can tell me what's going on."

I took a sip of the water, my hand shaking, then set the glass down on the small table at the end of the sofa. "I'm a horrible person," I whispered, violently wringing my hands.

She laughed softly. "No, you're not."

"That's not what you'll be saying when I tell you what I've done."

"I seriously doubt that," she replied.

"You're only saying that because I'm your client."

"Actually, not true. As your therapist, I will only tell you the truth. So, if I think you're a horrible person, I'll tell you that. But don't worry, that's not going to happen." She flashed an encouraging smile at me.

My mouth hung open, but no words were forthcoming—I couldn't bear the thought of her having a negative opinion of me. Deflated, I said, "I can't."

"Can't what?"

"Tell you about it."

"Why not?"

"Because you'll think differently of me."

"Hm. Well, I'm fairly certain that's not going to happen, though we won't know for sure until you tell me. But, if you aren't comfortable sharing, that's okay, too. However, judging by how upset you are, I think it would probably be helpful if we talked about it."

I was silent for a few minutes, and Selena sat patiently waiting for me to be comfortable. There was never pressure for me to rush when the words were having trouble leaving my tongue—it was one of the reasons I liked her so much. Lifting the glass to my lips again, I drank the rest of the water, noticing as I set the empty cup back down that I was absently rubbing a hand over my belly. That action served as a reminder that I needed to push through whether I wanted to or not; I owed it to my baby to be as emotionally balanced as possible so I could be a better mother than the one I'd been born to. So, without pausing, I related every detail of what had transpired the day before, starting when I answered the door to find Lucas standing on the porch up to watching him pull out of my mom's driveway a few hours later.

"Is that everything?" Selena asked after I'd fallen silent.

"Y-yes," I responded, confused.

"Oh—okay, then. I was waiting for the part that was going to make me think you were a horrible person."

"I already told you. Everything I did, everything I felt, everything I wanted with Lucas." The skin on my face was hot and tight. "It's all wrong and I'm everything Rob said I was... maybe even worse."

"Why was it all wrong?"

"Because I'm married to Rob!" I burst out, exasperated; she knew this already.

"Technically, yes—for now."

Forgetting my embarrassment at everything I'd just confessed, my eyes lifted to stare at her.

"Okay, let me ask you something," she continued. "Where's Rob?"

"I don't have a clue, I've told you that."

"Why not?"

"Because he left me, threw me out," I said, beginning to cry. It hurt to say the words even now.

"Have you talked to him? Heard from him? Since then, that is."

"Barely. I saw him at Lucas' brewery once, and at Lucas' house once, that's it."

"Okay, and what happened on those two occasions?"

"You know all these things—why are you asking me?"

She gazed at me for a moment, her eyes soft. "*I* know them, yes," she said, tapping her chest with her index finger. Then she pointed at me. "But *you* don't." She smiled sympathetically at my frustration. "Bear with me. It's not easy, but it'll be worth it. Okay?"

"Fine," I replied, using my palms to wipe the tears from my cheeks and sniffling loudly.

"So, tell me what happened when you saw Rob at Lucas' house."

"He yelled and screamed at me, called me a slut."

"Is that all?" she asked with her eyebrows raised.

My gaze fell to my lap, my face heating. "No," I whispered tearily. "He... he hurt me."

She nodded. "And at the brewery?"

My sobs made speaking nearly impossible. "He said the same kinds of things to me. Except that he told me he was divorcing me and that he was sleeping around."

"And how do you feel about all this?"

"I understand that he's hurt and thinks I did the same thing to him, that he's lashing out because of that. I know that he'd never have hurt me the way he did if he hadn't been intoxicated."

"But how do you *feel* about it?"

Reaching over to the side table, I snagged a tissue and blew my nose as I thought about her question, trying to remove the veil of understanding and just think about my feelings. "I'm disgusted. Furious. Hurt."

"Do you think if he came back today, right now, you could forgive him for everything he's done, everything he's still doing? Do you think you could ever trust him again?"

My eyes stared through the floor as an image of Rob from the brewery fiasco flashed through my mind, when he'd made the comment about other women never turning him down for sex like I had, and a wave of anger surged through me. "No!" I shouted vehemently. But in the same breath, guilt crashed over my head for that response. "I just want none of this to have happened."

"I know," she sighed, "but we can't go back in time, unfortunately. All we can do is make choices for our future. And do you think your future has a place for Rob?"

"No," I whispered, miserable. "I know it doesn't."

"And if there's no future between you guys, there's nothing for you to be betraying right now, is there?"

My knees pulled up around my belly and I cried into them. Everything I'd had with Rob was really gone. My chest caved in on itself as I wept, gasping for breath. Selena moved to sit next to me on the sofa and rubbed my back in silence, allowing me the space I needed to grieve for the rest of my session. Up to that point, I'd been angry for what he'd done to me. I'd been heartbroken over what he'd done to me. I'd accepted that we were going to be divorced. I knew I could never take him back. And yet I hadn't allowed myself to feel the pain of losing everything he'd meant to me over the years in a way I'd never lost him before. It felt like a part of me was dying.

"Annie," she said in a gentle voice when our time was up. "I would let you stay, but I have another client waiting, sweetie."

I nodded.

"We'll talk about it more on Monday," she continued. "But if you need to talk before then, you know you can call my cell any time day or night. Until then, remember your affirmations; they're going to be a little harder for you for a while, but stick with them." She gave me a tight hug once I'd gotten to my feet. "Don't hesitate to call me, okay?"

Speaking required too much energy, so I nodded as I pulled away from her embrace and left.

———————

"Honey, what happened?" Mom asked me as soon as I walked in the door after my therapy session, my red puffy eyes giving away the misery I'd been wallowing in for the last hour.

"I don't want to talk about it."

"You talked to Selena, though?"

"Yeah, Mom, I did."

"Okay. I'm glad you're seeing her. I wish you hadn't resisted therapy for so long, you could have been happier sooner and..."

I tuned her out, drawn back into my own thoughts and fears about the happiest days of my life already being behind me. Sighing, I knew I needed to go stand in front of a mirror and go through my affirmations; it was especially important when negative thoughts kept coming, but I just didn't feel up to the task—right then, I didn't believe a single one of them. But that was the whole point of them. And Selena had said that it was going to be harder for a while, but specifically reminded me to keep up with them before I'd left.

"I'm sorry, Mom, I need a minute," I mumbled, already walking into the bathroom and shutting the door behind me.

———————

Over the next several weeks, Selena helped me learn how to understand and accept that there was nothing wrong with my feelings for Lucas, nothing wrong with what had happened between us. And much to my surprise, when Haley and Carol finally learned about everything that had happened with him the day of my sixteen-week ultrasound, they were supportive and echoed what Selena had been telling me—that I hadn't done anything wrong. Even so, I wasn't ready to follow what my feelings were urging me to do.

Lucas and I exchanged an occasional text message. Even though I'd been the one to tell him we couldn't call or text, I'd broken the silence first, asking him about the expansion. He'd responded and asked how the pregnancy was going. I told him what the doctor said at the ultrasound he'd missed and mentioned when I was going back for the twenty-week visit. As the date approached, knowing he'd miss another ultrasound made me feel unsettled, but I couldn't bring myself to ask him to go after I'd demanded he give me space—especially since I couldn't tell from his short messages if he still felt the same way about me or if I'd succeeded in pushing him away for good this time.

At some point, I knew I wanted to fix things between us because I wanted my friend back, though any other kind of relationship would require a move to Clarksburg—a move that would take me further from my friends and family. With a baby on the way and no other system of support, that was something I couldn't contemplate right then. Though I also wasn't certain a friendship-only relationship with him was possible at this point, either.

In fact, it seemed all I did was go in mental circles. I needed something to do—not having a job was making me crazy. It was that craziness that pushed me to ask Nick if the Stockwood Brewery was still looking for help when I went down to discuss some details about the brewery hosting another Community Thanksgiving that year.

"Oh, hell yeah. Do you know anyone interested?"

"What positions are you looking for?"

"We need several servers out front, and with Lucas up in Clarksburg all the time now, I really could use an office manager to help me out with the office side of this job."

"What kinds of hours?"

"Anything I can get for the servers. And I'm guessing about thirty hours per week for the office manager. Please tell me you know someone!" Nick groaned.

"In fact, I do," I replied. "Me."

Nick stared at me for a moment, his expression inscrutable.

"What? Lucas offered to hire me to help in the office a while back."

"I know, but that was before he was in Clarksburg full-time. The job we need is a bit more demanding now."

"I am qualified and capable, I assure you," I said, offended he thought Lucas' offer had been a charity offer. "I'm a CPA and worked at one of the most prestigious accounting firms in the country for ten years. I'm pretty sure I can handle it."

Nick reached out, his hand engulfing my stiff shoulder as he heartily chuckled. "I didn't mean that you weren't capable, Annie, I promise. You're definitely overqualified for this job—you could do it in your sleep, I'm sure. I'm just thinking of the number of hours required."

Trying to shake off my irritation from the misunderstanding, I said, "I heard what you said. Thirty hours or so. I'm used to working hundred-hour weeks; this will feel like a paid vacation."

Nick shifted, clearly uncomfortable.

"What?" I demanded, still aggravated from the perceived insult to my ability.

"It's just that... I don't think Lucas would approve."

"What? Why not?"

"Before when he offered you the position, you were less pregnant and he was adamant about ten to fifteen hours per week tops for you, afraid you would overdo it. This is double that."

"Does he have to approve who you hire to work here?"

"Well, no," Nick replied, looking away from me, "Not anymore. But—"

"Then hire me, Nick. You need help, I need something to fill my time, and I'm qualified for the position."

"Fine, you made your case!" he exclaimed, throwing his hands up and grinning. "I'll hire you."

We spent a while talking about the details of what hours and days I would work, the exact responsibilities I'd be taking on, and reviewing the employment contract for the position. Once I'd signed and headed home on foot, my spirit was bolstered. I not only had something to do most days instead of sitting idle at home with Mom, but I'd advocated for myself. It was a unique and rewarding experience to have done so, recognizing my worth and what I had to offer... something I couldn't have imagined doing even half a year before. A hand moved to caress my belly as I walked, my chest fluttering with anticipation for the future.

Little one, I promise you'll always know your worth... and never know any other way to be.

chapter twenty-seven

lucas

I completely immersed myself in the brewery expansion after Annie demanded distance between us. But even keeping busy wasn't enough to dull how much I missed her, or how much it crushed me to miss her next appointments as well as the ones I'd missed the last day I'd seen her. But she had said she needed space, and I was trying to give her what she wanted. And at least I'd finally get to see her in a little over a week at Community Thanksgiving since we would both be there.

Though it was cold outside, I lowered the window in my car so the biting wind could help keep me awake as I made the trip back to Stockwood from Clarksburg, where I'd been for the last three weeks. There was so much to be done in a short period of time: agreeing on plans for the layout of the property, getting bids from construction companies, permits, the list went on and on. I had forgotten how much work was needed before anything could even begin, not to mention extra permits and red tape since the building was in a historic district. Just as I'd forgotten how tiring it was, and how short-tempered I could be when I was tired. If I wasn't careful, I'd end up losing contractors or pissing off someone with the power to cancel my permits.

Business was heavier than normal for a typical weekday afternoon at the brewery when I arrived. In the past, it picked up the following week when people took off for the Thanksgiving holiday. If there wasn't enough staff, Nick and I would have to catch up after closing. Which meant missing sleep I desperately wanted and needed.

"Hey, Lucas, long time no see," Nick said as we shook hands in the office. "You look like death," he snorted.

"Yeah," I sighed, "I'm tired as hell."

"We can do this later, man. Go home and get some sleep."

"No, let's do it today, though it looks busy out there. We got enough staff on today?"

Nick nodded, avoiding eye contact. "Yeah, we're covered."

"Great. Where do you wanna start?"

"Let's head out front so you can check out the new taps we got in before it gets any busier."

As we walked out to the main counter, customers were waving and greeting me, but I could barely muster a smile and wave in return, let alone any other kind of response. I was just too damn tired to care, though hopefully the customers didn't notice I wasn't as chatty as usual.

As we approached the taps, I caught a glimpse of dark brown curls serving at the far end of the bar. "Looks like you hired another new bartender out here?" I asked Nick as I grabbed two empty glasses.

His eyes darted down the bar, then back to me. "Well, I hired an office manager, and she helps out sometimes when we're short-staffed."

"Oh, that's right, you said you'd hired someone for the office. How's she working out?"

"She's amazing—almost too good at her job, and she's popular with the locals when she helps out at the bar, which means business is booming."

I laughed as the two glasses filled with beer. "Women behind the bar tend to do that. Guys coming in love having someone to flirt with."

"Hey, gorgeous, how ya feelin'?" someone called out from down the bar as I was inspecting the new connecting mechanism between the tap hose and the keg under the counter.

"Hi, Hank, a little tired today, but otherwise good, thanks," a woman's voice replied.

My heart skipped; I recognized that voice. Standing slowly, my head turned toward the end of the bar, watching as the woman with long curly hair I'd barely noticed earlier turned, giving me a glimpse of her face. She was none other than my Annie, who was very pregnant and serving beer to a small crowd of half-drunk men who weren't even trying to hide that they were checking her out.

Nick jumped in front of me as I took my first step toward Annie. "Don't, man, I mean it. She's fine."

I glared at him. "What were you thinking? Why the hell is Annie tending bar here?"

He glared back at me. "Not out here with the customers, Lucas," he said under his breath. "Back there," he added, pointing toward the office.

"Coming up, Jack," Annie's voice called to someone at the bar, reclaiming my attention.

I couldn't tear my eyes away, watching her deftly pouring beers and passing them out as she collected money. It was as if she'd been born to do exactly what she was doing right then, pregnant belly and all. She did seem to be fine with what she was doing, as Nick had said, but I sure as hell wasn't. Annie shouldn't have been tending a bar anywhere, let alone somewhere she'd get hit on. And should she even be working as much as the office manager position required to begin with at this point in her pregnancy? Didn't she need to rest more?

As Annie handed Jack his beer, he said, "Thank ya, darlin'. If you get tired of whatever yahoo you go home to at night, give me a call, alright?"

Who did these guys think they were? And Annie was letting them talk to her that way when she wouldn't let *me* talk to her at all? I stepped around Nick and started toward the other end of the bar, angry and aware I wasn't very much in control of it.

"Don't talk to her that way," I ground out at the men by the counter as I neared.

Annie's head snapped toward me as she jumped. The beer glasses in her hands started to fall, and when she tried to grab them, it was too late. They broke against the counter, slicing her palm.

"Ow!" she shouted, jerking her cut hand back.

"Oh my god, Annie!" I breathed as blood ran from her hand down her arm to drip off her elbow onto the counter.

Snagging a clean towel from under the countertop, I closed the remaining distance between us and quickly wrapped her hand.

"Nick! Take over!" I called as I put my arm around Annie's shoulders. "Are you okay?" I asked while I led her away from the front end, but she only scowled at me in response. "Sit down while I get out the first aid kit."

She walked into the office and sat, but didn't say anything, her scowl still in place whenever I looked at her. After retrieving the first aid kit and opening it up on the desk next to her, I grabbed her hand and carefully unwrapped the towel. There was a lot of blood, but the cut was on the fleshy part of her hand. It wasn't too deep—just messy.

"I don't think you need stitches," I murmured.

As I finished bandaging the cut, fuming internally about the fact that she was hurt—it never should have happened because she never should have been working at the bar to begin with, something I'd talk to her about in a minute—Annie yanked her hand away, jumped to her feet, and turned toward the door.

"Where are you going?" I huffed.

"To do my job," she bit out.

My head shook quickly side to side. "I don't think so. You're not tending bar here anymore. You never should have to begin with."

She narrowed her eyes. "You didn't hire me, Nick did. And part of my job description is helping out as needed everywhere in the brewery, including tending bar. So, yes, I am. Since when do you think you have a say in what I can and can't do?"

"Since I walked in here to see you—almost six months pregnant—on your feet at the bar while every drunk guy in here checks you out and flirts with you." I felt a twinge of guilt for my behavior as I stood there facing her, both of our chests heaving in anger. "They have no right to look at you or talk to you like that, you're—" I stopped abruptly, realizing I'd nearly called her mine... realizing that was how I felt even though it wasn't true.

"I'm what, Lucas? Huh? I'm what?" she yelled back at me.

Her eyes flashed and her curls tumbled wildly around her shoulders. Her whole body was soft and plump and her skin glowed. She was different from the last time I'd seen her: stronger, more confident, more independent. And, at the same time her arguing was frustrating, I felt more attracted to her than ever—an attraction that socked me in the gut and destroyed my ability to think clearly.

"You're not theirs," I finished.

"Not *theirs*? And what? You think I'm *yours*?"

"Yes!" I shouted.

I wasn't sure if I reached for her first or the other way around, but one moment we were glowering at each other and the next she was in my arms and we were kissing, desperate and feverish. I'd never felt a primal need for someone the way I did for Annie right then. One sweep of my arms cleared the edge of the desk, sending some items sliding to the other end and others tumbling to the floor, and then I lifted Annie to sit there. Still kissing her, I stepped between her legs and raked both of my hands into her hair.

Using my hands to tip her head up, I left her mouth and kissed across her jaw, under her chin. The frenzy that had been driving me started to fade and my movements slowed as my nostrils filled with her scent, my heart hammering in my chest. The last month and a half without her had been torture.

"I missed you," I whispered against her neck.

Her body stiffened and the hands that had been grasping my shoulders now shoved me backward.

"Screw you, Lucas," she said, her voice wavering. "You can't disappear for weeks on end and then just expect me to welcome you with open arms when you decide to reappear."

"Disappear?" I shouted as she slid off the edge of the desk. "You're the one who wanted space, the one who—"

"And I'm not yours," she continued over me. "I'm no one's. And that means that only *I* have a say in what I do or don't do. Not anyone else—definitely not you. I'm going out to do my job."

Her outburst was so unexpected that I simply stood there in stunned silence as she stormed out of the office back toward the bar. I was still standing there, staring at the empty doorway when Nick appeared several minutes later, his eyes taking in the disarray before he walked over and started cleaning up.

"You'd better explain to me why Annie is tending bar here right now, Nick," I snarled, as I helped him reorganize the desk.

"Calm down, Lucas," he replied. "We won't even have a brewery to argue about if you drive away all our customers. Which you'll do pulling shit like you did out there. She's here because I needed an office manager and Annie needed a job."

"Then why the hell is she tending bar?"

"Look, I know you're tired and stressed and that you're in love with Annie, but you're being a dick. I had no intention of having her out front, but she was very aware of her job description and just jumped out and started helping one day when we were swamped and understaffed. I told her she didn't need to, but she just recited her employment contract terms to me and insisted that she cared about the brewery and wanted to do her part. And then talked about how women all over the world, even in our own country, carry babies to term working twelve hours a day on their feet because otherwise their families wouldn't eat, so how could she possibly complain about a few hours here and there?" He chuckled, shaking his head. "I mean, come on, man, you know her better than I do—there's no keeping Annie away when someone needs help. Anyway, you know she grew up with most of our customers and they like having her behind the bar, so she's been really good for business."

"I don't give a shit how long they've known her, Nick—I don't want her out there."

Nick folded his arms across his chest. "She's the best thing to happen to this brewery in a long time, Lucas. She was so efficient with all the responsibilities for the office manager position that she started taking on other responsibilities to fill the hours, so she's also keeping the books for us now. She documented all our processes so we can use them to upskill the new hires in Clarksburg, implemented some controls to reduce our risk and exposure when hiring—she's seriously been a godsend." He paused. "Honestly, I think you should go home. Cool off, sleep, come back in when your head is level and you're not being such an asshole." With those words, Nick turned and strode out of the office.

chapter twenty-eight

annie

When I left the office at the brewery after going off on Lucas, I went straight back to the bar and started grabbing drinks, relieving Nick to disappear toward the office. As the customers called out what they wanted and I filled glasses, my mind replayed every second of mine and Lucas' interactions. And with each replay, instead of clarity, I found myself more confused about what exactly had happened and who was at fault. Lucas was being a jerk, undoubtedly, but what he said about me wanting space was true.

Except that I hadn't expected him to listen to me and actually stay away like he did. At least not for as long as he did. I'd broken our silence when I first texted him, but he'd stayed away anyway. And nothing about his responses had indicated he wanted things to be any different than they were between us. Though... my own messages had been just as neutral, even though it was the last thing I wanted.

"You okay, Annie?" Nick asked a while later after he'd returned and there was a lull in clientele.

"Yeah, I'm fine," I muttered on an exhale, glancing over my shoulder to see if Lucas had appeared. He hadn't.

Nick reached out, stopping me from turning to carry empty glass trays to the back. "Lucas was an asshole to me—I can only imagine he was to you, too. I'm sorry, Annie. If you need some time, you can have it."

"I said I'm fine," I bit out angrily. "Are you trying to make me leave, too?"

"No, no, not at all, I swear," Nick replied quickly, raising his hands in front of him. "The opposite—I don't want you to end up quitting because of Lucas. You've kept things running around here since you started. I don't know what I'd do without you anymore."

My face flamed into an uncomfortable blush at the compliment. I hadn't done that much, really, but something I was working on with Selena was accepting compliments. "Thank you," I replied. "And no, I'm not going to quit because of Lucas. But with the way he's acting, he might fire me."

"He won't, don't worry."

"How do you know that?"

"It's not just his brewery anymore. And his partner is going to keep you around," he added with a smirk.

"Thanks, Nick." A feeling of worth and pride began fully replacing my lingering frustration with Lucas.

"Don't take this the wrong way, because I like you, Annie, always have, but I want you around because you're good for business."

I laughed. "I understand making business decisions, don't worry. I'm flattered you think I'm good for the brewery. And I already knew you liked me—you used to ask me out every time I came in here."

Nick barked out a laugh. "I ask out just about every woman who walks in here because flirting's good for business—they know as well as I know that I'm not serious."

"So if I'd said yes, you would have... done what?" I asked, curious.

"Oh, I'd have taken you out, for sure," he replied, grabbing a fresh towel to wipe down the bar.

"Even though I'd come in with Lucas?" I asked, incredulous.

He finished wiping the countertop and turned to me, crossing his arms as he leaned back against the bar and studied my face for a moment. "When I first met you, you guys were only friends."

"And what about now?" I asked, leaning back against the bar next to him and looking up at him sideways. "Would you date me now? If I wasn't pregnant, that is."

He chuckled, shaking his head. "Hell no. I have no interest in trying to take my business partner's woman."

"I am *not* his woman!"

He laughed harder, pulling me into a side hug. "If you say so."

The rest of the day flew by as I obsessed about what Nick had said. That Lucas and I were involved... that I was his woman. Part of me bristled at the term each time I heard Nick's words, but another part of me relished the thought. Except that it wasn't true. If it were, Lucas would have a funny way of showing it: yelling at me and trying to tell me what to do.

Though I'd carefully watched my phone, anticipating a text from Lucas apologizing for how he'd acted toward me, I received nothing. Instead, I went home after my shift and stared at the box he'd given me the day we'd nearly slept together—the late birthday present. The same thing I'd been doing instead of opening it almost every night since he'd given it to me. After what had happened between us, it hadn't felt right to open a gift from him. And it still didn't.

Morning came too soon, the baby having kicked until late, then my sleep being interrupted often either because I had to pee or as a result of strange dreams about Lucas. None of them had been nightmares, exactly, but they were unsettling. The result was grogginess and grumpiness. What I really wanted to do was go back to sleep, but I was starving, so I rose and made my way to the kitchen, losing my balance and stumbling into the wall as I did.

"Oops!" I muttered to myself. As my belly was getting larger, I was having a harder and harder time with my balance, reminding me of my unsteadiness earlier in the pregnancy.

"Good morning, honey," Mom called out from the kitchen sink over the NPR program playing on the radio. "I'm getting ready to make biscuits if you want to wait a bit to eat."

"No can do, Mom, baby is demanding food now and won't be argued with," I laughed. "I'm sure I'll be hungry again by the time you're done with the biscuits, don't worry."

She turned, looking at my belly. "I can't believe you're really going to have a baby, honey. It seems so surreal." She looked up and frowned. "Are you feeling alright? You looked haggard this morning."

"I'm just a little more tired than usual. I got in late and then didn't sleep well, that's all."

"Is that a bandage?" she asked tipping her chin downward.

My eyes darted down to my hand. "Yeah, I broke a glass yesterday at work and cut my hand on it. I'm fine, though."

"Well, maybe you should take the day off today."

"Why would I do that? I love working. I'll take a nap after breakfast instead of my walk, then I'll be good to go for my shift. Besides, it's a short shift today because I have my appointment with Selena this afternoon."

"I know I've already told you this, but I'm glad you're in therapy, honey. It agrees with you. You seem happy."

"Thanks," I smiled. "I'm glad I'm finally doing it, too."

And I really was. I felt like a different person most days. There had definitely been some backtracking after what happened with Lucas six weeks earlier, but Selena had helped me to not only recover but continue to improve. Bad days still happened, and Selena assured me that would be a lifelong occurrence, but that with hard work, it would happen less and less often.

Having seen the truth in her words and how much I could heal already, I wasn't so afraid of the future anymore. Or of most things, really—I was less afraid of people around me, less afraid of feeling emotions, even negative ones, and less afraid of being alone. I had never appreciated before how much weight all that fear and self-distrust carried with them, so as they trickled away, I felt a buoyancy of spirit that was new and exciting.

The other side of all my inner work was a newfound anger, though. As I began to see that things I had blamed myself for were not my fault, anger—sometimes even rage—toward those who were responsible replaced my former shame and guilt. Selena assured me it was a normal and healthy reaction as long as I let it go over time. But in the meantime, I had more of a temper than ever before. Though it wasn't necessarily a bad thing; it meant I was sticking up for myself more, much like I had with Lucas the day before.

Lucas... even after sleeping on what happened at the brewery the previous day, I didn't know what to think or feel. For a split second before I processed that he was going off on our customers, I'd been so happy to see him, even though he'd looked worn-down and exhausted, with circles ringing his eyes that were missing their trademark twinkle. His easy smile had been absent, his face scruffier than I'd ever seen it. It was apparent he was working himself ragged.

His outburst and subsequent temper were surely a result of the fatigue that was so clear, but that didn't make it okay. He had no more right to treat me or the customers the way he had than to basically tell me I was his or to kiss me the way he did afterward. Though I'd wanted to kiss him just as much as he'd apparently wanted to kiss me. I hated his sudden attitude toward me, the way he talked to me—I wanted nothing to do with that side of him that was more like Rob than anything else. But his possessive outburst and the feverish kissing instantly set my blood on fire all the same.

I wasn't sure what to expect when I headed to work at the brewery and felt a mixture of relief and disappointment that he wasn't there when I arrived. After making some scheduling adjustments for the next few weeks based on recent business, I was just about to head out to the bar when Nick arrived.

"Good morning!" I called brightly as he stepped into the office. Really, morning was a stretch—a mere technicality—since it was almost noon.

"Hi, Annie. How are you feeling today?" he replied, smiling.

"Okay, I guess. I didn't sleep very well, so I'm tired today."

"I can manage if you want to take the day off."

"No way. I'm going to work my shift. People work tired all the time, and it won't hurt the baby at all if I'm tired for a day."

"Well, maybe you should at least stay in here and off your feet, then?" he suggested.

"Uh-uh. I'm wrapping up here and then I'll head out to the bar as planned. Really, I'm good." I smiled to punctuate my words, but Nick only looked concerned.

"Are you are sure? You don't look like yourself today. I know you're more than able, but I don't want you to wear yourself out too much."

"Is this because you're concerned about pissing Lucas off?" I asked, staring at him.

"No," he replied, wrinkling his brow. "Lucas can be pissed all he wants. I'm concerned about *you*."

I nodded. "Well, I appreciate the concern, but I'm fine. I promise I'll tell you if I'm not."

He studied me for a few seconds. "Okay," he finally assented, with a nod of his head.

"Thank you," I said, rising. "I'm done with scheduling, so I'll get us opened up."

It was normally very quiet right after opening, so after unlocking the doors, I got started on making sure everything was fully stocked and organized so the busy evening would go smoothly. After one trip into the back to grab napkins and coasters about ten minutes later, I heard voices as I walked out of the storage room on the customer side of the bar and my heart skipped when I recognized one as belonging to Lucas.

His eyes connected with mine as I came into view. I couldn't look away and didn't notice some coasters sliding off the stack I carried until I was tripping over them, landing hard on the ground. As I processed what had just happened, Lucas appeared, his arms helping me to sit up, and then stand.

"Are you okay, Annie?" he asked, worried. "Are you hurt?"

I shook my head, beginning to shake from the adrenaline in my bloodstream. Lucas slipped his arms around me, pulling me into a snug embrace as he released a loud exhale. My arms folded in front of me against his chest and I huddled there, allowing his heartbeat to calm mine.

"Annie," Nick said as he appeared next to us. "Why don't you take the day off today? You were already tired, there's not much left to do, and there's no one here. Go on. I'll see you tomorrow."

I sighed. He was right—I *was* really tired. And my legs still felt weak and wobbly. "Okay, thanks, Nick."

"I'll take you home," Lucas said, steering me toward the exit.

"I can get myself home, Lucas."

He shook his head and laughed. "No."

"Excuse me?" I asked.

"I said no. One, you're shaking like a leaf and could fall walking back to your mom's. Two..."

Tuning Lucas out, I walked out the door with him on my heels. It was a cold, late-November day, and as the wind cut through my shirt, I realized I'd walked out without my coat. Or my purse, for that matter. Without a word, I turned and started back inside to grab my things from the office.

"I don't think so," Lucas snapped, stepping around in front of me.

Glaring at him, I said through gritted teeth, "I need my coat and my purse, which are in the office."

Without breaking eye contact with me, he pulled his keys out of his pocket and shoved them into my hand. "I'll get your jacket and your purse. Go wait in the car where's it's warm."

His audacity left me speechless, standing there with my mouth hanging open as he turned and strode back inside the brewery.

chapter twenty-nine

lucas

When **I headed** back outside after grabbing Annie's coat and purse from the office, stewing because she never should have been in the bar in the first place, I saw with relief that my car was running and that she was sitting in the front passenger seat. I'd half expected her to be standing outside, freezing, to prove a point. My steps slowed to a stop as I studied her profile. Her head rested against the back of the seat and her eyes were closed, her face slack. She looked tired; she must have been working too much. I had to get Nick to understand so he would adjust her schedule.

Even considering the circumstances, seeing Annie in my car helped set the world back on its axis for the first time since she'd said she needed space. With a sigh, I walked to the driver's side, but the doors were locked. I tapped a finger gently on the glass and Annie startled awake, her eyes huge in fear for a moment before her face cycled through a number of emotions, some which made my heart race, before her anger and irritation set in.

"You really should go to the doctor," I said after climbing in and shutting my door.

"I don't need to," she replied, her voice clipped. "They told me before that the baby would be well protected with amniotic fluid for another month or so if I ever fell with how off-balance I get. As long as there aren't any changes to the baby's movement patterns, I'll be fine."

I shifted the car back into park just before I was going to pull out of my parking space and turned to Annie, my heart beating wildly. "Movement patterns? You can feel the baby moving?"

She nodded with a soft, almost dreamy smile overtaking her features.

"I... I didn't know. Since when?" I was excited and hurt at the same time. I had wanted to be there, to know about every little thing that changed in her pregnancy, but I'd been giving her the distance she'd asked for.

"About a month ago. She's moving a little bit right now, actually."

"Wait—you said 'she'—it's a girl?"

"I don't know for sure," she replied. "I just have a feeling."

"When will you find out?" I asked, thinking back over the pregnancy books Annie and I had read together. "I thought they could do that at twenty weeks."

She swallowed and looked away from me, her smile disappearing. "They can."

"But that appointment was a couple of weeks ago."

A few tears slipped down her cheeks and her breath caught. "I didn't want to find out without you. So I asked them not to tell me."

"You should have told me you wanted me there," I said, my voice starting low, but getting louder as I continued, and my anger ramped up. "I wanted to go—hell, I almost went anyway, thinking maybe that was the reason you'd told me when the appointments were. But you said you needed space apart, Annie—I was trying to respect that!"

"I know," she cried.

After several minutes of silence, I shifted into drive and headed toward her mom's house. Neither of us spoke during the short drive, and Annie steadfastly stared out the window while I got angrier with each passing second. If she had told me, I could have been there for her—she'd *wanted* me there for her. And if I had known, I would have put off the expansion in Clarksburg. But it was too late now. Contracts were now signed, and work had begun; I was stuck in Clarksburg and there was nothing I could do about it.

We needed to sit down and talk things over, get everything cleared up and figure out where to go from there. When we approached her mom's house, though, I saw Miriam's car. A private conversation would be impossible. Instead of slowing and turning into the driveway, I continued down the street.

"Where are you taking me?" Annie asked.

"My house."

"I don't think so, Lucas. I want to go home."

"You can—*after* we talk."

"We can talk here," she replied resolutely.

"No, we can't. Not with your mom around."

"I don't want to go to your house, Lucas!" she shouted.

"Then tell me where you want to go," I bit back. "We need to talk—there's too much unsaid between us right now, Annie, and we're going to get it all out. But we can't do that with an audience, so you tell me where you want to talk."

Annie stared at me murderously, but I was fairly certain I'd win a righteous anger award right then.

"I don't want to talk to you *anywhere*," she seethed. "I'm pissed off at you."

"I'm not sure I've ever been more pissed off in my life. And I'm not going along with the silent treatment again just so I can find out that you wanted me around anyway. We're going to talk and figure out this thing between us because things can't keep going this way."

Annie's mouth hung open as she first gaped—then glared—at me before turning to face out the window with her arms crossed over her chest. Guilt washed over me for a minute for having raised my voice at her again. But regardless of how I was handling my exhaustion, I had every right to be upset with her, so I pushed the guilt away as I pulled into my driveway.

"Do you want to talk here or somewhere else?" I asked in a low voice. "As long as we talk—alone—I don't care where it is."

She didn't reply or move for a minute, but then huffed out a breath while quickly undoing her seatbelt and grabbing the door handle.

"Wait!" I ordered as I turned the car off. Of course she didn't listen and was trying, unsuccessfully, to hoist herself up out of my low seat when I reached her. "I said to wait," I growled in frustration as I reached down and lifted her.

Once we'd reached the porch, Annie spoke. "You're being an asshole," she ground out.

"Oh, I think you've got me beat right now in the asshole department," I replied as we climbed the porch steps. Her eyes flashed in anger as we walked over the threshold into the house, and I closed the door hard behind us.

"Screw you! Quit acting like Rob!"

I froze in place, staring at her in shock.

"This isn't you, Lucas," she continued, her eyes softening some. "You're nice and thoughtful and gentle and considerate. Rob was the angry, brooding, bossy, asshole guy—not you. But that's how you're acting right now."

"Maybe that's a good thing!" I shouted, stepping closer. "Maybe if I'm more like Rob," I continued, more subdued, "you'll actually want me. Because when I show you respect and give you space to think for yourself and make your own decisions, you just push me away."

I was so close to her that we were only separated by a few inches, but we weren't touching. Our eyes were locked, waging a silent battle to see who was going to back down first. After a few moments, she looked away, her jaw clenched as she swallowed. When she turned back, her eyes rested on my mouth.

Crossing the few inches that separated us, I lifted my hands to cradle her face and placed a soft kiss on her jaw. When she gasped, I stepped forward until our bodies were pressed together, and touched my lips to hers. She clung to my biceps and kissed me back passionately.

Annie whimpered, her hands clamping down tighter on my arms, and I leaned further into her, sliding one hand down to circle her lower back and hold her against me. Our arguing had led to an intense desire I'd only ever felt for Annie, including the day before at the brewery and the day we'd almost had sex, and it seemed to have done the same for her.

"You have to tell me what you want," I whispered, breaking our kiss to press our foreheads together as we panted. "You have to be open with me."

"I was scared," she whispered back.

"Annie, sweetheart," I started, my thumb caressing her cheek. "You never have to be scared with me. I promise. And I'll show you. But you have to talk to me. You have to tell me what you want. I'm not going to do something you've asked me not to, so if you change your mind, you have to tell me that."

She nodded and our noses bumped.

"Promise?"

"Promise," she breathed in reply.

"What do you want right now?" I asked softly.

Her breathing accelerated, and then she pressed her lips to mine. But just as we began to kiss again, I remembered she had told me moments earlier that I was acting like Rob. She was desiring *him* right then—not me.

Immediately distancing myself, I stared at Annie where she was leaning back against my front door, her face and neck flushed as she breathed heavily. She looked confused and disoriented and my heart constricted. Turning my head to the side, I scrubbed my hands over my face. I loved her more than I could even understand, but I couldn't be there just because Rob wasn't.

"I can't do this," I said, deflated, as my eyes returned to her face.

She stiffened noticeably. "Can't do what?"

"I can't be just a Rob substitute, which is what I am to you. I need more than that. And I'm already committed to moving away from here for the expansion, anyway—I can't do anything about it at this point. Whatever's happening between us right now... we should stop. And I'm not blaming you. I'm the one who should have stayed away a long time ago."

"You're not a Rob substitute," she whispered.

"You tell me I'm acting like him. And then you want me. How am I not?"

She started crying but didn't respond. After several minutes of waiting for her to tell me I was wrong, her silence made the answer clear. My chest felt like it would split apart.

I swallowed, my eyes glassy as I avoided eye contact. "That's what I thought."

chapter thirty

annie

I **relayed to** Selena everything that had happened with Lucas when I arrived for my appointment later in the afternoon, though I was still trying to process the events myself. Through it all, she nodded thoughtfully, not speaking once until after I'd finished.

"Well," she started, "how do you feel about everything you've just told me?"

My head shook from side to side as I stared absently in front of me. "I don't know. I think I'm in shock? I can't believe Lucas is really walking away from me... just like Rob did."

A thoughtful expression came over Selena's face. "Interesting that you're making another comparison to Rob."

"I wasn't making a comparison. I was just saying that—" I stopped when Selena raised an eyebrow at me. "Okay, I guess you could call it a comparison, but I didn't mean it that way."

"What about what Lucas said to you? About him acting like Rob getting your attention?"

My hands moved around in search of lint but found none on my clothes. Clasping them tightly together in front of me instead, I responded, "I don't know. I mean, it's true, he's all angry and brooding and bossy, which was Rob at least ninety percent of the time, and Lucas, like... well, never. It pissed me off, really. But I also wanted him. I don't understand it. I mean, I don't like anyone being an asshole to me—not Rob, not Lucas."

Though Rob had left me before I'd started seeing Selena, so I hadn't really thought of the way he treated me in those terms before or considered if I was okay with it or deserved it or not—it was just the way it was with him. The way it always *had* been. And I couldn't imagine having the type of arguments with Rob that I'd had with Lucas the last two days—just the thought made my heart race, and my hands start sweating.

"Okay, so it pissed you off," Selena said. "But you also said you wanted him. In what way?"

My face leapt into flames. Even with Selena, it was hard for me to articulate anything about sexuality. "Well, I mean like..." I paused, my breath shallow and vision tunneling. When I continued, my voice was thin and quiet. "I dreamed about having sex with Lucas last night. I've never dreamed about sex before— *ever*. Well, not in this way, anyway."

"In what way is that?"

"Oh." I laughed a little in my discomfort, anxiety making my eyes water. "I mean I have bad dreams—nightmares—about... rape... all the time. But this wasn't like that at all. It was... good, I guess you could say." I swallowed, mortified. "It's probably just pregnancy hormones, though, right?"

"Could be," she replied noncommittally with a small nod.

"I just... I don't know. I was so mad at him for being a controlling asshole, but something about it made me feel... wanted? Not in *that* way, but as a person. I mean, I have never doubted that Lucas cared about me, but I'd never felt like he felt that strongly about it, I guess. Like he cared enough to act possessive and protective like that."

As the words were leaving my mouth, it hit me that I equated Rob's possessiveness and protectiveness with care and love, as if that was the only way to show those things. Or as if those things excused the way he'd always treated me.

"And is that how you felt when Rob behaved that way?" Selena asked, apparently thinking the same thing I was.

I nodded. "I felt desired and loved and cared about when he acted like that. But I never really thought about whether I had a problem with his angry outbursts or controlling tendencies until recently—it's just how he's always been, ever since I met him in high school. It never occurred to me until just now that even if he loved me, it wasn't okay for him to be that way toward me."

She nodded again, slowly this time, her expression thoughtful when I glanced up at her.

"I meant it when I told Lucas to stop acting like Rob," I continued. "But I *did* respond to it. What does that mean?" I asked, my voice cracking and my cheeks dampening with my tears. "Does it mean I secretly like it or something? Or that I won't be happy in a relationship if I'm not being treated like shit? God, I'm seriously screwed up."

Selena handed me a box of tissues but remained silent.

"What are you thinking?" I asked when I couldn't stand the silence any longer.

"Well, I don't think you're screwed up, that's for sure. And I don't think you like being treated poorly. I think you're confused. Confused because you had two conflicting reactions to something, and you don't know what that means. Confused because you don't know if it was the similarity to Rob that you liked or not. Confused because you have a new perspective on a relationship that has defined much of your life."

My head bobbed up and down. "So... what do *you* think?"

She studied me for a moment. "I think your response to these behaviors—both Rob and Lucas—wasn't to them being assholes exactly, but rather to the realization you had about how deeply they cared about you when it was happening. That doesn't mean you enjoyed the way they were treating you."

"I don't know," I responded quietly. That's what I'd thought a few moments ago, but what did that say about me if I only felt cared about if I was being treated that way?

"It's something to think about." She took a sip of her water, then continued. "Let me ask you something."

"Sure."

"If Rob showed up on your doorstep today saying he was wrong and sorry and asking you to take him back, what do you think you would do? How would you feel?"

It was a question she'd asked me a few different times since I'd started seeing her. But, as always, I tried to imagine the scenario right then, shifting uncomfortably as I thought back over our entire history, seeing his pattern of outbursts and losing his temper, his near-constant threat of violence just below the surface, his intense jealousy and controlling tendencies, his pattern of losing his sanity and lashing out to intentionally try to hurt me when he was hurting, and how a fear of all of those things drove my behavior and decisions with him.

And then, most recently, he'd even left marks on me. My hands slid up my arms over my biceps where the bruises had been as I remembered seeing the marks for the first time when I was sitting on the floor in Lucas' entryway. My tongue darted over my lip where it had bled. I'd have sworn he'd never do something like that to me... and then he had. I still loved him, anyway, I knew. But I also deserved a life in which I wasn't perpetually afraid of how someone else might behave or react.

"I'd thank him for apologizing. But it wouldn't matter. I won't ever take him back."

Beginning that night after the blow-up with Lucas and my realizations in therapy, my dreams became ever more disturbing—horrifying combinations of reality and fiction, including everyone I had ever cared about and everyone who had ever hurt me. Each morning left me more exhausted than when I'd gone to bed, but I wasn't sure what to do about it.

Lucas was avoiding me at the brewery, closeting himself in the office when I was at the bar, and going to the bar when I was in the office. We needed to talk—I needed to tell him what I'd worked out in therapy—but I didn't know how to even start. Instead, I kept my eyes averted when we passed each other so I wouldn't have to see his face missing the life and warmth he used to have.

And because I was so tired all the time and wrapped up in my thoughts about Rob and Lucas, Mom was worried about me and hovered whenever I was home. I couldn't stand it and just wanted to be left alone to think, but she was my mom, and I was living under her roof, so I tried to just accept her concern.

Needless to say, I was practically ecstatic when Haley came down to visit a few days earlier than expected for Thanksgiving, giving us a few days alone before Carol and Linc arrived as well.

"Surprise!" she shouted with open arms when I opened the front door the Sunday before Thanksgiving.

"Haley!" I threw my arms around her, muffling my voice. "What are you doing here? I thought you weren't coming until Wednesday?"

"Well, I worked some miracles and got our merger closed early so I could come spend some extra time with you and my soon-to-be niece or nephew. Hi, baby. Super awesome, ultra-fun Auntie Haley is here!" she said, pulling back enough to rub my belly. After a second of talking to the baby about how awesome an aunt she would be, she looked at my face for the first time and hers fell.

"What's wrong, Haley?"

"What's wrong with *me?* More like what's wrong with *you,* babe? You look like shit."

"Thanks a lot."

She waved dismissively. "Whatever. Seriously, what's going on? Is everything okay with the pregnancy? It better be, because I'll lose my shit if there's something wrong and you didn't fucking tell me."

"No, nothing's wrong with the baby. I just haven't been sleeping well. Something... happened last week and I've been having a hard time sleeping since then, that's all."

"Last week? Why didn't you call me?"

I shrugged. "I know how much time this merger has been demanding from you and I didn't want to add to it by whining about my life drama. I figured we could catch up this week when you came."

She rolled her eyes. "You know you're fucking annoying, right? Goddamn call me next time! I can always make time for you if you need me—you know that, babe. But tell me inside, it's fucking freezing out here."

We sat on my bed across from each other, just like we used to when we talked in college. There was something comforting about the familiarity of it, making it easier to talk about the rollercoaster the last weeks had been, from starting my new job to everything with Lucas and my realizations in therapy. Getting everything off my chest to Haley had an unexpectedly relaxing effect on me, though, so I was yawning by the time I'd finished talking.

"We can talk more about it later, babe," she said, stretching her arms on the tail end of her own yawn. "I'm fucking tired, too. Let's take a nap."

We both lay down on my bed on our sides, and Haley snuggled up behind me with a hand on my belly. Within a few minutes, I was asleep.

***

After we woke up, Haley asked me what I wanted to do.

"I don't know," I replied with a sigh. "I'd usually be over at the brewery, but Nick told me yesterday that he didn't want to see me until Monday, and only then if I was well-rested."

"Good guy, I like him already. Is he fuckable?"

"Seriously, Haley?"

"Well, yeah, duh," she laughed.

I rolled my eyes, though I wasn't surprised or even bothered. "You'll think he's hot, yes. You probably met him last year, but we can go over if you want to meet him again, just not now because it'll be getting busy."

"So what? We'll go over as customers."

I snorted. "Right, pregnant woman as a customer at a brewery."

"Of course not. You'll be my wing woman. Come on, it'll be fun."

It was a packed Sunday evening at the brewery when we arrived—much busier than we had staffed for, I knew. There was no way I could sit out there at a table with Haley and let the brewery staff deal with the onslaught alone. Besides, it was crowded in there—I'd be much more comfortable having the bar counter separating me from the throngs of people.

"Haley!" I shouted in her ear over the deafening noise around us.

"Yeah, babe?" she called back as she continued to move us through the crowd toward a line for the bar.

"I'm going to go behind the bar for a bit and help out."

"What? No! You're off today, don't leave me hanging!"

"Seriously—look at them—they're drowning. They need help. And honestly? I want out of this crowd. It's too much."

"Yeah, yeah, I get it, babe. If I don't find a hookup, though, I'm blaming you!"

I laughed. "Don't leave without me or without at least telling me first!"

She nodded and I beelined for the end of the bar so I could slip behind and start helping out. Just as I reached the end of the counter where I'd be able to step out of the crowd, though, a pair of hands grabbed my hips and pulled me backward.

chapter thirty-one

lucas

The brewery was noticeably short-staffed with business booming and Annie off, so it was all-hands-on-deck at the bar. Taking and filling beer orders and answering questions about the brews was second nature to me, and I easily went through the motions without much thought. In the past, being behind the bar had been an opportunity to share my passion for the different brews with each and every customer. Inevitably, conversation flowed as easily as the beer, and I made a point of memorizing faces and names so I could provide individualized greetings when they returned, flirting with women who wanted to be flirted with. But I'd long since lost interest in flirting and now couldn't even drum up enough desire to chat with people. The only thing I could think about was Annie, wondering what she was doing, what she was thinking. Wanting to talk to her, to hold her, to erase Rob from our lives as if he'd never been a part of them so we wouldn't be in the situation we were.

Shit. Distracted thinking about Annie, I overflowed the glasses I was filling and there was now beer everywhere. I needed to focus. A glance around revealed no clean towels. After using some bar napkins to dry the glasses and pass them to the customers waiting on them, I started down the bar until I found a stack of clean, dry towels under the counter at the very end. Standing, a flash of curls caught my eye and I froze—Annie was on the other side of the bar, squeezing her way through the crowd toward where I stood, though she didn't appear to have seen me. As I watched, she was suddenly pulled backward—someone's hands were on her hips.

In a matter of seconds, I'd cleared the bar and was propelling Annie away, the offending man flat on his back trying to catch his breath. By the time I had Annie safely on the employee side of the counter, the asshole who'd grabbed her was on his feet, a small crowd watching to see what would happen next.

"What the fuck, dude?" the guy roared as he stood.

With Annie safely behind me, I shouted, "If you're not out of my brewery in two minutes, I'm having you arrested for sexual assault. Get out now and don't ever step foot in here again!"

Once he was gone, I spun around and scanned Annie for any sign something was amiss. Cupping her head and lowering my mouth to her ear so she could hear me over the din, I asked if she was okay.

"Yeah," she replied, her eyes still in a daze. "He didn't hurt me. I'm a little shaky, but I'm fine—I just need to sit down for a few minutes, I think."

I gave a short nod, grabbing her hand. "Come on."

We headed toward the office, pausing for me to tell Nick I'd be back in a few minutes. With the crowd we had, behind the bar was where I needed to be, serving the customers who were the reason I even had the brewery, but I wasn't ready to leave Annie's side yet. Or to stop touching her skin where our hands were clasped.

"What are you doing here when you're not on the schedule?" I asked more harshly than I'd intended once I'd closed the office door behind us.

"Haley's visiting and she wanted to come out," Annie replied.

"Where the hell is she, then?" I demanded. "Why weren't you guys together?"

Annie stiffened. "She was in line for a beer. When I saw how busy it was, I decided to help out since I was here. That guy grabbed me just as I was about to walk behind the bar."

"Damn it, Annie—"

"Lucas, please don't," she interrupted. Her tone was defeated and beat up and kept me from continuing. She stared at the floor as she continued in a soft voice. "I know you think I like it when you act like Rob, but I don't. I actually *hate* it." Her eyes shone with tears that I could tell she was trying to hold back as she turned her head up to look at me. "I understand if this," she gestured at herself and her belly, "is too much, and I know you're moving, but I don't want to miss out on having you in my life in some way because of something that's not even true. And it's not true that I want you to be like Rob."

She turned away as a few tears slipped free, using the palm of her free hand to wipe them away. I wanted to believe her, but I'd seen for myself how she responded differently to me. I needed some time to think.

"I'm sorry for all this," she whispered in a watery voice, wiping more tears from her cheeks as she continued to stare at the wall.

I gaped at her. "Annie, look at me." I used a hand to turn her head to face me, my thumb smoothing back and forth across the soft skin on her cheek as I searched her eyes intently. "What happened isn't your fault. At all. If it wasn't you, it would have been some other woman that asshole assaulted. What he did wasn't okay—and that's all on him. You did nothing wrong. *Nothing.*"

She nodded, looking down. "I mean for everything else. It's my fault you think I want you to be like Rob. And I'm the one who pushed you away to begin with." Her eyes came back up to mine, full of emotion, and her voice shook when she continued. "I'm sorry I did that. I wish I hadn't."

It was suddenly hard to breathe in the small room with Annie that close to me, thinking about how the last nearly two months might have unfolded if she hadn't pushed me away. How many things I could have done differently that I couldn't now undo. It was too much, and I stepped back, my hands falling to my sides. Clearing my throat, I told her we'd handle the bar, that she should get Haley and go home to get some rest when she was ready. After speaking, I hesitated before leaving; my body wanted, desperately, to pull her into my arms again, to kiss her, to tell her that I loved her. But I couldn't get out of my mind how she'd reacted to me when she thought I was acting like Rob. So, instead, after a moment, I left the office, gently closing the door behind me.

chapter thirty-two

annie

It was Thanksgiving, my favorite day of the year. Luckily, preparations for the Community Thanksgiving had been much easier thanks to having the previous year for a reference and Mom to help out with the cooking this time. As I putzed around the kitchen trying to help, my phone vibrated with a text from Lucas asking me to open my birthday gift if I hadn't yet.

I thought back to seeing Lucas at the brewery a few days earlier, how after dozing off for a while in the office, I'd searched for him only to find out he'd left already. My heart had crumpled, even though Nick had assured me it was only because he had to drive some drunk customers home. I'd been sure he'd left because he didn't want to see me, that he hadn't believed what I'd told him in the office. But he'd just texted me, so maybe I'd been wrong.

Slipping out of the kitchen to my room, I pulled the box out and plunked it onto my bed. The gift he had given me for my birthday stared back at me as I eyed it, unsure if I really wanted to open it or not.

"I can show you how to open a present if you forgot," Haley said, plopping down next to me.

"Ha-ha, smart ass."

She snorted. "Open it, then."

"It's from Lucas," I replied. "For my birthday. I haven't wanted to open it since things have been... how they are. But he texted me about it just now."

"Open it."

"You think?"

"Definitely," she replied, nodding. "If he wants you to, you should."

Gently, I pulled the end of the ribbon, undoing the bow tied around the box and lifting the lid. Carefully folding back the tissue paper revealed a note in Lucas' handwriting.

Annie—

You have spent your life thinking about others, feeling guilty when you think of yourself, always aware of what you have that others don't, unaware of the light and happiness you bring to everyone around you. Like a sunrise after a long night, or field of wildflowers by the side of the highway, you're a wonderful surprise to all who meet you. Look at this whenever you have any doubt about how you have touched the lives of others, including mine; we're all better for having known you.

I love you,
Lucas

Under the note was a scrapbook with every note from the Jar of Thanks at the previous year's Community Thanksgiving. I'd read only a few before we left that day and forgot entirely after Charlie had attacked me that night. The more I read, the more my hands shook.

"Oh my god, Haley," I breathed out, my voice shaking as tears slipped down my cheeks.

She wrapped an arm around my shoulders and pulled me into her side. This cry was different from what I'd become accustomed to recently—it was a mixture of happiness that Lucas understood me in such a way that he'd given me the perfect gift, and sadness at the state of our relationship. After a few minutes, I wiped the tears off my cheeks and grabbed my phone to send a message of thanks to him. Anything I could say via text would be insufficient to convey how much his gift meant to me—something that would be better handled in person—but it was all I could do at the moment.

After a short hesitation, I also sent him a link to an article I'd discovered two days earlier, *How to Love a Woman Who's Been to Hell and Back* by Kathy Parker. When I'd stumbled upon it, the world had stopped spinning for a few moments. It had felt as if the author knew me personally and had written the article about *me*. It also brought into my consciousness patterns I had that I'd never noticed before... patterns that were responsible for me having pushed Lucas away.

Hopefully it wasn't too late to repair that mistake.

Mom and Haley had refused to let me help set up for Community Thanksgiving, insisting I'd tire myself out if I did. And while I was sure I'd have been fine, it wasn't worth an argument I was likely to end up losing anyway. Instead, Mom and I spent the morning watching *Antiques Roadshow* reruns on television and arrived at the brewery shortly before the doors would be open to the public.

"Annie!" Nick called out as Mom and I walked inside. "You look much better. More rested."

"Thanks." I grinned, heading in his direction. "I *am* more rested, and I do feel much better. I hate to say it, but I think you were right about me needing to take some time to catch up on sleep."

"Of course I was," he replied with a smirk, reaching an arm out to give me his signature side hug. "I'm glad you'll be back, though, I didn't know how incompetent I was at all the office stuff until I had to handle it this week after you've been doing such a great job."

"I doubt that, but thanks," I laughed. "It looks great in here, Nick. Thank you."

He shrugged off my thanks, his lips tipping up on one side. "It's for a great cause."

"Yeah," I agreed, my eyes scanning the room for Lucas. I'd decided to do whatever it took to mend things between us, and while I was nervous about failing in that endeavor, I was also filled with an unusual excitement and optimism. Selena had said it was a sign my self-confidence was improving. The reason didn't matter as much to me, though—I was just happy I wasn't letting fear paralyze me again.

Nick cleared his throat and rested a hand on my shoulder. "He's not here," he said soberly. "There was an emergency at the Clarksburg site. He had to leave a few hours ago."

I blinked away the tears that rose to my eyes. *Today isn't about me, it's about hungry families in the community.* With a forced smile and bright voice, I said, "It looks like we already have a crowd out there. Let's get this thing started."

Even more people attended than the year before, and the brewery was bursting at the seams from the moment the doors opened. People were eating and drinking and enjoying easy camaraderie. New this year, Nick had blocked off a small area with games for the kids, and I wound up over there for a long time watching the kids play, imagining my own child there in a couple of years. The thought brought on a wave of emotion. As I wiped the moisture off my cheeks, an arm slid around my waist.

"Hey, babe, how you doing?" Haley asked.

"I'm good," I replied, wrapping an arm around her waist in return.

She snorted. "You're a shitty liar, but I'll pretend to believe you if that's what you want."

I laughed softly, tilting my head to rest on her shoulder. "I really am good," I said. "I'm sad about Lucas, but I'm okay. I know I *will* be okay, at any rate. And this—" my free hand gestured around us, "—is incredible. People have at least one day they don't have to worry about putting food on the table. Look at them—they're happy and carefree, if only for a day. I wish there was a way to provide that kind of relief more often." I swallowed, my eyes filling with tears again. "I remember what it was like to be hungry, Haley. No one should ever have to experience that. Especially children. They should be worrying about normal kid stuff and playing games. And for a day at least, they can do that. So, yeah, I'm good."

Haley let out a satisfied sigh and gave my waist a squeeze. We stood like that, both of us watching the kids play, and I felt... content. Rob and Lucas weren't in my life, but Haley would always be there for me. Really, one wonderful, caring, fiercely loyal friend was more than a lot of people could boast. And I knew that Carol would always be there, too. I was incredibly lucky.

"Ha-ley," I said in a sing-song voice as we searched for my mom a while later.

"Yeah?" she replied.

"Look who's right over there, near the end of the bar," I said, tipping my head toward the other side of the room where I'd spied Jax. She stopped walking and a glance at her revealed why. "Holy shit, Haley," I laughed. "You're blushing. You're actually *blushing*. This is a first."

"Fuck off," she muttered.

"Let's go talk to him."

"Hell no! He's already blown me off before. *Twice*."

"I know. But maybe three's a charm? Besides, maybe he's heard from Rob," I added, feeling a heaviness replace some of the lightness of spirit I'd been enjoying for hours.

"Who cares if he's heard from that asshole?"

I exhaled loudly. "I mean, it doesn't matter, I guess. Our time together is forever over. But I still want him to be okay."

She sighed and grabbed my hands, swinging them slightly. "Look, if Jax is in contact with Rob, he's only going to have bad news for you, and you don't need to hear it." She paused. "Babe? I owe you an apology. I fucked up. I tried to run Lucas off and push you back to Rob, and I shouldn't have. I was wrong about them both. And I shouldn't have been trying to make your decisions for you, anyway. I'm really sorry."

I nodded absently. "It's okay," I said. "I'm lucky you love me enough to care. And I don't really need either of them, anyway, do I? I've got *you*."

Haley laughed, giving my hands another swing.

"Well," I added, "now that that's settled, there's no reason for us to *not* talk to Jax, right?"

Her face turned pink again and excitement bubbled up inside me. This was the first time since we'd met that Haley was displaying anything other than carnal interest in someone, and it was long past due for her to let someone in. Maybe Jax could be that person. Setting aside any lingering sadness from our conversation so I could be there for her, I pulled her toward Jax, greeting him once we were within earshot.

"Annie!" Jax called back, his face lighting up. "I was looking for you! How you been?"

I laughed uncomfortably, deciding against asking if he'd heard from Rob. "Ah, well, you know, ups and downs. How about you, how have you been?"

He gave me a warm grin. "I'm good. Busy. Apparently, everyone wants a tattoo this year." He chuckled.

"You've met Haley, I believe, my closest friend?"

"Yes, I certainly have," he said, his lips tipping up on one side as he peered intently at Haley.

Haley glanced away and steadfastly looked everywhere but at Jax as her blush deepened from pink to red. There was a palpable tension between them. I beamed back and forth between them, wanting to bounce in my excitement for Haley. She deserved to find someone who could get past her barriers and make her happy, and if my gut was right, this was the guy who would do it.

"What the fuck are you grinning so smugly about?" Haley muttered.

With a hug, I replied, "I love you, Haley."

"I love you, too, asshole, but what's with the fucking face?"

I laughed. "You know that once this baby's born, you'll have to stop saying the f-word all the time, right? I won't have a toddler running around cursing like a sailor."

She rolled her eyes.

"Well," I continued, "you two are still young and decidedly *not* pregnant, so I'll leave you to have fun and drink for me. I'm going to find my mom and head home. I'm so tired I'm barely standing."

Before either of them had a chance to reply, I spun around and walked away. When I found Mom a few minutes later, she was predictably engaged in a wine-induced conversation about feminism and politics and was not amenable to leaving just yet.

"Hey, Annie, I was looking for you," Nick said as I was heading back to the office to lay down while I waited for Mom. "Great turnout this year. Better than last year, even."

My lips curved slightly, too tired for a full smile. "I know, it's wonderful. But also tiring. Or maybe that's just because I'm pregnant. I was just going to lie down for a bit in the office."

"Why don't you go home?"

"My mom is my ride home, and she isn't ready to go yet, and I don't have enough energy to walk right now." *Not to mention it's too dark for walking through the streets alone, even with Charlie locked up for another month.* I shivered.

"I'll tell you what, how about I drive you home, and then I'll make sure your mom gets home safely whenever she's ready?" Nick suggested.

I gazed at him, undecided. The offer was tempting. I was exhausted, both physically and emotionally, while my mom seemed like she was gearing up for a night out on the town.

Nick put an arm around my shoulders. "Come on, I can tell you're beat. I'll take you home real quick. Where's your coat?"

I yawned, closing my eyes and imagining for a moment that the warm frame supporting me was Lucas'. "Okay. My coat's in the office."

chapter thirty-three

lucas

After dealing with the construction issues in Clarksburg, I'd intended to just stay up there; originally, I wasn't due back for two more days, but there was no reason I had to return to Stockwood. However, after what Annie had said in the office earlier that week, it had been rolling around in the back of my mind how different Rob and I were... and that maybe I really wasn't a Rob substitute to her and I was already considering returning. Then Annie had sent me an article via text that changed everything. As soon as I finished reading, it was like puzzle pieces falling into place; I suddenly understood Annie's push-and-pull with me. I hated she'd had a life that made it so hard for her to love and trust, but it all made sense now. And I was going to love her harder, just like Kathy Parker's writing said to do. I'd immediately gotten on the road back to Stockwood once I was no longer needed on the site.

About ten minutes out, I called Annie, but her phone must have been turned off because it went straight to voicemail. I crossed my fingers she was still at the brewery and headed there. I parked and made my way to the back entrance to avoid the crowd, almost running into Nick and Annie as they were about to exit. Annie's eyes rounded and her sharp inhale hung in the air as we held each other's gazes.

"Hey, Lucas," Nick said eventually. "Weren't you in Clarksburg?"

I nodded, my eyes never leaving Annie's as I responded. "I was. I left to come back as soon as I could."

"Well," Nick said, "I was just about to run Annie home."

I swallowed, my breath stuttering as I inhaled. "I can do that," I said. "If that's okay with you, that is," I added to Annie.

Her head moved up and down slightly. "Yeah, that's okay," she said faintly, her face steadily reddening.

"Alright, I'll see you guys later, then," Nick said with a smirk, turning and heading back toward the event.

I cleared my throat, shoving my hands in my pockets and looking away. "If you want to wait, I can drive up here to get you. I had to park a ways down the street."

"That's okay," she said. "I don't mind walking."

I nodded again, lifting an arm to wrap it around her but running my hand through my hair instead. Then I turned and held the door open for her to pass outside. We walked side-by-side down the street in silence, though we were so close that it felt like there was an electric current running between us. After helping her into the car, I took and released a deep breath as I made my way to the driver's side.

"How did it go?" I asked as we pulled onto the road. "It looks like it's still really busy."

"It is," she replied, looking out her window toward the building. "The turnout was huge. I'm not sure the brewery will be big enough to keep hosting it."

"We'll figure something out," I said. "I'm sure we will."

Awkward silence fell, and before I'd figured out what to say, I was pulling into her mom's driveway. I shifted into park, but she made no move to exit the car aside from removing her seatbelt. Snippets of the article I'd read kept running through my mind as I tried to come up with what to say to her.

It requires a relentless love, one that is determined and not easily defeated... she will swing between fear of suffocation and fear of abandonment... sometimes she may not know what she needs... and you will need to be what she needs when she does not know herself... ashamed to be herself for no one has loved her both when she is small and also when she is tremendous... she does not understand a love with no conditions, one that is powerful enough to withstand hard times... love her because you understand with every damn fiber of your soul the gift of her love, what it has cost her to offer you her fragile heart.

"Thank you for driving me home," she said, breaking the silence as she turned toward me with her eyes cast downward. "I know you have to get back, but maybe... maybe we could talk sometime. When you have time."

I released my seatbelt and turned my body to face hers. "I don't have to get back to anything right now. I drove back tonight just so I could see you. But I know you're tired. You should go in to bed."

She nodded, then turned slowly to face her door. As she did, an unease settled over me. I desperately wasn't ready to say goodbye again. I reached out and grabbed her hand.

"You *should* go in to bed, Annie. But I don't want you to."

Her breath caught loudly. "I don't want to, either," she whispered, shifting around to face me. My fingers wove between hers and she stared down at our hands. "Thank you," she said. "For my present."

"You're welcome." I cleared my throat and ran a hand through my hair. "I heard a song today that made me think of you." I swallowed. "Would you like to hear it?"

"Okay," she replied.

I grabbed my phone from the cupholder and within seconds "Falling Like The Stars" by James Arthur filled the inside of the car.

"Do you want to come inside?" she asked with a soft sniffle after the song had ended, her free hand picking at the cloth of her jacket. "I mean, we shouldn't keep running the car, the exhaust is so bad for—"

"Yes," I replied, pulling my hand from hers to cut the engine. "I'll help you," I added as I opened my door.

After stepping quickly around the car and swinging her door open, I leaned down and helped her to stand. On her feet, she was only inches away—so close I could feel her breath on my face. For a moment it felt as if none of the last two months had happened;

it felt like the day we'd walked in the rain. Except more intense. Every atom in my body was screaming out for me to pull her into my arms. To kiss her and touch her and tell her how in love with her I was. Tell her how the last months felt like I was walking around directionless without her, how dull life suddenly was. But it was freezing outside, so instead, I stepped back, clearing my throat, and let her lead the way to her front door.

chapter thirty-four

annie

My heart felt like it was going to split my chest open as Lucas followed me to my mom's front door, then inside. I wished it would calm down so I could think clearly; as things were, I couldn't even figure out how to form words, though I knew there was a lot that needed to be said.

Lucas built a fire in the fireplace while I made us tea. Listening to the sounds of him moving around in the living room from the kitchen brought back memories of when he was practically living with me a little over a year ago, and for a moment I yearned to go back in time. Before Charlie attacked me, before I ended up with Rob, before I was pregnant. When it was just Lucas and me and no hurt existed between us.

Once we were settled onto the sofa near the fire, Lucas broke the silence. "Twenty questions?"

I smiled. I'd been about to ask him the same thing.

"Do you want to ask first, or do you want me to?" he asked.

I always answered the same way when he asked that question—I told him to go first. But this time, I had a question ready. "I'll ask first." He nodded and I continued. "What's the best gift someone has ever given you?"

"An actual object?"

"Yeah," I replied.

Lucas shifted around on the sofa for a moment before closing his eyes. "When I was really little, my mom gave me an enormous wool blanket for Christmas one year. I was so excited about opening the present because it was huge, and when I tore open the box, I was confused about the itchy dark gray thing inside. I thought maybe it was wrapped around my actual gift, so I pulled it out and shook it, but there was nothing else. Mom's eyes were twinkling as she watched me, and I tried so hard to hide my disappointment because I didn't want to hurt her feelings. Mom always picked the best gifts, so I couldn't believe she'd gotten me a big wool blanket for my birthday. She could tell I wasn't thrilled, but it didn't seem to bother her. She just winked at me and said that sometimes you don't realize the worth of something right away."

His features softened, his lips curving at the edges, and I watched his face while he was lost in his memory. I loved listening to him talk about growing up and imagining the kind of loving parents he had. Imagining what it would be like to have had that. Every now and then I felt a twinge of sadness while listening because I hadn't, but it always passed as quickly as it appeared. Even if I couldn't have had a caring household, at least *he* had.

"The next morning, Mom woke me just before dawn, a thermos of hot chocolate ready to go. I was surprised she was waking me up because it was too cold in the dead of winter for spending time sitting still outside, but I followed her down the stairs anyway. After donning my winter gear, she pointed over to where my new blanket was folded on the dining table and told me to grab it. Turns out, that blanket was big enough for both of us to be wrapped up in it, and warm enough for us to sit huddled together long enough to watch the sunrise even in the coldest time of year. The density of the blanket warded off sharp winds and it repelled moisture, keeping us dry. It meant I didn't miss my mornings with Mom for part of the year anymore."

"That's beautiful," I murmured, picturing a little Lucas cuddling with his mom under a large blanket.

"You?" he asked, opening his eyes, his face relaxed as he gazed at me.

My stomach fluttered and the skin on my face was now too warm. "A scrapbook."

The air between us suddenly charged like a live electric current. Lucas hadn't moved, but it felt as if he was now closer to me, so intent was his focus as he waited for me to continue.

"Not just a scrapbook, though," I continued. "Its contents told me things words never could have. They told me the person who gave it to me understood me in ways not many do. That the person saw the deepest parts of me. Like, really saw them—the parts that can't be explained. And that the person both grasped and cared about those parts of me, too."

"And what person was that?" he asked softly.

"You," I breathed.

Something flared in his eyes, and he swallowed. "The best intangible gift I've ever received was you knocking on Grams' door a year and a half ago."

My jaw trembled. "Mine is you teaching me that I could love again, and that love doesn't have to include fear."

"Sweetheart," Lucas whispered, the word scarcely off his lips when he was there, his arms pulling me into him, his mouth on mine.

Everything was a tangle of tongues and bursts of breath for several minutes before Lucas pressed our foreheads together. As we panted for air, he rubbed my nose with his, cradling the back of my head, and my hands clutched at the material over his chest.

"I missed you," I said, my voice unsteady.

"God, I've missed you, too," Lucas replied, kissing my cheek and pulling back.

We studied each other for long seconds, and then his face split into that cheesy, boyish grin that made my heart flutter. Smiling in return, I leaned into him again, pressing a kiss to his neck. For that moment in time, everything else in our lives fell away, leaving just the two of us and the way I felt right then: blissfully content and filled with love.

Just then, the baby started moving, the same as every night, though I was usually already asleep and the movement woke me up. I reached behind me to turn on a light and situate a pillow at the end of the sofa and laid back. Lucas' face scrunched in confusion.

"Watch," I breathed out as I lifted my sweater, tucking it under my breasts, and then rolled down the high waist of the maternity leggings to expose my belly. "Just... watch." About 15 seconds later, it happened. A knee or foot or elbow plowed into my abdomen, causing a quick distortion in my belly, followed by several more.

"What the hell was that?" Lucas asked, his head drawing back in surprise.

I laughed at the consternation in his voice. "She's kicking the crap out of me right now. Or elbowing me or something. If you put your hands on my belly, you'll be able to feel her, too."

I moved my own hands that had been on the sides of my belly up to my shoulders, out of the way. Lucas scooted closer, resting his hands gently along the sides of my belly where mine had been, watching intently. There was a sharp kick to my left side and then Lucas jumped a little.

"Oh my god, Annie," he said, his eyes wide.

"I know—at this rate, she'll put a hole in my side by the time she's born," I laughed.

My eyes fluttered closed, and I willed the baby to keep moving for Lucas, which she was more than happy to do for the next twenty minutes or so. When there'd been no movement for several minutes, Lucas sat up straight again, his eyes still on my belly with an expression of wonder. As I sat back up, though, the baby put pressure on my bladder. After I used the bathroom, Lucas stood from the sofa as I walked into the living room, stepping closer when I stopped. He reached a hand up and gently lifted a curl from my cheek, tucking it behind my ear, his fingertips whispering along my jawline before his hand fell to his side. My entire body broke out in goosebumps, and I shivered.

"It's really late," he said. "As much as I don't want to, I should probably go. You're exhausted. I'm exhausted. And I've heard I'm a bit of a jerk when I get too tired." His lips quirked up on one side at his self-deprecating remark.

I nodded, though I was disappointed. I didn't want him to leave, but I couldn't ask him to stay, either; Haley was already sharing a bed with me since Carol and Linc were taking the spare bedroom. And I wouldn't be comfortable asking him anyway without talking to Mom first since it was her house.

"I'm sorry for everything," he said soberly.

"Me, too," I replied.

"I don't go back to Clarksburg until Sunday. Can I see you tomorrow?"

I nodded. "I'd like that. But in the afternoon, after Haley, Carol, and Linc leave."

He leaned forward and pressed a lingering kiss to my forehead, one arm wrapping around my lower back and holding me against him. My body melted into his and I wanted to stay there forever, feeling the wonderful, delicious electricity that existed between us and surrounded by his smell and steady heartbeat that simply felt like coming home.

He pulled back, his hands finding mine and lacing our fingers together. Then he lifted my hands, one at a time, and pressed a kiss to the backs of them. My sweater and leggings were now too hot, my breath too loud, and I wanted to beg him to keep kissing me like that. I wanted to ask him to take me home with him. But I hadn't gathered up enough courage before he spoke.

"Good night, sweetheart."

I swallowed, trying to calm the blood rushing through my body. "Good night, Lucas."

As soon as I saw him pull out of my mom's driveway from the sidelight, I turned and leaned back against the door, my body sagging into the wood. The night played on repeat through my mind, a rush of images and feelings as I tried to sort everything out. But my heart didn't care right then whether or not we'd discussed anything we really needed to.

I tried to stop grinning like an idiot as I supported myself against the front door alone in the dark, but I couldn't. My stomach fluttered and clenched, and my chest felt like it was lifting me into the air. He hadn't said the words, but I was pretty sure he still loved me. Which meant we had a future, because *I* sure as hell loved *him*.

chapter thirty-five

lucas

Before **I had** a chance to see Annie the day after Thanksgiving, another emergency had pulled me back to Clarksburg. My heart sank when I had to send the message to tell her. I knew it looked like I was just disappearing on her—she'd even told me it was fine if I couldn't make it after I asked when her appointments were so I could take her. And we hadn't actually resolved anything the night before. All we'd really established was that we missed each other, but that wasn't enough for a relationship. And damned if I didn't want a relationship with her.

How the hell I was going to make it work, I hadn't figured out yet, but I had to. I needed to show her that she could depend on me to be there when she needed—or even just wanted—me there with her. Make sure she knew how much I loved her.

As I drove to Clarksburg, I wracked my brain to find a solution to the problem I had with the brewery taking me away from Annie since I couldn't financially survive if I just walked away from the expansion at this point. Suddenly, I remembered something Nick had said when we were going over the contract terms to make him a partner and called him.

"Hey, Nick," I greeted. "Couple of things."

"Sure, man, what's up?"

"I remember a while back you mentioned there was a guy you were in college with, a business guy, you thought I should talk to first if I ever considered a third partner."

"Yeah, Scotty. You wanna to talk to him?"

I sighed. I'd never wanted to share my business with anyone—it had been my dream and I'd built it from the ground up. But my aversion to sharing it with yet another partner paled in comparison to the thought of a future without Annie in it. "Yeah. I am."

"Great—I'm sending his contact info over now. He'd be a good fit. You won't regret this."

I nodded to myself. "Unless the brewery goes under as a result, I think you're probably right," I said, my thoughts lingering on Annie. "I should have done this sooner," I muttered.

After ending the call with Nick, I called and left a message for Scotty. With any luck, he'd be as good a fit as Nick thought he would and soon I'd be able to show Annie that she was my priority.

***

Early Tuesday morning found me knocking on Annie's front door, a bouquet of wildflowers and lily of the valley shaking in my hands; the florist had said the lilies would represent regret and apology. Hopefully she and her mom were already up—I wanted to take Annie to breakfast before her first appointment.

I'd met with Scotty the day before and it had gone better than I'd hoped—Nick had been right that he'd be a perfect partner for us. The paperwork was being drawn up and would be sent to Scotty as soon as possible. Though he wouldn't be officially coming on until the first of the year, after the holidays, just having the paperwork signed would be a relief. Once that happened, I'd tell Annie. But not before, just in case something happened and Scotty changed his mind before signing.

"Hi, Lucas," Miriam said as she answered the door, interrupting my thoughts. She cocked her head at me questioningly.

"Hi, Miriam. I'm taking Annie to her appointments today."

"Oh, she didn't mention that you were coming. You can come on in, though. She was up a little bit ago but was going to lie back down—her nightmares have been keeping her up. But that wasn't very long ago. I doubt she's asleep."

"Nightmares?" I asked, following Miriam in. I'd had no idea they were back.

"Don't say anything because she wouldn't want me talking about it. But I hear her—she has them about every night."

My heart sank as I followed Miriam toward Annie's room. She knocked gently on the door.

"Come in," Annie said, her voice weary.

"Hey, honey. Lucas is here," she said, pulling the door open.

"He is?" she asked as I came into view.

"I am." I smiled.

Her lifted head dropped back onto her pillow as she looked at me. "You're here," she breathed out in surprise as Miriam headed toward the kitchen.

"I said I would be," I replied, my perpetual exhaustion making my irritation immediate.

"I didn't know," she said softly as she looked into my eyes. "I've barely heard anything from you, so I wasn't sure..."

"I know," I said, shame sweeping over me. She was right of course—what right did I have to be irritated with her? I walked to her bedside and studied her face, noting the dark circles confirming what Miriam had said. "I'm sorry. But I'm here. I wanted to take you out for breakfast before your appointments, but you look like you could use rest instead."

Reaching out for my hand, she tucked it under her cheek and closed her eyes, letting out a sigh. "I'm glad you came. And breakfast sounds nice."

We ended up at a diner near her appointments for breakfast and she told me about her calm, routine days, punctuated by work, therapy, mood swings, hunger, and the baby moving. I wished she'd stop working but knew that bringing it up would only guarantee an argument between us, so I bit my tongue and just enjoyed being in her company and listening to her voice.

"Okay, I've been selfish enough," she said after a while. "Tell me about you. I'm guessing from your unresponsiveness that it's been hell?" she asked, her voice full of sympathy.

I launched into all the issues we'd been encountering as well as why they kept cropping up.

"So, Stella is the construction manager?" Annie asked.

"That's right, and a damn good one, too."

"Good for her! I admire women who break through gender stereotypes and boundaries. I'd love to meet her one day."

"Sure," I replied, my thoughts straying back to the issues we'd been having at the site.

Annie reached across the table and grabbed my hand, dispelling my wayward thoughts. "Are you okay?"

I wove our fingers together, lifting her hand to press a kiss to it. A beautiful pink crept up Annie's neck to her cheeks and a grin stretched across my face. "No, I'm not okay," I replied. "I'm sitting here with you. I'm great."

chapter thirty-six

annie

I knew in my heart that I was having a girl, but now it was time to have it confirmed, and I was happy Lucas was there for the moment. He squeezed my hand and his knee bounced, his boyish grin wide and eyes bright. His excitement and enthusiasm were infectious, too—I couldn't stop grinning back at him. As usual, the ultrasound technician started with taking various measurements before taking shots that she could print out for me to take home. Each time she moved the wand, I thought she might be about to tell us the sex of the baby, but then she would take another measurement or another picture.

"Okay," she said at last. "Are you sure you want to know the sex?"

"Yes, definitely," I replied a little impatiently.

"Okay, you see here?" She pointed to a spot on the image that she had just frozen on the screen. "That means you're having a little girl."

My heart flipped in my chest. Tears slid down my temples, and a glance at Lucas revealed he felt the same.

"Time to think about names," he said when the ultrasound tech left, and we were waiting for the doctor.

"Oh, you think you get a say?" I teased.

His face fell, the warmth and joy from a second before gone. Releasing my hand, he stood, clearing his throat and avoiding eye contact with me. "I'll wait for you outside." And then he was disappearing through the doorway.

What just happened? In a split second, he'd gone from happy to... angry? Sad? Something. And then he'd walked out before I could even ask him what was wrong.

"What was that?" I demanded in the parking lot a while later. "Why did you leave?"

His eyes flicked up to mine, red as if he'd been crying, then looked away again.

"What happened?" I asked, sniffling. "You were happy and then... you weren't, and you left. Was it because I teased you about not having a say in naming the baby?"

He shifted to hold my gaze, searching my eyes, and my chest constricted at the thought of having hurt him.

After a deep sigh that pulled down his features, he replied, "I *don't* have a say, Annie. Because she's not mine."

———

After a quiet, tense lunch at an Italian restaurant next door, we were in the car and heading back to Stockwood. As we neared our entrance to the interstate, I asked if we could talk about us.

"Not like this," he replied distractedly as he merged onto the busy highway. "That conversation deserves both of our full attention, and I can't do that right now with all this traffic. Let's talk at my place when we get back into town. Why don't you rest while we're on the road?"

"Okay," I replied, my eyes closing.

I was perpetually tired and could always go for a nap. Within a few minutes, the gentle vibration from the car had lulled me to sleep. Ringing from Lucas' phone jolted me awake sometime later. Disoriented, I blinked, trying to clear the sleepy haze clinging to me and determine where we were.

"Shit," he muttered, frantically grabbing at his phone. "Hello?" he said in a tight, muted tone.

"No, I can't," he said, his voice hardening. There was a long pause as he listened, then he said, "I understand, but I can't be there before tomorrow morning." He swallowed slowly as the person on the other end continued to speak for several minutes, only muttering "damn it" under his breath a few times. When he finally spoke into the phone again, his voice was deflated. "I'll be there in a few hours."

My eyes gazed unseeing out the passenger window. Part of me wanted to tell him it was okay, to soothe the despondency emanating from him—seeing him hurting made my chest ache. The problem, however, was that it *wasn't* okay. It wasn't his fault, but that didn't change that he would have to leave again without us having figured anything out. And it was easy to predict what would happen next: he'd be gone all the time, barely even texting me. In a month, I'd agonize over whether or not he'd actually show up for my appointments, and if he did, he'd be gone in the blink of an eye—again. I'd always known the brewery was his life, but I'd never expected to be in a position where he'd have to choose... or that he wouldn't choose me.

chapter thirty-seven

annie

Officially **in the** third trimester, pregnancy was becoming ever more difficult. My exhaustion worsened by the day—even walking from one room to the next left me out of breath—my back hurt more often than not, my belly itched nonstop, I was starting to retain water, and it seemed I never stopped peeing. But that wasn't even all of it—Nick had cut back my hours at the brewery, so I had more time than ever to wallow in my discomfort.

"Would you like to watch *House Hunters* with me, honey?" Mom asked, just like she did every single day. And it wasn't that I didn't like *House Hunters*. I was just sick of watching it. All my mind would do is think about which parts of the houses and towns Lucas or Rob would like, which led me to thinking about my situation, which meant—thanks to my hormones—I ended up crying. The only reason I hadn't completely lost my mind at that point was because of my appointments with Selena. Though I didn't seem to be making progress anymore, which Selena said was—again—hormones. Fucking hormones. Since they seemed to be the cause of so many other issues, I'd decided to also blame them for the anxious, restless feeling that permeated my being, though who knew if they were really at fault.

"No, thanks, Mom. Would you mind taking me to the brewery before the show starts, actually?" I was weeks past being able to fit behind a steering wheel and drive myself anywhere.

"Sure, but I thought you weren't working today, honey."

"I'm not. I just want to go in for a change of scenery."

"Are you sure it won't tire you out too much?"

I shook my head. "I'll be fine, I just need to get out for a bit."

Mom drove me down to the brewery, dropping me off shortly after Nick would have arrived for the day, but before the doors were opened to the public.

"Hey, Nick," I greeted, walking into the office.

"Hey there, Anniebannie," Nick replied with a smile.

I laughed. "Anniebannie?"

"Sure! I hung out with my niece all morning and we made up nicknames for people and that's what we came up with for you."

"That's so sweet, Nick!" I said, grinning even though my hormones were making me tear up.

"It's not me, it's Jayden. She's the most amazing little girl. I wish I got to see her more often, but they don't live close enough for more than a few visits a year."

"I'm sorry to hear that, really."

A hint of sadness touched his smile. "Just how it is. But how are you doing? How're you feeling? And why the hell are you in here again today?"

"I'm... okay, I guess. I don't know. I'm restless. And the thought of watching another episode of *House Hunters* made me want to beat my head against a wall."

Nick and I both laughed as I sat down on the loveseat across from him, yawning.

"Why don't you lay down if you're tired? I'll keep the door shut once we're open so it's quiet and no one disturbs you. Sound good?"

Instead of responding, I nodded and stretched out on my side, tucking my purse and jacket around me to take the pressure off my hips and back. Sleep eluded me, however. I couldn't stop thinking about Lucas. After Nick had been clacking away at the keyboard for a while, I decided to ask him how the expansion was going.

Nick's fingers stilled as he gazed at me, his expression soft and sympathetic. "He's barely had time to sleep, he really has been busy. You know he'd be here if he could, right?"

"I asked about the expansion, not Lucas."

"Sure," he replied, raising an eyebrow. "Though that reminds me I've got some good news, there are four interviews lined up for next week after Christmas for your replacement."

His cheery voice seemed to mock me—that was not welcome news. The brewery was all I had anymore. My friends were all hours away, not to mention really busy—hell, they were also all traveling for Christmas and New Year's this year, so I wouldn't even get to see them for at least another month or two—even Haley, for the first time since we'd met. My sister... she was Lori. Lucas was in Clarksburg. So that meant all I had was Nick—who I'd gotten closer to and considered a friend—and the brewery. And once he hired someone to replace me, I wouldn't even have them.

"Earth to Annie," Nick teased.

I'd been staring at a spot on the floor while I was brooding and jerked my head up. "Sorry—what were you saying?"

"I was asking you if you would help me do the interviews. I could really use your input on the competence of the hires, especially for your replacement." He cocked his head to the side, his expression shifting to one of concern. "What's going on, Annie? We're friends, right? You can talk to me."

Right on cue, my hormones had me crying again. I shook my head, unable to fully articulate how I felt and why. Getting up and walking over to the loveseat, Nick sat down on the floor in front of me and extended his arm for me to cry on his shoulder.

"I don't want to be replaced," I whispered through my tears.

"You know you'll always have your job here if you want it back, right?" Nick responded, his voice quiet and soothing. "We can hire someone on a temp basis. And if you decide not to come back, we can offer them a permanent position. Don't worry about having your job when you're ready for it."

"It's just... the brewery is all I have left."

"That's not true, Annie."

"Yes, it is. My friends are nowhere near here, my sister is never around, and Lucas..." I swallowed, unable to finish that sentence. "You, the brewery, and my mom, that's all I have. Once you have my replacement... it's just my mom and me. And then this baby in a few months."

"You can come in here every day if you want, even once we have a replacement, Annie. You're always welcome here. And just because I hire someone doesn't mean you and I aren't friends anymore."

"I know, but we've never done something outside of the brewery. We're work friends—not outside-of-work friends." I felt so dumb and childish as soon as the words were out of my mouth, but it was too late. My face leapt into flames.

"Well, let's hang out, then."

I snorted. "You don't really want to hang out with a pregnant woman."

"Well, you're right, 'a pregnant woman,' no. But you? Sure. Tell you what. I have to go up to Caperton to finish my Christmas shopping—why don't you come with me? I'd love to have your company."

"Okay," I sniffled. "I'd like that. I have a bunch of stuff I need, and I hate shopping with my mom. When are you going?"

"I was thinking tomorrow, since it's the slowest day for the brewery and it'll be the first day I leave Chase alone here." Chase was the new manager that Nick had hired a few weeks before so that he could take off a day every now and then. He hadn't had one since Lucas had disappeared to Clarksburg.

"Okay." I gave him a weak smile, though my mood was already improving. "Thank you."

chapter thirty-eight

lucas

My phone buzzed in my pocket while I was talking to Stella about the work schedule for her crew over the next couple of weeks. I'd been pushing hard for us to get ahead of schedule so I could take a long break for Christmas. That meant, unfortunately, that workdays had become even longer. However, we'd finally wrapped up with a plan that would get us all an extended break for the holiday, though it meant working nonstop until then... including right through Annie's appointments that Friday. A call to talk to her would be more appropriate than sending a text, but I couldn't bring myself to do it, a mixture of guilt over what I had to tell her and trying to avoid being a jerk to her; I was exhausted and well aware that meant I had a short fuse.

Like every time I texted her nowadays, her responses were short. And then after typing that I couldn't make it back for her appointments, she'd only responded with 'okay' as if the news didn't matter to her at all. I waited for her to say something else—anything else—to indicate she cared, but she never did.

 Back in the hotel room late that night, I was looking at my calendar and suddenly realized that Charlie would be out of prison the next day. After a moment of panic as I remembered that I didn't have any information from Joel yet, I called Nick.

"Hey man. I need to talk to you about something. The asshole who assaulted Annie last year is getting released from prison tomorrow."

"I know. Charlie, Rob's brother. The rapist," Nick said.

"She told you about that?" I asked, incredulous.

"Yeah," he replied. "We see a lot of each other around here," he laughed. "We talk."

A twinge of jealousy ran through me that Nick was able to spend time with her when I desperately wanted to and couldn't. I ignored it and continued, telling him about the letters I'd found from Charlie and about having Joel do some investigation. I also shared my worry for Annie's safety in the meantime and Nick agreed to keep a close eye on her, but insisted I tell her everything.

"I will. I meant to at least tell her about the letters sooner, but everything has been a clusterfuck since we started work on the new site and I've barely had a conversation with her about *anything*. And now... it's been so long. She's gonna be pissed."

"She might, but you have to tell her anyway." He paused for the span of a breath. "You're really fucking up with her."

My heart constricted. "I know she's upset that I'm missing her appointments," I said.

"She expected you to bail, man." Nick said.

I sighed. "How is she?"

"Not bad, but not great. She's lonely and scared. And uncomfortable. She's got that same swollen look my sister had."

"Didn't you say your sister had complications?"

"Yeah, she got... preeclampsia, I think it was called, and went into labor really early. Jayden was like two months premature, and Jessica nearly died."

I suddenly had a vision of Annie in the hospital, her and the baby not surviving because she hadn't gotten there soon enough. Annie and I had learned about preeclampsia together at the last appointment I'd been to with her, how it could progress to eclampsia quickly and undetected, how that could be fatal for both her and the baby.

"You there, Lucas?"

Nick's voice startled me out of my vision. Clearing my throat, I swiped off the moisture on my face. "Yeah. Hang on a minute."

Muting the phone, I stepped into the bathroom and blew my nose. Imagining losing Annie and the baby made me realize how misaligned my actions had been in relation to my priorities. I didn't want to lose the brewery… but I *couldn't* lose Annie. Yet, I'd been acting for so long as if that was reversed. Hopefully it wasn't too late to set things right.

"How's the new manager working out?" I asked, changing gears.

"Chase is great. Doing better than I expected. I know it hasn't been long since he started, but I'm letting him fly solo tomorrow and we'll see how things go."

"That's soon."

"I know, but he can handle it, trust me."

"Good. I know you need a day off. Going to see your sister?"

"No, she just left this morning, actually. They were visiting over the weekend. I'm going to finish up my Christmas shopping in Caperton." He cleared his throat. "With Annie."

"You're taking Annie to Caperton?"

"More or less. I need to go anyway, and I invited Annie to come along. She needs to go by the maternity shops there, so it works out. We're friends, Lucas."

"I know," I replied, taking and releasing a deep breath. "I was just thinking I'd come see her tomorrow after meeting with Scotty to get the paperwork signed."

"Why don't you meet us in Caperton?" Nick suggested. "You guys should be done by lunchtime. I'll let Annie know in the morning that you're coming to meet us for lunch."

I nodded as I thought through what he was saying. "That should work." I sighed. "I'm exhausted. I'm going to bed. I'll let you know once everything is wrapped up with Scotty in the morning."

I glanced at my watch as I spoke and saw that I had about four hours before I needed to be up again. Hopefully it was a good four hours of sleep.

———

"Hey Stella. How're things looking for today?" I asked as I approached the next morning.

"Morning, Lucas," she called back. "Not bad, knock on wood. It looks like the wiring issue in the lower level might not be as extensive as we'd thought."

"Finally catching a break!" I exclaimed, relief buoying my mood.

She flashed me a bright smile and laughed. "Yeah, finally. Maybe we can grab lunch or dinner together at an actual restaurant to celebrate."

"Actually, I need to leave in a little over an hour, and I won't be back until tomorrow. I have a meeting in Sperryville and then some personal business in Caperton after."

She used the back of her wrist to clear some sweat from her forehead and put her hands on her waist. "Okay."

"I'll have my phone if you need to reach me, but I'll be out until tomorrow even if there's an emergency."

She nodded, studying me with her brow slightly furrowed. "Everything alright?"

Everything *wasn't* alright—not really. But I was hoping to fix that. I never talked about my personal life with Stella but decided to share when I saw the genuine concern in her eyes. "Not really. This project is costing me an important relationship and I need to fix it. That's what I'm hoping to do today."

Stella's eyes clouded and she looked down at her left hand for a moment. She had no ring on that hand, but I noticed right then for the first time the tan line there where one used to be.

"Do what you need, Lucas," she said after a moment, her mouth in a straight line. She suddenly looked tired and a bit sad. "And tell me what you need from me—I'll do what I can to help."

chapter thirty-nine

lucas

The meeting with Scotty and the lawyers had taken longer than expected, and I was late for meeting up with Nick and Annie for lunch. After arriving in Caperton, I texted to find out which store they were in and jogged there from the car. Every second felt like hours; I could finally show Annie what I was doing to put her first and I wasn't off to a good start running late for lunch.

"Annie, wasn't it?" I said softly as I walked up to her in the maternity store Nick had texted they were at.

Though I'd been approaching from the side, she hadn't seen me and startled so severely she started to lose her balance until I reached out and caught her.

"Lucas!" she called out breathily, surprised. There was a flash of excitement in her eyes before her expression became neutral. "You're late. Really late."

"I know, and I'm sorry." I replied. "My meeting ran over. I got here as quickly as I could."

"That's nice of you, Lucas, but I'm sure you have work to get back to. I don't want to use up time you don't have. It was good to see you, but you really don't have to stay. You should get back to the brewery."

Thanks to the article she'd sent me, I knew that she was trying to protect herself from getting hurt again by pushing me away before I left. Dad's words about loving her the best I could paraded through my mind. I'd been failing at that, but I was determined to repair the damage I'd done and do a better job from then on. As she turned away from me, I reached out and gently stopped her, stepping around so we were facing each other again.

"Please. Just spend a few hours with me? I just wanna talk—there's a lot I need to say to you."

Her eyes rounded with tears. "What's the point? I'll see you for a few hours, and then you'll disappear for another month," she said, her voice cracking as her tears broke free. "I can't do this anymore."

She used her palms to swipe at her cheeks, rushing away from me and toward Nick. Rooted where I stood, I watched them walk out of the store, my heart ripped out of my chest and dragging along with them. But what else could I do if she wouldn't talk to me?

I can love her by not giving up so damn easily—that's what I can do.

"Wait, Annie, please!" I called as I caught up to them on the sidewalk. "Please just talk to me, that's all I'm asking."

She stopped walking and turned to me, still crying, every tear accusing me of failing her.

"Please." My eyes searched hers, imploring. Everything in me was waiting for her to respond; I wasn't breathing, my heart wasn't even beating. It couldn't be too late—it *couldn't*. She finally gave an almost imperceptible nod of her head and my breath rushed out of my lungs. "Thank you," I whispered, dizzy with relief as I cradled her face and touched our foreheads and noses together for a moment.

"I think I'll just catch up with you guys later," Nick said. "I have some more shopping to do, and I'll get some food after. Annie, do you want me to grab anything else for you?"

She sniffled as she stepped back and wiped at her eyes again. "Um," she swallowed, "No, I don't think so."

"Okay. I can put your bags in the car if you want."

"I can take her bags," I said. "I'll bring her home. Well, if that's okay with you?" I asked Annie.

"Yeah," she murmured. "Okay."

———

It was bitterly cold outside, but we were in a local restaurant, tucked cozily into a corner near a fireplace, providing both warmth and privacy. It was romantic, even. Though, now that the time had come for Annie and me to have a conversation about our relationship, I was nervous as hell, especially since I'd been screwing up so badly. She had no reason to believe anything would be different, that I'd be around more than I had been, but I needed her to trust me anyway.

Annie had barely spoken since we'd parted ways with Nick, watching me warily and silently. But she was letting me hold her hands across the table now, her expression less guarded as she waited for me to speak.

"I've been wanting to tell you something for a while now," I started. "Weeks ago, I met with someone to bring on as another partner. I didn't want to tell you until it was finalized, and it is as of this morning. Meeting with him and the lawyers to get the paperwork signed this morning is why I was late."

"Really?" she asked, her eyes widening. "You never wanted partners at all. It was a difficult decision for you to bring Nick on. Do you even know this guy?"

"No. I just met him a few weeks ago, but Nick has known him since college."

"Why are you doing this?"

With a slow, deep breath, I searched her eyes for a moment before answering. "For you. For us. I don't care about anything— not the brewery or anything else—if I don't have you in my life."

"Lucas—how can you say that? You've worked so hard for the brewery. It's your dream!"

"It *was* my dream—but you are my reality, sweetheart. I know I've been doing a crappy job of showing you that, but I'm asking you—begging you—to give me one more chance to show you how much you mean to me, how important you are in my life. Another chance to be there for you—the way you need. Another chance to love you."

Her hands slid out of my mine and covered her face as she sobbed. I jumped up and around the table to sit next to her, pulling her into my arms. We sat like that with me holding her even after she'd stopped crying—all the way until our food arrived. And then she held my hand as we ate, but she looked miserable and still hadn't said anything. While waiting for our bill, I decided to break the silence—it was killing me.

"You haven't said anything."

"I... I don't know what to say, Lucas," she replied, quiet, staring down at the tabletop. "I'm so confused and conflicted."

I nodded, my breathing stilted. "Just give me a chance to show you?"

"I don't know..."

"One more chance is all I'll need. Tell me what to do and I'll do it, I swear, just give me a chance to show you that you are my number one priority. You don't owe it to me, and I definitely don't deserve it, but I'm hoping you'll give it to me anyway."

She studied me for a while before her expression softened and she spoke. "Okay."

The waitress appeared right that second with our bill. Huffing out a frustrated breath, I quickly handed over my card and turned my attention back to Annie.

"Come back with me?" I rushed out, realizing I wasn't ready to take her home and be away from her again. "Come back, see the new site, spend some time with me. You can stay for a few days, and I'll take you home after your appointments on Friday and spend Christmas in Stockwood with you."

"You already said you couldn't make it to the appointments," she murmured, looking away.

"I know... but I'm doing it anyway. Being there with you is more important to me."

"I won't cost you the brewery, Lucas—I would never be able to live with myself."

"You won't, I promise," I rushed out, still trying to figure out how I was going to manage it. "I'll figure something out. Just... will you come back with me?"

My breath was stuck in my lungs as she held my gaze for a moment. Then something sparked to life in her eyes and the corners of her mouth lifted almost imperceptibly. With a small nod, she spoke.

"Okay—yes."

chapter forty

annie

On the drive toward Clarksburg, I gazed out the window, the scenery passing in a blur as I tried to sort my thoughts into some semblance of order. I'd said yes to spending at least the next few hours with Lucas, but was that the right thing to have done? What if things weren't different this time and he disappeared on me like every time before—could I handle going through that again?

And what if things *were* different—would he lose the brewery because of me? Even if he didn't, was I ready for that kind of relationship with him? I was still married to Rob, though that was just a technicality, I reminded myself. What if I jumped in with both feet with Lucas, but then he left me one day, just like Rob had? I couldn't say he wouldn't. I'd said that about Rob and had been so very wrong. And being abandoned like that again wasn't something I could come back from, I was sure of it. I wanted Lucas in my life—I wanted all of him—but did he feel the same way about me? And could I trust that he would stay?

And what about my baby? Was Lucas ready to take on both of us? Did he really even *want* to? And in what capacity? No matter how much I cared about Lucas, I needed to make sure my decision would also be the best one for my daughter.

"You live here?" I asked in disbelief as we parked and headed inside. "In a hotel?"

"Well, for now," Lucas replied. "I've been meaning to find a rental house, but I haven't had the time."

"I can look around online for you if you want, just tell me what your must-haves are."

Lucas' lips twitched like he was trying to hold back a smile, and my face leapt into flames as his arm slid around my waist, pulling me into his side and pressing a kiss to my temple. Despite the distance over the last month, it all felt so natural being there with him. With my eyes closed for a moment, the feeling of calm and normalcy spread, loosening some of the tension in my body.

As the elevator doors slid shut, I was suddenly nervous and could feel my heartbeat in my throat. When I glanced up at Lucas, my eyes got lost in his; he was watching me intently and that electric pull between us was there. He leaned down and touched his forehead to mine. It felt like I could taste his want for me in his breath washing over my face, and my own breath caught as an answering want for him engulfed me.

"Lucas," I breathed, not sure if I was going to tell him yes to everything or that we needed to talk first. My mind was at war with my heart and my body.

The elevator dinged as it came to a stop and the doors slid open. Even though the person standing in the hall waiting for it was looking the other direction, my face reddened as Lucas let out a rush of air.

"So," he said, as we started down the hall. "I do have a kitchenette in here with a hot plate, but no stove or oven, which makes cooking nearly impossible. We'll have to go out or get takeout for our meals."

"I don't mind. I know you like to go out anyway."

"I've eaten out enough for a lifetime these last few months," Lucas said. "Besides, I'd much rather stay in where I can keep you to myself." He winked and flashed me his cheesy grin.

My stomach flopped and I blushed again. "If we're going to see the site today," I started, ignoring his comment, "can we go before it gets dark? And I need to find something to sleep in if I'm going to stay—I didn't think about it while we were still in Caperton, unfortunately. I bought clothes, but not any pajamas."

His eyes warmed and suddenly looked hopeful, and his grin morphed into something less playful and more joyful. "So you're staying?"

"I think so. For tonight, at least," I said, looking away. "But I need something to sleep in."

"I've got you covered. I've got plenty of clean shirts."

"Um, I doubt they'll fit me over this giant belly," I said.

Lucas laughed. "They'll fit, trust me."

My eyebrow lifted as my hand pointed to my belly, the skin on my face surely beet red. "You're looking at this belly, right? And I've put on some padding all over, so I'm quite a bit larger than I used to be." It wasn't until the words were out that I realized how insecure I was about my body right then. I'd never been comfortable with how I looked, and pregnancy hadn't helped, even if I'd had a few fleeting moments, like after I'd gone shopping with Haley during my first trimester.

"You'll see," Lucas assured me. "And you've never been more beautiful, sweetheart."

After dropping off my stuff, we headed straight over to the new site, though the way Lucas was looking at me made me kind of want to stay in. But I kept those thoughts to myself. Once parked, Lucas kept an arm around me as we picked our way over the uneven ground until we reached the building entrance.

"Wait here—don't walk around until I get back. We need hard hats inside. I'll run and grab some from the trailer real quick."

"I can go with you," I offered, nervous about standing there alone for however long it would take him to return.

"No. You could fall or step on something sharp. Just wait here and I'll be right back."

With a quick kiss to my cheek, he was off. The building in front of me was a very large, very old church in the Clarksburg historic district. I knew from talking to Nick that the ample grounds around it would be converted to outdoor seating areas connected by walkways and lush gardens, complete with a bar and stage area for performances. Lucas had left me standing in a large entry vestibule at the front of the building. The walls were comprised of wood panels that had been carved into scenes depicting people and animals and nature. Hopefully, they'd preserve those panels and incorporate them into the brewery somehow. They were beautiful. Rob would have loved to see them, I thought with a sharp pang. The air seemed to thicken and the walls felt like they were shrinking down around me. I needed to get out of that vestibule.

Lucas had asked me not to walk around, so I wouldn't, but I did step through the next door into the main room of the church. Whether from the temperature inside the building or the anxiety thoughts of Rob had generated, I was now hot and shrugged off my coat, draping it over my arm as my eyes scanned the cavernous room that hummed with the sounds of power tools and hammering in the distance. Most of the pews had been removed, though a few remained, covered in dust, debris and tools. The walls were dominated by breathtaking floor-to-ceiling stained glass windows that I studied one by one, deciphering the scenes depicted.

"Excuse me," a woman's curt voice said, startling me as it echoed into the space. "This is an active construction site. You can't be here."

The woman moving quickly in my direction with a hard hat on her head had sharp blue eyes and blond hair pulled back into a ponytail. She wore jeans, work boots, and a gray t-shirt emblazoned with a company logo I couldn't quite make out, none of which detracted at all from how attractive she was; in fact, it seemed to enhance her beauty. It took only a split second for me to take all of this in and immediately feel inferior next to this confident, beautiful woman. Understanding who she was, however, I swallowed my apprehension and stretched out a hand, summoning the excitement I once had about meeting her.

"Hi. You must be Stella. It's so nice to meet you."

Her eyes narrowed at me, and her arms folded across her chest as she came to a stop in front of me. "Who the hell are you?"

"I'm sorry," I said, my face suddenly on fire. "I'm Annie."

She shook her head as she stared at me blankly, her mouth pulled into a slight frown. "I don't know an Annie. You need to leave. You're trespassing."

"Um, sorry for the confusion," I mumbled, trying to figure out why Lucas would have told me about Stella, but wouldn't have mentioned *me* to *her*. "I... I'm here with Lucas, he just ran over to grab us some hard hats."

She stared at me, her brows drawn in and my hand—which I'd still been holding out in her direction—drifted back to my side.

Just then, Lucas burst through the door. "Sweetheart," he rushed out breathlessly. "There you are." His eyes left me and landed on Stella. His arm snaked around my waist and pulled me into his side. "Annie, this is Stella, the construction manager," he said, nodding his head toward the woman. "And Stella, this is Annie." He turned back to me, a grin spreading across his face and saying the next words to me. "The love of my life."

My eyes were stuck on Stella, whose face grew even tighter. Her eyes suddenly looked glassy and she turned away from us. "I thought you were going to be in Caperton all day," she said, not looking at us.

"I was," Lucas replied, planting a kiss on my temple after smoothing some of my hair out of the way. "But I wanted to show Annie the site."

Stella nodded. "I don't think you need me for that, so I'll get back to work now that I know she's with you."

She walked away without turning back around and my mind spun with questions, filling in missing context with dozens of equally wild and unpleasant scenarios as my heart pounded against my chest.

"We should go," I whispered. *I just want to go home and get as far away from what just happened as I can.*

"Why?" he replied, his voice soft and full of concern. "I really want to show you around, and I know you want to see. Come on. Please?"

I looked at him; his eyes were so hopeful and full of love that I gave a nod of assent instead of insisting that he take me home.

"Thank you." He offered a small smile. "Here," he said as he placed the hardhats he'd been holding in his other hand on our heads, laughing. "You look adorable in a hardhat."

When I blushed, he snagged my hand and pressed a kiss to the back of it. Then, with his broad, cheesy grin making me forget why I'd wanted to leave, he began the tour.

chapter forty-one

lucas

Back at the hotel after dinner, Annie hopped into the shower. She had seemed mostly herself once we'd started the tour of the site, but I kept picturing her before that—all the confidence she'd built up since she'd started therapy nowhere to be seen. Something must have happened with Stella, though I couldn't figure out what it might have been. But I wasn't about to let it derail any progress Annie and I were making—we needed to talk about it.

After my own quick shower, I found Annie sitting up in bed, leaning against the headboard in one of my t-shirts. One hand rested on her belly, her knees were propped up on some pillows, and she was reading something on her phone. I became aware after a moment that my eyes were lingering on her bare legs and looked away quickly before she noticed, climbing onto the bed. Her feet and ankles were swollen, and while I couldn't make it completely better, I *could* do something to help. Shifting the pillows away from her legs and lifting her feet into my lap, I began to massage, starting at the bottoms of her feet like the pregnancy books we'd read together a few months earlier had said to do.

"You don't have to do that, Lucas," she said, her face turning pink as she set her phone down. "They're like sausages about to explode from their casings—it's gross."

"They don't look like sausages and there's nothing gross about them. Just relax."

She opened her mouth and I expected her to argue, but she moaned softly instead. "Holy shit, that feels amazing."

Glancing up with a smirk, I lifted my hands. "Magic fingers," I said, wriggling them and winking.

She snorted, laughing as she rolled her eyes and her face softened into a smile, her eyes shining as I grinned at her. There was an ease between us as I continued my massage, and while I didn't want to ruin it by bringing up whatever had happened earlier, I had to.

"So... Stella," I started.

Annie's body tensed. "I don't want to talk about her—it's not my business."

"Why do you think that?"

"I have no claim on you, Lucas," she said, pulling her feet out of my hands to be closer to her body and crossing her arms over her chest, staring blankly in the direction of her knees. "Whatever has or hasn't happened with her is none of my business. Besides, I really don't even wanna know."

"You have every claim on me, Annie—you and *only* you. Nothing has happened with Stella, and I don't want her getting between us. Not now, not ever. So, tell me what's on your mind, ask me whatever you want. But we need to talk about it."

Annie's chest was rising and falling noticeably faster as I waited. Finally, she asked, "Why was she upset that you brought me there?"

I scooted closer and put my hands on her knees. "I don't know why. I can guess, but I don't know for sure."

"What's your guess?"

"I told her today that I was losing a relationship that was really important to me, and noticed her left hand has a tan line where a ring used to be. I think she must be divorced."

She nodded slowly but didn't say anything.

"Annie," I said, reaching up to cup her cheek. "Whatever it is that upset her, it has nothing to do with me."

Annie's fingers began combing the blanket under her. I'd seen her do it enough times that I knew she was searching for lint balls, and that it meant she was anxious and stuck in her mind.

"Look at me, sweetheart." Her eyes darted up for only a brief moment before sliding away again. "Stella is the construction manager for the Clarksburg brewery location—that's all she is to me—all she *has* been to me, all she *will* be to me."

"Then why have you told me about her, but she's never heard of me?" Annie asked.

"We're not friends, Annie, we just work together. I'm not going to talk about my personal life with someone I only have a professional relationship with, and at the end of the day, that's all she and I have."

Annie's eyes were full of moisture when she turned to me, holding my gaze this time. "It's just so hard to believe, you know? She's a bombshell, Lucas! But she's not just gorgeous—she's also smart and successful and confident and ambitious. What man wouldn't be interested in her, especially when the alternative is a chubby, needy, pregnant, emotionally damaged, hormonal—"

"Stop right there," I interrupted before she could spiral any further. "The only true things you said were pregnant and hormonal. And you think *she's* the bombshell? *You're* the gorgeous one, sweetheart. And who cares if she's successful or not? You are, too. You're in no way inferior to her."

Her face contorted in a strange way as she half-laughed, half-cried for a moment. "Well, that would have been pretty close to perfect if you hadn't called me hormonal."

"I certainly didn't want to lie to you," I teased, winking.

She swatted at me but missed because her belly kept her from leaning far enough forward. "Damn it!" she muttered as she laughed. "I can't reach you."

Grasping her shins just above her ankles, I slid her down the bed until she was no longer leaning against the headboard, trying to ignore how the shirt she wore had ridden up, exposing her panties and the bottom of her belly. I shifted on my knees until I was straddling her and within easy reach. "How about now?" I grinned.

"You're such an ass," she muttered.

Eyes crinkling at the corners, Annie laughed, her damp curls spread around her head. As I watched, I was sure it was all a dream—she was too beautiful, the moment too perfect. I could feel my heart expanding with the love I felt for the woman in front of me—so much it hurt. The realization that I'd been missing moments like this because of the decisions I'd made was uncomfortable, but there was no use in dwelling on it—I'd be making better decisions from then on.

Annie's laughter faded and my heart raced as we held each other's gazes. Her chest rose and fell faster, her pupils widening. I wanted her right then in a way I'd never wanted anyone before— even her. It was a wanting that was in my blood, my breath. I didn't just want to make love to her, though—I wanted to merge into her until we were one. My stomach flipped; I loved her in a different way... she was part of me. I'd believed she was the only one for me for a long time, but it was right then that it went from a belief to something I knew as certainly as I knew my own name.

This was it—that different kind of love, the kind my parents had for each other. They'd always told me I would know one day if I'd found it, that any doubt would simply vanish, and they'd been right.

"I love you," I said, emphasizing each word.

The skin on her face and neck flushed deeply and her warm staccato breaths washed over my face when I bent to kiss her. We'd kissed before, but this felt different somehow, like it meant more after my realization, just as my declaration of love had. My heart pounded in my chest as I pressed my lips to hers, my breath hitching. And then our mouths opened, and our tongues began a sensual exploration of one another. My skin pebbled with goosebumps under Annie's hands when she raised them to my waist, then slid them up my back to my shoulders. Everything felt both familiar and new and it was as if some unknown part of me had been awakened.

"Sweetheart," my voice rasped. "Your hands on me..." I shivered.

She swallowed, holding my gaze, then trailed her fingertips—trembling as much as I was—slowly down my chest from my shoulders, grazing my abs. Shifting my weight back to my legs, I gathered the bottom of her shirt in my hands, but her body tensed under me.

"What's wrong?" I asked, pausing.

She glanced away, the rosy tone to her skin shifting instantly to bright red. "It's so bright in here..."

"Okay, sweetheart," I smiled. "I'll turn the lights off, but just know that you're breathtaking."

She gave a short nod of assent, but her body was still tense. I switched off the lights. In the darkness, my other senses were heightened; my pulse seemed thunderously loud, mine and Annie's breathing harsh and disjointed. The tension remained in her body, and I got an idea.

chapter forty-two

annie

"What are you doing?" my voice stuttered out. My whole body was warm and humming with desire, Lucas' fingers having left a trail of fire on my skin when he slowly, gently peeled off my shirt and panties. I'd never felt quite like this before. The closest had been the last time Lucas and I had been naked together before I'd stopped things from going any further. The feelings and desire Lucas ignited in me were so different from anything with Rob that I wondered briefly if it was simply pregnancy hormones that were making everything so intense it was almost too much.

Doubt crept in as I waited, naked, unsure of what Lucas was going to do next. Was I sure about this? Could I really do it? God knew I wanted to in that moment, but would I freak out again? And what would happen after? It had been hard before when he disappeared on me, but I'd also been okay... I wasn't sure I would be if we made love and it happened again.

"Lucas," I started, close to panic, part of me wishing I hadn't asked him to turn the lights off so I could see his face. "What happens after?"

Instead of answering, his hands began massaging the soles of my feet. The sensation was so heavenly I was temporarily distracted from my concerns.

"Well, for starters," he replied several minutes later, his voice deeper than normal and smooth and calming, "I'd like to sleep with you in my arms until the last possible second in the morning. I miss falling asleep and waking up with you." His hands trailed along my skin to my ankles a moment later. "And then I'd like to come back and have lunch with you," he continued. "And after a few more hours of working, we'll have dinner together."

Lucas was now working on my calves, and I was dizzy from the onslaught of physical sensation and powerful emotions.

"After dinner, I'd like to relax with you, doing whatever you choose. Maybe make us each a cup of tea. Definitely more of all this. Every time we kiss, every time we touch, I feel things I only ever feel with you, and I want that all the time."

I'd been watching him in the dim light from the alarm clock as my eyes adjusted but had to close them against the spinning of the room when he reached my thighs. I couldn't think, could barely even follow what he was saying over the sensations in my body.

"In fact, I don't want to waste another day in my life without being able to see you, talk to you, touch you, kiss you." He paused, his hands still on my legs. "Let's roll you onto your side."

With a hand under my back, Lucas pushed to make it easier for me to shift onto my side as far as my belly comfortably allowed me to go. I listened to him adjusting on the bed and my heart raced in anticipation, knowing his warm hands would be on me again soon, touching me in that tender and gentle way so characteristic of him. That soothing way that coaxed every ounce of tension from my body. And then my breath stalled when his hands made contact, smoothing from the base of my tailbone outward toward my hips—it was unclear if the relief to my sore muscles or the arousal his touch stirred up was stronger. Regardless, the combination was nothing short of blissful.

"Then," he said, picking up where he'd left off as his hands worked their way up my back, "once I have a house rented, I'm going to ask you to move in with me."

He reached my shoulders. "I'll be forever happy and content as long as I have you."

He had just finished massaging my arms and I felt like jello—both mind and body—as he helped me roll onto my back again. After straddling himself over my thighs, he started smoothing his hands across my belly before moving to my sides, stopping just short of my chest. Shifting, his mouth hovered above mine—my eyes were still closed, but I could feel his warmth as well as his breath sliding across my cheeks.

"And always lots of this," he whispered, cradling my cheek.

His mouth was soft and hot, the slow way he kissed me as if his lips were seducing mine. As our tongues touched, his hand smoothed from my cheek to my jaw, pressing lightly as our kissing deepened. His mouth left a trail of small kisses from the corner of my mouth toward my ear as I dragged air into my lungs and tried to calm my raging hormones.

As his mouth traveled across my cheek, his hand slid down further over the side of my neck and I stiffened slightly, the haze of want beginning to clear as memories I'd almost forgotten I had tried to surface.

Immediately, Lucas' hand lifted and his kisses paused for one second... two... then he used it to brush some hair from my temples before pressing a kiss there.

"It's me, sweetheart," he murmured, his lips still against my temple, his fingertips whispering over the skin on my arm, similar to the way he often touched me when we talked. He pressed his lips against me again.

I nodded, the threat of the memory already fading; he'd responded so quickly it didn't have time to take root, and the way he was touching me grounded me into the present moment, leaving no doubt who was there with me.

He lips brushed down my cheek, over my chin, then dotted soft, slow kisses down the side of my neck where his hand had traveled only moments earlier. He trailed the fingers of one hand down my side to the crease between my thigh and hip where he began to trace small, agonizingly slow circles. I was completely, utterly lost in the moment, Lucas having shredded into oblivion every hint of doubt I'd had about making love, every threat of a flashback, leaving me feeling drunk with desire that intensified with each passing second.

His fingers continued their small circles, though I could feel them beginning to tremble, while his lips traveled across my clavicles. It suddenly occurred to me that he was worshipping my body and I wanted to do for him what he was doing to me, make him feel the way I felt right then. Raising my arms, my palms and the pads of my fingers skated slowly over the skin of his back and chest, exploring every ridge and dip until his body tensed—even the small circles ceased as his hand shook against my hip—and his breath burst violently against the crook of my neck.

"Annie," he panted out, raising his head to press his forehead into mine and rub our noses together. "I love you. So much."

My breath caught at the words spoken against my lips. "I love you, too, Lucas."

chapter forty-three

lucas

The next morning, I was reluctant to release my hold on Annie so she could get up to use the bathroom; it meant leaving for work sooner than I was ready for. When she returned to the room a few minutes later, I spread my arms for her to come back to bed with me, but she ignored me, walking to the window and pulling the curtains open instead.

"What a beautiful morning," she said, looking through the glass.

"Yeah, it is," I agreed softly, following her gaze toward the sunrise. My thoughts strayed back to the story Dad had told me about him and Mom; maybe this was my first sunrise with Annie after what had appeared to be our last sunset together. Maybe this was the start of many more sunrises—as many as we were alive for. My heart felt steady and erratic simultaneously, and there was a flutter of excitement in my chest as I took in the sight before me—Annie in one of my shirts, silhouetted by a bright, spectacular daybreak.

After a moment, I slid from the bed and walked up behind her, sweeping her hair back off her shoulder and pressing a soft kiss there. She inhaled sharply, leaning back into my chest as my arms encircled her. The sound transported me to the night before, to every moment I heard the same sound come from her. Everything had been so different from the only other time we'd slept together when I had been horny and nervous, not to mention ignorant about what she needed the first time she was having sex after she was raped, and I'd rushed everything. But the night before, we hadn't had sex—we'd made love, a new experience for me. Everything had been so intense, every movement an expression of how we felt about one another. Slowing down, I could read her body—not just her words, but her breathing and her movements—and know when I needed to do something differently, when she needed a reminder of her safety with me. I'd felt this deep desire to merge with her, and merging was what we had done.

"Thinking about last night?" I asked quietly, nuzzling her neck.

"Yes," she breathed, her voice catching.

"Me, too." I smiled against her skin.

Too soon, it would be time for me to get ready and leave for the jobsite, but for a few moments, we could simply enjoy being there with one another. Once the sun had cleared the horizon, Annie leaned back and tipped her head up to look at me. Her face was serious, worry lines in her forehead and her mouth drawn. My heart skipped.

"I'm scared, Lucas. I want the future you described last night, but I'm so damn scared. What if you change your mind? What if you decide that taking us on is too much? Or I do something to make you so angry you leave us?"

"I'm not like that," I replied, trying not to get frustrated. "I wouldn't just leave you, even if you made me mad."

"But how do you know that?" she asked, lifting her head to look out the window again. "That's exactly what—"

"I'm not Rob, damn it," I interrupted as my jaw clenched and my arms dropped from around her. We were back to the comparisons between him and me. I couldn't spend my life knowing that was always under the surface, knowing I was always competing against her history with him. "Is that what you want, Annie?" I asked after a tense moment. She spun slowly to face me as I continued. "It's okay if it is, but for the love of god, tell me now. Am I just a consolation prize since Rob is out of the picture?"

"No," she said, her voice watery. "I swear. I want nothing to do with him ever again." She sniffled, a few tears slipping out as she hesitantly reached out and clasped my hands. "I want to be with *you*, Lucas, not anyone else. I'm just scared because I believe he meant it when he said he'd never leave me, and yet he did."

My hands framed her face and I held her gaze steady. "I'm *nothing* like him. I would never refuse to talk to you and just leave instead. *Never*."

Her eyes faltered, quickly darting back and forth between me and the wall. "And what about the baby?" She stepped back away from my touch, her hands on her belly as she put several feet between us.

The seconds ticked by slowly as I waited for her to continue, my heart pounding. I knew what I wanted, but it wasn't my decision to make.

"As much as I wish it wasn't true," she started, quiet, "she's Rob's. I can't change that, ever." She paused, her chest rising and falling rapidly, her eyes watering as she stared through the floor in the space between us. "I also don't think he'll ever want to be part of her life, though I can't know for sure."

Again, she paused, but this time she looked up at me. The corners of her mouth were turned down and her jaw trembled. My heart skipped at the depth of pain I saw in her eyes. I wanted to hold her and fill her up with love until there was no more space for things that could hurt her. She opened her mouth, then closed it without making a sound. Then she did it again, but this time her tears began to fall, and she buried her face in her hands.

I closed the space between us and folded her into my arms as her body shook. I lowered us to the floor, and we leaned back against the side of the bed, the window in front of us as she cried into my chest and I stroked her hair, my other arm holding her tight. After a while, she sat up, lifting the neck of her shirt to dry her face before looking at me with determination.

"My parents didn't want me," she said. "I always knew that. I felt like a burden from my earliest memories, like I didn't deserve the air I breathed or the space my body took up. I can't—" she stopped abruptly as her voice started to crack, taking and releasing a slow breath. "I won't let my daughter ever feel that way. If someone is in her life, it needs to be because they want to be there.

And if they don't—if they don't *want* to be a part of *her* life—they have no place in mine."

I shifted so we were facing each other cross-legged on the floor with our knees touching and slowly took her hands in mine, resting them between us as my thumbs stroked across the backs. When she finally looked up and held my gaze, I spoke.

"I wanted to be a father, like my dad, when I was little. I wanted to get married to someone who made me as happy as my parents were and have lots of kids. I always wanted a big family. I buried that dream when I shut myself off from relationships after Mom died. But that dream came back when you were staying with me a few months ago. I realized I do still want to be a parent, and that I want to do it with you. I know she's not mine, but I'll love her like she is. It's what I've wanted since I heard that first heartbeat with you."

She nodded and swallowed. "And I'm afraid of being a mom—afraid of being like *my* mom. My biological one. I'm afraid I won't be able to handle the stress and I'll fall apart or shut down and won't be able to even care for *myself*, let alone my daughter. I'm afraid I'm going to need a lot of support, more than is fair. I don't know how to be around babies or children. I... I don't even know how to just be around myself sometimes. I'm already needy without a baby in the picture, and sometimes life just gets to be too much, but what if it's like that all the time and I can't handle it? What if I can't even be enough for my daughter, let alone you? There's so much in my genes, so much in *hers* that most people want nothing to do with. What if she and I become too much of a burden for you?"

I looked deep into her eyes the whole time she was speaking, and I could see the turmoil inside her, the fear and doubt and worry. I could also see her beautiful heart, the love she had inside her to give, all of it. Her *soul*. It was the most vulnerable she'd ever been with me, and it took my breath away that she was giving me that kind of trust. It wasn't a burden; it was a gift.

"Oh, sweetheart," I whispered. "Thank you."

"For what?"

"For not hiding yourself. For telling me everything. It's not a burden—never a burden. And it changes nothing about how I feel about you or the baby. It doesn't matter how much support or help or love or assurance or care you need, it'll never be too much, and I'll always be here for you. Everything I can give is yours. I'll be there through it all, holding your hand or carrying you—whatever you need. As long as we have each other, we can make it through anything life decides to throw our way—now and for the rest of our lives."

"Well," she said, glancing toward the ground, "let's just start with the next few days and see how they go, okay?"

I nodded. "Of course. I understand I need to show you that I mean everything I've said and that you can depend on me—*both* of you."

After standing, I helped Annie to her feet, then wrapped her in my arms. We stood, holding each other for a long time before I pulled back. I used my fingers to lift a few tendrils of hair from her face and wiped away some moisture that remained on her cheeks with my thumbs. Her eyelids lifted and my heart stuttered at the love staring back at me, her eyes clear with it. With her face resting in my palms, I leaned in, pressing a soft kiss to her lips. I wanted so much more in that moment, but I didn't want to push her.

"I'm going to get dressed now," I whispered instead, pressing my forehead to hers and rubbing our noses together for a moment.

As I began to pull away, however, Annie's hands clasped my arms, a gentle pressure urging me to return. Slowly, I obliged, bending over to press my lips to hers. She deepened the kiss, her hands sliding up my arms to rest on my shoulders when my cell phone began to ring. I froze, part of me wanting to answer the call while another part urged me to ignore it.

"Lucas, your phone," Annie breathed out heavily, her eyes closed.

My attention returned to the woman in my arms, and I chose to ignore the phone. Instead, my mouth returned to hers and I lowered us to the bed. As the second ring faded, Annie turned her face to the side and spoke through panted breaths.

"It might be important."

I reached over to the nightstand and saw Stella's name on the screen when I lifted my phone. I flipped it to silent, then tossed it back down. "*This* is important, sweetheart. You and me. More important than whatever that call is about."

Turning, I looked back down at Annie lying under me, her face and neck flushed, her chest moving up and down as she breathed. Her eyes luminous and open, her hair messy and spread over the pillows. Her hands on my arms.

"What is it?" she asked.

I lifted a hand and used my fingertips to smooth the furrow in her brow, then kissed that spot. "You're just so damn beautiful."

chapter forty-four

annie

I was lounging on Lucas' bed in the hotel room, my back and knees propped up with pillows, when Haley's call came in within minutes of the text I'd sent telling her I wanted to talk when she had time.

"Alright, babe, talk to me," Haley said when I answered, my cell on the speakerphone setting and resting on my knees. "I only have about thirty minutes, tops, for lunch today. Is everything okay? Fuck, hold on a sec." I smiled and shook my head, listening to her muffled voice for a moment. "I'm back. What's up?"

"What, I can't talk to my best friend the day before she abandons me for the holidays?" I teased, though it was true—it would be the first time since we'd met that we wouldn't at least see each other over the Christmas and New Year's holidays. And to top it off, she wouldn't even tell me what her plans were, though I had a hunch they had something to do with Jax.

"Yeah, yeah—I'm done feeling guilty, asshole, nice try. Seriously, though—is everything okay with my little niece?"

Her reference to the baby made me feel warm and gooey, and thanks to the hormones, that meant I started crying when I responded that the pregnancy was fine.

"Is there something actually wrong, or are you just being emotional and crying again?"

"Screw you, I can't help it," I laughed. "My hormones and your sentimentality toward my unborn baby bring me to tears without fail."

I took a slow, deep breath as I organized my thoughts, the events of the last twenty-four hours rushing through my mind at once.

"Oh, this is gonna be good," Haley said, drawing out the last word.

"You know there's seriously something wrong with you?"

"Yeah, but you knew that a long time ago and still chose to befriend me, so now you're fucking stuck with me. Anyway, I'm running out of time—tell me already!"

"Short or long version?"

"Start with short. If it's interesting, I'll ask for the long version," she said with a snort of laughter.

I shook my head with a small giggle, glad to hear my best friend in such a good mood. "Guess where I am."

"Well, you sound happy, so there's only one place you can be right now: in your mom's living room, watching your five-hundred sixty-seventh episode of HGTV's *House Hunters International* with her."

We both burst out laughing—she knew I would be happy to never see another episode of that television show for the rest of my life after the last few months.

"No, thank god," I said with a final chuckle as my heart started to beat faster. "I'm with Lucas."

There was a pause before Haley spoke. "I thought Lucas was in Clarksburg and you guys weren't really talking?"

"All true," I replied. "But then he showed up when I was shopping with Nick yesterday to take me to lunch. Then, over lunch he talked me into going back to Clarksburg with him. He wants me to stay for the rest of the week, and I think I'm going to."

"But I thought you'd written him off, babe?"

My face burned. "Also true. But he did something else, too— he's brought on a third partner to take on some of the workload from the expansion so he can be around more. He said he's been messing up, but that he has his priorities straight now, that the brewery can go to hell for all he cares if he doesn't have me in his life. He said that one chance was all he'd need to show me, and I agreed to give it to him." I swallowed and took another deep breath before continuing. "He wants me to move in with him."

"Well, that was fast. What did you tell him?" Haley asked.

"That everything sounded wonderful, but that I was scared. He said he understood and all he was asking for was a chance to prove himself. And so far, he has. He spent all afternoon and evening with me yesterday and then went into work much later than normal this morning. Even when Stella called him."

"Stella?"

"Yeah—she's the construction manager."

"Your voice makes me think you don't like her," Haley said.

I sighed, the day before flashing through my mind. "I mean, I don't even know her. She's gorgeous and apparently very good at her job."

"You don't like her because she's smart and gorgeous? Sounds like you're just jealous, babe," Haley said in a tone of amusement.

"I'm intimidated by her because she's smart and gorgeous, Haley," I replied, annoyed. "When Lucas introduced us yesterday, she got upset. Like, she looked like she might cry and turned around and didn't look at us again. Why would she do that unless she has a thing for Lucas?"

"I don't know. Sounds like she must like him. Did you ask Lucas about it?"

"Yeah... he said he's pretty sure she's divorced and it's related to that. But I don't know."

"You're just jealous, babe. Trust Lucas. Besides, it doesn't matter what the reason is, does it? He's with you, not her."

I nodded, though Haley couldn't see me. "Fair."

"So where is Lucas?" Haley asked a moment later while I was still thinking about what she said. "I'm assuming he's not there with you right now."

"No, he's at the site. But he'll be back soon. At least he said he would be," I added dubiously, doubt trying to wriggle its way in. "No," I said firmly. "He will be. He said he would, and I believe him. He's coming back to have lunch with me."

There was silence on the other end of the line, which was unusual for my chatty friend.

"Haley? You're being weirdly quiet."

"I'm thinking, babe, that's all."

"Do it out loud?" I laughed. "I want to know your thoughts. Everything feels right, but I think we both know I've had questionable judgment my whole life, so I want to know if I'm an idiot for considering jumping into a life with Lucas—a relationship, living together, parenting, the whole thing."

"I'm going to be honest and, for the sake of time, blunt."

I snorted and rolled my eyes.

"Okay, maybe I'd be blunt anyway," she joked, lightening the sudden solemnity of the conversation. "Anyway. When I met Rob, I was immediately drawn to him. And before your mind goes there, as I know it will, I'm not talking about sex. Yes, of course, he's hot, but that's not what I'm talking about. I recognized what he tries to keep under the surface—that agony and rage—and felt an immediate kinship with him. That blinded me. I was so damn certain he wouldn't take things this far or ever hurt you, but I was wrong. Just as I was wrong about Lucas. I thought he was trying to take advantage of you when you were vulnerable. He doesn't have any of the kind of damage I can connect to in people, so I didn't understand him and misjudged his motivations. I was totally wrong about them both—more wrong than I've been about anyone since I've met you—since I was wrong about my ex, that motherfucker Albert."

"So, what're you saying?" I asked softly, my fingers searching for lint balls to collect on the bedspread. "Do you think it's a good idea? Or am I being hormonal, stupid, desperate, something along those lines?"

"None of the above. Well, you *are* fucking hormonal, but..."

I snorted. "Seriously—what do you think?"

"Honestly, babe? I think you shouldn't be asking other people before you make a decision like this. I think you should rely on your own judgment, not someone else's. Hell, I pushed and shoved you toward Rob, and look how that turned out. And if you recall, *you* were the one who was reticent to jump in with Rob from the very beginning. So, if you think you should do it, go for it. If you think you shouldn't, don't."

"Well, shit, Haley, that's not helpful," I laughed, though my heart beat painfully in my chest at the thought of having to rely on my own judgment alone to make such a big decision.

"Tell me: what do you want?"

"What do I want? I want to be with Lucas. I love him, Haley— like, really, *really* love him. He's the one I dream about, the one I think about, not anyone else. Not even Rob. At least not that often, anyway. That's been fading for months as I've become more aware of how controlling he was and accepted that he hurt me in ways I can't forgive. I've had a lot more clarity about my relationship and feelings for both him and Lucas."

I paused, thinking about Rob for a moment. What I'd said was true, though that didn't mean I loved him any less than I always had. It was just different because I understood now that love wasn't always enough. It couldn't undo the unhealthy parts of our past together, and it couldn't change the ways he'd hurt me. It also didn't mean I had to accept the way he'd always treated me. Just as it didn't mean I couldn't love someone else. And not just anyone, but a man who made me feel things I'd never felt before.

"Being with Lucas since yesterday, it's just made me more certain of my feelings for him. And he must be more rested or something because he's been himself—not the grumpy version he was for a while. I'm in love with him, Haley."

"You do sound happy, babe."

"I *feel* happy, but I'm also scared. Rob meant it when he said he would never leave me no matter what—I *know* he did—but then he did anyway. For something I didn't even do. What's to stop the same thing from happening one day with Lucas? Or what if someone better comes along? Or the baby and I are more than he bargained for? Or my daughter and I end up taking a back seat to the brewery? It would be hard enough if it was just me, but with a baby? I can't risk it. I *will* be a better parent than mine were,

Haley, and that means making sure she's my priority before she's even born."

"You have to figure that out with Lucas, babe," Haley responded soberly.

"Seriously—that's it?"

"Christ, Annie. I'm trying to be a good friend. In all seriousness, I don't want to sway you like I did before in case I'm wrong again."

"Okay," I replied. "But assuming I completely disregard your opinion—what is it?"

She sighed. "I think Lucas would be good to you. I don't think he'd ever do something like what Rob did. And he seems like the kind of person who could see past genetics and love a baby that wasn't his as if it was. I think you guys could be happy together."

"That's exactly what I think, too," I said, my voice cracking. "But what if I'm wrong, Haley?"

"Trust yourself, babe. Your judgment has always been better than you give yourself credit for. And if you're wrong? Well, I'll always be here for you, no matter what happens or what you need."

I nodded. "Well, I guess the next few days will help me figure it out."

"Yeah, they will. You'll get to—hang on." I heard her voice, muffled and annoyed. "I have to go. I'm sorry, babe. I'll text when I can on my trip, and I'll call you when I get back, okay? I'm so sorry I'm going to miss *another* appointment—I'm such a shitty best friend and auntie."

I laughed. "You are the *best* best friend and auntie. I'll text you pictures from the ultrasound, don't worry. But before you go, you have to tell me who you're going to the Bahamas with. I know you're not going alone like you wanted me to believe. You wouldn't skip out on New Year's for no reason."

She huffed out an annoyed breath. "I had a moment of weakness when I had the realization I'd been wrong about Rob and Lucas... I thought maybe I was wrong about other people, too.

So I called him. Just to have a conversation, not for sex this time. And somehow we're going on vacation together now."

"It's Jax, isn't it?" I asked, giddy. *Please let me be right.*

"Yes, Jax, asshole, now leave it alone. We'll probably have lots of hot sex while we're there and then never talk to each other again. That's why I didn't want to tell you, because you're gonna make a bigger deal out of it than it needs to be. I gotta go. Love you."

"Love you, too. Have fun," I said in a sing-song voice. I touched the end call button, then shouted into the empty room. "Haha! I knew it! I freaking knew it!"

"Oh, yeah?" Lucas asked, grinning as he approached the bed, followed closely by the divine smell of Thai food.

"Where the hell did you come from?" I asked, startled, adrenaline pumping through my veins as my heart raced.

"Right there," he replied with a smirk, pointing to the corner of the wall as he set the food down in the kitchenette and began to untie his work boots. "And before that, the hallway."

I rolled my eyes at him but couldn't keep from smiling and letting out a small laugh. "How long were you there?" I asked, tipping my head to where he said he'd been standing, hoping it wasn't more than a few seconds.

"Long enough," he replied, flashing his cheesy, boyish grin and a wink. "Pad Thai, green curry, or fried rice?" he asked.

"You bought all three?" I asked in disbelief.

"And eggrolls."

I laughed. "Some of everything."

He served me a little of each dish. "I realized when the restaurant answered the phone to take my order that I didn't know what you liked. I thought this would be a good enough variety to ensure you'd like *something*. But it made me think about other things we still don't know about each other."

"Pad Thai and Green Curry are tied for my favorites," I said. "You?"

"Fried Rice."

He set three small bowls of food down on the nightstand next to me, one of them also containing an eggroll, and a fork, then returned to the kitchenette to serve himself. Once he was seated next to me on the other side of the bed, he continued.

"Are you up for a round of twenty questions?"

I smiled at his question. When he'd first introduced the game when I was in the hospital after my aneurysm scare, I'd been aggravated, but I now understood he wanted to know so much because he loved me, and it gave me a thrill and surge of love every time he suggested we play.

"Absolutely."

chapter forty-five

"What would you like to do with our extra time?" I asked Annie when her second appointment on Friday was postponed last minute.

"Want to grab an early lunch? I could eat."

"You can *always* eat," I teased with a wink.

"Ha-ha, very funny." She deadpanned for a moment before her face broke into a grin, her eyes crinkling at the corners. "We could look for a house together," she suggested.

"Sure," I replied. "There's a restaurant with a fireplace within walking distance from here. It's the same chain as the one we went to in Caperton the other day. How does that sound?"

"Perfect."

Once we were settled into a booth close to the fire, both of us sitting on the same side, our food ordered and hot teas on the table in front of us, I booted up my laptop.

As the desktop loaded, a new song started through the restaurant speakers: "Love Me Now" by John Legend. I looked over at Annie, my heart swelling, and smiled.

"Do you know this song?" I asked, pointing toward the ceiling.

"I've heard it before, but I don't know the words," she replied.

"Listen to them," I said.

She tilted her head toward the ceiling and listened until the song ended, her eyes watery. So were mine.

"I love you," she whispered, her eyes intense.

I returned her gaze, hoping she could see just how much I loved her in return. "I love you, too, sweetheart."

Annie's hand shook as she pulled the laptop closer to her a moment later and began typing the real estate search web address into the address bar and I worried for a moment that something was amiss.

"Are you alright, sweetheart?"

"Yeah, I'm good," she replied quickly, smiling up at me.

She seemed nervous or excited or something, but I decided not to push and give her a chance to tell me on her own.

"How about this one?" she asked as she turned the laptop so I could see the screen.

Wrapping an arm around her shoulders, I kissed her temple and looked down at the computer. The house she had pulled up was a newly renovated four-bedroom Victorian home in the Clarksburg historic district, only a short walk from the new brewery site. The pictures revealed that in addition to the several bedrooms, two offices, a sunroom off the kitchen, and a small but beautifully landscaped yard, the back had well-placed, lush mature trees that gave the impression of seclusion and privacy even though it was in the middle of town.

There wasn't anything about it so far that I disliked, and it was definitely an Annie kind of house. Its proximity to the brewery would mean more time home—hopefully with Annie one day. That was all I really needed to know about it, as long as the rent was affordable.

"I love it," I said as I scrolled to search for the rental rate. "But it's not for rent. It's for sale."

Her eyes darted up to mine, then away again, then she turned to face me and lifted her gaze, holding it steady this time. "I know." She took and released a slow, deep breath. "I want to buy this house... with you." As soon as she finished speaking, she looked down toward the computer.

My heart skipped. "Annie, sweetheart—look at me? I want to make sure I understand."

Her eyes lifted back to mine. "I'm saying yes to everything, Lucas. I want a future with you, so let's get something and put down roots—together—before this baby is born. We can keep your house in Stockwood as a rental property—I still have a lot of money from selling my house in the city, so we can put a hefty down payment on this house and then buy it together."

"Yes," I rushed out as soon as she stopped speaking. With my hands cradling her face, I tipped her chin toward me when her eyes darted away again. "Are you sure, sweetheart? I'd love nothing more than to do this together, but *only* if you're sure. I can wait for you if you need more time—I don't want to rush you into something you aren't ready for."

Her lips pulled up on one side, her finger still sliding back and forth along the table edge. "Honestly? No, I'm not sure. I'm terrified. But I want to give us this chance more than I want to stay in my comfort zone."

My laughter bubbled up from my chest as I pulled her into my arms. "She said yes!" I shouted. "She's moving in with me!"

"Lucas, stop, this is embarrassing," she hissed, her face bright red as her eyes scanned the other tables.

My forehead pressed into hers, our noses rubbing together in an Eskimo kiss. "You just made me so happy, sweetheart, and I don't care if the whole world knows it."

chapter forty-six

annie

Lucas **was on** the phone in the sunroom at my mom's house while I was in the kitchen making tea and Mom was baking cookies for her knitting group. My face was on fire after asking if Lucas could spend the night—I felt like a teenager. It was worth it, though, to have a few more hours to spend with him before he left for Clarksburg; I wasn't ready to part ways after having suggested we buy a house together just that morning.

Mom glanced at me sideways, her expression inscrutable, before looking back down to what she was doing with the cookie dough. "Why is he here, honey? What's going on with you two? He was gone, and now he's back? It's one thing for *you* to jump around from place to place and person to person, but kids need stability, honey."

"What? You really think that about me? I have spent most of my life alone, Mom, and I've barely even had friends. How can you say that?"

"And then what happened? In the last two years, you've dated Lucas, then married Rob, and now you're dating Lucas again? I'm just saying that I think you don't know what you want, honey, that's all."

My face continued to burn, for different reasons this time. Mom was right about the last two years and having everything that had occurred in that time reduced to just those three events was uncomfortable. What did that say about me that I loved two different men and could so easily adjust to life with one when I'd been with the other?

What would Selena say? I wondered. If I said to her what I was just thinking about adjusting to life with Rob and Lucas so easily, she'd probably ask me if it was really all that easy and if my feelings had really waxed and waned for them. She'd ask why it was a bad thing to have enough love in your heart for more than one person. And she'd probably ask me what it was I really did want.

And what *did* I want? I wanted to love people who loved me as much as I loved them. I wanted to be around people who could help me be comfortable with who I was and help me stop feeling so afraid of everything. People who understood and cared about me, who helped me be myself and not some version of myself they wanted me to be. And I already had those things with Haley... but I also had them with Lucas.

He'd never tried to mold me into something I wasn't or tried to force me into facing things I wasn't ready for. More than ever, he seemed to really see and understand me, without me having to try to explain every thought or feeling to him. He wanted me to be happy, and the more I was around him, the more I felt I understood myself, the less afraid and more confident I felt. Thinking about it this way, I was even more sure of my decision to start a life with him.

"I think for a lot of my life, you're right—I didn't really know what I wanted," I said to Mom. "But this time, you're wrong. I know exactly what I want. And a life with Lucas is it."

She glanced at me, shaking her head without saying anything.

"I'm moving to Clarksburg in a few weeks," I added. "We're buying a house together. I was going to tell you in the morning when we had breakfast together after Lucas heads back."

Mom's hands stilled and she turned to fully face me. "Honey, stop and think before you do something so rash. He's young, he's successful, he's attractive. I've said it before: do you really think he's going to want to be tied down with a baby that isn't his?"

"He loves me, Mom. And he'll love the baby."

"Even if that's true, why do you think anything will be different than it has been? He's got a growing business. He's going to continue working a lot. He won't be there for you any more than he has been."

"He's committed. We're going to buy a house... *together*. And he's already stepping back from work a bit, and he and Nick brought in another partner so he doesn't have to work so much anymore. He did that so he can be there for me and the baby."

She turned back to her dough with more head shaking but remained silent.

"Why don't you like him, Mom?"

"It's not that I don't like him, honey, because I do. I think he's a wonderful young man, but things are different when you're having a baby. Especially when that baby isn't his."

I couldn't keep the tears back as I responded, her words tearing a hole in my chest because they were reflective of my own fears. "I know that. But I also know he loves me, and I believe him when he says he'll love this baby, too, regardless of paternity. And he's proving he'll be around by bringing in this new partner."

"Don't be naïve, honey, they're making a business decision."

"I'm not," I snapped. "Lucas has never wanted to have *any* partners to begin with. But was the only way he'd be able to have the time to be there for me, so he brought someone else in. The paperwork is already signed—the new partner begins the first of the year."

"If you say so, honey. I just don't want you to get hurt again. And I want to make sure you and that baby are secure and happy, that's all."

I nodded. "So, back to my original question. Can Lucas spend the night?"

"That's fine if that's what you want—you're an adult."

I went to the cabinet and retrieved two mugs, then paused, my hand in midair to close the cabinet door.

"Mom?"

"Yes, honey?"

"You keep saying that Lucas isn't going to stick around or love this baby because it isn't his," I began, steeling myself for what I was about to say. "But *I'm* not yours in that same way. And even though we don't always agree, you've stuck with me since I was eight years old, and you care about me anyway. Just give Lucas a chance to do the same thing."

Mom's eyes filled, but she blinked away the moisture, remaining silent. I took a deep breath, then turned to the stove for the kettle. After pouring hot water into our mugs, I walked out to the sunroom to tell Lucas he could stay, but he wasn't there. Instead, he was pacing in the driveway, gesturing wildly; whatever was happening on the phone, it couldn't be good. With a sigh, I set our tea down and got to work building a fire. But Lucas was still outside once the fire was roaring. With a last nervous glance out the window, I settled into a corner of the sofa with a throw and my tea, hoping Lucas wasn't about to leave suddenly again.

———————

I startled awake when something tightened around me. With my eyes open and heart pounding, it took a moment for the sleep fog to dissipate enough for me to realize I'd felt Lucas tucking the throw around me.

"You're still here," I said.

"Of course."

"I wasn't sure... I could tell something was wrong and you were outside for so long."

"I needed to step out to deal with something. I didn't mean to be out there that long, though."

"You must be freezing."

He gave a half smile, though his eyes looked sad. "I'm fine."

But when I reached out to grab his hands, they were icy. And when he leaned down to rub our noses together, his face was just as cold. "Lucas, you're frozen. You're not fine."

"I am now," he whispered, closing his eyes and moving my hands up to his face and pressing them into his cold cheeks.

"No, you're not." I leaned forward and gave him a peck on the lips. "Let's sit by the fire until you thaw." With a yawn, I pushed to my feet and then settled ungracefully onto the rug in front of the fire, patting the floor next to me.

He stared at me for a moment, then murmured, "I'll never get used to seeing you in firelight... so beautiful."

A blush swept up my neck as Lucas moved over the chest my mom used as a coffee table so he could lean against it. Then he sat behind me, scooting around so I was nestled with my back to his chest, and wrapped his arms around me.

"What happened?" I asked when he let out a loud sigh.

He bent his knees and planted his feet so that I was caged in on the sides by his legs before speaking quietly. "Do you remember when you were staying in the city with Haley, and you asked me to go up to Rob's to get your mail?"

"Yes," I replied, my mind racing to figure out what that mattered. I'd had a few bills, I remembered, and I'd paid them electronically after Lucas sent me pictures of them.

"Well..." Lucas squeezed me tighter but didn't start talking again, instead leaning his head down and kissing my cheek. "I meant to tell you sooner, I really did. It just got away from me and then too much time had passed and... anyway, none of that matters now. But I'm sorry I didn't tell you sooner." He paused. "Can you let me tell you everything before you get mad?"

"I'll try," I said. My body was already stiffening and my heart pounding in anticipation of having the rug yanked out from under me. Whatever was coming wasn't good. That alone was enough to give me the urge to walk away right then. But I wasn't going to run away from things anymore.

"Okay," he breathed out. And then he told me about the two pieces of mail that had caught his eye because they had change of address labels, and that he'd opened them to see if his suspicions about their source was correct. "The letters..." he swallowed loudly. "They were from Charlie."

I gasped, my stomach roiling, but before I could ask what he'd written, Lucas continued.

"Both letters were threatening you, though he did it in such a way that the police couldn't have really done anything about it. So, I did the only thing I could think of at the time. My college roommate, Joel, owns a private security and investigation firm now, and I asked him to look into Charlie's history when he had some time. Maybe something he dug up could help me figure out what Charlie might be planning. My first call this evening was from him."

"Give me a minute," I said weakly. I needed time to digest what he'd just said. All that time, I'd thought Charlie was only part of the past, but he'd actually been planning to get revenge on me. I'd thought I would most likely be safe once he was released... and I'd been wrong. And he'd been out for a few days now. My eyes went to the darkened windows and a shiver raced up my spine. He could be outside them right then, watching and waiting.

"You should have told me," I said, my eyes glued to the windows.

"I know. I didn't want to worry you. We read about how bad chronic stress is for the baby's development, that it could even lead to miscarriage, so I didn't want to make you worry if there wasn't a good reason to. And then, with the way things were between us, I forgot about them for a while because I was so distracted, and then it had been so long I didn't know how to bring it up."

"That's not the point, Lucas. I had a right to know."

"I know," he said, his voice flat and quiet. "I should have told you right away. I made a mistake. And I won't do something like that again, I promise." With a deep breath, Lucas continued. "I'm just going to tell you the gist of what Joel told me. If you want to know more, I think it would be better for you to read the documents yourself another time. Anyway, because their history is tightly intertwined, Joel dug up information on Rob, too."

My heart skipped. "I don't care," I said. "I don't want to know anything about Rob."

"That's fine," Lucas replied, his voice pained. "But there's one thing you *need* to know, Annie. He... Rob married some showgirl in Vegas about ten years ago... and they're still married."

"*What?*" I asked, shaking my head in disbelief. Rob was married to someone else? But that would mean... "My marriage was never even legal?"

Lucas was quiet and still, in stark contrast to the intense sensation of motion within me. My heart was beating fast and hard, my blood was pumping quickly, my mind was racing in an effort to assimilate this new information and everything it meant. How was my marriage even possible? How did no one know?

Except that one person did—Rob. He knew. He knew he was married to someone else and that our marriage was a sham. I'd thought he was making a mistake about the pregnancy, but he'd still actually loved me. But how could you love someone and do something like that to them? My face burned—I felt so stupid. And furiously angry that he'd made me think we were married when it wasn't even possible. How the hell could he do that to me?

"No," I breathed out, pushing away from Lucas. "It can't be. I was so wrong about him, more wrong than I ever would have thought because I was wrong about the one thing I'd always been certain of." I looked over my shoulder at Lucas. "If I was wrong about *that*?" The rest of the words got stuck on my tongue and I started crying.

Lucas scooted forward, gingerly pulling me back into his arms. "You're not wrong about me," he said tenderly, having understood the words I hadn't said.

He smoothed one hand up and down my back as my body shook with my sobs for long minutes. And after a while, his steady heartbeat and soothing touch calmed me, and my crying tapered off. I felt utterly drained, body and soul. It was still several more minutes before either of us moved, Lucas using a gentle hand to turn my face toward him.

"Are you okay?" he asked, searching my eyes.

"I don't know," I replied. "But I just want to get through this conversation right now. Tell me whatever else I need to know— just get it over with."

He kissed my forehead, then continued. "Charlie has some serious drug connections that he made a lot of money for before he was incarcerated. It's likely they just replaced him after making sure he kept his mouth shut, but it's possible they're unhappy about it."

"Oh my god," I exhaled, trying to fight the terror that was threatening to take over. That couldn't be good for the baby. "I don't think you needed to tell me that part."

"I did," he replied. "Because I need you to understand what I'm doing with that information. Joel recommended hiring a bodyguard for a while—"

"Absolutely not!"

"—but I knew you would never agree. The next best thing until I can be there myself is Nick. He's huge, he's good in a fight, he cares about your safety, and you're comfortable around him. So, I called and told him everything and he agreed to keep you safe when I'm not around."

"No, I can't—"

"All we're asking is that you don't go anywhere without him when I'm not around. He's happy to take you anywhere you need to go, whenever you need to go."

My eyes filled with tears again. "But, Lucas, he's got a life of his own, he doesn't want—"

"Sweetheart, he cares about you and your safety. He wants to help any way he can. Okay?"

I nodded, not trusting my voice.

"Does that mean you agree? I really want you to—Nick wants you to—but it's *your* decision. Not ours."

"I'll think about it," I whispered.

"Okay. And of course, make sure you check who's at the door before you open it, and you should probably keep the doors locked at all times."

Oh god, the door. My eyes widened and I scrambled to get to my feet.

"I already locked it," he said softly.

I collapsed into his arms, burying my face in his chest as the tears spilled over. My breath was coming in violent hiccupping gasps despite my efforts to keep calm for the life growing inside me. Lucas remained silent, his arms holding me tightly as the panic and fear washed over me.

"I'm so scared," I whispered between sobs.

He began smoothing a hand up and down my back. "I know, sweetheart," he replied quietly. "I am, too. We can keep you safe, though—this plan will keep you safe. I promise. Do you trust me?"

His heart beat steadily under my cheek, and I felt the confidence in his touch, heard the determination in his voice. Slowly, methodically, that gentle, confident touch was drawing out my fear and replacing it with a sense of calm. Thinking about Charlie wanting to hurt me again made me feel like I was lost and drowning, but Lucas felt like solid ground.

I nodded, realizing I did trust him... with my life, and with our future.

chapter forty-seven

———

annie

Deciding I'd be fine in broad daylight, I had my mom drive me to the brewery shortly before they opened instead of asking Nick to come get me; Lucas had already left to return to Clarksburg earlier in the morning. I didn't have a set schedule anymore since Nick refused to let me serve at the bar at this point, but I'd said I would come in sometime that day to work on scheduling and bookkeeping.

"Hey, Nick!" I called as I walked in.

I'd expected to find him stocking the bar like he usually did on Saturday mornings, but there was no reply. I made my way to the office, but he wasn't there either. Shrugging out of my coat, I decided to call his cell phone, but before I had a chance, Chase walked into the office. We greeted each other as my heart rate picked up—I didn't know Chase that well, and being alone with him made me nervous.

"Did Nick decide to take the day off?" I asked, suddenly wishing I'd called him *before* leaving my mom's house the way he and Lucas had wanted me to.

"Not that I know of. Isn't that his coat hanging there?" Chase pointed toward the coat rack in the corner behind the door.

"Yeah, but he doesn't always wear it home. I'll just give him a call."

When the call went straight to voicemail, I sat down at the desk to start working; keeping busy was the best thing I could do right then to keep myself from imagining scenarios that would likely never come to pass. Then, just as Chase was about to walk out after reviewing schedules for the day and pulling cash drawers for the registers out of the safe, Nick walked in, stopping short just inside the doorway.

"Annie? I didn't know you were here."

"Hi, Nick," I said, relief flooding my body. "I got in a little while ago. I didn't see you when I came in. I tried to call you but got your voicemail."

He sighed. "I forgot to charge my phone last night, so the battery is dead. It's charging," he said, pointing to a stack on the corner of the desk where I hadn't noticed his cell phone sitting. He looked at me for a moment, his mouth poised to speak, but then turned to Chase instead. "Hey, Chase, can you start stocking the bar while I get Annie caught up on what she's missed this week? I'll be out in a few minutes to help."

Nick closed the office door behind Chase as I stood and walked over to the small sofa. I assumed he wanted to talk about his phone call with Lucas the night before and I couldn't really see him around the computer screen. He stepped over and wrapped his arms around me in a tight hug.

"That's the first time you've given me an all-out hug," I said, half-laughing. "Everything okay?"

He stepped back, his face drawn. "I'm fine, Annie, I'm just worried about *you*. Are *you* okay? I'm assuming Lucas told you everything?"

"He told me enough," I responded. "And I'm fine, though I feel bad because you have better things to do than basically babysit a grown woman when she leaves her house. At least I don't have much of a life, right?" I joked.

Nick gave a small smile. "You're my friend. And I want you to be safe. So no, I don't have anything better to do. Besides, I don't have much of a life outside the brewery, either. You're okay with the plan, then?"

I nodded. "So what have I missed?"

After Nick filled me in on the happenings at the brewery over the last week, he went out to the bar to help Chase with stocking and to pull in the counts we needed for me to make the supplies order.

Before long, the doors were open, and the bar was full. And while Nick wouldn't let me serve anymore, he couldn't do anything about me replenishing supplies for them as they got low. With how busy we were, time flew by, and suddenly it was late afternoon and the brewery was bursting at the seams as the evening rush began. Nick had long since insisted on taking me home—more than once, actually—but I'd ignored him. It was nice to feel needed and to have something to do. With a grunt, I stood, lifting a partially full tray of dirty beer glasses, a task that used to be easy but was now difficult around my ever-growing belly, and found myself face-to-face with a pair of unforgettable ice-cold blue eyes.

Charlie.

Everything in my body froze as every bit of fear he'd ever instilled in me hit me at once, suffocating me. As his mouth curved into a sneer that promised violence, the tray of glasses I'd been holding slipped from my fingers, creating a colossal crash that silenced the immediate area.

"Annie!" Nick's voice shouted. "Don't move—there's glass everywhere!"

My eyes darted in the direction Nick's voice was coming from and when they returned to the space in front of me, Charlie was gone. I scanned the crowd frantically as I struggled to breathe, and the room started to spin. Where did he go? Where was he? How did he appear and disappear so quickly?

"Annie, what's going on?" Nick asked from my side.

My body started to shake and a wave of nausea passed over me. Then my lower back and abdomen seized as the room darkened into blackness.

Nick was holding his cell phone to his ear and had started talking to me when my eyes fluttered open. I looked around, realizing I was on the sofa in the brewery's office. My abdomen and lower back tightened suddenly. "Aah!" I shouted, my body feeling like it was going to split in half. The pain felt like it lasted for days before it began to subside. Charlie's face flashed before my eyes, and I turned just in time to throw up in the small trash can adjacent to the sofa.

"Fuck, I don't know!" Nick shouted into the phone. Then he set it down next to him and pressed a button to put it on speakerphone.

"Annie? What the hell is going on?" Lucas' panicked voice came across the phone.

"I saw Charlie," I rushed out. "He was here—at the bar. I think. I don't know, it happened so fast. He—aah!" Another round of painful tightening overtook me.

"What's happening, Nick? What's wrong with her?"

"I don't know!" Nick yelled, his face full of panic.

"I think I'm in labor," I gasped out as the pain began to subside again. "I'm having contractions, but it's too early, Lucas—she's not ready yet. Please, she can't come yet."

"Everything will be okay," Lucas said.

"I'm scared," I sobbed. "I can't do this. I need you."

"Annie, listen to me," Lucas responded. "You need to call your doctor. I'll be there as soon as I can, but you have to call your doctor right now, okay?"

"Okay," I replied, though my voice was garbled from my crying.

"Call them now, sweetheart. Nick, take me off speaker."

While Nick talked to Lucas, I dug my phone out of my pocket. My hands were so shaky, I couldn't even unlock my screen, and then another contraction was coming on. Once it passed, I forced myself to take a deep breath, reminding myself that I had to calm down so I could keep my baby safe, and then I called my doctor.

The doctor told me to go straight to the hospital. Then everything happened so quickly that it was all a blur. They had done an ultrasound and confirmed that I was in fact having true labor contractions. I was waiting on the arrival of my doctor to discuss my options, Nick standing next to the hospital bed.

"You look as scared as I feel," I said, attempting to make a joke to ease his discomfort.

He gave me a tight smile, but didn't say anything, his eyes distant. But he stayed by my side and even held my hand after the doctor came in and explained that they thought my labor was caused by having an incompetent cervix and that, if they were right, performing emergent cerclage combined with IV medication to temporarily stop the contractions could possibly resolve the pre-term labor. However, there were also down sides to both the procedure and the medication, particularly if the treatment wasn't successful.

"This is a big decision to make, but we feel fairly confident this has the highest chance of success. And the sooner we do it, the better since you've already begun to dilate. I'll leave you to think it over and return in a few minutes."

As soon as the doctor left, I curled into a ball and started crying, even as another contraction passed through. "I need Lucas," I hiccupped.

"He's coming as quickly as he can, Annie," Nick said gently. "Until then, do you want me to try calling your mom again? And we can get Lucas on the phone, too. Just tell me what I can do, and I'll do it."

"Call my mom, please. I'll call Lucas."

chapter forty-eight

lucas

When Nick called about Annie, I dropped everything and was on the road before I was even off the phone with him. After he promised not to leave Annie's side until I arrived, I hung up and called Stella, explaining quickly that Annie was in the hospital, and I didn't know when I'd be back. Nick had kept me updated, so I'd known they were at the hospital before Annie called, telling me what the doctors had told her: that she was in pre-term labor, and they needed to sew her cervix closed to make sure she didn't go into pre-term labor again. They'd just given her a medication that would make her contractions stop.

"I'm almost there, Annie," I soothed into the phone, working to stay calm for her sake. "Everything is going to be just fine, I promise. Trust the doctors, they know what they're doing."

"I'm so scared," she cried into the phone. "I can't do this alone, I need you here—"

"It's okay," I interrupted before she became even more upset. "Is your mom there yet?"

"Nick's calling her again right now."

"Okay. She'll be—"

"Aah!" Annie screamed into the phone.

She was having another contraction. The fear and pain in her voice ripped my heart to shreds. I wanted to take it all away for her. I wanted to be there with her, helping her through everything, not on the road and talking to her over a damn phone.

"I'm coming, sweetheart, I'm coming. I'm almost there, now, I promise. Only a few minutes away."

When I ran into her hospital room less than ten minutes later, she was on her side with her back toward the door,

"I'm here, sweetheart," I said, out of breath from sprinting inside from the parking lot, rushing to the other side of the bed so I could see her face.

"Lucas..." she cried, the sound making my chest constrict.

"I'm here," I whispered, wrapping my arms around her.

When I glanced up, Nick raised his eyebrows at me, and I knew he was asking if he should get the doctor. I nodded and he disappeared into the hallway. He returned a minute later, and then everything happened very quickly. Nick had given Annie's hand a squeeze and left, tears in his eyes as he asked me to please keep him updated. A swarm of nurses and doctors appeared, driving me out of the way as they pushed more medicine into her IV and prepped Annie for the epidural she needed before they could do the procedure.

As soon as there was space, I pulled a chair close to the bed and clasped Annie's hands in mine. With our foreheads pressed together, I distracted her by murmuring into her ear about the life we were going to lead together, how excited my father would be to finally meet her. My words had a calming effect on her, and while she never really stopped crying, the tears had slowed, her body was still and restful, and her expression was shifting to be more tired than fearful. As her calm increased, it became easier for me to breathe.

The doctor explained normal short-term and long-term side effects for both the medications and the procedure, as well as warning signs to look out for. She explained that she was still high risk for another bout of pre-term labor and that once she was discharged, she'd need to take it easy, physically and otherwise— there would be no more working at the brewery for the rest of her pregnancy.

Annie was asleep when her mom arrived, so I stepped into the hall with her to fill her in on everything that had happened. "They'll discharge her in two days—three at most—if it appears the risk of labor is over."

"Cervical insufficiency? How is that possible?" Miriam asked.

"From when Charlie raped her," I said quietly. "There was a lot of damage."

"She never told me that," Miriam said softly, her eyes watering and her mouth turning down into a soft frown. She nodded absently for a moment. "Thank you for being here with her. It means a lot to me, and I know it means a lot to her. I'll make sure she gets home safely and follows the doctor's orders—you can go back to Clarksburg if you need to."

"What?" I asked, drawing back. "I'm not going back to Clarksburg and leaving Annie while she's in the hospital. I'm staying right here."

I knew Miriam didn't think it made sense for Annie and me to be in a relationship together, but I couldn't believe she really thought I'd leave while Annie was in the hospital. Without waiting for a response, I turned and walked back into Annie's hospital room, taking up my spot next to her. Miriam followed me in a few minutes later and sat on the other side of the room in another chair and knit. After a few hours, Annie was still sleeping soundly, and Miriam said she was going to get some coffee and would be back. Before she returned, Grams shuffled in.

"Hi, Grandson," she whispered with a small smile.

"Hi, Grams," I responded in a quiet voice, realizing that in all the chaos I'd never thought to call her. "I'm so sorry I didn't call and tell you what happened... all I could think about was Annie."

"That's okay," she replied. "Miriam called me."

"Let me guess, she wants you to talk me out of staying here," I bit out.

Grams gave me a sharp look, tilting her head at me in warning. "Watch your manners. She only called to tell me what happened. So how's Annie doing?"

Miriam returned while Grams and I were speaking in hushed tones. After we'd stopped talking, I noticed how much better I felt having Grams in the room, how comforting her silent presence was. Since the expansion project, I'd barely seen her and had forgotten what a force she was. Annie wasn't the only person I'd neglected the last few months.

"I'm sorry, Grams," I whispered.

"For what?"

"For being absent the last few months. Things will be different from now on, I promise."

She smiled. "Lucas, you'll discover one day when you have kids and grandchildren of your own that as long as they're happy, you're happy. You've been pursuing your dreams, and that's enough for me."

"My dreams being possible is thanks to you, and I haven't done a good job of showing you that I know and appreciate that recently. But I promise I'll do a better job."

"Just be happy, that's all I really want for you. Life is too short to spend it any other way."

"I am, Grams. I've finally gotten my priorities straight and I've made amends with Annie. We're buying a house together in Clarksburg. Can you believe it?" I looked over at Grams and she was smiling and nodding as if she was pleased with the news. "I just hope we can keep this baby in a while longer. But even if we can't, as long as Annie is okay and safe, we'll get through whatever happens. She's it for me, Grams. Meeting her was when my life story became worthwhile, and with her is where it'll end."

chapter forty-nine

annie

“**W**hat is *that*?” I asked when Lucas got out of the driver’s side of a new, rugged, gray-blue Toyota 4Runner. I had just been discharged from the hospital, the doctors confident my pre-term labor had been stalled, and I was waiting near the hospital entrance in a wheelchair with a nurse behind me.

He wore his trademark cheesy grin, his eyes twinkling as he winked at me. “Do you like it?”

“Is this the surprise you said you had?”

“One of them.”

“But... what happened to your car?” I questioned, glancing around as if it would somehow be there, too.

“I traded it in, of course.”

“Are you serious?”

“Yes, but it’s freezing out here, let’s talk in the car.”

I stared at the SUV in disbelief as Lucas helped me out of the wheelchair and over to the passenger door. The vehicle was gorgeous—sexy, even—and suited Lucas perfectly. But he’d been attached to his sports car, so I was baffled about why he would have gotten something new.

“Why the hell would you get rid of your car?” I asked once we were both buckled.

“Well, sweetheart, we’re buying a house together, if you recall, and I’m building a new brewery, so it would have been financially irresponsible of me to keep it when buying a new car. You like it?”

"What's not to like about it?" I laughed, glancing around at the luxurious interior. "I love it. It's the exact car I wanted before I moved to the city. I just don't understand why *you* bought it."

"This is a family car," he replied, his grin back in full force. "My sports car wasn't. I've been meaning to replace it for a while. With this scare, though, I couldn't put it off any longer, so that's what I was doing for most of the day yesterday while your mom was with you."

My heart fluttered in my chest that he was so committed to us becoming a family, but I worried he'd regret his decision. "But you loved that car, Lucas."

"No. I *liked* that car. I also *like* this one. I *love* you and that baby, who still needs a name, by the way." His eyes shifted meaningfully to the back seat, and he asked, "Do you think she'll like it?"

Taking off my seatbelt for a moment and turning to look as best as I could with my belly in the way, I saw a brand-new rear-facing infant car seat installed in the back seat, the material soft shades of pink and gray. Tears came to my eyes and my words stuck. *He really does care about this baby already.*

When I still hadn't spoken, his cheesy grin widened and he continued, "There was no way a car seat would fit in the sports car, and I don't want anything in my life that doesn't involve you anymore. Besides the fact you could barely get in and out of it already and still have two and a half months to go. So, as long as you are comfortable and like this one, I'm happy with my decision."

He certainly sounded happy. "Okay, I believe you," I said, smiling back and replacing my seatbelt. "And yes, I'm very comfortable and I like this car *a lot.*"

"Good," he said, putting the car in drive to pull out of the parking lot. "We'll get you one, too, then, once you can drive again in a few months."

He was strangely peppy, all things considered, even for having a new vehicle. And while his happiness was infectious, I wanted to understand where it was coming from.

"Why are you so upbeat right now?" I asked, narrowing my eyes.

"Why shouldn't I be?" he cheesed. "I made a good car purchase according to the woman I love, who happens to be sitting right next to me, healthy. The baby is still right where she should be for now, and I have nothing on my agenda for at least the next week except to spend time making sure the love of my life knows that's what she is."

"Hm."

"Oh, and I almost forgot," he said mischievously. "I heard from the agent that we can close on the house even earlier, and our lender confirmed they can accommodate the accelerated timing. Which means we can move into *our* new home together in just over two weeks from today. Three weeks, tops."

"Really?" I exclaimed. "That's incredible news! I can't believe you waited to tell me that!"

Instead of responding, he remained silent and cranked up the radio, which had started playing a new song. "Say You Won't Let Go" by James Arthur. His eyes darted over to me repeatedly as the song played until we approached a red light.

"I won't let you go—ever. I promise. Say you won't either," he said as he slowed.

"I won't," I said, my heart racing.

Once the car came to a complete stop at the light, he shifted into park. Then he leaned over and cupped the back of my head, pulling me toward him for a kiss that lasted until someone behind us blasted their horn because the light had turned green.

I laughed as we pulled away from the light—we'd also created a small traffic jam the summer we started dating when he'd stopped his car beside me until I hopped in with him. "Holding up traffic seems to be a habit of ours."

"They'll get over it," he laughed in return, grabbing my hand and lacing our fingers together. "And if they don't?" He shrugged dismissively, a wide grin stretched across his face. "Who cares?"

rob

I was driving through town to head back home for the first time in weeks after a trip to the liquor store when I saw them. I almost missed them because they were in a different car, but once I saw them, I couldn't look away. They were driving the opposite direction and we were both stopped at the front of the line of cars at the stoplight. We were facing each other. But they didn't notice me—they were too busy kissing. The longer I watched, the more tempted I was to jump out of my truck, walk over there, and drag Lucas out to beat the shit out of him. My fists tightened around the steering wheel and my teeth felt like they would crack from the tension in my jaw. When the light turned green, I drove past, and they still didn't notice. They didn't even notice the light had turned green. They were still fucking kissing.

How the hell had she ended up with fucking Lucas? I was the one who'd loved her so damn hard I practically killed myself when she left me. Why would she choose *him*? When I was the one who was there for her when she had fucking no one when we were kids. When I was the one who knew what she needed when she was suicidal the year before. It was me—not him. And yet *he* was the one she was with. I gave her everything and she destroyed me. She betrayed everything we'd ever had together.

I had been driving on autopilot, not noticing where I was headed, and found myself parking at the old cross-country course. In a way, it was where everything began. It was where I fell in love with her, where I realized I loved her more than life. Where we spent so much time together. Where I'd wished to have her come back into my life; a wish I never should have made. It was all because of that tree—that fucking willow tree.

Slamming my truck door after I jumped out, I pulled out a bottle of whiskey I'd just bought, opened it, and downed about a third of the bottle. Then I fished out a machete I kept in my truck in case I needed to clear downed trees along my driveway and hit the path. It wasn't long before the willow came into view atop the hill, its leafless branches hanging around the massive, twisted trunk. I ran the rest of the way, gasping for breath by the time I reached the top, the months of drinking heavily having already taken a toll on my body. Dropping the machete as the world spun around me, I leaned a hand on the tree to keep myself upright and was immediately transported back in time.

"This is my special spot. I come here... well, a lot, really, but especially when I'm upset or just need a little... inspiration, I guess."

"Inspiration? From this old thing?" I asked, incredulous, as I eyed the ancient trunk, twisted and knotted with age, not a hint of symmetry in its form.

"Don't you see it?" she asked breathlessly, her eyes lit up and more alive than I'd seen them before.

Fuck, I wanted to make her eyes light up like that every day.

"She's beautiful. This is a weeping willow, and she really does look like she's weeping softly, some unspoken tragedy in her past, doesn't she? And yet, she grows bigger and stronger every year. She's on top of this hill, and I like to think that she's up here for a reason, to catch the sadness from everything she can see, taking on that burden, so others don't have to." She reached out impulsively and grabbed my hand, placing my palm on the trunk next to hers. "Can't you feel it? Her power, her compassion? How she's drawing out the hurt?"

I felt something, alright, though it wasn't the damn tree. It was that moment, as Annie gazed into my eyes so earnestly, her walls down, allowing me a glimpse into her heart, into her beautiful fucking soul, it was that exact instant that everything I'd ever been, everything that'd ever driven me just stopped. Even my heart refused to beat for a moment.

And when it started up again, it beat for her and her alone. I knew right then, with a clarity unfamiliar to me, that I was standing in front of the only girl I would ever love.

My body crumpled to the ground as the pain took over and I cried, hunched over my legs. How had things gone so wrong for us? I loved her—god, I loved her. And at some point, she must have loved me, too. It was right where I sat that she'd told me those words for the first time.

We were both leaning with our backs against the massive trunk, Annie with her eyes closed. It was time. My heart in my throat, I stepped away from the trunk, pivoting so I was standing in front of her with my feet straddling hers. Christ, my breathing was erratic, bordering on panting.

"Annie." I was close enough that I could feel her warm breath bathing the cold skin on my face as she replied.

"Hm?"

I took a deep breath and pulled my hands out of my coat pockets. I was so nervous my hands were shaking—big, jerky movements—but I didn't have a choice. I couldn't risk losing her; I had to tell her. So, I gently cradled her face and neck in my shaking hands. As soon as my fingers touched her skin, her eyes flew open.

"What're you doing?"

I leaned in as I struggled for air, touching my forehead to hers. After a dry swallow, I forced the words past my lips, praying they would be reciprocated.

"I love you."

After the words were out, I thought I might actually be sick, so acute was my terror that she didn't love me back. After a short pause, her breathing became ragged and under my hands, I could feel her heart beating a rapid, irregular rhythm. I allowed myself a glimmer of hope and pulled my head back a few inches so I could see her face. She held my gaze as I searched her eyes, trying to figure out what she was thinking since she hadn't yet spoken.

Her eyes were glassy with unshed tears as the seconds continued to tick by until she finally whispered a response.

"I love you, too."

At what point had that changed? Was it when she met Lucas? Was it because he wasn't as fucked up as me? Or was it because he was more successful than me? What was it about him she thought was so much better than me? Or was it earlier? Was it when I didn't protect her from my brother? Had she stopped loving me then? Or maybe she'd never really loved me. Maybe I'd always just told myself she did because I loved *her* so fucking much. Maybe she'd cared about me, but never felt the same way I did, and I only saw what I wanted to see.

What did it even fucking matter? She was gone. She was with *him* now. I bet she didn't even think about me. While I had to blackout to stop thinking about *her*. I didn't want to think about her anymore, I didn't want to love her anymore. I didn't want to remember I'd ever met her.

"Take it all back," I growled at the tree. "Fucking take it back!"

My anger returned, pulling me to my feet. That tree was responsible for everything I was feeling right then, responsible for so many memories I didn't want anymore. Bending over, I snatched up my machete, raising my arm high. Then, with a shout, I took the first swing at the closest branch. The metal hit with a dull thud, slicing into the branch but not severing it. With a grunt, I yanked it back and swung again, this time harder. I continued to swing, hacking off branches until I could no longer lift the machete.

But when I was done, I didn't hurt any less.

chapter fifty-one

annie

It was just shy of three weeks since I'd left the hospital after my pre-term labor scare when Lucas and I were headed to Clarksburg to spend our first night in our new home. Those weeks had simultaneously flown past and crawled by. Aside from Christmas festivities and a resurgence of nightmares about Charlie, the first week had been blissfully uneventful—I stayed at Lucas' house in Stockwood with him and our days were primarily spent taking short walks, long naps, reading, and playing Lucas' twenty questions game to continue learning about each other. We also spent some time watching HGTV with my mom, who seemed to finally accept that Lucas wasn't going anywhere, and having tea with Mrs. Renner. And I'd decided to name the baby Mary—a form of Miriam—for my mom, but had yet to decide what her middle name would be.

Lucas' friend, Joel, hadn't discovered anything new about what Charlie might be planning, and we hadn't seen him since the incident at the brewery, so we decided to be hopeful he had decided I wasn't worth his effort. Even so, Lucas was insistent I didn't even walk outside without him or Nick accompanying me. And after what had happened at the brewery, I was more than happy to comply with that request.

Saying goodbye to Selena had been difficult, but she'd assured me that her friend and colleague based in Clarksburg—Jasmine— would be a great fit since Selena's practice didn't offer virtual sessions, and I trusted her. Enough that, before I'd even moved, I was on the schedule with Jasmine.

After that first week, Lucas drove back from Clarksburg every few days to spend a half day and a night with me. All the travel took a toll on him; I could see the exhaustion on his face, and he was grumpy and a bit short-tempered, but he'd insisted on it. And aside from knowing he needed more rest, I was glad to see him that often.

Lucas hired movers to do the bulk of the packing, moving, and unpacking; there wasn't really anything to be done when we arrived at our new home for the first time except to unload our one suitcase each that we'd been living out of for the previous week. I was equal parts excited and nervous as we neared the house, and Lucas seemed to feel the same way, our anxious laughter filling the car when we caught each other stealing sideways glances.

"Welcome home, sweetheart," he said softly as he swung open the front door and we stepped inside.

Looking around, I was shocked—all the walls had a fresh coat of paint in the color scheme I'd mentioned to Lucas over Christmas, a medium slightly greenish-blue with a hint of gray and cream trim. My eyes slowly took in the furniture placement in the foyer, landing on a frame on the entry table with the words "Our Story Is Just Beginning." The photo inside was a candid photo of us someone must have taken right after I'd opened my Christmas gift from Lucas which my fingers immediately found around my neck. It was a delicate rose gold necklace with a small heart charm stamped on one side with the same words as the frame and on the other side with a miniature bouquet of wildflowers. In the picture, we were beaming at each other, happy and in love.

I couldn't hold in my emotion and started crying as I turned and wrapped my arms around his waist. "I love it."

He laughed softly, hugging me back and kissing the top of my head. I could tell when he spoke that he was feeling as emotional as I was. "Come on, there's more."

I wiped my eyes, laughing. "Of course there is."

I shrugged out of my coat, hanging it on a wall hook in the foyer, before slipping my fingers between Lucas' and letting him lead me unhurriedly through the house. The last room we entered was the one we'd chosen to be the nursery. As the door opened, I froze, amazed at what I saw. The room was already set up—all the furniture in place, the bookshelf already full of baby books, everything in pinks and greens and browns and orangish-yellows. Not only that, but there was a mural on one wall of a sunrise shining on a field of wildflowers. It looked almost exactly how I pictured the meadow Lucas used to watch the sunrise from with his mother from the stories he'd told me, except that there were also butterflies with tiny dashes behind them to show their path, that looped into the word "joy." I had mentioned to Lucas my vision for the room and that I wasn't sure how I was going to find the energy to set it up, and then he'd done it for me so I wouldn't have to, except even better. My heart swelled with gratitude and love as Lucas ushered me gently into the room and wrapped his arms around me, his hands resting on my belly. And then I knew exactly what Mary's middle name should be.

"Lucas... what about Elizabeth?"

"Elizabeth?"

"For her middle name. Mary Elizabeth."

"That was my mom's name," he said quietly.

"I know," I replied. "She'd be named after our moms."

He lifted a hand to my cheek, turning me to face him as he searched my eyes. "Are you sure?"

I nodded. "Yes."

"This is your room, Mary Beth," he said, his arms tightening around me as he used the same nickname I'd just thought of myself before angling his head down toward my belly. She immediately began kicking at the sound of his voice. "Ha!" Lucas half-shouted excitedly. "She loves it already!"

"Of course she does," I whispered. "It's perfect."

As we stood there, I imagined us standing just as we were, but with Mary Beth sleeping soundly in the crib ahead of us and my eyes watered again. In that moment, there was no doubt that I was exactly where I should be.

Over the next two months, we fell into an easy, quiet routine, and since Scotty had legally become a partner, that routine involved Lucas spending a lot more time than I'd expected at home with me, often going into the site only for a few hours in the morning and a few hours after lunch and driving into Stockwood for a day or two every other week.

Most evenings before bed, Lucas insisted on getting me propped up on pillows against our headboard while he sat near the end of the bed with my feet in his lap and massaged from my toes to my thighs to keep the massive amounts of fluid I was retaining from pooling in my lower legs and ankles. Arguing had been fruitless and I'd given up after less than a week.

It was one of those evenings when Lucas said, "I just got off the phone with Nick, and he and Chase are coming up to see the site and for Chase to meet Scotty. I thought they could bring your car up with them. Is that okay?"

"Why wouldn't it be?"

He shrugged, glancing at me before looking back down to my feet. "I don't know, but I wanted to check."

I snorted. "Do I really have a choice?"

He tilted his head up, pretending to think about it. "No." He barely stifled his laugh when I rolled my eyes at him.

"Of course it's fine. It's not like I'll be doing anything anyway."

Lucas turned serious. "I'm sorry, sweetheart."

"I was just joking, Lucas."

"But it's true," he said soberly. "And I wish it wasn't."

"Really, it's fine. I'm as large as a house anyway. Doing just about anything is impossible." And it was true; I was exactly thirty-eight weeks pregnant and had just had the cerclage stitches removed a few days earlier, so I could go into labor at any time.

"A really beautiful house..." Lucas murmured.

"Go away!" I laughed as he stopped rubbing my feet to climb over me.

He rubbed his nose against mine, careful not to put weight on my belly, before cupping my head and kissing me deeply, a hand skimming slowly up my side under my shirt. After a few minutes, when I'd lost all train of thought except what he was doing, he whispered into my ear, "You know what all the books say can help you get labor started, don't you?"

chapter fifty-two

lucas

Annie and I had just climbed into bed together for the night when she began shifting around, fluffing and re-fluffing and positioning and repositioning pillows. This went on for several minutes before she groaned.

"What's wrong, sweetheart?"

"I'm hungry," she grumbled.

I tried—and failed—to stifle a laugh.

"It's not funny," she fussed. "We just got comfortable and ready for sleep, and now I have to get up."

I leaned forward and kissed her cheek. "Don't be ridiculous, sweetheart. *You* don't—*I* do. What would you like?"

"No, Lucas, I don't want you to have to get up. You're tired, too. I know you are. I'll get up. I'm just whining about it first."

Again, I couldn't hold back my laughter. "Sweetheart, we both know that you're going to whine, and then I'm going to get up and get you something anyway. Wouldn't you rather just skip straight to me getting up to get you something and eat ten minutes earlier?"

She snorted, trying not to laugh. "You're an ass," she hissed.

"You love it," I teased.

Not even trying to hide her laughter this time, she replied, "It makes me nuts sometimes, but I *do* love it. I love *you.*"

"I love you, too," I replied, no longer joking. I almost didn't like saying it because I felt like the word love was inferior to the strength and depth of feeling I had for her, but I had yet to find a better word, so love it was.

Scotty and I were standing outside the new brewery location the following Monday discussing some of the exterior modifications we hadn't agreed on yet. Nick had been right that Scotty would be a great business partner; he was shrewd, had fresh ideas, and was endlessly enthusiastic and energetic.

He interrupted our debate to tilt his head toward the street. "Is that the famous Annie coming down the street with Nick?"

I spun around to see Annie was, in fact, slowly making her way down the street, her arm linked through Nick's, Chase on her other side. "It is," I grinned, rushing off to meet the group.

"Sweetheart, what are you doing?" I asked when I reached them. She wore no hat or scarf, and her cheeks and nose were bright red from the bitter cold wind. "It's freezing out here, and there's ice everywhere."

The bright, beaming smile she gave me as I yanked off my own hat and pulled it down over her head was disarming and my worry melted away entirely when she threw her arms around my neck and kissed me.

"Nick and Chase said I could walk over with them. Nick made sure I didn't slip. You make lunch for me every day, and I wanted to return the favor. So, I've brought lunch for us. Well," she added laughing, "I made it, but technically Chase brought it." She pointed to the bag in Chase's hands. "Thanks again, Chase," she said in his direction.

"You're welcome," he replied cheerily.

I considered her for a moment. She was so full of life, so animated. Her eyes shone brightly, and her face was positively glowing. She looked happy, I realized, a grin spreading across my face. "You're adorable, you know that? You didn't have to make anything. I'm sure it wasn't easy. But thank you. It means a lot to me that you made me lunch." Cupping her head, I kissed her, more deeply this time. "I love you," I whispered against her lips.

"I love you, too."

There was a crunch of feet on ice and snow behind me; Scotty had walked over. With a final kiss, I stepped to Annie's side and wrapped an arm around her. "Scotty, this is Annie," I said, kissing her temple. "And Annie, this is Scotty, the brewery's newest partner."

"Nice to meet you," Annie said, sliding off a glove and holding her hand out.

"The pleasure is all mine," he replied, shaking her hand.

"Also, this is Chase, the GM from the Stockwood location; he was out the day you were down there, Scotty. Chase, this is Scotty."

Scotty turned and held out his hand. "Nice to meet you, Chase."

"Okay, let me get Annie settled inside where it's warmer and then we can walk you guys around," I said to Nick and Chase.

"Oh, I brought enough food for them, too," Annie said. "Since I was coming over here, I thought it would be rude if I didn't bring enough for everyone."

We all headed for the trailer through the frigid air. It wasn't meant for a crowd, but we managed to find somewhere for everyone to sit, though Annie had to sit on my lap on the chair behind the desk. By the time everyone was situated the entire trailer was filled with the aroma of whatever food was packed in the bag Chase had carried.

"What is this, sweetheart?" I asked, opening the bag. "It smells like heaven!"

She smiled and blushed again. "It's nothing special. I couldn't stay on my feet that long. It's just canned tomato basil soup and bacon grilled cheese sandwiches."

"Nothing special?" I balked. "I can't believe you did any of it, this is a wonderful surprise," I replied, nuzzling her neck until she swatted at me.

"Enough, Lucas," she laughed. "You guys should eat it while it's still hot and fresh and before the sandwiches get soggy."

After unpacking and distributing the individual soup containers, spoons, and sandwiches, I saw there wasn't a portion for her, amid choruses from the others about how delicious everything was. "You said this was for all of us—where's yours, sweetheart?" I asked.

Her face flamed red. "I was too hungry to wait—I ate it right before we left."

I laughed. Of course she would have been hungry after spending enough time to cook. And she was probably hungry again by now. I kissed her cheek. "Share with me, I'm not that hungry yet anyway," I told her. It wasn't true—I was famished—but she didn't need to know that. I could find something to eat later.

The other guys were talking about the expansion, Scotty giving updates on the status of the renovations in advance of walking them through the site after lunch. There was no reason I needed to chime in—Scotty was more than capable of filling them in—so I let their voices fall into the background and instead focused on the beautiful woman in my lap.

"Are you sure you didn't overdo it?" I asked so only Annie could hear me. She was bored and uncomfortable most of the time, so I knew she was desperate for something to do, but I worried about her doing too much.

She shifted to sit sideways on my lap, making it easier for us to look at each other while we talked. "I promise. And even if I did overdo it, what does that even mean at this point? That I'll go into labor?"

"That's true... so maybe you should be cooking all day. I mean, for the sake of starting labor, of course," I teased, grinning.

She deadpanned, though the corners of her mouth were twitching. "Ha-ha, very funny, Lucas."

"*I* thought it was."

"You're impossible," she replied, shaking her head as her smile broke free.

"Only for you," I said, giving her a peck on her nose. "You bring it out in me."

"Oh, really? Lucky me," she giggled.

My chest expanded as I listened to her first laughing, then groaning in appreciation as she took a bite from the sandwich and chewed. How had I gotten so lucky in life that I'd not only found a woman like Annie, but that she was mine? A woman who was endlessly generous and kind to every living creature, a woman who understood not only the love I'd had for my mother, but the pain I had from losing her. A woman who supported my dreams as if they were her own, and whose heart was so pure and innocent and beautiful.

I'd spent so many years closed off to attachment, sure I didn't really want it, but I couldn't have been more wrong. I did want it, desperately; more than I'd ever wanted anything else in my life. At least with Annie, I did. No matter what the future brought—even if it one day brought tragedy and heartache like it had for my dad— each moment I had with her was worth it.

After nearly losing her a second time, I had a deeper appreciation for Annie's presence in my life. We were definitely in our first sunrise after what I'd been afraid was our last sunset, but my father had never told me that first sunrise would be the most amazing one in my life.

chapter fifty-three

annie

Lucas had walked me back home from the brewery while everyone else was finishing up their lunches, his own food left half-eaten on his desk, and then we'd made love.

"I love you so much it hurts," I breathed out as we laid in bed together.

"I know what you mean," he replied softly, tucking my hair behind my ear. "I feel the same way, sweetheart."

I enjoyed lying there in his arms for another few minutes before I remembered he needed to get back to work. "Everyone's going to be waiting on you, Lucas."

"Let them wait."

"But they'll know *why* you're late," I hissed, my face leaping into flames.

Lucas' laugh started as a rumble deep in his chest. "Sweetheart, they knew as soon as I said I was walking you home without finishing my lunch what we were going to be doing."

I wallowed in my embarrassment for a moment, and then I had to pee. Lucas rose first, helping me to the edge of the bed and then to my feet. But as soon as my feet hit the floor, there was a strange pinching sensation between my legs, followed by a warm rush of fluid.

"Oh, shit, Lucas, I think I just peed myself," I said mortified as the fluid started rushing down my legs. I moved as quickly as I could into the bathroom to try to keep anything from making it to the floor. "But I can't make it stop!" I added after I'd sat on the toilet and the liquid kept flowing.

"Um, Annie, are you sure it's pee?" Lucas asked, his eyes round.

"I don't know!" I shouted, frustrated because I couldn't seem to stem the flow. And then I began to pee. "Oh my god, Lucas—my water just broke!"

"It's happening!" Lucas exclaimed, his eyes lighting up.

It wouldn't have been a shock if he'd started bouncing up and down, there was so much excitement on his face. He leaned down and kissed my forehead while I sat on the toilet, the water still rushing out from between my legs with no signs of slowing. My heart was already racing so fast it felt like no more than the flutter of a hummingbird's wings in my chest. *I'm actually having a baby.*

I watched in a state of detachment as Lucas rummaged around in the under-sink cabinet, then pulled out a postpartum pad we'd stocked up on for when we got back from the hospital. After he placed it on the counter and disappeared into our bedroom, my abdomen began to tighten, and intense pain radiated in a band around my lower belly and back. I gripped my knees and breathed through the contraction, mentally preparing myself; I remembered from the pre-term labor fiasco that it was going to get a whole lot worse.

Lucas returned a moment later with a pair of panties, a pair of his sweatpants, and one of his t-shirts. I narrowed my eyes at him as he set the stack of clothes on the bathroom counter. I'd picked out an outfit specifically for wearing to the hospital that consisted of maternity pants and a sweater and Lucas had smiled and shook his head, telling me no one was going to care what I was wearing when I was having a baby. He said what mattered was that I'd be comfortable on the way there, reminding me that I'd be wearing a hospital gown once we arrived, but I'd insisted on picking out the outfit. Right then, though, as another contraction started, I couldn't imagine putting on anything except what Lucas had picked out for me.

He quirked an eyebrow at me, a hint of his mischievous grin at the corners of his mouth as he waited, also a hint of concern as my contraction faded. I grabbed at the clothes on the counter.

"You were right," I mumbled, rolling my eyes. But when I saw Lucas desperately trying not to grin, I laughed.

He kissed my forehead again, then began efficiently helping me to dress. He called the doctor as he helped me out the front door toward his car. The hospital bag as well as the diaper bag had been in the car already for nearly two weeks, the car seat since he'd bought his new car; the only thing missing for the trip to the hospital had been us.

As calm as Lucas was, I was the opposite. My breathing was erratic, and I had tears permanently waiting to spill over. He had an excitement buzzing around him, but while I was excited to meet my daughter, I was even more scared. Scared of giving birth, scared of being a parent, scared of Lucas deciding this was too much for him.

The miles passed under us both too quickly and too slowly, me crushing Lucas' hand with every contraction. He played gentle music in the car to help and seemed to be smiling at me, his eyes full of love, every time I looked over at him. Between contractions, his thumb was smoothing across the back of my hand, and I welcomed the soothing sensation.

My mind flashed for a moment to a different scenario if things had been different with Rob. I imagined what he would have been like right then and was sure his tension would have been smothering, that I'd have been trying to calm *him*. My chest filled with a warm rush of fresh gratitude that I had Lucas, with his gentle love and calming presence.

"I love you," I said, wishing there was some way I could show him how much I meant it.

"Oh, sweetheart, I love you, too," he said, lifting my hand to press a kiss to the back of it.

———

"Annie Weller, she's pre-registered, her water broke about an hour and a half ago and her contractions are about four minutes apart and strong," Lucas rapidly fired off the second we walked up to the registration desk in the labor and delivery center. Some of his calm was beginning to fade, worry slipping into his eyes with each of my strengthening contractions.

"We're ready for you guys," one of the nurses replied as she walked around the desk. "Let's get her into a wheelchair and we'll head back to her room."

Another contraction, stronger than the last one, tore through me just as I was sitting down in the chair, and I squeezed Lucas' hand until it had passed. "Sorry," I panted out as the pain subsided.

"Sorry for what?"

"Crushing your hand."

"Don't worry about me. Just focus on you and Mary Beth," he responded.

I scrutinized his face and saw a mix of excitement and worry, which was a pretty accurate reflection of my own feelings. "I love you," I said for at least the tenth time since we'd left the house.

"I love you, too."

"I'm so scared," I confessed, my jaw trembling.

His other hand tucked my hair behind my ear, then rested on my cheek, looking intently into my eyes. "There's nothing to be scared of, sweetheart. Everything's going to be just fine. Before you know it, you'll be holding this beautiful little girl in your arms for the very first time. And then we'll be going home together as a family." He kissed my cheek.

"You promise?" I asked, though I knew most of what he said was out of his control. For some reason, I still needed that assurance from him.

"I promise."

chapter fifty-four

lucas

"You're about seven centimeters dilated, so just hang in there. Are you sure you don't want an epidural? This might be your last chance to get one." The doctor was speaking sympathetically to Annie after examining her again.

We had been there for about nine hours already. Annie was dilating, but it had slowed down significantly after five centimeters, even though her contractions were strong, and she'd been fighting an urge to push for about an hour already. She was between contractions for a moment, her whole body limp and drenched in sweat. I'd supported her decision to forgo the epidural but was hoping she would change her mind. I could never understand what she was experiencing, but it was agony for me every time her face contorted, and her body tensed from a contraction.

"Annie, sweetheart, did you hear Dr. Martinez? This might be your last chance to decide you want an epidural. You're seven centimeters. Do you want one?"

"I shouldn't need one," she replied weakly. "We've been doing this for thousands of years."

"You're not less of a woman if you want some relief from the pain," I said gritting my teeth. That sounded like something Miriam had told her, probably so many times Annie would think she was failing her mom if she didn't have a natural birth. "I promise you."

"I will be, though," she cried out just as another contraction started to peak, crushing the same hand she'd been squeezing for hours.

"If you want one, get it. I know how strong you are, and the epidural doesn't change that. If you don't want it, I support you, but if you do, I don't want you to sit here in pain because you're worried about what people might think about you or because you think you'll be a lesser person."

"Lucas…" Her words trailed off as another contraction started, and she was sobbing once it passed. "Okay, I want it. I can't keep doing this. I'm so sorry."

"Annie, you have nothing to be sorry for. Let me go tell a nurse and I'll be right back."

Flooded with relief, I pressed a quick kiss to her sweaty forehead, then jogged to the nurse's station to let them know she was ready to get an epidural. When I returned, the sight of Annie lying in the hospital bed sobbing gutted me.

"Oh, sweetheart," I breathed, rushing to her side. "It's going to be just fine. The doctor will be here soon for your epidural, and then you'll feel much better, I promise. And then at some point, when she's ready, you'll push this baby out and we'll be a family."

―――――

It had been seven hours since Annie's epidural—sixteen hours since we'd arrived at the hospital—and we were in the final stages. Despite her exhaustion, Annie was alert and pushing with everything she had. Mary Beth's head was now out, and one more big push was all that was needed to get her little body to follow. Growing up on a farm, I'd seen many animals birthed, and it was always a moving experience. But nothing could compare to watching Annie deliver Mary Beth—it was the most beautiful thing I'd ever witnessed.

With a loud groan, Annie pushed when directed and the tiny, slimy body of the baby she'd been carrying and nourishing for the better part of a year slid out into the waiting hands of Dr. Martinez.

"You have a girl!" Dr. Martinez shouted.

"Is she okay? What's going on?" Annie panted out, her head turning from side to side as she frantically searched for the baby.

My eyes switched back and forth between Annie and the baby, who had yet to make a sound. Suddenly, Dr. Martinez called out a code and within seconds the room was filling with more nurses and another doctor, all talking at once as they huddled around Mary Beth, blocking her from view.

"Annie," Dr. Martinez said, her voice calm. "I need you to give me one more push so we can get the placenta out, okay?" Dr. Martinez said.

Annie's forehead was creased as she took in all the activity around us, but she pushed as instructed before asking again about Mary Beth.

"She should be fine, she's just stunned," Dr. Martinez said as she turned around to examine the placenta in a metal bin on a rolling cart. "It happens sometimes after a long labor. I called in our neonatologist just to be on the safe side. They'll take her up to get some vital signs on her and monitor her for a while before she moves into the postpartum room with you guys."

Pale, Annie nodded, closing her eyes.

"Everything's going to be just fine," I whispered to her as I watched the army of medical personnel—all but Dr. Martinez— disappear with Mary Beth. "Okay, sweetheart?" When she didn't respond, I tore my eyes from the doorway to look down at her. She seemed even more pale and didn't appear to have heard me. Turning to ask the doctor if what was happening was normal, I saw a river of blood flowing out from between Annie's legs.

"Dr. Martinez! Something's wrong! Please!" I shouted.

The doctor turned in our direction from her examination of Annie's placenta, and before I even had time to process, I'd heard the words "hemorrhage" and "surgery" and a flurry of scrubs and white coats had rushed from the room with Annie, leaving nothing but a lake of blood where her bed had been.

chapter fifty-five

rob

It **was a** rare, mostly-sober moment that morning as I searched the liquor bottles scattered around me for any that weren't quite empty. During the last sober moment I'd had, I'd decided to have my semen tested so I could prove I couldn't have kids and stop the cycles of self-doubt that were fucking killing me. All I did was go in circles, oscillating between thinking I'd made a mistake and being convinced Annie had an affair. The test results would make those circles finally stop, and I was expecting a call from the doctor at any time.

My phone chimed with a new text message and I glanced at the screen. It was from Haley.

> Not that you fucking deserve it, but letting you know you're about to be a dad. Annie's in labor right now.

The doubt washed over me, but I'd soon be able to end it forever. As if my thoughts summoned it, a call came in on my phone from a number I suspected was the doctor just as I poured a tall glass of whiskey. I tapped to answer the phone and confirmed I was correct. I listened carefully as he explained the results of the testing. I had a normal sperm count—in fact, it was high. *My vasectomy was ineffective.* I stood staring through the wall, my phone shaking in my hand even after the doctor had hung up. I'd never hated myself more than I did right then. I threw the glass of whiskey against the wall, shattering it and sending liquor and glass exploding in all directions. Turning, I picked up the stools that sat tucked under the island countertop and threw them across the kitchen where they left holes in the wall. Then I punched the refrigerator door until I'd broken enough bones the pain prevented me from continuing. Sliding down the front of the cabinets, I thought about the last months, everything that had happened since the morning Annie told me she was pregnant, and threw up onto the floor between my legs.

Oh my god, what the fuck have I done?

———

After many cycles of rage and despair, I cleaned up the vomit, liquor, and glass on the kitchen floor. Then I took a shower after responding to Haley and begging her to tell me where Annie was. None of my clothes were clean—I couldn't remember the last time I'd done laundry—so I threw on a shirt and jeans that seemed to smell less than the others. I had no plan, no idea what to say or do as I sped down the highway toward Clarksburg Medical Center, but that was my family—my wife and my child. No matter what it took, I had to fix what I'd done and get them back.

I flew across the parking lot, then down the halls of the hospital, slowing only to call out to the nurses Annie's name to get her room number, since Haley had refused to tell me more than what hospital she was at. As soon as they said the number, I'd started running down the hall. The nurses were shouting after me, but I didn't care what they were saying—no one was going to stop me from getting to Annie.

In every scenario that had played out in my mind during the drive to the hospital, I hadn't even considered the one I encountered when I turned the corner into the room. In the middle of the space, near a puddle of blood taking up most of the open floor, was Lucas sobbing loudly into his knees. My eyes searched around again, not wanting to believe what I'd walked into, but there was no one else in the room—no Annie, no baby, no medical personnel. There was only evidence of a birth and tragedy.

"No," I said softly to myself as I backstepped out of the room where Annie and our baby had died. "This can't be."

I gave a sharp shake of my head, but nothing in front of me changed. Not the bloody puddle or bloody receiving blankets. Not the absence of Annie and the baby or the presence of Lucas in despair.

Turning, I fled. If only I had fucking done things differently. If I'd been with her, maybe I could have gotten her to the hospital sooner and they'd still be alive. It was my fault they hadn't survived... I'd killed them by kicking her out of my life, by refusing to listen to reason.

In my truck, I sped in the opposite direction of home. That was a place I could never go back to—it would only serve as a reminder of what I'd thrown away... of what there was no possibility of ever getting back.

chapter fifty-six

lucas

I wasn't sure how much time had passed since they'd wheeled Annie out of the room when a nurse appeared. She walked over and squatted down next to me.

"Are you okay, sir?" she asked kindly.

"I don't know where they took them or if they're okay," I cried.

"It's okay, sir. Your daughter is in the nursery and doing well. She'll be allowed to go with you to the postpartum room soon. Your wife just came out of surgery. She was hemorrhaging, but they found the source of the bleed in time to save her and her uterus. She needed a blood transfusion, but she'll recover. You'll be able to see her within an hour."

I grabbed the nurse and clung to her as I wept, this time in relief. "Thank you. Thank you so much," I whispered.

She hugged me back. "That's why we're here, sir. Your family will be just fine. Would you like me to show you where the new room is and then take you to the nursery?" She glanced at the floor. "This room needs to be cleaned. Someone will be here in a few minutes to do that."

As we walked, I sent an abbreviated update to our friends and family. I didn't have the heart to relive all the details right then. Once my phone was pocketed and we neared the nursery doors, there was a bubble of excitement in my chest to see Mary Beth. The nurses in the nursery told me her vitals weren't quite where they wanted them to be, so she wouldn't be able to go anywhere for a while, but I was allowed to hold her. My heart raced and my arms trembled when the nurse placed her tiny body in my arms.

She was sleeping, her petite pink mouth in the tiniest little pout, her skin as soft as silk as I stroked her cheek with my finger. I'd imagined doing that so many times during the pregnancy as I stroked my finger across the ultrasound picture of her cheek, and it was surreal to be doing it in real life. I could see some of her full head of black hair peeking out from under the little hat that was keeping her head warm. She looked just like Annie.

"Hi, Mary Beth." I grinned. "Your mommy and I have been so excited to meet you. We love you so much already."

I continued to whisper to her, telling her all about the life we were going to have together and about how I met her mommy and fell in love with her. Every now and then she'd make little sucking movements with her mouth and sigh, but she never woke. With every word I spoke, the tiny baby in my arms claimed another piece of my heart. No matter how she'd come to be, I was desperately in love with the tiny, perfect being.

"Sir, Ms. Weller is in recovery now if you'd like to go see her. Your daughter should be able to join you by the time she's moved to the postpartum room."

I nodded, my eyes still drinking in the baby in my arms. With a soft kiss to her forehead, I whispered, "I love you, Mary Beth. I'll see you again soon, and then you'll get to meet your mommy."

Annie hadn't woken up yet when I arrived in the recovery room and my heart constricted with worry. Despite the assurances I'd received that she was okay, every minute that passed without her waking increased my fear that she wouldn't wake up at all, though I hadn't realized how tense I'd become until she started stirring and my shoulders slumped forward in relief.

"Lucas?" she asked groggily after looking around, blinking slowly for several minutes.

"Hey, sweetheart," I soothed, touching her cheek lightly with my fingertips and giving her a bright smile.

"Where's Mary Beth?"

"Mary Beth is fine. No, *better* than fine. She's incredible, she's amazing. Oh, sweetheart, just wait until you meet her." I sniffled and tried to blink away the tears that welled up as I talked about the new life Annie had brought into the world. "She's perfect," I breathed.

"What happened?"

I swallowed, trying to banish the image of Annie gushing blood in the delivery room. "You hemorrhaged right after she was born. They had to do surgery to find and repair the bleed, but they did, and everything is fine now. You're in the recovery room. We can go to your postpartum room soon, and Mary Beth will join us there."

Tears slipped down her temples, and she squeezed my hand. "I was so scared, Lucas," she whispered, her voice watery.

"I know, sweetheart. I know. But everything is fine now. You're both fine. And in a few days, we can go home—you and me and Mary Beth. You did it, Annie. You did it. You brought the most perfect little creature into this world, sweetheart, you can't help but to love her with your whole heart when you see her. You can just tell she's going to do wonderful things, you know? And she looks just like you, sweetheart, she—what's wrong?"

"Nothing, it's just... what you're saying... you sound so happy and in love with her."

"Oh, god, I am. In love with her and in love with you. I'm so lucky to have you two as my family."

"*I'm* the lucky one," she sobbed. "Because I have *you*."

chapter fifty-seven

annie

It **was the** second morning after Mary Beth was born and the room was quiet—just Lucas, Mary Beth and me. Mom and Mrs. Renner had stopped by the day before, though only for a few minutes; I hadn't been ready for any more excitement than that. I was still recovering physically and emotionally from the birth and surgery as well as the news I likely would never conceive again. The plan was for everyone else to come visit today.

My eyes clouded as I gazed at Lucas while he rocked Mary Beth, and I thought back to the story he'd told me about his parents—a beautiful story that tugged at my heart on its own, not to mention how he equated it with us. He was the man I'd always thought Rob was; the man I wanted and needed and then so much more. Looking at him now, seeing the love in his eyes, for both Mary Beth and me, it was hard to believe there'd ever been a time I thought my feelings for Lucas and his for me were somehow inferior to what I'd had with Rob. Our love wasn't lesser—it was simply different. And it was the kind of different that I both needed and wanted.

My heart swelled as my eyes shifted to the vases of wildflowers Lucas had delivered to the room the day before. He'd said one was for me, and the other for Mary Beth, that he wanted to give us joy so we'd understand what we'd given to him. He called it his wildflower promise—that he'd always strive to bring joy to our lives.

"Hey, babe. How're you feeling?" Haley's voice floated in as Lucas pulled away from my side. She walked up to me and gave my hand a squeeze as she scrutinized my face, creases in her brow indicating she was worried.

"I'm wonderful," I beamed back up at her.

She smiled, a shadow crossing her face before she bent and hugged me.

"I love you, babe, and I'm glad you're okay."

"I love you, too, Haley. I'm better than okay, though. Look at that little bundle of perfection right over there, how could I be anything else?"

Haley stepped over to where Mary Beth was sleeping and gazed down at her, an unexpected warmth and softness creeping into her features. "Hey there, little one," she whispered. "It's your Auntie Haley. It's so nice to finally meet you. A little secret, just between us: you have the best mom in the whole world. But don't tell anyone, because then they'd all be jealous."

Tears stung the backs of my eyes as I listened to Haley, and I rolled my eyes at myself. I'd be happy once my hormones were back to normal and I stopped crying so easily.

"Hey everyone!" Carol called out softly as she and Linc walked into the room. "How are you feeling, Annie? Where's the wee one?"

"Hey guys," I replied. We all exchanged hugs the best we could with me lying on the hospital bed and then they joined Haley to see Mary Beth. They were all crowded around the tiny box and cooing and whispering gently to her and I couldn't help but think again how lucky I was.

"Let me know if you need a break or to rest and I'll kick everyone out, okay, sweetheart?" Lucas spoke into my ear.

"Thank you, I—"

"Annie, I'm so glad you're okay!" Nick called out loudly as he barreled into the room to a chorus of hushing from everyone standing around the baby. Lucas and I glanced at each other and broke into quiet laughter.

"It seems everyone had the same idea about what time to visit," Lucas said to no one in particular.

And sure enough, as Nick was giving me an awkward hug, his huge frame bent over my hospital bed, Mom, Lori, and Mrs. Renner all walked in as well.

"Holy cow, guys, I don't know how you're all fitting in here," I laughed.

But I was also getting uncomfortable. Even though I was surrounded by people who loved me, there were a lot of people in a very small space. Lucas floated over to talk to his grandmother, everyone else focused on Mary Beth, and I closed my eyes against the beginnings of panic. As I fingered the necklace Lucas had given me that I never took off, I conjured in my mind a large, open field and began silently counting my inhales and exhales. A few moments later, I startled when someone grabbed my hand and opened my eyes to find Lucas hovering over me, his forehead creased.

"You okay, sweetheart?" he asked, his thumb smoothing over the back of my hand.

I stared back at him, not wanting to admit that being surrounded by people I loved was making me so anxious.

"It's all this, isn't it?" he asked, raising a hand to gesture around the room before smoothing some hair from my forehead with his fingertips. With every passing day, it seemed he was better able to understand me even when I said nothing.

"It's wonderful, really, I feel so loved. It's just..."

"Too much at once," he finished for me. "That's okay—I'll clear the room out for you."

"No, don't—not yet. Just stay here and keep holding my hand?" I didn't want to ask everyone to leave when they'd just arrived. Besides, having Lucas nearby and touching me was helping... as it always did.

"Of course, sweetheart," he murmured, bending to rub our noses together, then press a kiss to my lips.

I closed my eyes and focused on the image of an empty field again, but this time I was walking through it hand-in-hand with Lucas, Mary Beth running around ahead of us, chasing butterflies. I didn't even have to count my breaths that time—the image was enough to tamp down my anxiety. My chest filled with optimism for a future untainted by the past—one filled with happiness and laughter and security, and far removed from the experiences I'd spent most of my life battling. If my ability to stop the panic that had always before been inevitable was any indication, that future was certain.

While I could never undo the life I'd lived to that point, the decisions I'd made and the hurt I'd endured, the sun had set on that version of me and the relationships I'd let define my life for most of it. Now I was looking into a new future where I had the space to figure out and be whoever I was, a future where I could do things differently and be the kind of mother I didn't have. A future where I had the tools and support to handle whatever life threw my way instead of running away and hiding. A future filled with sunrises and the promise of joy.

A wildflower promise.

acknowledgements

This is *always* the hardest part of the book to write because I'm perpetually afraid of missing someone, not to mention trying to figure out how to thank everyone who maybe didn't have a direct impact on the publication process, but indirectly had a vital impact on my idea coming to fruition. I truly couldn't do it without every person in my life providing the support, comic relief, and reality checks I needed along the way. I love you all.

Joe, we really are soulmates and I think I've always known it. Even when life threw mountain-sized boulders in our way, this crazy connection we have held strong. So grateful we never gave up on one another.

Olivia and Kayli, you have helped me, yet again, to communicate my ideas in a manner that is not only coherent, but beautiful. You ladies edit for me, you get me, and you love me... maybe almost as much as I love you guys. I've said it before, and I'll say it again: I'm so grateful to have met you both and have you in my corner in life.

Melissa, I find myself struggling for words more than usual here. Thank you is so insufficient for everything you've done for my writing career as a whole and especially for this book. So much has changed because of your feedback and I'm eternally grateful for your willingness to read for me repeatedly, continuing to make insightful suggestions to improve this story. Yet again, what readers hold in their hands is better in ways they'll never know thanks to you.

Of course, I have to give an enormous thank you to my amazing cover designer, Murphy; yet again, you've exceeded my expectations and I couldn't be happier. Likewise, a huge thank you to Jo for bearing with my date changes and providing a beautifully formatted e-book—you rock.

And thank *you,* my dear reader—without you, I wouldn't be here. You make everything worth it.

resources

"Trauma is perhaps the most avoided, ignored, belittled, denied, misunderstood, and untreated cause of human suffering."
-Peter Levine

I have included here a few resources related to the topics of sexual assault, childhood trauma, and the associated mental health impacts and challenges. You can find a more comprehensive listing on my website at www.kturnerwrites.com/resources.

RAINN
RAINN (Rape, Abuse, & Incest National Network) is the nation's largest anti-sexual violence organization.
www.rainn.org
800-656-HOPE (800-656-4673)

National Suicide Prevention Lifeline
National Suicide Prevention Lifeline provides free and confidential support for people in distress, prevention and crisis resources, and best practices for professionals.
www.suicidepreventionlifeline.org
800-273-TALK (800-273-8255)

ACA
ACA (Adult Children of Alcoholics World Service Organization) provides information and a safe environment to foster healing from growing up in dysfunctional homes with abuse, neglect, and trauma.
www.adultchildren.org

ADAA

ADAA (Anxiety and Depression Association of America) works to prevent, treat, and cure anxiety disorders and depression.
www.adaa.org

NIMH

NIMH (National Institute of Mental Health) is the lead federal agency for research on mental disorders and aims to transform understanding and treatment of mental illnesses.
www.nimh.nih.gov

NSVRC

NSVRC (National Sexual Violence Resource Center) provides leadership in preventing and responding to sexual violence.
www.nsvrc.org

about the author

Katherine Turner is an award-winning author and a life-long reader and writer. She grew up in foster care from the age of eight and is passionate about improving the world through literature, empathy, and understanding. In addition to writing books, Katherine blogs about mental health, trauma, and the need for compassion on her website www.kturnerwrites.com. She lives in northern Virginia with her husband and two children.

By Katherine Turner

Fiction

<u>Life Imperfect Series</u>

Finding Annie

Willow Wishes

Wildflower Promise

Non-Fiction

moments of extraordinary courage

resilient: a memoir

www.ingramcontent.com/pod-product-compliance
Lightning Source LLC
Chambersburg PA
CBHW061048190726
48286CB00006B/1662